GARRY KILWORTH

THE WELKIN WEASELS

THE SECOND TITLE IN A RIVETING TRILOGY

CASTLE STORM

BOOK 2
THE WELKIN WEASELS

GARRY KILWORTH

THE WELKIN WEASELS

THE FIRST TITLE IN AN INVENTIVE NEW TRILOGY

THUNDER OAK

Three rats went in as many minutes. The others paddled for all they were worth, towards the distant shore. Ripples followed them as the monster gave chase. It propelled itself across the lake at an alarming rate by forcing a jet of water out of the bottom end of its body. It had six legs but these lay flat and streamlined against its sides. It skimmed across the water after the hapless rats, who must have known that more of their number were going to be eaten before they reached the distant shore.

The weasels simply remained where they were for the moment, still too horrified to do anything but stare. Then they came to their senses and everyone started yelling at once.

'Grab the pole!'

'Push, push.'

'Get us out of here.'

'Paddle with your paws.'

'Use anything – anything.'

They raced for the distant banks of the lake as if they had an army of monsters behind them . . .

GARRY KILWORTH

CASTLE STORM

Book Two of
The Welkin Weasels

CORGI BOOKS

THE WELKIN WEASELS:
CASTLE STORM
A Corgi Book : 0 552 545473

First publication in Great Britain

PRINTING HISTORY
Corgi edition published 1998

Set in 11/12pt Palatino
by Phoenix Typesetting, Ilkley, West Yorkshire

Corgi Books are published by Transworld Publishers Ltd,
61–63 Uxbridge Road, Ealing, London W5 5SA,
in Australia by Transworld Publishers (Australia) Pty. Ltd,
15–25 Helles Avenue, Moorebank, NSW 2170,
and in New Zealand by Transworld Publishers (NZ) Ltd,
3 William Pickering Drive, Albany, Auckland.

Made and printed in Great Britain by
Cox & Wyman Ltd, Reading, Berkshire

FROM THE 'HISTORY OF WELKIN'

In the Year of the Dormouse, by mammal calendar, the humans suddenly left the great island of Welkin. The stoats who were the most organized of the beasts of the field quickly seized power under their King Redfur. The weasels, smaller cousins of the stoats, were pressed into service as serfs and underlings. Here and there around Welkin small bands of weasels rebelled. All but one group were quickly put down by the ruthless stoats. This small band lived in a place called Halfmoon Wood, in County Elleswhere. Their leader was a weasel called Sylver, whose father had disappeared in Castle Rayn, home of King Redfur. These outlaws harassed the stoat rulers to distraction in the desire to be left alone in their woodland home.

One year after the human evacuation, King Redfur was killed in suspicious circumstances. Some say it was an accident, some say it was suicide, others say it was assassination. Prince Poynt, Redfur's brother, became the ruler of Welkin. He appointed a High Sheriff, by the name of Falshed, whose job it was to keep the law of the land. Falshed immediately set out to hunt down Sylver and his band of outlaws.

Lord Haukin, ruler of County Elleswhere, had some sympathy for Sylver and the weasels, being a kindly and intelligent stoat. He supported their bid to remain free of servitude. One day Lord Haukin received reports that the sea walls around Welkin were crumbling and would one day soon break down to allow the sea to flood most of the land. He saw the need to find the humans and persuade them to return to repair the sea walls. At about this time Lord Haukin found a diary in the library of Thistle Hall, written by a human girl called Alice. Alice and her child-hood friends had left a number of clues as to the whereabouts of the humans.

Lord Haukin determined to employ Sylver and his band of outlaws in finding the location of the humans. It was the lord's intention to discover their whereabouts and send Sylver to persuade the humans to return to Welkin. Without the use of their 'hands' and superior earth-moving power the sea walls could not be restored. Sylver was only too willing to assist the stoat lord in his aim and he and his weasel friends set forth on various adventures to secure the knowledge necessary to carry out Lord Haukin's plan.

By the paw of –
CULVER THE WEASEL

Chapter One

Something horrible was stirring in the depths of the unnamed marshes in the north of Welkin.

It was as if there were a volcano that was just coming to the boil. There were trembling movements in the reeds, in the grasses, in the yellow celandine down by the murky waters. Swiftly these stirrings increased to frenetic energy, until the whole area of the marshes was covered in moving creatures, scrambling here and there, doing things with bits of string and cut reeds, making things, preparing for the moment when they would soon overflow the edges of the river Bronn and swarm southwards.

Rats!

Hundreds and thousands of rats.

Their faces had been painted with red ochre, circles around the eyes, bars across the bridges of their noses. Their wicked-looking teeth glinted in the morning sun as they continued with their feverish plans for the conquest of Welkin. Their leader, an old wizard-stoat by the name of Flaggatis, pored over charts and maps in the dank rooms of his fort on stilts, which stood in the shallows of the swamps.

'This time, this time,' he muttered to himself, 'I will destroy that upstart Prince Poynt and take what is his and make it mine . . .'

'*Yerrrssshhhh, massgggerrr,*' snarled the rat attendant at his side in that almost-language which rats used to communicate with their leader and one another.

Not for the first time Flaggatis flinched when he heard the foul harsh sounds which came out of the rat's throat. It was he, the great wizard, who had taught the rats how to speak, but you could only do so much with a creature whose brain was like a mushy yellow porridge with burnt bits at the bottom. Weak thoughts and poor reasoning were a rat's inheritance from its parents. Flaggatis sighed. Even his dark magic had not helped him defeat the sluggish sloppy activity of a rat brain.

'Let's face it,' said Flaggatis, more to himself than the dull-witted creature at his side, 'one can't expect miracles of a species which has eaten nothing but garbage since the beginning of time.'

'*Yerrrssshhhh, massgggerrr.*'

Flaggatis coughed roughly. His throat felt as if it had a sandstone lodged in it this morning. His lungs were raw and full of phlegm. Living in the marshes had not been kind to the stoat who had been banished by Prince Poynt to the outermost reaches of the kingdom. Damp had entered his bones and made them ache, even on a bright summer's day. His head forever felt twice its size. He had difficulty in sleeping. The marshes were not a place which fostered good health and a happy life. The air here rotted clothes and lungs alike.

'I shall not live in Castle Rayn,' mused the old wizard, 'for the weather there is inclement most of the year round. No, I shall move the seat of the kingdom to the middle of the country.' He stared down at the map before him. 'This place,' he said, pointing with a claw to a green patch. 'Halfmoon

Wood. This looks like a nice sunny spot. Belongs to Lord Haukin at the moment, I believe, but we'll soon change that.'

He stared at the markings on the map as he schemed in his warped and twisted mind, now close to madness through living too long with savage creatures and their barbaric culture.

'I'll raze the woods to the ground and build a strong fort from the trunks of the trees. I'll dam up this stream and use the water for my moat. And those who live in the wood – whoever they might be—' he tapped his claw on the spot, 'they shall be my personal slaves – or they shall die terrible deaths.'

'*Yerrrssshhhh, massgggerrr.*'

'Oh, shut up,' snapped Flaggatis, irritably. 'Can't you see I'm thinking?'

The rat by his side cringed and looked down at the floor.

Flaggatis went to the window of his room and stared out at the marshes. Activity. Activity everywhere. The rats were building little coracles out of reeds, ready to cross the river Bronn and invade the civilized areas of Welkin. Their efforts at boat-building were poor, but then Flaggatis did not expect too much. All that was required was that the transport should get them across the river quickly, so that the element of surprise was not lost.

'We must overwhelm the stoats while they are in their beds,' he snarled. 'Tomorrow. We attack tomorrow.'

The rat waiting in the middle of the room to be forgiven for his trespasses, lifted its head now.

'*Haaarrrgghhhh!*' it shrieked. '*Tooomarrraagggghh.*'

In Halfmoon Wood, spring always brings a welcome respite to the end of winter. Weasels do not exactly *detest* the cold months: their coats are warm and their spirits stoical. But of course food is scarce during the short days and long nights, and one can get tired of the sight of snow and ice. Once the snowdrop blooms have wilted and the wood anemone opens they begin to look forward to warmer days. Then the scent of meadowsweet tickling their nostrils tells them that the cold days are well and truly behind them and summer is only next door.

Halfmoon Wood was the home of the weasel Sylver and his band of outlaws, who were forever battling against the tyranny of Prince Poynt's sheriff, the stoat Falshed. Since the stoats ruled Welkin, the weasels – smaller, slimmer creatures – were treated like serfs and vassals. They were there only to see to the comfort of the stoats, whose leader Prince Poynt never changed his white winter coat for the brown summer pelt, because he felt that ermine was more regal.

No other stoat in the land was allowed to wear winter white now and had to struggle against nature to remain brown through the cold months. Some of them, those who could not manage to remain brown, coloured their fur with clay and had to stay out of the rain.

The pelts of weasels do not turn white during the winter, like those of stoats. Some would have thought this fortunate for them. However Icham, one of the outlaws and Sylver's closest friend, sometimes covered his coat in bird lime so that it went white and thus flouted Prince Poynt's laws.

Besides Sylver and Icham, there were Bryony, Luke, Wodehed, Miniver the little finger-weasel, Alysoun-the-fleet, Mawk-the-doubter and finally the newest addition to the band, the grubby, disrespectful but indomitable Scirf, who cared for

10

neither manners nor cleanliness and who adored his fleas.

One day in mid-spring, when the sun was slanting its rays through the trees, creating golden bars of light with dancing flecks, Sylver made his way to Thistle Hall, the home of a kindly old stoat named Lord Haukin who ruled County Elleswhere. Sylver came across the lord before even covering half the distance to the hall. He was with his weasel servant Culver on an old dump of sorts. Culver was boring down through the dirt with a metal rod.

'Morning, my lord,' said Sylver. 'It's not often I see you outside your study.'

The old stoat with greying whiskers looked up and frowned. 'Ah, yes, it's what's-his-name, isn't it? Morning?' He looked up at the sky and seemed surprised to see it light and bright. 'Yes, yes, good morning, young fellah.'

Lord Haukin had an appalling memory for names, but he knew the band of outlaws and was helping them in a quest.

'What are you doing, Culver?' asked Sylver of the hall's servant. 'Looking for gold?'

'Bottles,' grumbled Culver, clearly out of sorts over this exercise he was getting. 'You know how his lordship loves bottles of all shapes and sizes. We've discovered a bottle dump here.'

'Yes, yes,' said Lord Haukin, enthusiastically. 'One fiddles about with a metal rod. When you hear a particular squeaking sound you know the metal has touched glass. Ingenious, eh, young fellah?'

Just at that moment there was a grating squeal from Culver's direction. The rod in his paws refused to be pushed further down. Clearly he had struck glass. Culver then took a trowel and began digging carefully, until he finally unearthed a blue bottle

11

with ridges running vertically up its body. Lord Haukin seemed mildly pleased by the find.

'Poison bottle,' he explained. 'You can tell by the shape and colour. I suppose the ridges are there for blind creatures, so they can feel they have a dangerous bottle in their claws. Perfectly harmless now of course. Empty.'

With that the lord invited 'what's-his-name' to accompany him back to Thistle Hall where they could talk in more comfort.

In the lord's study, his favourite place, surrounded by books, charts, brass instruments and weaponry left behind by the humans when they went away, the two were able to talk. The smell of old leather and damp paper filled the room. In the corner a fire was smoking away quietly and damply to itself without any visible flames or friendly glow, adding to the already thick atmosphere of the study.

'Lord Haukin,' said Sylver, hoping to jog the memory of the old stoat, 'you know we have to find the humans and bring them back to Welkin . . .'

'Yes, yes, the sea walls are crumbling. We need their hands and brains to repair the dykes or many of us will drown. If you remember, young Sylver, I was the one who helped you find the first clue to the whereabouts of the humans. I was the one who pointed you towards Thunder Oak, where you found the carving of the dormouse. You really ought to polish up that memory of yours.'

As always, once into a subject, Lord Haukin was as sharp as the next stoat. He even started remembering names. Sylver choked a little on being admonished for a bad memory, but he swallowed his pride and continued.

'Yes, I remember. Well, the thing is, we have to start seeking the second clue. I wonder if you could look in that diary left by the child, Alice. Perhaps it will tell us where to start searching.'

'I'm sure it will. I'm sure it will,' replied Lord Haukin, peering at the books that lined the walls. 'Now where did I put it . . . ?'

Sylver groaned inwardly with dismay. Surely the old stoat had not just stuck the precious diary on any old shelf when they last used it. It would take for ever to find it amongst all these tomes. Some of them were so thick with dust you could not see the colour of the binding. Others were just parchments, rolled tight, with faded ribbons wrapped around them.

There were pyramids of parchments, sometimes being used as book-ends, behind which were more and more books.

'Culver?' called the lord.

The house weasel entered; his paws were covered in flour.

'You yelled, my lord? I was trying to bake.'

'Do you remember a diary by a child . . . ?'

'Third shelf to the left – little green book,' said Culver, sailing out again with a look of disgust on his face.

They found the diary and Lord Haukin opened it on a table full of bottles which made a tinkling noise every time the table was joggled.

'Ah, yes, here it is,' said the old stoat, peering through a magnifying glass at the words. 'It's in code of course but the gist of it tells of a building with a secret passage. The structure lies far to the south of Welkin, in the deepest part of the moors. At the end of this passage Alice's cousin, a boy called Tom, has left the second clue.' Lord Haukin looked up and peered into the middle distance. 'I don't remember any building in the moors.'

'Are you sure that's what it says, my lord?' asked Sylver. 'There couldn't be any mistake,'

'Young weasel,' replied the stoat sternly, peering from underneath bushy white brows, 'I do not make mistakes of that kind.'

'No, of course not, my lord. A child called Tom, eh? The vital clue. Well, I'd best get the band together and prepare to go on the road. Hopefully we can be well on our way before Sheriff Falshed arrives with any troops to delay us. You know he has a habit of turning up just as we're about to depart.'

At that moment, Culver came scurrying back into the study. He still held his flour-covered paws away from his nice leather apron, but his eyes were wide and plainly showed the whites. There was a small tremor in his voice. Beneath his metal slave-collar his throat was working hard as he swallowed.

'Lord Haukin,' said the faithful serf, 'something terrible has happened.'

'Ah, right on cue,' said the lord, nodding at Sylver in respect. 'I expect Sheriff Falshed has arrived.'

'No, my lord,' cried the weasel, dramatically. 'Not that.'

'Then what?'

Culver cleared his throat before delivering the chilling words, 'The rats have invaded Welkin.'

Lord Haukin whirled. 'How do you know this, Culver?'

'A messenger has just arrived from Castle Rayn,' replied the servant. 'An amnesty has been declared by Prince Poynt, for all outlaws, provided they assist in helping to stem the tide of rat hordes pouring down from the unnamed marshes.'

Sylver said, 'You mean, if we fight for Prince Poynt we'll be given our freedom.'

'That's it. You and your band – and any weasel

14

who is not yet in the army – have got to help the stoats and ferrets. Otherwise we shall be overrun by savages.' Culver sniffed and suddenly looked devastated. 'Oh, no,' he added.

'What is it?' asked Sylver. 'Do you think you should come with us too?'

'Certainly not,' replied the indignant servant. 'I'm no fighting weasel. I cook, clean and keep house. I'm upset because I can smell my bread burning. Now if you'll excuse me, I must get about my proper business.' And with that he left the study swiftly but in a dignified fashion.

'Well, young thingummyjig, I suppose you'll fight?'

Lord Haukin had asked the question which Sylver was asking himself at that very moment.

'Welkin is in danger from the barbarians. We *must* help. I'm not sure I trust this amnesty thing, promised by Prince Poynt though.'

'No,' agreed Lord Haukin, 'he's not the most trustworthy of mammals – but do you have any choice?'

'You mean with the whole of Welkin in danger? I don't think we do have a choice. Our beloved prince can be as sneaky as a rat himself, when he wants to be, but there are others to think of besides him.' Sylver sighed. 'Anyway, once it's all over we'll be on our way south, to look for this mysterious building.'

'The diary said something about bad weather,' added Lord Haukin, enigmatically. 'Something to do with a name.'

'Thank you, my lord – now if you'll excuse me?'

'Quite, quite, young thingummy. In the meantime I must put my mind to the problem of the rats. I fear Prince Poynt will run round in circles as usual without seeking intelligent advice. We must find some way of driving out the rats . . .'

Sylver left Lord Haukin deep in thought, knowing that great stoat's brain would worry the problem of the rat invasion until he came up with some sort of an answer. Sylver went out of the great open doorway of Thistle Hall and towards the woodland path which led to the glade where he and his outlaws had their hideout.

Chapter Two

When Sylver arrived in the glade where his weasels were to be found he discovered the messenger, a ferret from Castle Rayn, captive of his outlaws. They had the ferret tied to a tree and were tickling him with a crow's feather. The ferret could not speak to them for laughter, tears running down the creature's nose.

'All right,' ordered Sylver. 'Untie him.'

'Eh?' cried Scirf. 'We was just about to have some fun, squire. We caught this rabbiteer sneakin' through the wood. Thought we'd use him as a hostage or somefink.' Scirf scratched the white fur on his belly as he spoke.

'Did you hear what he had to say?' asked Sylver.

'No,' Bryony admitted. 'We didn't give him a chance.'

'Better do so now.'

Thus the ferret was released. He was a slim narrow fellow, built for running speed, which was presumably why he had been chosen as a messenger. He first explained that he was one of three who had tried to get out of the castle at night and sneak through the camps of rats circling the moat. Two of his companions had been caught and their dying screams had terrified him into diving down an old rabbit hole and waiting there until the night had calmed down around him. Then he had made his escape. His descriptions of the firelight, flickering on the faces of the savage rats as they did unspeakable things to his companions, chilled the blood of the most hardened of the outlaws.

'. . . they're all over the north of Welkin and heading southwards fast,' he babbled. 'Lord Ragnar is doing his best to hold them but they may break through soon. I've never seen anything like it. They just came down in swarms. I was on the battlements of Castle Rayn at the time and I saw this dark tide, like a flood, flowing over the land. I was just about to sound the alarm for a break in the sea wall, when I saw there were small gaps, patches in the flood. It was then I realized that what I was looking at was thousands, tens of thousands, of bodies with hairless tails and glinting eyes . . .'

'Rats,' breathed Icham.

'Yes – a sea of rats – coming in great waves over the land to swallow everything in their path.'

'Yuk!' muttered Alysoun.

'Yes,' repeated the ferret, pleased to have an attentive audience, 'and Flaggatis has given them a war god. I saw it – it's huge and monstrous and ugly. It's made of wicker, painted with white birdlime. They call it "Herman" or something. You know how difficult it is to understand these rats. That's what it sounded like to me. I was hidden in a patch of reeds when I saw them carry it by on a litter, chanting horrible words to this Herman.' The ferret shuddered.

'What's it supposed to be? This god called Herman?'

'A monster white rat, I think. That's what it looks like – a white rat with sharp front teeth made of peeled-wood spikes. The inside of its mouth is red and it has a long lolling tongue. It stares at you

18

something awful. I was sure it had seen me in the bushes and was going to give me away.'

The ferret swallowed hard, the memory obviously rekindling his fright at the time, before continuing with his tale.

'Then Flaggatis came by. I heard Flaggatis tell his rat warriors, ". . . our great and savage war god shall serve as a guiding light, a beacon, to rats on their glorious invasion of Welkin. He will frown darkly on any coward who leaves the field alive after a defeat. He will swallow their souls and they will travel down through his belly into his dark guts, there to rot for eternity. When we have won, when we are the conquerors, we shall take our god back to the unnamed marshes and burn him on a huge pyre as symbol of our victory. We shall return him to his pure state, a smoky spirit in the sky, for his work as our war god will then be over . . ." '

'Nasty beggar,' said Scirf. 'He's no slouch, this Flaggatis, is he? I mean, there's nothin' like a big staring war god to rally warriors to the cause, whatever it is, and put some bristle in their whiskers. Puts the fear of defeat up 'em. Gets 'em throwing themselves into the battle, not caring whether they live or die, just so they don't lose.'

Sylver briskly got down to the main business. 'So where are we needed? If they're as numerous as you say, won't they reach *here* soon? Shouldn't we stay and help protect Lord Haukin and Thistle Hall?'

'At the moment the barbarians are fighting on two fronts. Castle Rayn is under siege. Flaggatis hates Prince Poynt so much he'll not move on from there until the castle is taken. To the east of the country Lord Ragnar is holding back the tide. Help is needed to stop them coming any further. If they do take the castle or break through Ragnar's lines, then nothing on earth will prevent them from overrunning Thistle Hall. You'd be overcome in a single day.'

The ferret paused for breath.

'My advice is this,' he continued. 'Castle Rayn can't hold on much longer without supplies of food. They're starving in there. If you could somehow get some supplies in . . .'

'Oh, right,' said Scirf, sarcastically. 'We just put baskets of grub on our heads and stroll through millions of rats, saying, "Mornin' lads, fine day init?" '

After long consideration Sylver said, 'No, I think the ferret is right, Scirf. We should try to get supplies in to the castle. Once the castle falls, the rats besieging it will be free to flood south, east and west, and the beleaguered Lord Ragnar will be overrun, as well as places like the Hall. We have little choice.'

'Is this wise?' said Mawk-the-doubter, quickly. 'I mean – we could sort of ask some birds to drop in supplies. Do we have to go ourselves? Maybe some of us should stay here and guard the wood. I don't mind volunteering for that.'

Mawk was not the bravest of the weasel band.

'Birds?' said Wodehed, disgustedly. He was the wizard of the band, whose spells never turned out quite the way he expected. 'You know what birds are like. Balls of feather. Twitter-brains. How are you going to get them to remember what they're supposed to do, even if you could get close enough to one to ask it?'

'Yes,' added Luke, the holy weasel, 'let's have some sensible suggestions, Mawk.'

'What – what about me staying here then?'

'Right,' said Luke. 'You stay here all on your own and when the rats send down a vanguard, you fight

20

it off all by yourself, with no-one to help you.'

'I'm coming with you,' Mawk replied, quickly. 'I don't – don't want to miss the fun.'

Sylver nodded. 'Fine, we're all agreed then? Now, obviously we few can only carry so much food. On the way we must recruit more weasels, and even stoats and ferrets if we can, to join us. And we must think about the best sort of food to take. Nuts are very nutritious – acorns, that sort of thing. If we take meat it'll only go rotten in this weather before we get there. Similarly fruit. Nuts have got lots of goodness in them – and they're easily carried. We should make knapsacks out of sticks and cloth. Culver at the Hall will help out with those. Bryony, Luke and Scirf, you set about making knapsacks.

'The rest of you scatter through the woodland, pick up any of last season's nuts you can find, acorns included. I'll speak with Lord Haukin, he usually keeps his cellars stocked well from his orchards. He has walnut, chestnut and hazelnut trees. No doubt he'll let us have some of his stores. He's not a great nut-eater himself anyway, so I'm hoping there'll be plenty. Right, set to all of you. We need to be on our way before evening.'

The weasels went about their various tasks. Lord Haukin did indeed have a good store of nuts which he was happy to relinquish. When evening came round the band all had heavy packs on their backs, full of nuts and corn cobs. What they were carrying would not feed an army, but it was the best they could do with the numbers. They set off, towards the north west, heading for Castle Rayn.

'I never believed,' said Scirf, voicing the thoughts of them all, 'that I'd willin'ly trudge over the countryside towards Castle Rayn. Wild humans wouldn't have dragged me there in the past. Just

21

takes a few outsiders to come pourin' down, and everythin' changes.'

'The common enemy,' said the learned Luke, 'always unites squabbling cousins.'

'Stoats might be our cousins,' remarked Mawk, 'but I'd hardly call their treatment of us a squabble.'

The band stopped that night in a village a league from their wood. They decided to rest at the inn, whose keeper was an old friend of Scirf's. (All innkeepers appeared to be 'old friends' of Scirf's, even though he had told everyone he'd never been more than a league from the village of his birth before joining the outlaw band.) The inn was full of weasels, stoats and ferrets, all whispering together about the invasion.

'Well, if it isn't the old dung-watcher hisself,' said the weasel innkeeper, on seeing Scirf come through the door. 'How's the rhubarb-growin' profession these days?'

'Gave all that up,' said Scirf, to the inn as a whole. 'I'm one of Halfmoon Wood's dreaded outlaws now.'

Several stoat and ferret heads swivelled and stared at Scirf and then the other weasels. Sylver inwardly groaned. Scirf tended to be indiscreet at the best of times, but this was plain foolishness.

'We've been pardoned for the time bein',' continued Scirf, giving the stoats and ferrets a defiant glare, 'by Prince Poynt hisself. We're on our way to relieve Castle Rayn.'

'All by yourselves?' asked the innkeeper, cheerily.

'When they hear us comin', them rats will run a hundred miles,' replied Scirf, his natural bravado coming out. He then turned to face the tables of stoats, some still wearing pieces of armour and helmets. 'Wass this lot then? Deserters? Why aren't you all up on the front, eh?'

The word 'deserters' had the stoats and ferrets looking away and down into their honey dew mugs. Sylver realized that Scirf was right. Many of these stoats must have run away from the fighting. They *were* deserters. Sylver saw an opportunity to recruit more carriers of supplies.

Once the band had finished their dinner and had ordered honey dew, Sylver took his mug and went over to the nearest table full of stoats. They looked aggressive as he sat down without an invitation. One of them, a big fellow with strong-looking shoulders, spoke in a nasty tone. 'You're Sylver – I recognize you by that white lightning streak down your face – what do you want with us?'

'You're runaways, aren't you?' said Sylver.

They looked uncomfortable at this, but the one who had spoken before said, 'So what?'

'Why did you run? You, big-fellah. Why did you, personally, desert?'

The stoat took a swig of his honey dew and looked up again, shame-faced. 'I dunno. It happened so fast. Sort of split-second decision, without thinking too hard. I expect half the castle would have run if they could've. I was outside, see, supervising a work-party of weasels weeding the vegetable plots. Then I hears a cry from the battlements and looks to where the sentry's pointing. Up over the hill comes these rats . . .' He paused, shuddered and took another quick swig of his drink. 'I could *smell* 'em. Horrible musty smell of old dry drains and unwashed pelts. It made me gag. They swarmed over the downs in their thousands, heading straight for us.

'The serfs panicked. They dropped their hoes and

23

rakes straight away and began running for the forest to the south. I – I sort of got caught up in them. Couldn't help myself. There was this kind of fever in the air. I just ran. Had to get away from them hordes of stinking rats, with their painted faces and their squealing, shrieking noise. You never heard anything like it. Drums too. Drive you crazy.'

All the other stoats nodded at this and muttered to each other about the drums and whistles, the hollow-sounding moan of rat horn-blowers, the bullfrog-roarers they whirled around their heads and the cymbals they clashed in their claws.

'Terrible noise,' agreed one, 'enough to drive fear into the most stalwart heart.'

'So really, what you're saying, all of you, is that you kind of ran by *accident*?'

By this time other stoats and ferrets had crowded around the table, listening to the conversation. They had been nodding their heads when they heard of the 'stink' and the 'noise' which they obviously recalled.

'How can we go back now?' asked the big stoat.

Sylver pointed to his knapsack, on the floor beside him. 'You join us in transporting supplies to the castle, to help protract the siege until Ragnar has defeated the rat hordes in the east and can turn his attention to the besiegers. If the castle falls, then we are in real trouble. You can stop that happening. You can turn yourselves into heroes overnight.'

'We're still deserters,' replied a dubious stoat at the back. 'He may still have us punished.'

'You can say you planned it this way all along. You retreated, regrouped, and worked out this plan to save the inhabitants of the castle. I'll back you up. All you have to do in go out into the woods tomorrow morning, make yourselves some

24

knapsacks, and we'll fill them with whatever stores the villagers on the way can spare us. What do you say?'

The big stoat slammed his mug down hard on the table. 'Rabbit's blood! I think this weaselly outlaw has saved our pelts for us. Here, give me your paw, fellah. I once fought against you in the Battle of Stocky Hill, where you used clay grenades full of ants against us. I cursed you that day for a pig's orphan, but I think you've made us see the light this evening. What say, stoats and ferrets? Do we give it a go? Are you with me and this skinny weasel?'

A great cheer went up and the mugs foamed with honey dew as they toasted their new alliance.

Chapter Three

Sheriff Falshed stood on the battlements of Castle Rayn, looking down on the encampments of the rats which surrounded it. The invaders' leafy bivouacs stretched as far as he could see. At night their camp fires were as numerous as stars upon the ground. The smell of their unwashed fur was overpowering. Their screeching and scratching was horrible to the ear. How were the stoats ever going to rid themselves of this menace?

'Sergeant-at-arms?' he called.

A fat stoat came running out of a room in a tower. 'Yes, sir?'

'What are they doing down there? Those rats with the baskets?'

The sergeant stared at where Falshed was pointing. 'They're carrying dirt, sir.'

'I can see that. What are they going to do with it?'

'They're piling it up against the south wall to make a ramp. They've already filled in the moat at that spot, with rocks, now they're dumping clay on top of the rocks and earth on top of the clay. Once the ramp is finished I expect they'll come running up and into the castle. Then it'll be all up with us.' The sergeant shuddered violently. 'I expect they'll cook us slowly over one of their fires. I hear they eat stoats.'

Falshed raised his eyes to the heavens. 'I suppose

26

no-one has thought to try to *stop* them making their earth ramp?'

'Captain-of-the-guard said we was to keep an eye on them – ah, here he is now, sir – with Prince Poynt.'

Out of a door which led to a spiral staircase came the captain, followed by an irritable prince. One of the many reasons he was upset was because the siege prevented him from obtaining fuel for his many fires. The woodsheds were running low.

'Falshed,' snapped the prince. 'What are we doing about this earth ramp?'

'I've only just been informed of it,' replied Falshed, a little too testily for his own good when speaking to his lord and master. He glared at his captain. 'No-one thought to inform me. I had to find out for myself. If I hadn't come up here for a breath of fresh air . . .'

'Yes, yes, but I don't want excuses, Falshed – I want action – and quickly.'

'I shall get some stoats and weasels on it right away, my prince.'

'Doing what?'

Falshed stopped to think. He was not an altogether unintelligent stoat. There were some flecks of inventiveness amongst the grey matter which filled his skull. He looked over the wall again, at where the rats were piling the earth. They seemed to be about halfway up the wall now. Another two or three days would see them to the top. Rats could work at fever pitch when they wanted to.

'I suggest, my liege, that we go downstairs to the wall against which they are piling their dirt. We then remove a few building blocks from the foot of the wall. Once we have a hole we will be in contact with their dirt. We then shovel the earth out from inside their ramp. Once we have taken enough the

27

ramp will collapse and they'll have to start again. If we keep doing that, they'll eventually give up and try something else.'

Prince Poynt ran his claws down his pure white ermine coat with the tar-tipped tail. He stared at Falshed for a minute, taking all this in. His brain cells worked at a slower rate than Falshed's and it was some time before a light gleamed in his eyes.

'Brilliant, Falshed. No wonder I had the common sense to make you sheriff. That makes *me* brilliant too.'

'My prince, just being in your presence generates ingenuity and resourcefulness.'

'Quite so, quite so. I wasn't looking forward to hanging you by your heels from the battlements, which of course I would have had to have done if you hadn't come up with an answer pretty snappily. Good, good.'

At that moment the prince's stomach began gurgling and the royal stoatage winced. He put a foreleg around Falshed's shoulder. Falshed hated being touched by the prince and stiffened a little.

'Falshed,' whined Prince Poynt, 'I'm so hungry. I'm cold and hungry. The two worst things a stoat can be.'

The prince always felt cold, no matter what the weather, probably due to the fact that he would not change out of his white winter coat. In his mind, in his subconscious, it was winter all the year round. Even when the sun was blazing down on the castle walls he had fires in every room and went through the corridors and passageways shivering violently.

'I'm sorry you are hungry, my liege.' Falshed gritted his teeth before adding, 'We're all very hungry.'

'Yes, but I'm not worried about everyone else,'

snapped the prince. 'I'm concerned about *me*.'

'I meant, we're all concerned about you, my prince. No-one else really matters.'

'Quite. Now, are you going to get those workers moving the dirt, or do I have to do it myself?'

Falshed took his leave of his prince and went down to the courtyard below to organize a work-force. Soon he had had three blocks of stone removed from the bottom of the curtain wall and his stoats were tunnelling through the dirt piled against the outside. They carried the earth and put it on the allotments, where the peasants – all weasels, of course – were hurriedly trying to grow potatoes and carrots.

Once things were moving Falshed decided it was safe to leave and let the peasants get on with it. He went back to his room in one of the towers. There he flopped into a chair and called for his stoatservant.

'Spinfer?'

'Yes, sir,' said a lithe, slim weasel flowing silkily out of the shadows of the room. 'You called.'

'I thought you might be there, lurking some-where.'

'I never *lurk*, sir – I simply hover, waiting to answer your every beck and call.'

'Be a good weasel and go and get me some water, would you? Fresh stuff, from the well. I'm so thirsty.'

'Haven't you just been down by the well, sir?'

Falshed blinked hard. He was very fond of his body-servant, the faithful Spinfer, but the creature could be rather dense at times.

'I wish to be alone, Spinfer. I have thoughts. Dark thoughts. You understand?'

'As you wish, sir,' replied Spinfer a little haugh-tily. 'I shall fetch the water.'

Once Spinfer was out of the room Falshed leapt from his chair and went into his garderobe, which is a lavatory with a long drop, and pulled out a loose brick above the doorway. Reaching in he came out with half a packet of chocolate biscuits. Lovingly he tore away the wrapping and took out a single biscuit, putting the rest of the packet back behind the brick.

Falshed took his biscuit into his room, where he intended to nibble it slowly, savouring its goodness.

Fortunately he had his back to the door when it opened, for all edible materials had been pronounced property of Prince Poynt, under a new law which had recently been proclaimed, and to have undeclared food in one's chambers was punishable by death.

'Ah, Falshed,' said the prince's voice. 'This is where you are . . .'

Falshed fainted right away at the sound of his master's voice with the chocolate biscuit touching his lips.

The sheriff came to, still face-down on the stone floor. For a moment he was electrified with the thought that he had been discovered eating contraband food. But on moving ever-so-slightly he realized the biscuit had slipped from his claws and was hidden under his body. Wisely he decided to remain where he was and try to brazen it out.

'Awake?' said the prince, standing above him. 'Well, get up then.'

'I – I'm too weak with hunger, my liege. Perhaps if you could assist me.'

The prince wrinkled his nose. 'Assist you? My dear sheriff, what do you think I am? A peasant with muscles and things?'

'In that case,' replied the relieved Falshed, 'I hope

30

Your Highness won't mind if I remain here on the floor for a while, to recover my strength.'

'If you must,' said the prince, walking around the chambers and staring at ornaments. Suddenly Prince Poynt stopped and sniffed hard. He looked down again at Falshed. 'You haven't got food in here by any chance?' he said, suspiciously.

Falshed was almost hysterical with fear by this time. 'Food? Me, my prince? How could that be?'

Prince Poynt sniffed again. 'I can definitely smell something . . .'

'Perhaps it's coming from outside. Those rats have plenty of food. Their camp fires are just below my windows.'

The prince went to the windows and inhaled. A strong aroma of cooked fish and meat was coming from below. He immediately started salivating, dribbling all down his bib. The faint scent of chocolate was gone from his nostrils now, overpowered by the heavier smell of cooking meat. He stared down in envy on the camp kitchens of the rat hordes, wondering whether it was possible to change sides and join them.

At that moment his sister, Sibiline, burst into Falshed's room, wringing her claws. 'Brother, here you are – I was told I would find you in Falshed's chambers . . .'

Falshed was beginning to think he lived on the crossroads to the universe, with stoats rushing in on him from every direction. The stone floor was very cold, despite the summer weather outside, and his bones were beginning to ache. He wanted everyone to go so that he could get up.

'What do you want?' snarled Prince Poynt, who was not especially fond of the princess. 'Can't you see I'm busy?'

'Busy? Doing what?'

'With affairs of state,' said the exasperated prince. 'Things. Important things.'

'I thought you were staring out of the window and dribbling.'

'I came up here to see my sheriff, in order to – in order to—' He suddenly remembered what he had come for. 'In order to find out if my plan for removing the earth ramp was progressing satisfactorily.'

'Oh, very, my prince,' replied Falshed, in a sarcastic tone. '*Your* plan is going very well.'

'I hope I don't detect a note of annoyance in your voice, Falshed?' said the prince.

'Falshed,' interrupted Sibiline. 'What are you doing kissing the floor?'

'I'm not kissing it, Your Highness. I was overcome with giddiness through hunger. I fainted. But don't worry, I shall be all right in a minute, once I get my strength back.'

'I'm not worried at all. Stay there for ever if you want.' She turned again to her brother. 'I just came to tell you we are under a major attack on the other side of the castle. They have platforms and siege machines. They're catapulting some very nasty-looking dollops of something from that field of cows to the east, over the wall and onto my little patio. Are you going to do something about it?'

'What do you expect me to do?' said the prince, waspishly. 'Clean it up for you?'

'Brother, if you don't do something about it, then I will! Of course I shall require you to pass the kingdom over to me first, but then if you're going to be worse than useless the kingdom would be safer in my paws anyway.'

There was a clattering sound above, which had all three staring up at the ceiling.

'There,' Sibiline said, 'they're using rocks now. When those platforms on wheels reach the edge of the wall, they'll be coming in here to do unspeakably savage and primitive things to us educated and cultured stoats. We're not made for it, you know. I had a genteel upbringing. I'm sensitive.'

'You, *sensitive*?' snarled Prince Poynt. 'Sib, you're my sister, but you're as blunt as a battering-ram.'

Sibiline, who was a very capable and determined female living in an age when jills were supposed to be weak and insipid, narrowed her eyes. 'Someone has to do something to stop them. What about my cockleshell collection? I expect they'll crush those straight away. Rats are such horribly uncouth creatures. Pointy, if you don't try to do something about them – this instant – I'll organize a revolt and wrench the whole kingdom from your incompetent claws. I can do it and you know it. It's only my feeling for family ties that prevents me.'

The prince hated being called 'Pointy' in front of other stoats, especially rough, tough ones like Falshed.

'I'm coming, I'm coming. In the meantime, Falshed, get up off the floor and organize the troops. We have to get some forked twigs or something to push over those platforms. Listen, is that a battering-ram I hear? Come on, stoat. I'll expect you in less than three seconds flat.'

The prince left the chambers with his sister.

Falshed eased himself off the floor. Looking down he saw that his body weight had crushed the chocolate biscuit to a thousand crumbs. He picked up the biggest of these and popped it into his mouth with a sigh. At that moment Spinfer came through the doorway and saw the crumbs on the floor.

33

He stared at his master and said with a smirk on his silky features, 'Don't worry, sir, I'll clear up that mess. You go and sort out your soldiers.'

'Thank you, Spinfer,' growled Falshed, knowing he had been caught with illegal food and could do nothing about it. 'I appreciate your help.'

'Glad to be of service.'

Falshed went through the doorway and began yelling for the captain-of-the-guard and the sergeant-at-arms.

'Boiling oil!' he yelled. 'Hot coals! We must throw things down on the rats before they get inside the castle.'

The captain appeared. 'We've got no boiling oil or hot coals,' said that able officer. 'Used 'em all up on the prince's last barbecue.'

'Anything then. Bricks. Furniture. Conkers. Throw it down. Drive them back.'

He heard the cranking and squeaking of wooden wheels, coming from the eastern side of the castle.

When Falshed reached the battlements, there he saw high rickety platforms on wheeled towers moving closer to the walls. The platforms stuck out in front so that when the towers reached the edge of the moat, the platforms would be touching the top of the castle walls. The little housings on these platforms were crammed with armed and grinning rats, who would no doubt leap from them onto the battlements and begin fighting the stoats.

Fortunately the rats were not very good carpenters and already one or two of the platforms had begun to fall apart. As they got closer, a good push or two from the battlements with a long pole ensured their total collapse. Rats fell yelling and shouting from their perches, most of them landing in the moat below. Most rats can swim and they

34

reached the bank without difficulty. Stoat soldiers jeered at them from above and threw lumps of earth onto their heads.

Next Falshed had blocks of stones, cannibalized from storehouses in the castle grounds, piled up against the main doors. The rat battering-rams were now obstructed by solid rock and could not break down the doors.

Finally, Falshed began using his own catapults, firing at those used by the rats. Soon the air was full of stones and clods of earth among other things and a lively battle was in progress which kept the stoats busy and their thoughts away from their stomachs.

Prince Poynt came up to see how things were progressing.

'Everything under control, Falshed?'

'Yes, my liege. We have them at our mercy. Well, not quite at our mercy, but we're giving as good as we get.'

'Fine, fine.'

Falshed could not help noticing, as he was talking to the prince, that his master had brown stains down his white front. The prince caught the sheriff staring. He nodded slowly and reached into a pouch at his waist.

What came out was a chocolate biscuit. The prince began to nibble it. Falshed saw it out of the corner of his eye but said nothing. Finally the prince said, 'Well, I'll be going down. By the way, I found these biscuits, hidden in your loo . . .'

Falshed evinced surprise. 'In *my* garderobe, my lord?'

'Behind a loose brick. I went back after you left and sniffed them out. I *knew* I could smell chocolate, you see. Your servant, what's-his-name?'

'Spinfer,' murmured Falshed, trying to keep the croak of fear out of his voice.

'Yes, Spinfer. He seemed quite shocked. Said that neither of you had any idea the biscuits were there – that they must have been hidden by someone in the dim and distant past. He suggested Sir Badarock might have hidden them. Is that right, do you think?'

'Oh – oh – *yes* – yes, that has to be it.'

'I'm inclined to agree. One of my dead brother's sieges probably accounts for them being hidden there. That was his sheriff's chambers before yours, you know. The stoat known as Sir Badarock. Never did like Sir Badarock. Dead too, now. I had him executed when I became prince. Didn't trust the creature as far as I could throw a cathedral. Hung his pelt from a gibbet in Long Meadow, south of Didcott Wood. Probably still there now, hanging in the wind and the rain, all crisp and brittle like a worn scrubbing brush.' The prince paused before adding, 'Carry on, Falshed, with your warlike activities.'

'Thank you, my liege,' said the sweating Falshed. 'I shall endeavour to do my best to protect you.'

'Of course you will – mmmmmmm – delicious biscuits, despite their being so *old*. I'd let you have one, but there's only six left in the packet. Never mind, I've arranged for your room to be thoroughly searched. If any more turn up, you can have one of those, providing you have a good explanation as to why they are there in the first place. *Old* biscuits won't work a second time you know,' the prince said with narrowed eyes. 'I am a lenient, forgiving stoat, but I can go only so far.'

'I'm – I'm most grateful, my prince.'

'So you should be, Falshed. So you should be.'

Chapter Four

Not only were there stoat runaways to contend with, but also some of the rats had deserted their lines and were out pillaging and looting in the country villages. Such things happen in war. The stoats and ferrets had deserted because they were afraid of the enemy, and the rats had deserted because they thought there were better pickings elsewhere.

In the event it was difficult to enter an area without coming across bloated rats drunk on honey dew, staggering around wielding short swords and creating havoc amongst the peasants of country towns and villages. There was a gang of the creatures in a village called Walberswit on the road to Castle Rayn. They were plundering weasel hovels, carrying away anything they could lay their claws on, especially if it looked like food.

During the night, out in the fields, an idea had come to Sylver on how to get inside Castle Rayn, carrying the supplies, without being caught by the besieging army. In a particular village called Walberswit – the one in question – a bronze horse roamed the streets. It had once had the statue of a famous human general in its saddle, but that particular gentleman had parted from his charger and had proceeded out into the world on foot. The reason for this was that they had been cast separately and were from different First and Last Resting

Places; they had been smelted from ore taken from different copper and tin mines.

It is a fact that the statues of Welkin came to life once the humans went away. Some say this was because the presence of humans keeps magic at bay. Once the humans were no longer around, magic began to flourish again, growing like invisible mushrooms in the air, and this magic was responsible for giving statues animation and some power of thought. All the statues wanted to do was find the place from which they had been mined or quarried and to remain there. Their First and Last Resting Place was where they felt happiest.

The general had gone off looking for his, leaving his horse behind to clatter about the streets of Walberswit, not yet ready to go out and look for its own ore mine.

'I noticed,' Sylver told his outlaws and the stoat deserters, 'some time ago, that the old horse has one or two holes in its bronze. Holes that are big enough to allow weasels to get inside its hollow body. You will all climb up and crawl inside the horse.'

'Then what?' asked one of the stoats.

'I shall ride it to the castle.'

Bryony said, 'But the castle gates are closed. Once they're opened the rats will swarm inside.'

'Not if the gates are only opened for a few moments, right on the stroke of midnight, and the rats don't expect it.

'I propose that two of our number sneak through the rat lines, leaving their haversacks with us of course, and signal us once they're inside. When I see the signal I'll gallop the bronze horse through the rat lines. The rats will be caught by surprise and won't be able to stop us. We'll arrive at the castle gates just a few seconds before the last chime of midnight.'

'Who're going to be the ones to sneak through the rats?' asked Scirf. 'Bit of a job, that.'

'Care to volunteer?' asked Icham, with an edge to his voice. Icham and Scirf did not get on well together.

'Yerse! All right, I'll go,' replied the bold Scirf. 'An' I'll take my friend Mawk with me.'

'No you won't,' interrupted Mawk-the-doubter, quickly.

Scirf said, 'Right. You'd rather be lumped in with this lot: half a dozen weasels, two dozen stoats, three ferrets, and the nut harvest for the whole of Welkin. All in the metal belly of some half-mad horse that's got the brain of a brick. You'd rather go careering over hill and through dell, at breakneck speed, hoping the gong doesn't put a hoof in a rabbit hole and crash to the ground in a welter of metal and bodies.'

Icham said, cruelly, 'Come on, Mawk, make up your mind – are you going with Scirf or do you come with us?'

'With Scirf,' replied Mawk, eventually. 'I – I wish to volunteer my services for a hazardous mission.'

'Good,' said Sylver, 'that bit's settled. When night-fall comes, Scirf and Mawk will head towards the castle. The rest of you will deal with the renegade rats, then catch the bronze horse and climb inside it. Is everything clear?'

Everyone said 'yes' except Mawk who made a non-committal squawk in the back of his throat.

Once darkness fell, Scirf and Mawk set out towards the distant downs where lighted fires could be seen. At first they drifted swiftly through the gloaming, but when they came on the first line of rat bivouacs they had to get down closer to the ground and snake through the grasses.

Mawk could smell the greasy sweat of the rats as the pair of them inched their way between the camp fires. He could hear the guttural sounds of the rats' almost-language, as the creatures called to each other in the half-light of the evening. Once or twice the two weasels had to lay dead still while a bunch of rats went by, usually squabbling, their painted faces clearly visible in the light from their fires.

The circles around their eyes and the stripes across their noses gave them the appearance of ghouls. During these times Mawk's heart was either racing ten to the dozen, or it was so deathly still it was in danger of seizing up on him and giving him a cardiac arrest.

Those rats who were of the common soldiery had leaf-and-stick bivouacs, but there were those amongst them of higher rank who owned leather tents framed with staves. At one point one of these tents was in the way of the two creeping weasels. Scirf signalled silently to Mawk that there was only one way through and that was under the flap of the tent, through the middle of it, and out the other side. The alternative was to go between a clutch of several fires, all close together.

Mawk's heart fluttered like a terrified bird as he followed Scirf under the leather tent-flap into the darkness within.

Inside the tent the awful stink of sleeping rat mingled with half-cured animal hide. The air was fetid enough to make Mawk gag, the bile in his stomach rising. Something was rotten in the state of Welkin. Many things. And they were all in this tent. Unwashed hide, dirty leather underpants, stale-sweat jerkins, muck-encrusted socks, cheesy sandals – they were all here in this tent – along with the stench of plates full of tidbits: dead slugs and snails that had gone off and cockroaches that had been off to start with.

The weasels remained on one side of the tent, absolutely still, to let their eyes get used to the darkness. Once they could see a little, Mawk was aware of a sleeping form on a mousehair rug in the middle of the tent.

By this creature, which was clearly a large roof rat, was a tub of rancid lard. Mawk knew that rat chieftains insisted on being paid in slabs of lard, rather than money, which they ate in order to make themselves bigger, fatter rats and therefore more feared amongst their kind.

What they had here was clearly a fierce chieftain, a massive creature with a great belly, who would no doubt bite the eyes out of Mawk's head as soon as look at him.

Scirf indicated that they had to skirt by the chieftain in order to reach the other side of the tent. The dauntless Scirf led the way, with the trembling Mawk in his wake. As they passed the rat chieftain, whose snores resembled the sound of starving pigs eating swill, Mawk could not resist a glance at the horrible face of the creature.

What he saw almost made him leap out of his skin!

The rat chieftain had one eye open, staring at Mawk as he crept past him.

'Gaaahhhhhhh,' moaned Mawk in fear, then in panicky undertones, 'Scirf – he's awake.'

'Ssshhhhh!' hissed Scirf, sternly. Then he whispered, 'That's a wall eye. Can't you see how milky it looks? He's blind in that one. He obviously can't close it.'

Mawk looked into the glazed white eye and realized Scirf was right. It was a sightless orb. But how it glared at him! It was only with difficulty that Mawk believed the owner's stare was not fixed on him, following him, waiting for the moment when the rat might leap up and tear out his throat! The creature's foul breath, smelling of rotten meat trapped between its teeth, engulfed the weasel and he almost choked with the odour.

The strange eye in the great thick-skulled head followed his progress right to the door of the tent, yet the heaving body of the chieftain continued to remain inert, slobbering occasionally, licking its lips in its sleep and muttering nonsense the way a dozing body does.

Looking around the walls of the tent, just before following Scirf outside, Mawk recognized the dried scalps of weasels and stoats, hanging as decorations. And there, in a bunch from the centre pole, dangled a clutch of magpie beaks and feathers. This barbarian chieftain was clearly a savage killer of beast and bird, and poor gentle Mawk had passed by this ugly brute within the thickness of a rat's tail!

Outside the tent the blessed air was fresh – as fresh as it could be in a camp of ten thousand rats – and Mawk gulped it down gratefully. A few moments before he would have given his eye-fangs to have been with the other members of the weasel band, but now the castle was close by. Mawk could see lighted brands behind arrowloops. He could see movement high up among the crenellations on top of the walls. Scirf had led him through a place of horrors safely enough. Now they had to scale the walls of the castle to bring their mission to an end.

Scirf slipped into the waters of the moat and began swimming towards the castle walls. Mawk followed him into the cool inky waters, hoping there were no pike awake at that time of night. The pair made the other side and followed the damp mossy stones around until they found some blocks which were pitted with age and into which they could get their claws. Scirf began the perilous climb up the sheer face of the castle.

Mawk watched where the ex-dung-watcher put his claws and did the same. Together they scaled the building blocks, one by one, resting when they could cling on to some soft mortar between the stones. When they were halfway up, they were spotted by some rats who were doing some night fishing amongst the reeds of the moat.

'*Thhhaarrrr – oooop thhharrr!*' cried one of the rats, pointing.

The rats took out some slingshots and began to pelt the climbing pair with pebbles, which struck the stonework and went zinging off into the night. The rats' activities fortunately roused the sentries on the castle walls, who started throwing down clods of earth onto the rats, driving them away from the edge of the lake. Finally, Scirf reached the edge of the battlements and was pulling himself, exhausted, over the top when a stoat soldier with a halberd rushed at him, crying, 'Die, rat!'

'I'm a weasel,' gasped the slick, wet Scirf. 'Give me a second to get me breath.'

Fortunately the halberdier stayed his paw and in the next moment Mawk also tumbled over onto the battlements. A sergeant came to see what was the matter. The two stoats stared in amazement at the fatigued weasels.

'We made it!' cried Mawk, joyously, at the same time as fighting for oxygen. 'We got here. As leader of this expedition I order you, stoat sergeant, to take

43

us to Prince Poynt. We have urgent news. There is food on the way. Prince Poynt, I say. Immediately!'

'I think I'd rather put you in the dungeons,' said the sergeant, 'unless you can convince me otherwise.'

Scirf, ignoring Mawk's attempt to grab all the glory, now stood up on his hind legs and regarded the stoat sergeant with some disdain, walking round him.

'Yep,' said Scirf, eventually, 'you'd look very pretty, all torn and ragged in a gibbet, you would. All right then, take us to the dungeons if you want to be stripped of your rank, then have your head axed from your shoulders and stuck on a skewer by the castle gates. Otherwise, take us to your prince – *now.*'

'Yes, sir,' replied the sergeant, quickly.

'Very good, sergeant. I'll tell the prince to go easy on the Iron Maiden – that's a box thing with spikes what they chuck you in and close the door – when I gets to speak with him. Now lead the way, marshal – lead the way.'

The stoat sergeant did as he was bid.

As the pair of weasels were being led down a stone spiral staircase, the peeved Mawk asked, 'How do you do that?'

'You works on their imagination, squire,' replied Scirf, clacking his teeth in mirth. 'You gives 'em a picture of themselves, which ain't very pretty. They can't stomick it, these stoats. They've got no grit.'

'Them and me both,' muttered Mawk, remembering his crawl through the rat camp. 'Them and me too.'

'All we got to do now,' added Scirf, 'is to get Prince Poynt to believe what we've come to tell him.'

Mawk could hear, from the tone of Scirf's voice,

44

that this was not going to be at all easy.

When they reached the bottom of the staircase, a stoat was hurrying along the passageway. The stoat stopped and stared hard when he reached the sergeant leading the pair of weasels. Mawk noticed with apprehension that the stoat had a burn mark on his bib. This nasty scar had been put there by the leader of the outlaws, Sylver, with a flaming brand. The stoat suddenly clicked his teeth in amused satisfaction.

'Well, well, well,' said Sheriff Falshed, for the creature was indeed this stoatage. 'If it isn't Mawk and Scirf. Captured some outlaws have we, sergeant? Take them to the torture chamber. I'll join you in a few minutes, after I've attended my prince's call.'

'No, you got it wrong,' cried the alarmed Mawk. 'We're working for you now. There's been an amnesty. We're all against the rats now.'

Falshed's eyes hardened. 'An amnesty for *most* weasels, but not you lot. Oh, no. Never. Anyway, we'll talk about all this in a few minutes, over a red-hot branding iron. Can't stop now. Away with them, sergeant. Don't let them fool you with any talk about amnesties. They're for the boiling pot, those two – and any more outlaws from Halfmoon Wood you can find. There's a captaincy in it for you, if we can manage to make them talk – scream or talk, I don't mind which.'

With that the sheriff hurried away, with the cold eyes of Scirf on his back and the panic of Mawk hovering in the passageway, ready to give its owner the screaming habdabs.

Chapter Five

The outlaws and their stoat confederates split up into several parties before entering the village of Walberswit. The intention was to search out rats and render them harmless by binding them with cord. Alysoun, Luke and Wodehed found themselves together as they made their way between the weasel hovels. They passed vole pens where the cattle were snuffling and snorting, eating from troughs. Suddenly the trio came up against a huge rat who was leaving a house. The creature looked bleary-eyed and bad-tempered. He stared hard at the three weasels, probably believing they were villagers come back to protect their property.

'Weeeshhhels,' snarled the rat. 'Meee-eeeett weeeeshhhels.'

'Stand back,' Wodehed said to the other two, as the rat hunched on all four legs, ready to spring. 'Time for a bit of magic.'

Wodehed faced the hackled rat without fear.

Stormcloud black from mountain peaks
Swollen big with rains and sleets,
Let your belly burst above us,
Drown this rat who does not love us.'

'Rhyming's a bit dodgy,' muttered Luke.

The rat looked up to the heavens, as did all the

46

three weasels, to see what was to occur. The evening sky looked as quiet and tranquil as a weasel grandmother working with her crochet hook. No dark stormclouds came scuttling across the pink sunset. No threat was visible from the weather at all.

All four creatures stood as if in a tableau for a few moments, waiting for the magic to work.

When nothing happened the rat sneered and jeered something unmentionable at Wodehed. Then the fat bristly creature began to move in Wodehed's direction. Rats are much bigger creatures than weasels and this bully was prepared to use all his strength and viciousness in ridding the world of poor magicians like Wodehed. As the rat lumbered forward, his bulk nudged a tower made of timber struts, which stood next to the house from which he had emerged. A creaking sound came from the tall structure, as if its spars were under heavy pressure.

Just as the rat bared its horrible yellow teeth, ready to sink them into Wodehed's throat, the creaking structure collapsed and came crashing to the ground. The tank on top of this wooden tower burst open on contact with the ground and a flood of water came rushing out to sweep the big rat off his feet. The now gibbering creature was taken away in a swirling flood and jammed up hard against the wall of a building opposite.

Once the waters had receded the three weasels ran in and quickly trussed the creature with cords.

Wodehed was triumphant. 'It worked – it really worked – my magic!'

'I'd hardly call accidentally knocking over a water tower the result of bad weather brought on by magic,' scoffed Luke. 'The tower looked on its last legs. The rat itself did the rest by banging against it.'

'Yes, but right at that moment?'

'That moment, or any other. It was ready to go.'

'Oh, give Wodehed the benefit of the doubt, Luke. The result was the same,' said Alysoun. 'We've got the creature. Now let's go and look for another.'

All over the village, rats were being pounced on and bound with cord by various small raiding parties. The attacks were swift and competent. Before long every rat had been caught and trussed and dumped in the vole pens amongst squealing voles.

'Right,' said Sylver, 'now for that bronze horse.'

In every weasel village there is a shop which sells staves, this being the main fighting weapon of peasants, an aid to walking when travelling long distances and a tool for various other uses including forming the main pole for a bivouac. Sylver took his weasels to the staffseller's house and there they found sheaves of good sturdy rods. Sylver had them lash the staves together in four latticework squares which, when held upright, their ends touching, formed a cage.

This cage was placed in the middle of the village square, leaving the door to the cage open.

'Now, we have to round up the gong,' said Sylver, using the nickname weasels and stoats employ for hollow metal statues. 'Spread out, everyone. If you find the horse, shoo it this way – but *gently* – we don't want to scare it out into the open countryside. Just sort of usher it into the square and then into the cage if you can.'

Weasels and stoats scattered throughout the village.

It was Bryony and two stoats who found the metal creature ambling around at the south-east corner of the village where the rats had probably chased it. It was green with corrosion and the two holes

48

mentioned by Sylver were clearly visible. The bronze creature viewed the weasel-stoat party warily, watching with hollow eyes their every movement.

'Go-away-snakybody-things,' said the slow-thinking horse, in its limited language. 'Keep-from-me.'

Bryony broke a willow switch from a crack willow and got behind the horse. The two stoats held a staff each horizontally, forming a wide avenue. Walking forwards Bryony gently urged the metal beast back through this moving avenue towards the village. As she did so they came across other parties who now that the creature had been found, assisted in driving it gradually towards the cage Sylver had built.

The cage had cleverly been placed around the stone dais. This was the site on which the horse and general used to stand when they could not move. Thus the bronze creature experienced a comfortable, familiar feeling when herded onto that spot.

'It's all right,' Bryony told the general's charger, 'we're not going to harm you. We just want your help.'

With a little persuasion from Sylver the bronze mare went inside the cage and the gate shut. She seemed nervous, but in fact only became really agitated when a pigeon alighted on top of one of the staves. The sight of a pigeon is enough to enrage any statue, who over the centuries have had to put up with being used as a toilet by these feathered pests.

Now that they could move around, statues were no longer prepared to put up with such treatment from the pigeons. The horse snapped with bronze teeth at the bird until it flew off with a shout of alarm.

Once the metal animal had been soothed, Sylver was able to speak to it and explain what they wanted. 'We need you to carry us and some stores to the great castle at the place where it always rains,' he said. 'Will you do that for us?'

'What-you-give-general's-horse?' asked the other, practically.

'Our, ahem, wizard here will help you find your First and Last Resting Place by using his, ah, great magical powers.'

'Not-yet-ready-to-go-to-First-Last-Rest-Place.'

'No, but you will be, one day, and when that day comes you'll know exactly which way to head.'

The bronze horse pawed the ground and thought about this for a long time, before nodding slowly. 'I-take-you-to-castle,' she said.

A great cheer went up from weasels and stoats and the cage was removed.

The stores were loaded inside the bronze horse without any great difficulty. The metal creature seemed quite tickled that its hollow shape should be deemed useful. A couple of staves were tucked through the stirrup straps, in case they came in pawy. Then the weasels, ferrets and stoats climbed inside. Finally they were ready to leave.

Sylver leaped up from the dais on to the neck of the charger and took the metal reins in his paws. He stood on his hind legs for a better view of the countryside before them.

'Giddyup,' Sylver said. 'Off we go.'

The bronze horse began to trot, finding it rather comfortable to have a creature on its back once again, just as she had borne the general for so many years. Of course this weasel was much lighter in weight, but still the feeling was there.

Outside the village was a yellow-dust road across a moor along which the bronze mare cantered.

Sylver, tall and slim on the creature's back, kept a wary eye out for any rats. By bog and past peat hag went the crew. Darkness fell over the moor and the landscape turned to purple. The moon came out and rolled amongst the banks of high grey clouds.

Midnight was still a few hours away.

After some while the sound of the horse's hooves on the roadway set up a rhythmic sound. But there came a point when that sound was interrupted by another such rhythm, a heavier noise, not quite in tune with the bronze hoofbeats. The two sounds set up a discordant cadence.

Soon, out of the mists on the road ahead, came a figure on horseback.

Sylver reined his own mount and waited until the shape was clearer.

The other rider stopped too and silently regarded Sylver.

It was a stone knight on a stone horse. The block – a nickname weasels and stoats give *stone* statues – was fully armed, with a lance, a sword and shield, and a mace. These were all made of marble, like their owner, of course, and gleamed in the lemony light of the full moon.

'Out-of-me-way-ye-prune,' called the knight.

'Who are you calling a prune?' asked Sylver, indignantly.

'Don't let him get away with that,' came a voice from inside. 'Call him something back.'

The knight was not going to wait for a return insult. It was as if this were the opportunity for single combat he had been waiting for all his life. He set his lance point at Sylver's chest, lifted his shield and spurred his charger's flanks. 'If-ye-won't-get-out-of-me-way-I'll-have-to-knock-ye-out,

51

eh,' cried the stone warrior. 'Have-at-ye!'

With that the knight came thundering forward, his lance levelled at its target.

Seeing they were in a war situation the bronze horse beneath Sylver felt a rush of battle fever to her hollow head. Far from being timid about such combat, she sensed an old faintly familiar excitement in the air. She too surged forwards, her nostrils flaring. She would have been spouting sprigs of steam through those nostrils had she been a real horse with breath, but as it was the bronze charger had to make do with a snort.

Alarmed for the safety of those inside, Sylver drew out one of the staves from under the stirrup leathers. He held it just as the knight was holding his lance, level with the ground and poking between his mount's ears. The two jousters then bore down on one another at full tilt.

The enraged knight's stone lance missed Sylver by a whisker and struck the bronze horse with a noise like a rock hitting a dinner gong. The sound echoed over the moorland. The blow created a huge dent in the mare's neck.

Sylver's own 'lance' clipped the side of the knight's head and knocked off an ear. The end of the staff broke off on impact, leaving Sylver with an even shorter weapon. It was now more like a sword than a javelin or spear.

Sylver would have kept on riding, now that he was past the knight, but the bronze horse would have none of it. This creature whirled, ready to tilt again. Sylver could see the stone knight pulling on his bedraggled moustaches in great fury.

'Ye-busted-me-ear-ye-impudent-weaselly-charac-ter!' cried the knight, getting ready for another charge. 'I'll-have-your-guts-for-sock-elastic-so-I-will.'

Again the two combatants went thundering at one another, the wind whistling through the holes in the bronze horse's head. She was having a fine time. Not for a thousand years had she been used for such purpose. It was both exhilarating and exciting, and she wanted so desperately to win.

The stone charger coming at her was clearly an inferior mount who had to be checked and turned at every moment by its rider, while it was the bronze horse who was the dominant partner of the other pair.

Inside the bronze charger, all the others were now yelling and shouting, being jostled by the gallop.

This time the knight's lance struck the bronze horse on the rump with the sound of a dustbin lid hitting a brick wall. The stone shaft of his lance shattered. The bronze mare gave a whinny of triumph at having bested the knight and his charger at the joust.

The knight checked his own marble horse and drew his sword in great anger.

Again and again the knight came at Sylver, the stone blade whistling this way and that, never quite managing to hit the weasel. The enraged knight certainly managed to hit the bronze horse though. It was as if a mad cymbal-player had continued to strike his instrument, even though the rest of the orchestra had got up and left. What a symphony there might have been, on that lonely, desolate moor, if only the violins, woodwinds and brass sections had been there to fill in the gaps between sounding bronze and clashing stone!

Sylver was able to use his shortened staff to make a good show of fencing with the big knight. Stone and hardwood staff struck several times, both somehow managing to survive the glancing blows without breaking. The furious knight's moustaches bristled as he fought; his marble eyes glinted. He too was having the time of his life.

As they fought they left the narrow road and battled out onto the moor itself.

Suddenly, at one point in the combat, the knight held up his hand for a pause in activities. He stared down at his horse's legs, which were now up to the knees in marsh mud. It was obvious the knight and his mount were sinking fast, in a bog that was not going to let them go.

'Come-no-nearer-worthy-opponent,' warned the knight. 'We-sink-in-the-mire.'

Sylver and the bronze horse saw what he meant and wisely went no deeper into the moor.

Gradually the stone knight began to disappear, down into the oily quagmire in which he and his horse were trapped. The knight suddenly seemed resigned to his fate – which was not a death, for a stone warrior cannot die – and put his sword back in its stone scabbard. He gave Sylver a sad wave.

'Tis-not-a-chosen-end-but-such-is-the-way-of-things,' said the knight, calmly. 'Goodbye-fellah-me-lad.'

'Goodbye,' said Sylver, then as an afterthought, 'How are you called?'

'Sir-Percy-of-Castle-Storm,' replied the knight. 'The-castle-grounds-in-which-we-stood, Blinknot-and-I, are-far-to-the-south-beyond-a-turquoise-lakeland.'

'My name is Sylver,' said the weasel, remembering what Lord Haukin had said about the place which contained a secret passage leading to the second clue. 'You say your castle is called Storm?'

'Aye-so-it-be.'

Lord Haukin had mentioned something about a mysterious building having to do with bad weather . . .

By now the mire had covered Blinknot and was up to the knight's neck. The pair were almost gone. If they found solid ground beneath they might have a chance of travelling slowly through the mud on the bedrock bottom, moving as if through a sluggish sea, and finding their way to a slope which would lead them back up into the fresh air again.

'Castle Storm,' repeated Sylver, 'beyond the turquoise lakeland. Thank you, Sir Percy.'

'You're-welcome,' were the knight's last words, as the mud covered his brave moustaches, though he had no idea why he was being thanked. The stone plume on top of his helmet was last to disappear.

Sylver said, 'Goodbye, Sir Percy.'

This was echoed by a dozen or so voices, which resounded around the bronze horse's hollow chest.

Wodehed was muttering, 'Turquoise lakes? I'm sure I've heard something about them, from someone. Now who was it? I wish I could remember things – but – no, it's gone. Perhaps it will come back to me later, when I'm not trying so hard.'

But no-one was listening anyway. He might as well have been speaking to himself.

Chapter Six

Having been delayed on the moor road, Sylver and his crew of weasels, stoats and ferrets arrived within sight of Castle Rayn at about a quarter to midnight.

He halted the bronze mare in a copse of trees on a hill overlooking Rayn valley, staying hidden from prying eyes. The copse was eerily silent. The creatures who had once lived in it had long since run away to escape the rats.

'Are we near yet?' called Wodehed from inside. 'Can you see anything?'

'I can see the flags flying from masts on the towers of Castle Rayn,' said Sylver by way of reply. 'The stoat emblems are clearly visible in the light of the moon.'

Between himself and the castle however was a sea of dark bivouacs and hide tents flapping gently in the night breezes. Around these dwellings, out in the open, slept thousands of rats. The embers of their evening fires glowed red in the darkness like the eyes of a many-headed monster. Here and there stood a yawning sentry, some poor rodent chosen to watch over the landscape while his comrades slept. It was not a job taken too seriously, since the enemy was safely locked up in the castle.

Sylver studied the mass of rats and worked out a path through them. It was not easy. They were sprawled all over the place. In general however they appeared to avoid the dips in the ground. This was probably because those shallow earth basins filled with water when it rained, which was quite often in this western part of Welkin. What he had to do was ride like mad, sticking to the lower ground, heading for the castle gates.

'Is the drawbridge up?' asked Bryony, from inside the horse. 'What about the portcullis?'

'It all looks pretty well shut up tight to me,' replied Sylver, 'which is as it should be. If Scirf and Mawk have got through they'll have the gate open just before we reach it. I expect we've missed their signal, if they ever made it, by getting here so late in the evening. We'll have to take a chance and just go for it.'

'What if they're not there?' cried a stoat. 'We'll be at the mercy of the rats.'

'Well, we'll confuse them by riding through their camp. They probably won't gather their wits for a few minutes. In which time we can escape – I hope.'

'You *hope*?' muttered the stoat. 'I hope so too!'

It was quiet out on the plains in front of the castle. The group in the copse on the hill could clearly hear the castle clock chiming out the quarter hour.

They waited, counting away the seconds and minutes, until it was just one minute to midnight.

'Here we go!' cried Sylver. 'Hang on, everyone!'

With Sylver flicking the reins to urge the bronze horse forwards, they began their gallop towards the castle gates.

And what a run it was! The bronze mare went hurling forward. She dashed across the rat-covered ground keeping to the dips and hollows. She was a sprightly creature, even after her battle ordeal earlier in the evening. She had many wounds, many dents. These uneven places on her metal coat gleamed in

57

the moonlight. She wore them like badges of courage.

Her bronze hooves flew, kicking up divots at the stars. Her bronze mane and tail flowed like burnished founts in the light of the moon. Here was more great excitement! After decades of wandering aimlessly around a village of weasel peasants with nothing to do but sigh, here she was at last doing what military chargers do. Riding into the enemy.

But not all the rat sentries were dozing.

'*Aaaaalllarrrm! Aaaalllarrrm!*' screamed one, more awake than the rest. '*Unnndddrr aaaatttark!*'

The savage rats leaped from their beds with great alacrity. Far from being thick-headed they looked wide awake and eager for battle. They snatched up sharp, hooked sickles and staves with ugly-looking curved blades bound to the end. True, they were a little confused, dashing this way and that, looking in vain for an army of stoats. But they soon regrouped. Many of them had jumped up and had gone to the drums, beating out their unhealthy rat rhythms. Others had grabbed horns and bullfrog-roarers, and were making as much noise as they could.

The bronze mare decided to ignore Sylver's advice about sticking to low ground. Now that the rats were awake it made no sense. She galloped through the middle of them. They scattered before her charge, yelling and screaming terrible oaths. Missiles began to whizz through the air: knives, iron-spiked balls, metal discs with sawtoothed edges, lumps of clay full of nails.

Sylver, high up on the back of the horse, had to continually duck as these objects went whistling past him. The mare cared nothing for such weapons. They clattered against her metal flanks, falling uselessly away without harming her.

The castle loomed ever nearer as she trampled down tents and bivouacs in her tempestuous run to the gates. Shrieks of fury came from within these temporary dwellings. Stew pots were knocked over and sent flying. Scattering rats were covered in the greasy remnants of last evening's supper. Coals from camp fires showered into the night like clouds of blacksmith's sparks. Weapons, stacked like sheaves of corn, ready to grab in case of battle, were kicked high into the air and came down like spent sky-rockets. These often landed point first, to quiver in the ground. The air was full of deadly flying objects.

'Nearly there!' shouted Sylver, as he could see the stoat sentries on the castle walls, peering down with round amazed eyes. 'Hold on inside!'

The castle drawbridge was in sight. However, it showed no signs of being lowered. In front of the drawbridge stood a great fat rat, a giant of a fellow, with a wide leather belt ringed with spikes. In his claws he held a stone club. He wielded this weapon with narrowed eyes, ready to smash away a bronze shin.

Sylver realized this was quite a dangerous situation. If the rat bent one of the mare's legs, they could all go tumbling down. Those in the horse would be at the mercy of the multitude. Around him were hundreds of rodents, their eyes burning with hate and their claws itching for revenge.

'OPEN UP! OPEN UP!' yelled Sylver, at the faces which leaned over the castle walls. 'CAN'T YOU SEE WE WANT TO ENTER THE CASTLE!'

If they heeded the call or not, it was surely too late. The bronze horse was almost at the moat's edge. Another few metres and the giant rat would swing his club. A few more metres beyond that and they would all be in the murky waters of the moat. Those inside the horse would most likely drown. The wounded bronze mare would fill with water and sink.

At the last moment the mare swerved away from the giant rat. One of her hind hooves caught him right on the belt buckle. With a wail of dismay he shot out over the moat. He landed a moment later with a big splash. Sylver saw him bob to the surface, clutching at pondweed with panic on his face. Clearly he was not the good swimmer his kind were supposed to be.

The mare continued round the edge of the moat, pursued by a blood-thirsty, howling mob of rodents. Sylver felt that surely all was lost. Once the metal steed which carried them tired or fell, he and his brave companions would be clubbed and hacked by those horrible creatures around them. He could not remember being more anxious about a situation.

Then suddenly he spied something ahead! An earth ramp, reaching up the castle walls. It had collapsed in on itself close to the wall, but half the ramp remained, like an unfinished bridge. Sylver urged the bronze horse up this slope, while the rats followed, still shrieking like lunatics.

'Come on, my beauty,' said Sylver. 'You can do it.'

The bronze mare had not heard these words in many years. They were just the right thing to say to her. The old general used to use the same phrase. That was before he dismounted and went off wandering on his own. Any weariness she had felt before now left her. She picked up speed towards the top of the ramp, seeing the gap between it and the top of the castle battlements.

She launched herself from the edge of the ramp, flying out over the chasm. Down below was the muddy mess which used to be the moat. Her hind legs had lost none of their strength. Over the dark gully she soared. Then her forehooves struck the battlement walk between two towers. There she skidded to a halt, a stream of sparks flying from her feet. It was a glorious jump and one of which any horse would be proud – metal, wood, stone, or even flesh.

Sylver unfortunately went flying from her neck, to somersault through the air. He landed at the feet of a stoat with a burn mark on his chest. The others, inside her belly and chest, were shaken up but unharmed. No-one had suffered any really serious injuries.

Many of those rats who had followed the mare full pelt up the ramp could not stop on reaching the top. They went spilling over and dropped like lemmings into the deep mud below. Some managed to cling to the edge and dangled there, eventually to be rescued by comrades. A few even sailed across the great divide, only to smack into the stone wall of the castle. These too fell to join those struggling in the morass below the battlements.

'Such entertainment,' mused the stoat with the scarred bib. 'I only wish my prince could have witnessed it.'

Sylver looked up to see the face of Sheriff Falshed peering down at him. The sheriff wore an amused expression.

'I did, I did,' cried an excited voice, as an ermine swept out of a doorway onto the battlements. 'I saw it from the arrowloop in my room – most of it – couldn't see it all, of course.'

This figure was indeed Prince Poynt, one-time arch enemy of all weasels, Sylver's band especially, until they had all been united by the common enemy – the rats. He was wearing a startling-looking red sash around his middle, vivid against his white fur, onto which he had tied the scabbard of his dagger. The material appeared so light it was ethereal. The ends of this sash flowed behind him like misty trails of blood. The sash looked garish and kitsch on the stoat prince.

Sylver got up and dusted his pelt down with his paws. 'Why did no-one open the gates?' he asked. 'Didn't my two weasels get through? We've brought stores with us – food in plenty – they were supposed to ensure we got in at the stroke of midnight. We nearly lost everything to the rats.'

Prince Poynt raised a brow at Falshed who said in a creamy voice, 'The weasels we threw in the dungeon, my prince. Those we put on the rack this evening. They said something about opening the gates for the outlaw Sylver, but of course we didn't believe them. They were lying to save their pelts.'

Light dawned in the prince's eyes as several other noblestoats came out onto the battlements – Earl Takely, Wilisen, Lord Elphet and Jessex – followed by a weasel in a silly hat, blowing silently on a whistle and dancing as if he were at a festival.

This latter creature was Pompom, the court jester, who kept His Highness amused in times when the prince was assailed by dark thoughts involving his deceased older brother.

'Ah, yes,' said the prince. 'You informed me that they didn't even change their tune when we used the red-hot branding irons. Obviously they were *not* lying, Falshed. We'll speak more on this subject later . . .'

Falshed sighed and shook his head as if to say, How was I to know?

'You tortured them?' cried Sylver. 'They came to

help you. We were told of an amnesty. We were informed that you had made it law that if weasels helped against the rats all charges against them would be dropped.'

'Did I say that?' asked the prince with a wave of his claw at the noblestoats. 'Thanes, knights, my dear Pompom – did I say anything like that?'

Laughter came from the thanes, but it was Pompom who replied to his master.

'I think you had your claws crossed behind your back,' cried Pompom. 'You were lying when you made the proclamation, your stoatitude.'

Prince Poynt frowned. 'I never *lie*, you stupid little weasel. Truth is merely pliable in my paws. Flexible. I mould it like clay. I'm allowed to do that. I'm a prince.'

Pompom danced up to Sylver and looked into his face, his expression jubilant. 'Silly outlaw, fancy believing a stoat.'

Prince Poynt frowned again, not being sure he really approved of the way Pompom was putting things.

Sylver however, glared at Pompom. 'You ought to be ashamed of yourself – call yourself a weasel?'

Pompom's face dropped. His expression suddenly became one of abject misery. His shoulders drooped. 'We all survive the best way we can,' he said, in a quiet tone.

Stoat soldiers then dragged the other outlaws and the deserters from the holes in the mare's bronze body. They were lined up against the wall. Then the stores were found. Joyous shouts greeted the baskets of nuts and dried fruit. Prince Poynt was immediately offered a pawful of hazelnuts. He gave them to Pompom for that weasel to crack them between his teeth and to return the kernels to the ermine.

'Do you know of any reason,' asked the prince, sneering at outlaws and deserters alike, 'why I should not have you thrown over the battlements, down to those blood-thirsty creatures below? If so, speak now.'

'We brought you food, Your Highness,' croaked one of his returned stoats. 'We saved your life.'

'Saved my life?' squealed Prince Poynt. 'Saved *my* life, you impudent stoat. Do you think I would be the first to die of starvation here – or the very last? Speak up!'

The stoat turned to his companions for help, but finding none in their eyes, said, 'I – I think – the last, Your Highness.'

'Well, you're wrong,' said the prince, crunching on a walnut kernel. 'I'm much more noble than that. My sister means more to me than my own life. She would be the last to expire. Throw this oaf over the wall . . .'

The guards stepped forward, but Sylver shouted, 'Stop!' He was enraged. 'How dare you! How *dare* you! You puffed-up animal! This stoat risked his life to save your castle from falling into the paws of the rat hordes of Flaggatis – and you reward him with his death? Do you not know there is a higher authority – that place where your dead brother waits for you – which will judge those actions you take this night?'

Falshed gasped and stepped away from the prince, knowing a forbidden subject had been thrust in the royal face.

The prince snatched a mace from a nearby noblestoat and stood eyeball to eyeball with the angry weasel leader. A dark area of the prince's memory had been thrown into the light. He shivered as he stood there, seeing a mental picture he did not want to see. The mace was raised, ready to crush the head of the weasel who had illuminated that picture. The prince was in the grip of terrible dreams, things he wanted to forget.

'Never – never ever – mention my brother,' he hissed, the ugly visions burning into his brain.

Gradually, having been through this torment many times, the prince regained control over his horrors.

The outlaws – Bryony, Luke, Icham, Alysoun and Wodehed – waited in apprehension for Prince Poynt to strike.

However, the prince finally lowered his weapon and with a sideways smile he turned to the stoat deserter he had ordered to be thrown over the walls.

'Now that,' he pointed to Sylver, 'is a sound argument. Take heed, soldier. Learn.'

Then to Sylver, he said slowly, 'Never, ever, call me names again, weasel, or I'll have your eyes burned out of your head and your liver fed to the pike in the moat. The only reason I don't throw you to the rats right now is because I believe you're in league with them. Yes! How else could you have got through their lines unscathed? They let you through, didn't they? It was all a cunning plan, no doubt devised by Flaggatis. The second I turn my back you'll open the gates and let in a flood of horrible hairy rats . . .'

Sylver saw that it was useless to argue with the paranoid prince.

Falshed cried triumphantly, 'You are conspiring with the rats to overthrow your rightful lord and ruler, but your reward for treachery will be to spend the last few days of your life in my dungeons.'

Prince Poynt turned to Falshed and ordered, 'Have the weasels clapped in irons.' He waved a claw at the deserters. 'These stoats can return to their barracks. Remind them they're back in the army. A few fatigue duties in the castle kitchens, cracking nuts and washing dried fruit, will help them to remember. Now, bring a sack of dried fruit and one of nuts to my quarters. The rest can go to the store-room until morning. Return the key to me after they're safely stacked. If I catch anyone chewing so much as an acorn I'll make him eat his whiskers.'

'Yes, my prince. What about the horse?'

The prince stared at the mare, who was now wandering up and down the battlements, in the way that she used to stroll about the village of Walberswit. Her task for the weasels now over, she was content to indulge in idle dreams. She was once more without purpose.

'Let her stay – she doesn't eat anything.'

With that the ermine swept off the battlements, his noblestoats and jester in tow.

Chapter Seven

The weasel band were taken and chained to the walls of the dungeons by a stoat jailer with a patch over one eye. There they met Scirf and Mawk. There were burn marks on their fur. Both their expressions told the other weasels they had been subjected to pain. Mawk looked frightened and miserable, but Scirf was putting on his usual show of bravado.

'Got you lot too, eh? Well, they won't hold us long.'

'That's what you think,' muttered the stoat jailer, who had had just about enough of this ex-dung-watcher. 'You'll stay here until I'm good and ready to execute you.'

'You?' said Scirf contemptuously. 'You got about as much say round here as a fly. Who do you think you are? A greasy minion with few grimy keys, that's what you are. It's the prince what says who gets the chop and who doesn't.'

'My keys ain't grimy,' said the jailer, lovingly stroking the ring attached to his belt. 'They're my badge of office, they are. They're specially made with special tools. They're like a work of art, they are. Don't you say anythink against my keys, you grubby serf.'

'Grubby? Look who's talking.'

The jailer rubbed one of the bare patches on his pelt in irritation. There were bald bits all over him.

Sparks from the wood furnace where they heated the branding irons had spat onto his coat numerous times. They had burned holes in it. His tail looked mangled as well. This had once caught in the winch on the rack and had been chewed up. And one of his claws was crooked where he had trapped it in the door of an Iron Maiden. And a foot had been flattened when a pressing stone had been dropped onto it. In truth it appeared as if he himself had undergone all the tortures the dungeons had to offer.

It was a fact that more accidents happened in the torture chamber than anywhere else in the castle, including the kitchen and the garderobe. The jailer was a pathetic creature who looked as if he were held together with bits of string and glue.

He said nastily, 'If you don't watch your mouth I'll get out some o' my more int'resting torturing irons.'

Mawk said, 'Shut up, Scirf, for heaven's sakes. He's bad enough without you baiting him all the time.'

Sylver spoke now. 'So, Falshed had you manacled the minute you got inside the castle?'

'Yep,' replied Scirf. 'Had some adventures gettin' in here too. Not worth it, is it? You treat these stoats like proper animals and they just cheat you at every turn. They're a bunch of dishonourable ruffians.'

'Not all of us are like that,' said the jailer, jangling his keys. 'Some of us are honourable stoats.'

'Like who?' sneered Scirf.

'Me for instance,' replied the jailer, hotly. 'We're not all like . . .' The jailer suddenly stopped in mid-sentence, realizing he was being goaded into saying something which would get him into trouble.

'Yes?' cried Scirf, triumphantly. 'Like – the *prince*? That's what you was goin' to say, wasn't it?'

'No, no, I wasn't. I wasn't going to say that at all. I was going to say like . . .'

'Sheriff Falshed,' murmured Bryony.

'Yes – like Sheriff Falshed,' replied the jailer, clutching at the first thing that was thrown at him. Then he realized what he had said. 'I mean, no – no, not like him – not like the sheriff at all.'

At that moment Falshed flowed down the slimy stone steps into the lower dungeon. 'Not like who?' he asked.

The jailer looked panic-stricken as Scirf crowed, 'This peasant said you were a creature without honour.'

Falshed eyed the trembling jailer, who had backed away from the sheriff holding his paws over his head. 'Did he now? Well, I'm sure he was put up to it, and I don't have to look very far to find the weasels who tricked him into saying it, do I? Scirf, you will find yourself in a pot of boiling oil if you don't behave. The rest of you will learn over time that you will either come to respect me, or you'll thirst, starve and be subjected to horrible acts. It's as simple as that – you give, I take, and no buts.'

Falshed stayed in the dungeons for some time, walking up and down, occasionally tweaking a nose or twisting an ear. He seemed as pleased as punch that he had at last got the outlaws in chains. Sylver, looking around the deep dungeon, with its thick walls, stout wooden nailstudded door and no windows, was inclined to think that escape was going to be very difficult.

'. . . no prisoner has ever left these dungeons alive,' Falshed was saying. 'None has ever escaped and inmates who did not die of old age lost their lives under the pressing stones, or in the Iron Maiden. All have ended up decorating the prince's gibbet, blowing stiffly in the wind and the rain.'

There did not seem to be much to say to this and Sylver kept his own counsel until Falshed had left, not without the stoat giving the jailer a cuff around the ear for his earlier remark about the sheriff being dishonourable.

The jailer sat at his table, rubbing his ear. His candle had melted down to a stub, so he took another one out of a cupboard and lit it. Then he made himself a hot drink, using the torture furnace to boil the kettle. Finally he took up a leather cup and some hollyhock seeds and began to play a game of solitaire hollyhockers, which was not a great deal of fun since he had no-one to bet against.

'I used to be an expert at that,' said Mawk. 'I once played against a gang of moles for my freedom.'

The jailer looked up, interested. 'What moles?'

'Some bandit called Jaspin.'

The jailer's brows shot up. 'You played against *Jaspin*? He's supposed to be unbeatable. I heard he can go into any game, anywhere, and wipe the table with any other player.'

'Well, I won against him,' retorted Mawk, a little immodestly. 'Just once. If it hadn't been best out of three I would have walked away winning.'

'It's *always* best out of three.'

'That's what he said. But I threw a jabby-knocker on my second throw. Otherwise I would have beaten him.'

The jailer shrugged and threw his seeds. He stared at the pattern on the table.

'Widdershins,' Mawk said. 'Void game.'

The jailer stared at him for a moment and said, 'You want a game then? I get bored down here on night shift. The hours go so slowly.'

70

'Can't do it from up here,' replied Mawk. 'If you let me come down I will.'

The jailer cocked his head to one side. 'You won't try to escape, I suppose.'

'Where would I go? In any case, I'm a coward. I never do anything against authority. Ask anyone here.'

'Coward,' confirmed Scirf. 'Yellow as a daffodil.'

'That's right, you are, aren't you?' the jailer said, remembering. 'You yelled like a baby before I even touched you with one of my red-hot irons. Scared to death, you were.'

'So would you be,' retorted Mawk. 'I've got a lot of imagination.'

The jailer ummed and ahhhed for a bit, got up and carefully locked the outer door to the dungeons, then eventually he took one of his little shiny keys and opened the manacles on Mawk's forepaws. Mawk rubbed his joints where they had been made sore on the rack. He spat on his paw and rubbed his wounds where the red-hot irons had touched. This smarted and made him wince and blink his eyes.

Then he went and sat at the table with the jailer. Before long they were deep in a game of holly-hockers.

'Hurdygurdy!' cried Mawk. 'I get to throw again.'

'You'll be throwing Molly Maguires next,' grumbled the jailer. 'Come on, hurry up.'

Mawk put down the leather cup and rubbed his hindleg joints again. 'What about a glass of something? I'm getting thirsty.'

'What do you think this is, a minstrel's den? I got no honey dew here, if that's what you're after. We're not allowed to get drunk on duty.'

'I'll get some soup. You sit there. That's right. You

deserve to be waited on a little. You work hard. I saw the sweat pouring from you, when you was sizzling under Scirf's forelegs with your hot branding iron. It can't be all fun, your job, being a torturer and all that.'

'Too right,' said the jailer with a sigh. 'Animals don't realize what hard work it is. You have to carry logs, keep the furnace stoked, rake out the grate and get rid of the ashes afterwards. Turning those winches when you're stretching weasels on the rack's no picnic, either. You need all the strength and energy you've got for that. I'm pretty strong of course, and I've got the knack – it's all in the stance – but you still get worn out making other creatures suffer.'

'And all that screaming can't help any. It must jangle your nerves.'

'Tell me about it,' said the jailer, as Mawk poured some of the thin gruel into a cup – one for himself and one for the jailer. When they were sitting comfortably again, he made another suggestion.

'Tell you what,' Mawk said, 'it's a bit boring, playing hollyhockers for nothing. Why don't you share out those keys between us and we can use them to gamble with?'

'My keys?' said the motley jailer, clutching the items in question to his breast. 'I don't think so.'

'Oh, fair enough. Just thought we could liven things up a bit. But if they're too precious . . .'

An internal struggle went on inside the stoat jailer, who finally unhooked his ring of keys from his belt. 'All right then. But be careful with them.' He shared them out equally between the two of them. They began to play. Mawk lost steadily, relinquishing keys one after the other, much to the chagrin of the outlaws who were looking on in silence. Finally, the jailer had all his keys back.

'Hard cheese,' he said. 'I win.'

'Well done,' said Mawk, getting up and yawning, having a good stretch, 'but now I've got to get some shut-eye. Lock me up for the rest of the night, will you?'

'Sure,' replied the jailer, 'but how about another game tomorrow morning?'

'If you're up to it.'

'I'll look forward to it.'

The outlaws groaned as Mawk was once again incarcerated in his manacles and chains. The jailer got himself another cup of the gruel, which was not much more than water with a bit of pondweed dipped in it, and before long he was snoozing, his head resting on his table.

Once he had fallen asleep, Mawk seemed to fly awake. He winked at the others before tonguing something to the front of his mouth. He held it in his teeth. It was the small shiny key which opened the manacles. Somehow he had pawed the key and hidden it under his tongue, without the jailer noticing.

Using his mouth skilfully, Mawk used the key to open the locks on his forepaws. Then, when he was free, he skipped from outlaw to outlaw, doing the same for the rest of the weasels. Soon they were all free. They tiptoed to the nailstudded door, but when Sylver tried it, he found it locked.

Going back to the jailer he thought about removing the ring of keys from the jailer's belt, but it seemed an impossible thing to do, not without waking the creature. Then Icham silently pointed to a grating set in the stone dungeon floor.

The outlaws lifted the grating to see a deep channel below, in which water flowed. It was probably one of the ducts which carried the castle's waste water away. Certainly the water below looked pale and washy, as if it had lye soap in it. One by one the outlaws climbed down through the hole and lowered themselves carefully into the water. One by one they were swept out of sight of those still waiting above. The last to go down was Scirf, who managed to replace the grating quietly behind him, so that when the jailer woke it would seem as if his prisoners had just vanished into thin air.

'Poor ole devil,' murmured Scirf, hobbling a little where his joints had gone stiff from being stretched. He licked a few of the burn marks on his fur and nodded in a satisfied way. 'He's really goin' to catch it when the prince and sheriff find out.'

Then that weasel dropped into the fast-flowing stream below and was swept away into the darkness, travelling down the flume to some unknown destination at a heavy rate of knots.

Chapter Eight

Sylver hit the cold water with barely a splash. He grabbed an iron bolt projecting from the tunnel wall to avoid being swept away. Then he waited for Scirf to replace the grating. When he heard Scirf hit the water beside him, Sylver let go of the bolt. The two of them went sweeping down the narrow tunnel together. They tried to keep to the middle, where the current was strongest, thus avoiding being struck by the walls.

'Are you all right?' he called to Scirf, above the sound of the rushing flow.

'I don't like water,' yelled Scirf back to him. 'I hate it.'

Sylver was concerned for the other weasel. He knew how fear of drowning sometimes made creatures panic. He decided to try to calm his companion down a little. 'You won't drown in this. The speed of the flow will keep you up on the surface.'

'I'm not worried about *drowning*,' Scirf yelled, disdainfully. 'It's the washing part. I feel like I'm having a dozen baths at once. You know how much I hate washin' meself. But I must admit it's doing me joints good, where I was stretched on the rack. An' those burn marks. Cool water's good for some things, I suppose.'

Sylver clicked his teeth in amusement. It was true the scruffiest of the outlaws was Scirf, who had to be dragged to a stream to bathe by several strong weasels. Now here he was having to wallow in soapy water to save his life. It would make a good story for the others.

Their eyes became a little more used to the darkness as they were swept along. Very soon they came to the part where the stonework ended. This must have been where the castle met the countryside above. There had been an iron grate over this exit too, but it was thankfully hanging on its hinges, broken and open. The pair were carried over a little waterfall, which fell down into an underground river.

Here the water was clean and sweet and Sylver gratefully drank some as he went along. In the dungeons it had been very hot and they had been given no sustenance. He could hear Scirf doing the same.

On and on, for a very long time, went the two weasels. Sometimes Sylver fancied he could see one or two of the others ahead but it was so dark he could not be sure. Finally, the underground river slowed down to a meandering lazy walk. There was light from above where cracks and fissures in the rock allowed the day to seep in.

Eventually the river widened, flowing out into a cathedral-like cavern, then into a much larger cavern, and yet another larger still, and so on until they came to an enormous one where a long thin island appeared in the middle of a lake.

Along the sides of the monstrous cavern, as well as on the island, the pair could see lamps and flaming torches. The whole place was ablaze with light. Obviously they were entering an inhabited section of the underground world.

When the two weasels arrived at the island, they

found the rest of the band. But there were others there too. A large group of otters were surrounding the outlaws. Sylver and Scirf were quickly taken too. One large otter, carrying a cudgel, seemed to be the leader. She studied the outlaws with a grim expression.

'Why have you invaded the halls of the Guild of Otters?' she demanded. 'What did you hope to find here? Money? Treasure? Jays' feathers?'

'Jays' feathers?' said Scirf, in a surprised voice. 'What 'ave they got to do with anyfink?'

The female otter pushed her face close to Scirf's. 'Don't tell me you didn't know that jays' feathers are the most precious things in the universe.'

'What – all of them?'

'No, just the little blue ones on the wings.'

'Tshaw!' replied Scirf, contemptuously. 'You know where you can stick your little blue jays' feathers . . .'

Sylver shook his head and stepped in front of Scirf before that weasel landed them in trouble with his tongue. After all there were at least two dozen more otters than weasels. What was more the otters were all armed. Sylver suspected they had been driven underground by some tyrant like Lord Ragnar of Fearsomeshire, and having lived in isolation and near-darkness for so long, were not altogether right in the head.

'Listen,' he said, 'we want no trouble. We're not interested in treasure of any kind. We're escaping from the Castle Rayn dungeons. Can you tell us the quickest way to get to the surface?'

'Yes,' replied the otter. 'Go back the way you came.'

'Well, we obviously can't do that. For one thing the flow is too fast, and for another we would

77

probably be executed if we went back there. Surely this river must go up to the surface somewhere.'

'Yes, just before the Turq . . .' began a small otter on the side, but the female leader glared at it and it clamped its mouth shut.

Then the leader of the Guild of Otters replied coldly, 'We can't let you go. You have discovered the place where we have our workshops. If word should get out that this is where the famous blue-feather cloaks are made by Floe of the Guild of Otters – why we should be inundated with visitors. Animals would flock here from all over. And no doubt the jays would be after us . . .'

'How do you get their feathers?' asked Bryony. 'Do you pluck them from their wings while they are asleep?'

The little male otter on the side spoke up again, seemingly too bubbly to be kept down for long. His leader looked as if she would like to put the lid on him, but let him run on for a while. Her obvious pride in what he was saying overcame her annoyance with his interruptions.

'No, no – we take them from their nests. Feathers which have come loose and fallen out. We send agents out at night, into the countryside. Sometimes they find feathers from a fox-kill – we can use those if they're not too bloodstained. Our blue cloaks are worn by royalty and the nobility all over Welkin. We've recently started a new line in thrush-egg brooches to complement the blue of the feathers. Such a lovely blue. Blue is the colour, you know. Everyone adores it. Jason thinks it's something to do with the colour of summer skies.'

He paused and gave a little polite cough, before adding, 'Jason also makes very attractive snakeskin leggings, from skins sloughed by adders. But

78

those are for nobles who prefer *brown*.'

The word *brown* was uttered in such a tone of contempt it was obvious to the outlaws that anyone who wore such a colour needed to get a proper life. An otter, an elderly male, ducked his head in shame and tried to hide. This must have been the infamous Jason, who made brown leggings.

'You make new clothes,' Sylver said, now catching on and feeling relieved. 'You're workers in cloth – tailors.'

'Clothes? Cloth? Tailors?' cried the female otter. 'How utterly crass. We don't make clothes, we make *designs*. We work in *fabrics*. We are creators of beautiful garments. Please!'

'Well, be that as it may, we mean you no harm. No-one will be told of your location. You must let us go.'

'Sorry, can't do it. Part of the attraction of our garments is the mystery attached to their creation. No-one outside this place knows how or where the cloaks are made. If we let you go, one of you will be bound to blab sooner or later. You must remain here.'

'For how long?' asked Bryony, dismayed.

'Till the end of the world,' came the simple reply.

'That might come sooner than you think,' said Scirf. 'Don't you know Welkin's been raided by the rat hordes from the unnamed marshes? They'll eat everythin' that's not made of metal and take anythin' that's not nailed down.'

'We're safe enough down here,' replied an otter. 'No-one's ever found their way into here and left alive.'

The weasels were taken to a place on the underground island where there was a bank of caves. Here they were again imprisoned. A metal grate, very like the one the weasels had seen on leaving the castle, was used as jail bars. Two sturdy otters were put on guard outside.

The first thing Sylver did was to have the cave inspected from top to bottom and end to end. Unhappily all this proved was that they were indeed tightly enclosed. The weasel leader stared through the bars at the roof of the cavern through which the river ran. It was thickly covered in stalactites, joined by some kind of fluted shapes like limestone curtains or church organ pipes. There were no holes to the surface there.

'We're stuck here,' said Mawk gloomily. 'And we don't even know where we are.'

'I think I have a good idea where this river comes out now,' Sylver said, 'and it's just where we want to be. Gather round, jacks and jills, and I'll let you in on the secret.'

The others crowded round him.

'Where?' asked Scirf. 'Halfmoon Wood?'

'No,' replied Sylver. 'I'm sure that young otter – the one with all the enthusiasm – I'm sure he was about to say *turquoise* when he was stopped by that big female. I think this river comes out at the Turquoise Lakes.'

'The stone knight!' cried Luke. 'He said there was a Castle Storm just beyond a turquoise lakeland!'

'Precisely,' Sylver said, satisfied with his own deductions. 'I believe Castle Storm to be the place where the clue is hidden. Now if we could only get out of this blasted cave . . .'

'I'm *certain* there's something about those lakes,' Wodehed said. 'Something someone told me – I wish I could remember what it was. It just won't come to me.'

It was while Wodehed was muttering they received a visitor. It was the young bubbly otter. The

80

guards let him come up to the bars. He had a basket of food on his arm.

'We can't let you starve,' said the youngster. 'I've brought you some dried fish.'

'Dried fish?' snorted Scirf. 'I'd rather eat Mawk.'

'Thank you,' Mawk said, in a long-suffering voice.

However, the weasels did not have much choice. Sylver took the dried fish with grateful thanks and shared them out amongst the outlaws. The fare was a little salty, but not as bad as they expected it to be. The young otter watched them eat.

'My name is Sleek,' he said, after a while. 'Have you really escaped from Castle Rayn?'

'You think we go hurtlin' down subterranean rivers for fun?' said Scirf, sarcastically.

'No, what I mean is, you didn't come here on purpose, as Floe seems to think you did, to steal our designs?'

Sylver realized that Floe was probably the big female otter.

'We're here by accident,' he told the youngster. 'We have no interest in the garment industry of Welkin.'

Sleek looked as though he disapproved of this remark. He told the outlaws that it was impossible that other animals could not be interested in fashion designs. Why, dealing with fabrics and colours was life itself! When he, Sleek, woke every morning he could not wait to get his paws on some material or other. His claws were perfectly suited to using a needle and thread. A pair of cutter's scissors fitted them to precision. His eye was ever searching for new dyes.

'Natural colours are out at the moment,' he said. 'Nature is so limited in her hues. Look at a rainbow. Pretty insipid colours, wouldn't you say?

81

One can do so much better mixing ochres . . .'

'I thought you lot just did cloaks of jays' feathers,' Scirf interrupted. 'An' snakeskin leggings. They're natural enough, ain't they?'

'Oh, that's just *her*,' answered Sleek with disdain in his voice. 'That's just Floe. She thinks life begins and ends with jays' feathers. I'm into innovation! I want to revolutionize the fashion world. I've been secretly despatching little creations of mine to nobles on the outside. I recently sent Prince Poynt a scarf made of spider's web muslin dyed a beautiful crimson. Raspberry juice mixed with a secret fixing fluid. I shouldn't be telling you that, but you say you don't have any interest in these things and I think I believe you now.'

The youngster sighed, before adding, 'I should so like to see Prince Poynt in my beautiful scarf, wrapped loosely and nonchalantly around his aristocratic throat and drifting on the breeze as he walks the battlements of a morning.'

Sylver gave a cough, remembering a ghastly creased and knotted red sash he had seen Prince Poynt wearing tied around his middle like a swash-buckling pirate. 'I think – I believe I've seen the *creation*. The noble in question was wearing it when he called us traitors and renegades, and sentenced us to hang from chains in his dungeons. Fortunately, we escaped before he could make good his threat.'

'Oh, did it look fine on him?' breathed Sleek.

'Absolutely,' fibbed Sylver. 'Suited him down to the ground.'

Sleek looked sublimely happy. Then a change came over his face. He came close to the bars, so that the two guards could not hear what he was saying. 'What's your favourite colour?' he whispered, conspiratorially.

'Er, green?' suggested Sylver.

Sleek shrugged as if to say, every animal to its own, even if his own is rather naff. Then his eyes sparkled as he revealed his innermost secret: his reason for living. 'Mine's *orange*.'

The word was not exactly spoken. It wafted from his lips like incense smoke from the holes in a censer. Every syllable seemed to scent the very atmosphere. It was as if something sacred had been breathed into the air and hovered there as hallowed mist hovers about the head of an angel.

'There you have it,' he confirmed, after an appropriate interval. Then he looked melancholy, before adding, 'But it's so difficult to get the right shade. I wondered – you live in the outside world, don't you? – have you any ideas? Do you know of any plants, any herbs, that might produce a nice orangy colour? You help me,' he said, with another quick look at the guards, 'and I'll see what I can do for you.'

The outlaws all looked at one another. As a general rule they were not much interested in obtaining dyes from plants. But if anyone knew about such things, it would be Alysoun. She liked to colour their food sometimes, to add a bit of interest to a meal. They turned to her now and waited expectantly.

'There's only one or two things I can think of,' she said. 'One is the autumn-flowering crocus. Saffron. The dried stigmas are yellowy-orange of course, but if you could find some way of darkening them you might get a nice orange. The other is hibiscus. You get a sort of orangy stain on your bib if you brush against the stamens of the big red hibiscus blooms. Any good?'

Sleek thought for a moment and then nodded. 'Good enough. I'll give them a try. Now, I'll come

83

and let you out when the sentries fall asleep. Floe's good at setting these things up, but she'll forget to change the guard.'

'What about *you*?' asked Sylver. 'Won't you be in trouble for letting us go?'

'I'm coming with you,' said the determined young otter. 'As far as the outside world. Then I'm going off on my own. I'll find an abandoned water-mill somewhere and set up my own garment industry. You have not heard the last of Sleek. In a few months' time, every animal in the kingdom will be wearing my creations!'

'Provided they can afford them, of course,' said Sylver. 'They, er, won't be cheap, will they?'

'Oh, no,' Sleek shuddered. 'Nothing I ever do will be *cheap*. I don't even like using the word. It has a horrible, nasty sound to it, doesn't it? *Cheap*. Kind of word sparrows use. I'm sure even when it's written down it looks perfectly ghastly.'

'You could dye the letters purple,' muttered Scirf, 'and then it might be all right . . .'

But Sleek did not hear this sarcastic remark. He was gone, floating away towards the lamps of his kin. It remained to see whether he would be back later to set the outlaws free.

He did indeed return later, when the guard had fallen asleep, and let them out.

'There's some driftwood on the other side of the cavern,' he whispered. 'Swim over and grab a piece each, to use as a float. When you're coming to the end of your underground journey, you'll hear the roaring of a waterfall. That's when to strike out for the bank. There's quite a drop where the river leaves the cave mouth and becomes a waterfall, so don't leave it too late.'

'If there's a cliff,' said Sylver, 'how will we get down?'

'There's a goat track which goes down by the waterfall – it's fairly steep but we'll be able to manage it all right. I'll show you – remember, I'm coming with you.'

'How could we forget?' said Scirf.

Chapter Nine

Shortly after the escape of the weasels, Flaggatis arrived in the besiegers' camp, having been visiting the battlefields where Lord Ragnar was wreaking such havoc. Flaggatis sat in a massive chair on the back of a vole-cart drawn by six sturdy voles. He never walked anywhere, being frail of body. There was nothing wrong with his mind, however, which was as sharp as a needle. The Lord of the Rats was not happy to see that the ramp had failed and that food had entered the castle.

'You blithering idiots,' he railed at the rat warchiefs, 'can't you do anything right?'

'Nooooo, maaashtterrr,' they growled, as they cowed before this wizened and hunch-shouldered figure in its voluminous robe. 'Sooorrreeee, maaash-tterrr.'

'I can't have this,' cried Flaggatis. 'Carry me to my tent – I need my charts, my instruments. I shall have to conjure a punishment for those inside the castle, for ruining my earth ramps . . .'

They carried the frail figure into a mouseskin tent, where he steeped himself in his own kind of limited magic. Flaggatis could control elemental energies to a certain degree: enough to cause a little havoc and chaos when needed. Today he managed to raise a wind which created a dust storm. The storm was very localized, blowing four ways onto Castle Rayn.

The poor sentries on the walls began coughing and sneezing as red dust billowed around them. They began spitting gobbets of rust-coloured mud. They blew plugs of clay into rags. They had deposits all over their bodies, as the dust found its way under their armour and into their fur.

Clouds of dust entered windows and arrowloops, attacking the lungs of those within the rooms and towers. Ironically, only the dungeons escaped, being too far below ground level to be affected. Everyone else was subjected to thick, irritating dust and had to wear pawkerchiefs over their noses and mouths. Even so they were blinded by the dust. Prince Poynt was incensed at this cowardly attack which reached even his royal person.

'You could grow carrots on my back!' he wailed. 'I've got more soil on me than a kitchen garden. I feel like a walking slag heap. My lovely white pelt is as dirty as that of a scullery weasel's.'

His eyelids felt gritty. There was a mushy stuff between his toes. His teeth ground on soil. Whenever he breathed in he choked. Whenever he breathed out there were plumes of dust.

For weeks afterwards there would be a thin film of dust over every surface in the castle. The royal sheets would be full of it. Goblets gathered sediment in their bottoms. Machinery became clogged with dirt. Life, already intolerable in the damp confines of the castle, became muddier and muddier. By the time Prince Poynt sent for his sheriff, he was in a very bad mood indeed and the sheriff got the worst of it.

Sheriff Falshed kneeled before the throne of Prince Poynt, not afraid to grovel. Falshed had made cowering an art form. He could do it in his sleep. He quivered like an aspen tree in a valley breeze. His head hung in shame. A small tear, like a glittering jewel, trickled down his cheek. At the same time a lonely sigh, barely audible to those around him, escaped his lips as if he had tried to hold it in check, but failed.

'Odious, vile wretch,' muttered the prince, then as an afterthought, 'Abhorrent dunderhead.'

'Well mastered, master!' cried Pompom, dancing around the sheriff and striking him with an inflated mouse's bladder attached to the end of a stick. 'Such a way with big words and long language.'

'Thank you, Pompom. You know how I like flattery. But now, what do we do with *you*, Falshed?' said the prince, in mock despair. 'Once more you have let those outlaws slip through our claws. I've buried you up to the neck in the meadow outside the castle – no longer possible now the rats have temporary possession of it – and have hung you by your heels from the battlements. I can think of no more punishments. You will have to devise one of your own. Delight me with your inventive mind, Falshed. What shall I do with you?'

'My prince,' whined Falshed, desperately trying to think like a rabbit about to be thrown into a briar patch. 'Perhaps – perhaps you could put me on bread and water?'

'And that's supposed to be inventive, Falshed?' snapped the prince. 'Come, come. In these times of starvation, that's more like a reward. You can do better than that.'

Falshed's mind reeled, but he could think of nothing, especially since Pompom was leaping and cavorting in front of him, full of the joys of spring. The weasel jester kept battering Falshed in the face with that infernal balloon of skin. How could anyone think cleverly under such circumstances?

'Very well,' said Prince Poynt, after a suitable interval, 'in that case you will have to redeem yourself . . .'

'Yes, yes,' cried Falshed, hope welling up in his heart. 'I shall, my liege.'

'You shall indeed, sheriff. What I propose to do is put you down that hole in the dungeon floor, through which they obviously escaped, and send you after them.'

'But they've probably *drowned*, my liege. There's fast-flowing water down there.'

'But if they haven't drowned, then they'll be back with Flaggatis, conspiring to overthrow me, helping him work out ways to breach the walls of my castle. I'd like to send a regiment of stoats with you, Falshed, to make sure the job is done, but unfortunately I can't spare them. You'll have to go alone.'

'Alone?' wailed Falshed. 'My prince, even if I don't drown down there, the rats and weasels will have me quartered and the four bits thrown to passing wolves!'

'Alone, Falshed. You'll have to think of something clever to prevent being recognized. Disguise yourself in some way. Pretend to be a weasel. I'm sure it's possible,' the prince's voice became harder, 'since you seem to grow more like one of them every day. Now, no more whining. Get out of my sight. If you speak one more word I shall have Pompom beat you some more with his mouse's bladder.'

Pompom danced around the sheriff, joyfully beating him anyway.

When the sheriff was led to the dungeons by the captain of the guard, he found the jailer chained by his ankles, upside down, to the very wall where the outlaws had been.

'Hello, sheriff,' said the jailer, trying to turn his

head up the right way. 'You coming to join me?'

'I'll give you *hello*, you common-or-garden slug,' Falshed snarled, happy to find someone on whom to vent his wrath. 'When I come back it'll be *goodbye* – for keeps.'

'Where are you going?' asked the surprised jailer, not at all put out by these threats. The sheriff was always making promises he could not keep. 'Are you leaving us?'

Falshed stared miserably at the grating, which was now being lifted by a stoat soldier. 'Just for a short while.'

'You go down there,' said the upside-down jailer, 'and we won't be seeing *you* again.'

'No, I suppose not.'

'So goodbye to you too, you worm,' replied the jailer airily, feeling that if the sheriff was not coming back it was safe to fling a few insults after him. 'And good riddance. I never liked you much anyway. I used to throw darts at a likeness I made of you, so their points would give you shooting pains. I hope your teeth rot and drop out.'

'That was you, was it?' snarled Falshed. 'The sharp pains in the pads of my paws . . . ?'

The jailer smiled a wicked smile.

Before Falshed could reply further to the jailer's barrage of abuse he was pushed by the captain of the guard into the hole. He fell headlong into the water. Once in the flood, full fathom five deep, he was swept away down to where the river Alf ran through caverns measureless to stoats, down to a sunless lake. When he arrived however, half-drowned and in a wretched state, there were no gardens bright nor forests ancient as the hills, but a gang of bad-tempered otters who dragged him from the water.

A ring of torches surrounded Falshed.

90

'Here's another one, come to steal our secrets,' snarled a belligerent female otter waving a club. 'Let me at him. I'll paddle some sense into his thick skull.'

'Another one what?' cried Falshed, spitting out water. 'There are no stoats down here.'

'Weasels, stoats, whatever,' cried the otter. 'You've kidnapped our little Sleek.'

'I've never heard of your little sleek, let alone seen it, whatever it is. I've just been swept down from Castle Rayn. I'm on the trail of a motley crew of weasels. The leader calls himself Sylver . . .'

'Ha! He admits it!'

'It is my intention,' said Falshed haughtily, realizing the outlaws had not left a good impression behind them, 'to catch up with these villains and hang them from the gallows.'

This was enough to make the otter blink and the ring of torches to recede a little.

There was a long silence before the female otter replied. 'Alone?' she said. 'One stoat against half a dozen weasels?'

'I hope to recruit local help,' said Falshed. 'There are those who will do anything for gold.'

'You don't look as if you're carrying any gold.'

'I am High Sheriff of all Welkin. My word is my bond. Prince Poynt will honour any promises I make.'

'In that case,' she said, turning to her fellow otters, 'I suggest we let this stoat go about his business. Already several weasels have escaped to the outside world with knowledge of our whereabouts. It seems we cannot remain a secret. One more won't make any difference.'

Then turning back to Falshed, she added in a lower tone, 'Perhaps you'd like to see a few of our creations, before you go on? You might like a gift or two to be sent back to the prince. I myself have some very fine cloaks – blue as the summer sky – which you may find suitable . . .'

A few idle and unkeepable promises later, Falshed was on his way down the river Alf in a little coracle lent to him by the otters. They did not use such boats for themselves, but needed them to keep their raw materials dry as they transported the feathers and stuff up-river. It needed a little knack to keep the boat from spinning in circles, but Falshed was too intent on reaching the open air to worry about how dizzy he was getting.

Falshed smiled as he twirled on the current. He congratulated himself on his powers of persuasion. Not only had he got a boat out of the otters, he had also been given some nice snakeskin leggings, which he was now wearing, and a beautiful cloak made of blue jays' feathers. All that had been extracted in return was a promise to show those in high places the superior quality of the guild's craftottership.

'What a clever stoat I am,' he murmured to himself. 'How silver the tongue that rests in this mouth.'

He poked his little red tongue between his two front fangs for the benefit of any who might be watching his progress along the subterranean river.

Travelling through the darkness was not as scary as Falshed had first imagined it might be. There was something gleaming in the water and on the walls of the caverns occasionally: some mineral which helped give a shine in the darkness. Also, now that the Guild of Otters was behind him, there was nothing really which could harm a travelling stoat.

He began singing, the enclosed echoey space making his voice sound quite good. He fancied himself a minstrel-singer like the stoat Blondell, who went round the castles earning a piece of chopped liver or two with his golden voice. Falshed's voice was more like tin than gold, but not to his own ear.

'Fi-diddle-de-de, it's the stoatly life for me . . .'

A sudden storm of voices interrupted him. High squeaky voices, furious voices. 'We're *trying* to get some sleep!' seemed to be the main complaint.

Falshed looked up to see that the ceiling of the cave was covered in little black bodies. Furry bodies with hunched shoulders and wings that ended in little claws. Bats! Thousands of them, hanging upside down. They seethed. They simmered. They rustled like a single giant leathery net high above his head. Falshed shuddered. He did not like bats very much. Some stoats said they got caught in your fur. Thereafter he kept his fi-diddles to himself, humming softly instead, as he was swept along on the flow.

Eventually, to his great relief, he could see daylight. A roundish ball of light became closer and larger with each moment. However, he had noticed that the river was increasing in speed all the time and this puzzled him. A river, when it gets wider and closer to its mouth, should get slower. This one was not obeying the rules of rivers!

Then he heard the roar.

It was a few moments before he realized he was heading towards a waterfall. The river obviously came out of the ground halfway up a cliff or mountain. The reason why the flow was getting faster was because it shot out through that mouth to the outside world. Mist and spray was now clouding the opening, thrown back by the force of the water striking rocks.

'Oh no,' cried Falshed. 'It's not fair. Why didn't those otters warn me?'

It was as these words were coming out of his mouth that the coracle passed a landing stage. A path leading from this landing stage went winding up through a rock chimney to the open air. Had he been closer to the side, where the speed of the water was not as fierce, Falshed might have been able to throw a rope over one of the posts. He would have been safe.

He began paddling furiously in the opposite direction, but all he could manage to do was stay still. His forelimbs rapidly grew tired. Finally, through exhaustion, he succumbed to the inevitable. The little round boat rushed forward gleefully, happy to make the leap from the top of the falls. Falshed could do nothing but go with it.

Then, at the last moment, he looked down at the bottom of the coracle to see the feathered cloak. Snatching it up he just had time to grip the four corners in his forepaws and hindpaws. The boat flew out into open space – then fell to earth. Falshed hovered above the long drop for a few moments, then the cloak acted like a kite and he glided out of the spray. Soon he was high above a hanging valley, swooping and gliding as the currents of warm air took him.

'Whhheeeeaaahhhhrrrgggeeeaaaahhh . . .'

The sound of his voice went from elation to horror and back again, several times. He was not sure whether he liked it or not. He was alive, it was true. But for how long? He was not a flying fox. Controlling the flight was not an easy thing to do. There was the frightening thought that if he moved a paw the wrong way, the whole cloak might collapse. He would go plummeting down to those tiny fields below: a meteor for the last few seconds

94

of his life. He felt it best to let the air currents do what they wanted with him.

These same currents did their best to keep him circling above the landscape. He thought his paws would never touch ground. Then a sudden gust took him into a section between two cliffs. This was an area which local eagles called 'the doldrums' where the air was still. Falshed dropped like a stone, leaving his stomach behind. He screamed once before the ground winds caught him in their able hands, sweeping him towards a line of trees. Branches rushed to meet him.

Chapter Ten

The outlaws were on the banks of a turquoise lake. They had prepared rafts to cross the wide, glistening waters. Sleek, the young otter, was still with them but was preparing to say goodbye. His destiny lay in the world of the doublet and hose. Somewhere in the hinterland was an abandoned water-mill which would one day become a shrine for visitors interested in the history of the 'Sleekret Pocket', a device which was to thwart cutpurses and pick-pockets for several decades.

'Well,' said Scirf, 'let's get to it then!'

The outlaws began to file onto the raft, each saying his or her goodbyes to the otter. Suddenly there was a swishing sound from above. Several weasels ducked, thinking an eagle was coming in for the kill. A crash followed however as something smashed into the branches of a tree. There was a moment's silence, then a creature dropped from the tree branches to the ground. It was covered in blue feathers and had bits of twig and leaves in its fur.

Clearly dazed, the creature did not try to get to its paws, but lay looking up at the passing clouds above, which gently boated over the heavens.

'Falshed,' cried Sylver, recognizing the stoat straight away. 'Quickly, let's get out of here.'

The raft was pushed from the shore with a pole. Out on to the aquamarine waters went the outlaw band. Sleek stood waving from the bank for a while, then the little otter went over to the stupefied stoat and tried to revive him. The last the outlaws saw of Sleek, he was standing over the supine form of the sheriff, no doubt sympathizing with him in his plight.

It was pleasant out on the lake as they steered gently between two small islands. The sun glanced off the brilliantly coloured water, and glittered and flashed into the faces of the outlaws. The weasels shielded their eyes with their paws as they lay listlessly about the deck. Wodehed was poling the raft along like a punt, the only one of the band not idle. His expression showed he was deep in thought.

Insects like jewels hovered over the water. Silver fish broke the surface occasionally, to snatch a mayfly from the air. Otherwise, all was tranquil. Weasels relaxed and allowed their forepaws to dangle in the water, their claws causing soft velvety ripples to fan out behind the raft., A kingfisher went like a blue dart just above the surface, heading for the bank. Small flotillas of green weed, like mermaids' hair, occasionally became attached to the pole and had to be removed.

'That's it!' cried Wodehed, as he picked the weed off his pole. 'I knew there was something about this lake. I've just remembered. There's a monster in here – lives under the water. I remember some pedlar telling me about it. Apparently it was once a handsome fisherweasel, but a witch changed it into this immortal *thing*. It has a gargantuan appetite and never stops eating. It has reached terrible proportions . . .'

Immediately all the weasels were on the alert.

'Thanks, Wodehed,' said Scirf, now standing rigid

and scanning the lake. 'I was just enjoying a nice snooze. Now you've got all me nerve ends tingling. I s'pose you've got no idea what we're looking for, have you?'

'Something *unusual*, that's all I can recall.'

'Brilliant. I'll know *that* when I see it.'

Sylver said, 'Just keep your eyes skinned, everyone. Watch the lake for any kind of motion. If anything looks like it's going to surface, paddle like mad with your paws.'

However, after a half-hour of watching intently, no horrible *thing* broke the surface with a roar, water running from its scales – or whatever – spray snorting from its nostrils. The weasels began to relax again. That is, until they saw a long black canoe with rats in it. Once more they unrelaxed pretty quickly, arming themselves with darts.

'War canoe coming in fast to port!' warned Sylver. 'Everyone get ready to repel boarders!'

Mawk said, 'Port? What's that? Right or left?'

Then he saw the canoe – long, dark and sleek – being propelled through the water by twelve rats. The canoe, though lengthy, was so lean it had no room for the rodents' naked tails. These they had hung over the gunwales, alternately: the first rat one side, next rat the other side, and so on. These tails appeared like thin pink legs, trailing in the water.

It was as if some monstrous centipede were scurrying over the surface of the lake.

For weapons the rats had barbed spears – harpoons – which were clipped to the sides of the canoe and in easy reach of wicked claws. The rodents were showing their teeth, clicking their incisors in glee, knowing they had their prey at a disadvantage. Sylver told his crew to prepare for the worst. The canoe cut through the water with an alarming swiftness. It looked impossible to outrun.

When the rats got closer the outlaws used slings and darts, but standing on the raft to fire or throw missiles was not an easy thing to do. The raft was made of reeds and was waterlogged. Whenever someone moved violently it rocked, thus unsteadying those on board. Alysoun was just launching a dart when Bryony used her sling and because the raft dipped and rolled with their movements, both the jills missed their targets.

The rats on the other hand seemed to have it all worked out nicely.

One rat, right at the end of the line, stood up. The others steadied the canoe for her. She launched three harpoons, one after the other, which whistled through the air with alarming accuracy. Then she sat down, abruptly, having done her part. The next rat in line stood up, ready to do the same.

Of the first three harpoons, one landed in the deck at the feet of Wodehed. Another fell short, slipping into the lake in front of the canoe. The third struck Miniver in the shoulder, which was just bad luck since she was the smallest weasel and therefore presented the smallest target.

'Steady, weasels, steady,' cried Sylver, throwing a dart which struck the front of the canoe. 'Keep your balance!'

A second shower of harpoons came over and this time Wodehed was hit in the hind leg. 'Ahhh!' he moaned. 'Quickly, someone take the pole.'

Mawk leaped forward and did so, happy to have something to do while the battle raged.

It seemed that the raft would either be cut in two by the sharp dugout canoe, or the weasels would be overwhelmed. The outlaws were having to stand on their hind legs, throw their darts, then go down on to all fours to keep their balance. Icham seemed the most successful at this kind of warfare. His aim was true as he pinned a rat's ear to the gunwales of the canoe.

It seemed all was lost with the weasels at last.

Indeed the black canoe was now but a few metres away and coming in fast. The weasels clung to the reeds, waiting for the impact, waiting for their vessel to be sliced in two. At that moment something huge and utterly repulsive broke the surface of the water, muddy weed dripping from its ugly form.

It was sort of crispy-shelled and darkly shaded. A malformed giant larva with a death's-head mask and slicked-back body. Half its face then detached itself from the other half, to shoot forwards. It snatched a rat out of the canoe with two gruesome hooks which protruded from its lower lip.

It then proceeded with slavering mouth to draw its victim back into its jaws and then suck out its vitals. The rat's pelt was soon as flat as an empty wineskin. This deflated skin was spat away to float upon the surface of the lake.

'Good Lord of the Forest,' yelled Mawk, his eyes bulging out of his head. 'Save us, I beg of you!'

The other weasels felt much the same as Mawk but were too stunned to plead for help. This creature which had broken the surface was the ugliest and most grisly beast they had ever laid eyes on. Its face was a hideous mask which kept splitting in two, the lower part shooting forwards and snatching hysterical rats from their canoe. Once each victim had been sucked dry of all fluids, flesh and bone, he or she was discarded.

Three rats went in as many minutes. The others paddled for all they were worth, towards the distant shore. Ripples followed them as the monster gave chase. It propelled itself across the lake at an alarming rate by forcing a jet of water out of the bottom end of its body. It had six legs but these lay flat and streamlined against its sides. It skimmed across the surface at high speed after the hapless rats, who must have known that more of their number were going to be eaten before they reached the distant shore.

The weasels simply remained where they were for the moment, still too horrified to do anything but stare. Then they came to their senses and everyone started yelling at once.

'Grab the pole!'

'Push, push.'

'Get us out of here.'

'Paddle with your paws.'

'Use anything – anything.'

They raced for the distant banks of the lake as if they had an army of monsters behind them. The skins of emptied rats bobbed on the ripples of their wake. No-one looked back. No-one had any desire to see the horrible beast from the depths of the lake again. It would figure in the nightmares of every weasel on board for many months to come.

The weasels were not in the normal way too afraid of monsters. Dragons could come on in and be slaughtered. Sea serpents could have slid up and would be dealt with in due course. Fire-breathing lizards were ordinary monstrosities, next to the thing they had just witnessed. Cockatrices, krakens, leviathans, whatever. Those were but small horrors compared with that ghastly being which had chased the rats.

'What was it?' asked Sylver of Wodehed, once they had put distance between themselves and the brute. 'I've never seen anything like it.'

Wodehed and Miniver were being treated for their wounds by a resourceful Mawk, who always carried a couple of bandages in the dart-pouch on his belt.

'Dragonfly nymph,' replied Wodehed. 'Giant one, of course. Huge. Massive. But much the same as those you might find in any garden pond. This one has been growing for many decades, feeding on any poor traveller it can get its hooks into. I suppose one day it might change into a dragonfly. I think they're carnivorous too, if I'm not mistaken. Hunters. Pretty – but flesh-eating creatures all the same. A normal-sized dragonfly will eat something as large as a butterfly, so Lord knows what this one will eat, once it changes.'

'Cows?' Scirf said. 'Donkeys? Bulls? Horses? Weasels will be too small – probably – hopefully. Weasels will be just a mouthful. Did you know that your ordinary pond dragonfly can zoom about at sixty miles an hour? I don't think we could outrun that rotter, once he gets his wings.'

No-one really wanted to know any more about the dragonfly nymph. They were quite happy to remain ignorant. They paddled for all they were worth over the turquoise lake. Finally they came to the far shore. Here they alighted. Wodehed went off and found some medicinal herbs. With these as poultices Bryony bound up the wounds Miniver and Wodehed had received from the rat harpoons. Their injuries turned out to be not too serious, though Wodehed was in more pain than Miniver.

After that the outlaws rested on the bank. Before they left the shore however Miniver pointed to the middle of the lake and gave a sudden shout. The weasels all jumped and stared, thinking they were in for another attack by the nymph. All they could see was a dark figure on a coracle. The coracle had a blue sail made of what looked like a cloak of feathers. To assist the sail in the poor breeze, Falshed was paddling hard to reach the shore with a soggy and limp-looking dock leaf.

Luke peered. 'It's Falshed!' he exclaimed. 'And he's alone.'

'What?' Sylver said. 'He can't be expecting to take us back by himself. What's he thinking of?'

The coracle drew nearer and nearer to the shore. When it was within a stone's throw, the dragonfly nymph suddenly appeared on the horizon, shooting through the water with its tail jet. The outlaws started yelling, telling Falshed to paddle hard. They screamed at him as he drew closer. This had the opposite effect to the one they intended.

Instead of hurrying him up, their encouraging yells caused Falshed to stop paddling altogether. No doubt he was thinking these savage cries were being made in anger. It appeared to him that the weasels were in a blood-thirsty mood and could not wait to get their claws on him. Perhaps they were going to hang him from the nearest oak. Or roast him over a hot fire.

Whatever their plans it seemed to him they were eager to get hold of him and exact revenge for all the wrongs he had inflicted on them over the years.

In the meantime a ferocious and merciless monster sped silently towards the unknowing Falshed.

Chapter Eleven

At the last minute some survival instinct made Falshed look over his shoulder. What he saw made all his fur stand on end. His eyes started from his head. His heart began thundering in his chest. Letting out a mighty yell of absolute terror, as this frightful fiend did close behind him swoosh, he paddled for all he was worth. A fiend so ugly it stopped his blood in his veins. A thing like a giant brown shrimp with a carapace of plating like thick armour. A thing bristling with legs, its jaws see-sawing backwards and forwards, the lower half of its face shooting outwards in search of prey.

Fortunately the currents were with him. He flew towards the shore. No spinning of the coracle now. It went in a dead straight line. Weasels were there with paws thrust forward. A few moments previously he believed their claws were outstretched in order to grip him around his throat. Now he saw they were intended to save him from a grisly death.

The coracle bumped against the bottom.

He flung himself into the forelimbs of the waiting weasels, flying through the air. A set of vicious hooks detached themselves from the nymph's face, zooming out after him, fixed to a long elastic bottom jaw. There was a crunch from behind Falshed as his coracle with its precious feather-cloak sail was snatched from the water. It was caught up by the hooks on the mask of the nymph. A moment later it was flung past the weasels as the nymph angrily discovered it had an empty vessel in its ugly mouth. It spat out a cloud of blue feathers.

Falshed swooned in fright, knowing that had he jumped a second later, he would have been in the monster's jaws.

When he came to, he was lying on the grassy bank of the lake, at a safe distance from the water. A ring of weasel faces surrounded him, looking down on him. He closed his eyes again, as if only half-conscious, to give himself time to think of what he ought to do next.

When Falshed had landed in the tree following his accident at the waterfall, he had been battered and dazed. By the time he had rallied the weasels had bolted, sailing out onto the lake. He had decided to follow them. Sleek was still there at the time, attentive to the needs of an injured creature.

'Are you all right?' the otter had asked. 'Do you need any assistance?'

'Of course I need assistance,' the stoat had growled.

'Then let me help you.'

Falshed had gone back to the river below the waterfall and had found his coracle floating in the shallows of an oxbow lake. It had presumably landed there after being shot from the mouth of the cave below. Together he and Sleek had carried his little boat to the lake. There Falshed had found a dock plant and took one of its broad thick leaves to use as a paddle.

Sleek had spoken to him one last time before they parted company. 'What's your favourite colour?' the otter had asked, eagerly.

'Blood,' Falshed had replied, in a very nasty tone.

'Oh!' the little otter had exclaimed, 'mine's – mine's orange.'

Falshed had not even bothered to answer, ignoring the water creature from thereon in.

Before Falshed set out after the weasels he had added to the bits of twig and leaves already in his fur. He knew he could not – as his prince had suggested – disguise himself well enough to remain unknown to the outlaws. They would recognize him whatever he did to his outward appearance. For one thing he was a stoat and not a weasel. For another he had a burn mark on his bib which was like a sign that read 'I am Falshed'. Finally he had no real materials at paw to disguise himself.

He decided instead to pretend he was mad. It was, he told himself, a brilliant ruse. For no matter how much they questioned him, he need not tell them anything at all. He would just make out that his mind had gone. They would believe the fall into the tree responsible. (He did have a lump on his head!) So he daubed a bit of yellow clay here, a bit of red clay there, put a few twigs in his fur, stuck a dandelion in one ear, and set off across the lake in pursuit.

Now here he was, under their sympathetic gaze.

Scirf was the first to address him. 'Where *did* you get those leggings, corporal?'

A general snigger went round the outlaw band as they stared at his brown snakeskin hose. Falshed had forgotten his beautiful leggings, given him by one of the otters. He gritted his teeth. He hated being baited by ignorant peasants like Scirf. But he knew he would have to put up with it for now.

He decided to speak. 'How doth the merry moth of May dance upon the magpie's wing?' he cried, sitting up and staring about him wildly. 'You, sir,' he pointed to Scirf, 'form your answer and draw a plan.

106

I shall require seventeen copies, all in blue ink.'

He then started humming a popular tune and smiling inanely at the ring of faces.

'Bonkers,' Scirf said, with his usual bluntness. 'Pixilated. Cuckoo.'

'Hold on a minute, Scirf,' said Bryony. 'Maybe it's just a temporary thing. Give him time to come round properly.'

'Let us be bold and fight yon dragon,' yelled Falshed, leaping to his feet and grabbing a forked twig to brandish as a weapon. 'Let us spit him on this iron broadsword!'

He began to run down towards the lake shore, but Icham managed to do a flying tackle on him to bring him down.

'He is crazy,' cried the weasel, holding Falshed down with difficulty. 'He's off his beam.'

'Exactly,' Scirf said. 'Dappy as a grebe.'

Falshed sat up, his eyes wild and staring. 'Ho! See, a candle flame in yon window niche burns brightly, sire. It must be that Lady M walks at this midnight hour! Hey, ho, nonny-nonny-no. Here's a fine to-do. Young Lochinvar has stolen my bride, right in front of the wedding guest whose sleeve I clutch. What, sir, will you not listen to an elderly mariner? I have been to Xanadu and back.'

Scirf stared at the sheriff disgustedly. 'What are we goin' to do with him, Sylver?'

'We have two choices. We either leave him here, or take him with us. If we leave him, he won't survive very long. He'll probably go and offer himself to that thing in the lake. Or some wolf or fox will have him for breakfast.'

'Sounds all right to me,' muttered Mawk. 'A fitting end to a rotten stoat.'

Bryony said, 'No, we have to take him with us. I

know if things were the other way around, he wouldn't bother with one of us, but – well – we're not stoat sheriffs.'

Mawk said, 'I'd just as soon leave him here.'

The others came up on one side or another, but eventually Sylver made his decision.

'He'll have to come with us, until we can deposit him somewhere safe.'

Scirf said, 'That's fair, I suppose. I mean, he's not really the High Sheriff of Welkin any more, is he? He's a wanderin' idiot. Don't expect he knows his own name. Do you, squire?'

Falshed was silently fuming under the insults. He forced himself to smile in a silly, vacant way. He ignored the weasels for a moment. Then he realized he would have to answer Scirf's question. After all, he was supposed to be mad, not deaf.

'My name, good sir? My name is – is Rattlepate,' Falshed replied, bending to pick some wild flowers. He straightened and offered a bloom to Bryony. 'Here's bladderwort – that's for remembrance – and there's dandelions – they make you wet the bed. Or is it the other way around? And in your hand, sire, I place the herb robert, who was also known as The Bruce – and buttercups to shine yellow under this jill's chin – and over here are wolfsocks, or are they foxgloves? Heh, heh . . .'

'Someone shut that idiot up and let's get on,' grumbled Scirf. 'He's beginning to get on my nerves.'

Falshed shut himself up. He was finding it a strain, pretending he was mad. Sometimes his acting was so good it seemed as if he actually were going funny in the head. However, now that he had been asked to keep quiet, he did so with great relief. It was one thing to grin like a fool all the time and roll your eyes, quite another to have to invent drivel. He had not really wanted to call himself Rattlepate, but it was the only thing which came into his head. He gritted his teeth.

The outlaws now progressed across Darkmoor, the land beyond the lakes. They walked through ferny brakes and stepped over deep rills cutting through peat, until they came to a part of the country they never knew existed. The weather was foul and the ways hard. Black clouds loured above. Furious winds cut through their pelts and all but lifted them off their feet. The face of the land was firm and forbidding. This was no place for the traveller without a definite destination. It was no wonder the outlaws had not heard of anyone crossing the moor.

Eventually they came to a high tor, shaped like the skull of a badger. They stood in the badger's stone teeth and stared out over the hinterland. From this vantage point, their eyeballs smarting in the sharp winds, they looked down on a shallow basin of heather and bracken. In the middle of the basin was a huge lake, this time with slate-dark waters. On the near shore of the lake was a concentric castle: a structure ringed by two or more walls. The castle was stroked by water on three sides.

The fourth side faced Darkmoor, with its networks of drystone walls and swampy hollows. Forests of dwarf oaks filled the crevices between craggy uplands. This side of the castle consisted of two round towers set in the outer curtain wall in the middle of which was the gatehouse.

Joined to each of the two towers was a town wall which enclosed a number of half-timbered houses. There were figures in the streets of the town, and more upon the castle walls. It seemed as if this castle was inhabited by mammals of some kind. The weasels were too far away to see who or what lived there. By the time they reached the gates to the town, darkness had fallen.

Sylver hammered on the door with a stone. 'Open up!' he cried. 'We need shelter for the night.'

There was silence. Sylver knocked again, harder this time. A grumbling sound came from behind the gate. Someone jangled some keys. Then a voice called out, 'Who is it?'

'Some – some wandering monks. We're on a pilgrimage,' called Sylver. 'Is this Castle Storm?'

'No, it's Stormtown. The castle's a bit further on.'

'Can we come in? We need food and shelter. We are desperate for succour after our long journey. We were attacked by a dragonfly nymph and are careworn and weary.'

A little shutter flew back in the main doors and a face poked through it to glare at the outlaws. 'You don't look like monks,' said the face. 'Where's your habits?'

Scirf said, 'We gave 'em up for Lent.'

'What?'

'Our bad habits. I used to bite my nails . . .'

The great doors to the town eventually opened to reveal an irritable-looking red squirrel. 'What's all this about a dragonfly nymph?' he said, huffing and puffing after his exertions. 'You can get one of those things into a matchbox.'

'Not the one we saw,' said Sylver. 'It was massive. It could eat a cart-horse whole.'

'Well, come on in, if you're going to,' said the squirrel, looking a little shifty. He kept glancing to the side, but Sylver decided he probably had an unfortunate twitch. Sylver was always one to give a mammal the benefit of the doubt. Beyond the gates were the half-timbered houses they had seen at a distance, with lights twinkling in their windows.

'Ah, the beauteous handiwork of the lamplighter,' cried Falshed. 'As essential to the world as the man who comes to wind the grandfather clock.'

'What's the matter with him?' asked the squirrel, suspiciously, locking the gates behind him. 'Is he touched in the head or something?'

'Too much sun,' replied Sylver. 'Please, don't take any notice of anything he says.'

At that moment however, large shapes leaped from the shadows of the wall. They flung themselves on the outlaws. Falshed started shouting about phantoms of the night. Scirf put up a spirited resistance. Mawk begged for mercy. Sylver, Bryony, Luke and Alysoun fought back with vigour. The wounded Wodehed and Miniver went down almost immediately under the boots and fists of the attacking red squirrels.

Eventually all the weasels and their accompanying stoat were hauled off to a great house, a guildhall of sorts, where they were confronted by a large corpulent red squirrel. The two distinctive things about his appearance, apart from his being overweight, was a tail which curled inwards like a Catherine wheel and a black patch over his right eye. On his head he had a helmet of sorts. It was made from an old tin cup with a brush screwed to the top for a crest. The squirrel was armed with a sword made from a metal roasting spit.

'Who comes here, uninvited, to the town of Clive of Coldkettle?' He glared at Sylver with his one eye. 'You, sirrah – you seem to be the leader of this motley band – what's yer name? Speak now, or perchance we shall have you on the gallows before morning!'

This red squirrel strode about as he spoke in a very grand manner, while other squirrels moved aside for him. He was clearly a mammalage of some import. Every gesture was a flourish, every word spoken with precision.

'What? Ho? Are you spies of that foul knight of the grey order, Pommf de Fritte, or no?'

In circumstances such as these, the outlaws usually left Sylver to do the talking.

'Pommf? Who's he?' asked Sylver, rubbing a sore head.

The big red squirrel laughed and other squirrels joined in. 'Why,' he boomed, 'you must know your own master, Pommf de Fritte, leader of the grey squirrels?'

'No, I haven't heard of him – or you either, I'm afraid. We come from far away, across the Turquoise Lakes. My name is Sylver, leader of a band of weasels who live in Halfmoon Wood.'

Clive of Coldkettle's eyes narrowed. 'There's a gentlestoat who lives near that same wood – can you give me his name?'

Sylver clicked his teeth. 'That would be Lord Haukin, of Thistle Hall. He's a particular friend of ours, even though he's one of the ruling class.'

Clive of Coldkettle nodded thoughtfully and seemed a little less aggressive now. 'And this fellow?' he said, pointing to Falshed. 'He looks like one of your ruling class types too, even though he is wearing those silly-looking brown leggings.'

'The moving coffee pot pours, and having poured moves on,' babbled Falshed. 'Thereby curls a tale which no fellow shall gainsay. 'Tis a comic tale, yet 'tis a tale of woe. It turns within itself, instead of ending with a flourish.'

Falshed knew he was taking his life into his paws

by talking of Clive's tail, but he could not stop himself. Once he had started he could not cease. It was a fascinating appendage. The words seemed to well up inside him and come whooshing out in a fountain.

'Is he making fun of me?' cried Clive. 'Is he mocking my tail? We have a rule around here. Nobody mentions my tail. If they do, they get scaramouched. I'll accept this stoat is a simpleton – and so I'll let him get away with it once – but if he mentions it again he's for scaramouching.'

'No, the poor stoat has an addled brain,' Sylver told him. 'He doesn't know what he's saying. He used to be an enemy of ours, but he's only to be pitied now. It was probably because he came face to face with a monster dragonfly nymph. Horrible experience. We ourselves barely escaped its hooks.'

'Yet you all seem sane enough.'

'True, but weasels have stronger spirits and minds than stoats, who are basically weak creatures.'

Falshed said nothing but could not help grinding his teeth.

'By the way,' asked Sylver. 'What's *scaramouched*?'

'It means to have one's nose cut off.'

'Oh, well, anyway we're not spies of anyone, I assure you. If you'll give us a few moments to explain why we're here . . .'

'By all means,' replied Clive of Coldkettle, 'explain away – then we'll skin you alive and leave you to drip.'

Chapter Twelve

Sylver took time to explain carefully why they had come to Castle Storm. The squirrels listened patiently. When the explanation was over, Clive of Coldkettle nodded. He lifted his black eye-patch and scratched around the empty socket beneath with a thoughtful expression on his face.

'I have heard good things of Lord Haukin. He is a wise animal and his words are not to be taken lightly. If Lord Haukin says we are in danger of a flood, of many creatures drowning, then I believe it. You say we need the humans back to rebuild the sea and river walls – the dykes and such?'

'That's correct,' replied Sylver. 'Animals have no thumbs. It's not easy for most of us to use tools. Certainly the larger animals like cows and horses, goats and pigs, do not have anything even resembling hands. And those of us who can manage tools a little don't have the size and muscle of people. Building sea walls is not a light task.'

'Let's say I agree with you,' said Clive, 'what will be your next move?'

'To search for the secret passage.'

'You know from what you have already learned from me that the castle itself is inhabited by grey squirrels, while the town is occupied by red squirrels such as myself.'

'Yes.'

114

'So how do you propose to search, when the place is full of enemy squirrels?'

Sylver said, 'The grey squirrels are not *our* enemies. We have no quarrel with either of you, grey or red. I would hope you would have no quarrel with me.'

Clive stared at Sylver and the rest of the band as if they were not real. 'You think that now you have spent time with us, that Pommf de Fritte will welcome you into the castle? You think he does not have his spies everywhere? Even now some owl or nightjar is whispering in his ear, telling him that the red squirrels have recruited new soldiers, weasel mercenaries. I'm afraid you have already chosen sides, my friend, which is why I'm going to allow you to live. You are now allies of the red squirrels.'

'But we don't want to be anyone's allies,' gasped Bryony, indignantly. 'We are free agents.'

'Too bad,' said a female red squirrel. 'What's done is done – you must make the best of it.'

'And who are you?' asked Scirf. 'Isn't it time for a few introductions?'

Clive of Coldkettle proudly introduced his knights, both female and male. There was Blodwin, Imogen, Eric Rood, Wivenhoe, Will Splayfoot, Goodsquirrel and many others. He told them they would meet the grey squirrels at the next jousting tourney, when the two sides honoured a truce in order to test their mettle against each other. The war itself did not produce any great advantages for a real scrap, since the greys did not leave the castle and the reds could not get inside.

'You'll see Pommf de Fritte himself,' said Blodwin, 'and Derrière, Foppington, Poisson d'Avril, La Belle Savage, and a host of others. They

115

have little honour, those greys. Only here, in this town, will you find true squirrels – squirrels who are loyal and good, and hold the code of chivalry precious.'

Sylver, from what he had already heard and seen, was inclined to think it was half a dozen of one and six of the other. Lord Haukin had always maintained that when two close neighbours were at war it was usually over some half-forgotten battles or wrongs far in the past. Old wrongs, kept alive by hate, gave rise to new wrongs. So the cycle never ended, with one side accusing the other, and counter-accusations flying back in the opposite direction.

'You did this at such-and-such a time!'

'Well, that was because you did so-and-so!'

'Yes, but we were not as bad as you.'

'No, you were far worse, as well you know!'

And all this passing between animals that were not alive when the terrible things happened between their great-grandparents, or their great-great-grandparents, or even further back still in the mists of early time.

'Why are you fighting each other?' asked Sylver. 'Do you know?'

'Of course we know,' cried Clive. 'They are on our territory. The castle used to be ours until their ancestors stole it!'

Luke said, 'You seem to be managing well enough without it. Can I not smell the presence of walnut trees, and chestnut trees?'

'In the town parks,' said Imogen, nodding proudly. 'We have many groves of nut trees. But that's not the point. The castle was ours. We were driven out. We want it back again. What's the use of living in the town under threat of invasion? Once the greys have been slaughtered to a squirrel, then we'll sleep safe in our drays.'

'Seems a shame you can't come to some sort of an agreement,' Alysoun said. 'Never mind what used to be, in the old days; the greys are now in the castle. You seem comfortable here, they appear to be comfortable there. Why not just meet and agree to stay as you are, with each of you promising not to encroach on the territory of the other?'

Clive shook his big head. 'Wouldn't work. Can't trust a grey as far as you can throw the guildhall. Never have been able to trust 'em. Thoroughly untrustworthy creatures, greys, and that's a fact.'

The weasels realized they were getting nowhere and let the whole thing drop. It seemed they were destined to be regarded as allies of the reds, for the time being anyway. There was no telling that the secret passage might not be in the town itself, anyway, so they would have no need to go into the castle. Certainly the town was in essence a part of the castle, since the town wall was joined to the castle towers.

'Well,' said Sylver, 'it will be good to get some rest. Perhaps my band of weasels here could be given some food and drink, then shown a place to sleep for the night?'

'Now that you are red mercenaries,' Clive told him, 'you will be given good fare, parfit knight.'

'Parfait?' cried Falshed, suddenly coming to life again. 'I love parfait! A wonderful cold dessert of whipped cream, eggs and fruit! Almost as good as syllabub – lovely curdled cream mixed with wine. Not quite as nice as junket, that delicious dish of curds and cream served at blood temperature. I love exotic afters, don't you? Puddings, sweets, afters, whatever you call it, I just love it. Give me plenty of it that I may sicken and so die a bloated stoat.'

'What's he babbling about?' asked Blodwin. 'You'll get nuts and raisins, and like it.'

After the weasels had eaten, they were shown to various beds. The reds were keen to split them up, so that no rebellion could take place in the night hours. Sylver went with Clive to his dray, a huge copper kettle with a small hole in the bottom, now filled with warm soft hay.

'So this is why they call you Clive of Coldkettle,' said Sylver, settling down in a nice snug hollow of hay for the night. 'Well, goodnight, Clive – and on behalf of the other outlaws, I thank you for your hospitality.'

'You're welcome,' said the squirrel.

'One last thing,' Sylver said. 'You must know that the north of Welkin has been overrun by rat hordes from the unnamed marshes. Once they have taken Castle Rayn and defeated Lord Ragnar, they will be swarming down this way. You need to be prepared to fight them off.'

Clive of Coldkettle nodded, placing a paw on his sword as if to draw comfort from it. 'We have heard of the invasion. I and my knights would have set forth to do battle with the rats, had it not been for the fact that if we vacated the town the greys would take it over and we would have had no home to come to after our victories . . .'

Sylver could have added 'or defeats' but refrained from doing so. Instead, he said, 'And I suppose Pommf de Fritte and *his* knights won't leave the castle in case you arrive back first and overrun his territory?'

'Precisely. You have it in a nutshell.'

'Isn't it a shame you two can't get together on this thing? The stoats could do with some help.'

Clive said, 'I thought you hated stoats.'

'I don't like being ruled by Prince Poynt, but the rats are a common enemy.'

'The rats have done nothing to us yet,' replied Clive of Coldkettle, a little aloofly. 'When they do, we shall defend ourselves.'

Sylver saw that he was getting nowhere again and so dropped the argument and went to bed.

When Sylver woke the following morning the sunlight was streaming through several cracks in the walls of the guildhall. He lay there staring at these golden beams with a feeling of contentment. It had been a long time since he had slept so soundly and so peacefully. There had been no need to wonder whether there would be a night attack from Falshed's troops, or whether wolves might sneak into the camp, or whether some daft statue looking for its First and Last Resting Place was going to wake everybody up by stomping around the wood.

Sylver could hear the sparrows chattering to each other on the roof. It was just silly drivel, even worse than that which Falshed was spouting at the moment, but it seemed right. He could smell various scents, of warm hay, of brown earth, of old timber. Someone was having a fry-up somewhere. He could hear the fat sizzling in the pan and could smell cooking.

At that moment someone came bursting into the room and banged on the side of the kettle.

'Up, up, traitor in our midst!'

It was Clive. When Sylver poked his head over the lip of the kettle he saw an enraged squirrel waving a

119

sword fashioned from a human butcher's meat skewer.

'What's the matter?'

'That fellow-me-stoat you brought with you. He's gone over to the greys. Snuck out in the middle of the night. Were you aware that you had a viper in your midst, sir? Come, explain yourself.'

Sylver sighed. 'As I told you before, this stoat was once our enemy. It seems he still is. He's the High Sheriff of Welkin, Sheriff Falshed, and Prince Poynt's right-paw stoat. I think he must have been sent out after us, but has been in several accidents since. I was never really convinced he was mad – this proves it. Gone to the greys, you say?'

'Absolutely,' cried the enraged Clive. 'Taken his leggings with him.'

'Well, there's nothing much can be done about it. I wish we had not been so free with our tongues about the secret passage. We'll just have to hope he doesn't realize its importance. Is there another way out of the castle, apart from through the town?'

'Of course. They're not under siege. Three-quarters of Castle Storm is surrounded by lake. They can use the postern gate on the right side of the castle to reach a boat and cross the lake that way. That's how they get their supplies in and out.'

'Well, I just hope he leaves and goes back to Castle Rayn, so that we're free to search for the passage without interference from him.'

Clive of Coldkettle now seemed satisfied that there was no conspiracy going on. He had suspected, when he found the stoat missing, that this had all been planned. He did not see what could have been gained by such a manoeuvre, but you never knew what those devious greys were getting up to. There did not seem to be anything he could do about it now, so he decided to let matters drop.

'Come,' he said to Sylver, 'you have only seen our headquarters so far. Let us break our fast and then I shall take you on a tour of the town. There's not a great deal to see – our main defences are in our own mettle. We reds are renowned for our courage and skill in warfare. We need rely only on our bravery and brilliance with weapons, unlike the cowardly greys who need stone walls and iron gates to keep them safe.'

This lack of modesty reminded Sylver a little of the bragging of stoats, but he did not say so. 'I should be honoured,' was his reply.

Sylver found, on going down the stairs to the main hall, that his outlaws were being well cared for. Most had arisen – all in fact except Scirf, who always slept in late – and were tucking into a hearty breakfast. Scirf, it had to be said, was something of a sluggard when there was no real work to do. Left to his own devices he would stay in bed all day.

Sylver ate some food, drank fresh water, and was then taken out by Clive. Will Splayfoot, Imogen and Goodsquirrel accompanied them as far as the well, then left the pair to wander around the town. As Clive had said, there was not a great deal to see. There were the usual shops – leatherworker, candlemaker, ironsmith, nut-and-grainer, etcetera – but nothing Sylver had not seen before. That is, until they came to a tumbledown shack on the edge of town, just inside the great wall which surrounded them.

Clive tried to hurry past this dwelling, but Sylver unfortunately poked his head inside. There was a horrible smell inside, of rotting toadstools, poisonous plants such as deadly nightshade and rhubarb leaves, dried frogs' feet, bats' droppings, and various other unpleasant odours. Peering into the darkness, he could see such things, hanging from greasy strings which dangled from rusty nails hammered into overhead beams.

What he also saw in the dark, dank interior, were several large figures sitting in a circle. There was a pot on a fire in the middle of them – some kind of foul stew – which was being stirred slowly. A cracked saucer of live worms and slugs was being passed around the circle. The figures were taking one or the other and crunching them in their mouths.

Clive came up beside Sylver and gripped his fur with a firm claw.

'Come away,' said the red squirrel softly. 'You don't want to have anything to do with these crones. They'll steal the eyes out of your head and use them for bottle corks. Best leave matters of the darkness to these evil creatures, who are used to such nasty places.'

'Who are they?' asked Sylver.

'Hags,' replied Clive, and shuddered. 'They'll not only steal your eyes, but your soul too.'

One of the creatures, which Sylver could now see were moles with tatty velvet pelts, looked up and cackled.

'Hail, Sylver, Thane of County Elleswhere!'

The others around the circle then took up various chants.

'Hail, Sylver, Lord of Thistle Hall!'

'Halfmoon Wood is thine for all time, weasel Sylver, use it well!'

Sylver stood, stunned and aghast on the threshold of the ancient shack. How could this be? Lord Haukin was Thane of County Elleswhere. Thistle Hall and Halfmoon Wood were on Lord

Haukin's estates. Where did they get their knowledge, these foul creatures of the lower darknesses? Were they simply trying to goad him, with false prophecies, towards some unsavoury ambition?

Chapter Thirteen

Falshed had not gone over the castle wall in the middle of the night as Clive of Coldkettle had suspected. He was still in the town, hiding in an alley in the backstreets. He had seen Clive of Coldkettle and Sylver pass by just a few minutes before and his heart was still racing. It was clear he had to find some way of getting into the castle soon.

It was the sheriff's idea to get help from the greys in securing Sylver and his band. He obviously could not do it alone, but according to Clive of Coldkettle the greys hated the reds so much they would do anything to upset them. Falshed was sure that Pommf de Fritte would agree to imprison the weasels in his dungeons at the earliest opportunity, thus leaving the sheriff free to report their capture to Prince Poynt.

However, Falshed was not the kind of creature who was good at scaling vertical walls: he was no Scirf or Mawk. He only felt really comfortable with four, or at the very least two of his feet firmly on the ground. Now he was at a loss to see how he could get into grey squirrel territory. The only thing he could think of was to get outside the town, go down to the shores of the lake, and swim to the jetty which led to the postern gate.

A rubbish-cart came by, pulled by two scruffy-looking red squirrels in cracked leather aprons.

Falshed jumped on the back of the cart while the garbage collectors were fetching the rubbish from behind houses. Once there he burrowed under the cabbage stalks and potato peelings.

More slop and muck was thrown on top of him. Eventually the cart was full and the two squirrels, grumbling away to each other about their lowly position in the scheme of things, dragged the cart through the town gates. They trundled it to the edge of a sloping cliff and tipped it over.

The rubbish went sliding down the slope, Falshed with it. He rolled, head-over-heels, and came to a halt at the bottom of the slope. Fortunately he was now on the edge of the lake and he entered the water straight away, wanting to wash off the smelly garbage which matted his fine coat.

Falshed hated water more than he did rubbish. He was not a very good swimmer. Moreover, when he was halfway to the castle's jetty, he remembered the dragonfly nymph. This was a different lake, but it was not impossible for there to be two such creatures. In any case, most of these lakes harboured savage pike. He had visions of the cold dead eye of a pike coming in for the kill, its mouth open, the rows of razor-sharp teeth ready to rend the flesh from his legs.

He felt a chill go down his spine and increased the power of his stoat-paddle. Pretty soon he came up to the castle wall, where he found an arrowloop just above the surface. He decided to end his journey here, rather than carry on to the jetty some few metres ahead.

Falshed was now shivering violently, both with the temperature of the water and the thought that there might be a monster lurking beneath him. He had vivid pictures in his mind of a mouth open below, ready to chomp him in half. Trying not to wriggle his toes too much, in case the ripples attracted the attention of anything down in the depths, he pulled himself up to the ledge of the arrowloop. He crawled gratefully through.

He landed on the stone flags of a dim room.

Light came from several stained-glass windows, high up on the walls, as well as through the small arrowloop. There were signs of a religious nature everywhere in the dim room. Clearly he had landed in one of the castle chapels. He was not alone. There were three figures in the room with him.

Standing close to an altar three stoats turned to stare at this creature who had come in through the back window to land with a wet sound on the floor of their sanctuary.

'What have we here?' said one, wearing a gold-embroidered scarlet robe. 'An uninvited guest!'

Falshed was happy to see they were stoats, not grey squirrels. Here were his kin, creatures of his own kind. They would surely smooth his path to meeting with Pommf de Fritte and the greys. Stoats stuck together, where Falshed came from.

He stood up. 'Greetings, fellow stoats. My name is Falshed, High Sheriff of All Welkin, personal friend of Prince Poynt. Forgive this unfortunate entrance. I am fleeing from weasels and red squirrels, who would have my life.'

'Fleeing?' murmured the stoat in the red robe. 'In *those* pantaloons?'

Falshed, dripping all over the floor, looked down at his brown snakeskin leggings.

'I, er, can't get them off at the moment. They've shrunk a bit and now they're too tight. I agree, they're not the sort of thing a sheriff should be wearing.'

'Or anyone,' said the stoat in the scarlet robe, shuddering. 'I am Torca Marda, Grand Inquisitor. These are Cardinal Orgoglio and Monsignor Furioso, my assistants.'

'Your Grace,' murmured Falshed, bowing low. 'I – I have heard of you of course, as cousin to my liege, Prince Poynt, who is at this moment besieged by rat hordes from the unnamed marshes. I should beware, Your Grace, for the rats may soon be pouring southwards. You need to prepare yourselves.'

'I had heard,' murmured the inquisitor, 'that my cousin the prince was in trouble. I was tempted to raise an army myself and . . .'

'And go to his assistance?' suggested Falshed.

Torca Marda's face hardened. 'No, not quite, you stupid stoat. If you will let me finish? I was going to drive the rats back to their holes and take the kingdom for myself. Either that or from a strong position make a pact with Flaggatis. However,' he sighed deeply, 'I have earned myself a somewhat harsh reputation over the years. The only army I can muster is already present in this room and that excludes yourself.'

Falshed now remembered that the prince and his cousin, the Grand Inquisitor, did not get on at all well. They had each struggled for power when both lived in Castle Rayn. Falshed could remember Prince Poynt crying, 'Who will rid me of this meddlesome priest?' The inquisitor had eventually been banished and had fled to regions unknown. Well, they were not unknown any longer, for here he was, in the castle of the greys. Falshed did not know what to say next.

'Stuck for words are we?' said the Grand Inquisitor, gliding down the altar steps. He was a lean, hungry-looking stoat, with unholy ambition gleaming in both eyes. His movements were smooth and silky, with menace in every wave of his paw. In his years at Castle Rayn he had been more feared than his cousin, Prince Poynt, who at least tortured animals openly.

Torca Marda had always preferred to do *his* nasty work in secret. His evil doings took place behind thick closed doors. Only the screams of the damned were legacy to his cruelty. Prisoners vanished overnight when in his soft paws; no-one knew where, no-one ever dared to ask. One of these disappeared ones had been the father of Sylver.

Torca Marda was a stoat who had all the power of the Church of Redfur behind him. When King Redfur had been alive he had almost been a living god. Since his death, killed under mysterious circumstances, he had been confirmed as a divine being by his followers. Even Prince Poynt subscribed to the new religion, was a devout worshipper of his dead brother, and feared retribution if he did not say his prayers.

There were those who said Prince Poynt had murdered his only brother, in order to get the crown. There were those who said King Redfur had ordered *himself* killed, so that he might rise again out of the darkness of the earth, even more powerful than he had been before death. There were those who said his death was a hunting accident, but few believed in this last idea.

Finally, there was a growing group who wondered, without voicing it too loudly, whether the Grand Inquisitor himself might have had a paw in the death of the king. Torca Marda, after all, had gained in enormous stature after the death of King Redfur. Before that time he had been a mere lowly friar in some obscure monastery to the north of

Welkin, a place where mirrors were forbidden and the mention of scarecrows was a sin.

Torca Marda was the stoat who headed the dark Church of Redfur. Those who did not believe in the ex-king as a deity were tortured by the Grand Inquisitor, to purge them of the evil of unbelief. It was all right and proper. Even if you said you believed, your words might not be accepted, for you could be lying. It was the Grand Inquisitor's job to find out if you really *meant* what you said. The only way to do that was to subject you to pain and get you to confess to unbelief. Then you were put to death for your crimes against God.

It was no wonder that Torca Marda was one of the most feared stoats in all of Welkin.

'So, Sheriff, you have been sent to spy on me?' said the Grand Inquisitor, in smooth tones.

'By that oaf, Prince Poynt,' said Cardinal Orgoglio, nodding.

Monsignor Furioso, the third member of the inquisitors, looked like a walking map. He was a stoat with a very patchy coat, being chocolate in places, sandy in others. It was Furioso who voiced what was in the minds of all three inquisitors.

'We shall need to find the real truth behind those eyes of his. You can see by his look he is not willing to speak with the tongue of an angel, but with that of a demon. We must drive the demon from his head. What say you, Cardinal Orgoglio?'

'That is for His Grace to decide.'

The Grand Inquisitor nodded thoughtfully. 'A little game with the cage might not be out of place . . .'

'No, no,' cried Falshed wildly, 'I'll speak the truth without any need for pain or suffering. What do you want to know? Did Prince Poynt send me here? Yes, in a manner of speaking, but not to spy on you, Your

Grace. I was sent here to follow a band of outlaws. They are at this moment with the red squirrels. I swam the lake to get away from them and to enlist the help of the grey squirrels in capturing them.'

The Grand Inquisitor ignored this outburst. 'I think we should use the device I recently manufactured within the confines of these very walls. My new invention, patent number 101. Make ready the heretic.'

'I'm not a heretic,' shouted Falshed, as he was grasped by the two strong assistants of the Grand Inquisitor and pushed down into a strong wooden chair with stout arms. 'I believe in the divinity of King Redfur.'

'Nevertheless, we must be sure.'

Falshed saw that it was useless to struggle or protest. These three fiends were going to have their way with him. His forelegs were strapped to the arms of the chair. His ankles were strapped to the front legs of the chair. Torca Marda went to an oaken cabinet which he opened with a small key he kept on a gold chain round his neck. He reached inside and came out with a strange-looking helmet made of fine wire mesh.

'What's that?' cried Falshed, alarmed. 'What are you going to do with it?'

There were two bulges on the sides of the helmet: two small wire-mesh domes. Torca Marda held the helmet up to the light and peered into these domes. He nodded thoughtfully. Falshed, trembling from head to foot now, thought he could see movement inside the bulges. The helmet was obviously a kind of cage, which held captive some creature. Or perhaps *several* creatures. Falshed did not like the look of things at all.

'What's in there?' he asked, as the Grand

Inquisitor crossed the floor. 'Are they alive?'

Torca Marda said nothing. He simply fitted the helmet on Falshed's head. It wrapped around his skull quite comfortably, so that only his face was visible, his little black nose twitching with terror. Straps were fastened beneath his chin to ensure the helmet was not shaken off during any future exciting moments. It seemed the three inquisitors were expecting Falshed to become much more lively within the next few minutes.

'Now,' said Torca Marda, 'perhaps you will tell us why you are here, in this castle?'

'Wha – what's in the domes of the helmet?' wailed Falshed, trying to look out of the corners of his eyes but finding it impossible.

'Earwigs,' murmured Torca Marda. 'When I turn this wire loop, situated on top of the cage, it opens two little doors, one on either side of the cage. Such an action will allow two dozen earwigs to crawl into the orifices of your ears.'

'Your lugholes, he means,' explained Furioso, eagerly.

'Aggghhh! What will they do?' cried Falshed.

Orgoglio replied, 'Eat through your brain, send you stark raving mad. Maybe they'll come out the other side. I've yet to see that happen, but I'm told it's possible.'

Falshed went crazy with fright. He yelled and screeched, struggling furiously with his bonds. He shook his head wildly, trying to dislodge the helmet. All to no avail. It remained firmly fastened to his head. He could hear the earwigs scrabbling around inside their cages now. In a few minutes they would be scrabbling around inside his head. He bit his own tongue in terror.

'Please, please,' he wept. 'Don't do it.'

131

'Confess,' murmured Torca Marda. 'Confess that you are an unbeliever, that you are a spy, that your mother gave birth to you at Hallowe'en, thus making you a demon.'

'Yes, yes,' shrieked Falshed.

'Yes, what?'

'Yes to all of that you said.'

'Do you also confess that you came through the arrowloop with the intention of murdering me and my two assistants?'

'No . . .'

The Grand Inquisitor reached up for the little wire loop that would release the earwigs.

'. . . yes, yes, yes.'

'And that once you had committed your foul deed, you were going on to murder Pommf de Fritte, the owner of this fine castle, and usurp his position as leader of the grey squirrels, in order to further your grossly inflated ambitions . . .'

'Stop, stop. Anything, yes, everything. I'm the most devious creature on this earth, only don't let the earwigs out, please, Your Grace.'

'Perhaps you were even responsible for the death of our great lord, King Redfur, who even now is urging his priests to find his killer and bring him to justice.'

'Even that,' sobbed Falshed, hanging his head. 'I confess to everything.'

At a nod from Torca Marda the wire-cage helmet was removed from the head of the broken Falshed. The sheriff collapsed in the chair. He was a quivering mess. His brain was buzzing with the thought that it had barely escaped being eaten into by the pincer-tailed earwigs. He moaned. He blubbed.

'Pull yourself together,' said Cardinal Orgoglio, disgustedly. 'Call yourself a stoat?'

Falshed sniffled and looked up into the eyes of the Grand Inquisitor.

'Interesting,' murmured Torca Marda. 'Most interesting. My little invention works, does it not?'

Monsignor Furioso nodded in glee.

Torca Marda motioned for Falshed to be set free, but the stoat sheriff still remained sitting in the chair, even when his bonds were removed.

Torca Marda said, 'You would have confessed to anything, wouldn't you? Of course you did none of those things I accused you of. You couldn't possibly have murdered Redfur. You haven't the brains for a start. Yet you were prepared to accept the blame for his death. How curious. I do believe my cage is a great success. Now, Falshed. What were you saying about outlaws? Do tell me.'

Falshed could not believe he had just been a victim of a cruel experiment. He thought they were still trying to trick him. But there was no sense in lying, or making things up, just to please the Grand Inquisitor. He told the truth.

'Sylver and his outlaw weasels escaped from Castle Rayn. I was ordered by Prince Poynt . . .' Falshed stopped, abruptly.

'That's all right,' said Torca Marda, softly, 'you may mention his name now.'

'Prince Poynt ordered me to follow them and bring back Sylver's head on a silver platter.'

'Do you have a silver platter on your person?' asked Furioso, who was not that bright. 'It can't be in the pockets of your leggings – they're far too tight.'

Torca Marda said to his assistant, 'I believe it's just an expression, a figure of speech. Do go on, Sheriff.'

'Well, that's it. I ran into some otters on my way along an underground river. They gave me a jay-feather cloak and this fine hosiery you see on my legs. Snakeskin. A nice brown, don't you think? Anyway, I caught up to Sylver, after escaping a monster dragonfly nymph, and he's with the red squirrels.'

'Then you came here, to the greys, in order to obtain assistance in capturing Sylver?'

'Yes.'

'Hmmm,' murmured the Grand Inquisitor, who never raised his voice above a soft tone, even when he was angry or excited, neither of which were his mood at the moment. 'But what if *I* should capture Sylver instead? Perhaps my cousin the prince might forgive me my trespasses and allow me to return to Castle Rayn. He would reinstate me. Once again I would be Archbishop of Welkin, the most powerful – the *second* most powerful stoat in the kingdom. What say you, Sheriff?'

Falshed shrugged. 'I expect so.'

'Good, good,' murmured Torca Marda. 'This is how it shall be. I shall take the weasel's head to my cousin and put myself in his favour once more. After that, who knows what might happen? Prince Poynt cannot live for ever. I'm told he's been looking unwell lately. We must see he is attended to by a good physician. Someone like yourself, Cardinal Orgoglio. It might be we could cure him with a cup of something proscribed by an apothecary I know, the good stoat Grubelgut . . .'

Falshed knew that the chemist to whom the Grand Inquisitor referred was actually a clever poisoner.

'But perhaps there's no saving poor old Poynt, even with the most expert of attention. Sadly he has no small stoats in the castle nursery, no heir to rule after him. It follows then that my broad shoulders will be called upon to bear the weight of kingship.

Redfur would have it so, don't you think? What say you, Falshed? I don't think there's any rule which says the archbishop cannot be crowned king.'

'None that I know of,' replied Falshed, dully.

'I knew you would agree,' said the silky voice of the Grand Inquisitor in his ear. 'How clever you are, Falshed.'

Something occurred to Falshed. 'Wouldn't it be easier, if you want to take over the kingdom, to raise an army and drive out Prince Poynt and his supporters?'

'Fool,' replied Torca Marda. 'Do you think anyone would follow a mad priest into battle against a crown prince?'

There did not seem much that Falshed could say to this which would not get him into deeper trouble.

Chapter Fourteen

Sylver was considerably shaken by the words of the coven of soothsayers. The creatures themselves turned out to be moles. A mole called Griselda, with Mathop and Gowk, made up the central core of this coven. The place they lived in used to be the stables, when there were horses in Stormtown.

'Mark us, young Sylver,' cackled Griselda, leader of this baker's dozen. 'We speak only the truth of what we see in the jamjars.'

Sylver's eyes became used to the gloom.

Looking around he could see tack of all kinds hanging from nails in the rafters. There were old leather horse-collars, the kind cart-horses or dray-horses might wear. There were bits, bridles and stirrups, the metal parts tarnished, the leather parts cracked. Saddles were draped over trestles. Around the stalls were hay feeders, now empty. The whole place was running with spiders. Webs hung like holed linen from the ceiling and joined ring bit to girth strap. Most of these webs were old, had lost their stickiness, draped uselessly.

The soothsayers sat underneath all this junk, surrounded by jars of worms and other matter.

Griselda was lean and long-nosed and wore a tatty velvet coat. Mathop was small, scrunched and wrinkled, like a dried fig. Gowk was fat, with greasy-looking fur that hung in matted strings from his coat, as if he were in the process of unravelling. All together they looked a pretty ghastly bunch of clairvoyants.

'Er, thank you for your words,' said Sylver. 'I'll bear them in mind.'

'Goodbye until we meet gain, in rotten weather or in rain,' cackled Griselda. 'Until we cross each other's spoor, on some windy, barren moor.'

Sylver withdrew, happy to get out of the musty-smelling stables that had not been touched by sunlight or a real blast of fresh air since the heavens knew when. 'Bit worrying,' he said, 'that prophecy they threw at me.'

Clive of Coldkettle said the soothsayers were always flinging out prophecies to frighten people. 'It's their business. The funny thing is,' Clive told him, as they hurried away from the building, 'they mostly come true.'

'But Lord Haukin is alive and in fine fettle,' replied Sylver. 'And I have no wish to become Thane of County Elleswhere. That's a job for a stoat. My job is to find out where the humans are.'

Clive scratched under his eye-patch and shrugged his shoulders. 'Well, there's not much I can say to help you, except that maybe those soothsayers back there don't know what they're talking about. Maybe they mixed you up with someone. That sheriff for example. Maybe they thought you were him?'

'That must be it,' said a relieved Sylver. 'They saw in their glass jamjar that a stranger was coming and when they saw me . . .' He shuddered for a moment at the thought of Falshed becoming Thane of Elleswhere and settling in Thistle Hall in place of Lord Haukin.

'They took you for that stranger.'

'But then they used my name,' recalled a despairing Sylver.

'They must have been told it by someone – one of my squirrels perhaps – before you actually stepped over their threshold. It's easily done. You've been here quite a few hours now. Word travels fast in small towns.'

At that moment Sylver was distracted from his worries, for around the corner came a huge, magnificent figure. It was a suit of armour. It clanked and rattled as it walked. In its metal gauntlets it held a huge double-handed sword. From its helmet swept a high black ostrich feather like a plume of dark smoke. Its visor was down, so Sylver could not see inside. It seemed to menace the pair as they tried to pass it, but Clive of Coldkettle did not appear concerned by it at all.

'Is there anything inside it?' asked Sylver, recalling an earlier incident with one of these empty knights. 'Any ferrets, for instance?'

'No,' Clive replied, shaking his head. 'All the suits of armour in the castle came to life at the time the statues did – way back when the humans left us. But they don't bother anyone. Besides, there are only two ferrets in the town – they'd hardly fill up that hollow gong.'

'And these gongs – they don't attack animals?'

'Only each other. We catch them just before a tourney and pit them against each other. You should see them fight.'

Sylver was inclined to think that was rather cruel. Live statues – and the suits of armour – were not highly intelligent beings, but who knew whether or not they had feelings. To set them against one another just for sport just did not seem right somehow. He said as much to Clive but received the curt answer that he was 'new around here' and ought not to voice opinions on subjects he knew little about.

'When is the tourney?' asked Sylver. 'Is it soon?'

'Two days' time,' replied Clive. 'After which there will be a huge banquet. It's the greys' turn to give the feast.'

'Does that mean we'll get inside the castle?'

'That's right. The tournament has to be out here of course, because there's not enough room in the castle wards, but one side or the other has to provide the banquet.'

'But can you trust them, to let you out again I mean? What if they lock all the doors?'

Clive snorted. 'Then there'll be one ding-dong of a battle in there – but they won't. Pommf de Fritte does have a *tiny* bit of honour, even if he is a grey. If he sets a truce until midnight, then you can be sure we won't be attacked. The one you have to watch is that holy stoat.'

'Which holy stoat is that?'

'Torca Marda, the so-called Grand Inquisitor,' replied Clive. 'Now there's a rafter rat in wood mouse's clothing, if ever I saw one.'

Torca Marda! He was here, in this castle? This was the stoat who had called for the complete extermination of all weasels, when Prince Poynt came to the throne. 'Genocide. Wipe them out,' he was reported to have told Prince Poynt. 'Remove the weasels from the face of Welkin.' Fortunately the archbishop had tried to sieze power for himself and his threat had fallen upon unsympathetic ears. Even Prince Poynt was not that bad. The prince did not want to wipe out weasels altogether, but rather to make use of them.

Sylver knew that Torca Marda had started the religion of worshipping dead King Redfur. Sylver did not believe in all that rubbish. King Redfur had been a royal stoat, but had no divine powers. He had not even been a particularly good king. Some of his laws had been unnecessarily harsh and his judgements showed that he had been open to bribes.

Unlike humans, animals do not often look up into the night sky for their spiritual inspiration, it being too far for their eyes and just a fuzzy blur. They see the sun and moon of course, but the stars are like pebbles at the bottom of a lake, too dim and distant to mean very much. The tops of trees are the highest objects with which animals are concerned. Mountains do not really count because they are simply flat ground that has been raised and often have trees on top anyway.

So Torca Marda had spread the idea that King Redfur was now some sort of god who lived in the canopy of the tallest forests of the land. This was very hard to swallow for weasels like Sylver and his band, who had suffered even more under Redfur than they had under Poynt. It had been Redfur who had said there was a difference between weasels and stoats. Redfur had issued a proclamation saying the weasels were to be regarded as an underclass, fit only as slaves and servants.

Just because he did not believe Redfur was a god, did not mean Sylver had no faith in *any* Supreme Being. He believed in a force of Nature, some great spirit which was in every living creature, every bush, every tree, every blade of grass or piece of chickweed, perhaps even in the rays of sunlight which filtered through a forest. It was an invisible spirit which bound all living things together as one.

This spirit was mainly good, though there were bad parts of it here and there, like rotten logs in a flourishing green forest. A forest needs its rotten bits to nourish lower forms of life, like a fungus or a beetle, and eventually they rot into the earth to feed the trees themselves. It was when those bad bits got wildly out of control, when their rottenness spread throughout the forest, that the world experienced its terrible times, its dreadful troubles.

While these difficult thoughts were whirling through Sylver's brain he passed the village stocks. Locked in the stocks by her wrists and ankles was a bedraggled-looking red squirrel. She had bits of tomato, cabbage leaf and raw egg clinging to the fur on her face. Villagers had obviously been pelting her with missiles earlier in the day. Clive of Coldkettle ignored her, but the red squirrel clicked her teeth at Sylver as he passed.

'Awright, squire?' she said.

'Who's this?' asked Sylver. 'What's she done?'

'Nut poacher,' said Clive, giving the other squirrel a casual clip around the ear. 'Robbed my personal tree.'

The poacher seemed unconcerned by Clive's half-hearted cuff and clacked her teeth again.

'What's your name, squirrel?' asked Sylver. 'How are you called?'

'Why, they do call me Link,' said the other. 'Some say Link the Stink.'

'Why do you steal nuts, when they are not your property?'

'It's my belief the nuts belong to everyone. No animal should have personal property. It isn't right.'

Sylver had some sympathy with this point of view. 'Still,' he said, 'if you know you're going to be put in the stocks for it, that could be a reason not to do it.'

'I get tempted,' said Link, ruefully. 'You see them nuts, sweet as anythink, danglin' from a tree, and you just got to have 'em.'

This cheeky Link was a bit like a female Scirf and Sylver could not help but like her. If they let her out of the stocks later he would speak with her again. She might be a useful guide for the outlaws while they were searching for the secret passage. Clive was fine for a tour around the main areas and monuments, but he was a little too full of himself to be totally useful. And he would not know the back alleys, the dark cellars, the cryptic places of the town. Link would know all of these, being a member of the underworld.

When Sylver got back to the others he reported on all he had seen and heard. They were amazed when he told them of the coven of moles and their prediction, but like him they did not believe it. Lord Haukin was old, but he was not near death. And who would want to kill such a bumbling old creature? And if something *were* to happen to him, Sylver would be the last person Prince Poynt would consider promoting to a lord.

'Doesn't make sense,' said Bryony. 'I think they're just a lot of old fakes.'

The outlaws had been given an old house attached to the guildhall. They suspected this was not because Clive was being kind to them, but because they believed he did not fully trust them yet. The house was warm and comfortable, though not particularly leakproof. Clive had told them it was haunted, which Mawk said would give him nightmares

'You great softy,' growled Scirf. 'How can a

ghoulie hurt you anyway? They're not made of anythink but mist.'

'I just don't like them, all right?' replied Mawk. 'You don't like Brussels sprouts and I don't like ghosts. That's all there is to it.'

'The difference is, I don't have nightmares about Brussels sprouts and keep everyone awake.'

It was while this sparkling conversation was in flow that a figure came to the doorway. Looking up, Sylver recognized the creature. It was Link the poacher.

'I've just bin set free,' she said, trailing a rather unpleasant smell of rotten eggs in behind her. 'I thought I'd come an' look you up, see how you were settling in.'

'Look, it's rather useful that you've come,' replied Sylver. 'Thing is, we need someone to guide us about the town. Would you be willing to show us around? We'll pay you of course. We're particularly interested in secret passages.'

'Ten groats is my usual showing-weasels-over-the-town fee,' replied Link, quickly. 'That or a sackful of walnuts, whichever is the easier for you.'

They settled for the ten groats.

'Now, what would you like to see first off?' asked the red squirrel. 'You say you're looking for a secret passage. There's the one from the church to the guildhall. The one from the cottage-by-the-wall to the almshouses, where all the crotchety old red squirrels stay. Or the one from the nunnery to the mangers' graveyard. Which is it to be?'

'All of them,' said Sylver, congratulating himself on finding the one animal with the bits of local knowledge the outlaws required. 'Scirf, Bryony and Icham – you take the church passage. Luke, Wodehed and Alysoun – the cottage-by-the-wall.

143

Mawk, Miniver and I will do the nunnery.'

Link said she would go with the nunnery passage group, since it was hardest one to find. 'The church one is under the altar. Just go round the back of it and you'll find a hole big enough for a weasel to get down. Now, the cottage-by-the-wall. Go into the inglenook fireplace and turn right. The rest of you, come with me.'

Sylver proposed they use the back door, to avoid Clive of Coldkettle and any of his knights. As they went out it was dusk. The evening was slithering in as quiet and gentle as a grass snake. Mawk sidled up to Link and nudged her.

'Look,' he said, having been thoroughly frightened by a single word of hers. 'Mange. Is that rife here?'

The red squirrel looked into the weasel's eyes. 'Let's put it this way, squire,' she replied. 'If you see an animal wearing a ragged robe wiv a hood, and ringing a bell, an' wearing a sign hanging from its neck with the word UNCLEAN written on it – avoid that creature like the plague.'

'Because it *is* the plague, right?'

'Right.'

Mawk shuddered and might have let out a whimper if he had not been worried about what Sylver might say to him.

Chapter Fifteen

Mawk, Miniver and Sylver followed Link through the narrow streets of the town. High up on the hill lamps and candles were beginning to be lit in the castle. Before very long it would look like a fairy kingdom, with lights behind every window and arrowloop. Already the sentries on the battlements were carrying fiery brands which trailed flames like red comet tails in the evening breeze. It was so tranquil it was difficult to imagine that two sets of creatures were at war here.

The four mammals passed an inn called The Acorn Cup. It was a warm evening and doors and windows had been flung wide open. Clouds of midges peppered the lamplight which glowed from within. The passers-by could hear the sounds of animals enjoying themselves: the noise of clicking teeth, raucous shouting, mugs cracking together. Jollity spilled out onto the street along with the light.

Sylver noticed a wistful expression come over Link's squirrelly face. She seemed to waver as she glanced inside the inn, where squirrels were quaffing honey dew and playing hollyhockers. Her tongue came out and she absent-mindedly licked her lips. Sylver heard the squirrel jingle the groats now in the pouch on her belt.

'You have a job to do,' reminded Sylver, gently.

'You have to earn that ten groats before you spend it.'

Link sighed and nodded. 'I'm such a reprobate,' she said, clicking her teeth. 'It's just me. Won't be a minute.'

The red squirrel disappeared inside the inn, but to the outlaws' relief, reappeared within a few moments with something wrapped in brown paper.

Miniver, the little finger-weasel said, 'Your ten groats won't last you long that way.'

'Exactly,' said Mawk. 'You should heed good advice, squirrel, and save that money for a rainy day.' Mawk was good at pontificating and he did so now, as they wound their way through some tight snaky alleys between dark houses. 'My father always said, "Waste not, want not," and I've never forgotten that good advice. You would do well to listen to such sound words yourself, squirrel . . .'

He said no more, for a shout came from above. 'Look out below!' followed by a rain of vegetable peelings and dirty water, most of which landed on Mawk's head.

'Thank you very much,' he spluttered, standing there and shaking off bits of potato and carrot.

'Well, you should be alert instead of trying to lecture Link here on what to do with her money,' argued Miniver. 'The trouble with you, Mawk, is that you can't help interfering in other people's business.'

Eventually the four came to a low, sprawling building with a high wooden fence and a gate to match. On the roof of the building at the south end a weathervane in the shape of a dove turned and squeaked in the evening breeze. The smell of woodsmoke drifted from the northern corner, where the kitchen was probably located.

This was the nunnery.

Sylver asked, 'Are there nuns inside?'

'Yep,' replied Link. 'About four or five. All squirrels of the old order, before this business of Redfur came along.'

'Will the nuns mind us tramping around inside their building?'

'We won't disturb them too much.'

'It's very quiet in there,' Mawk said, looking at the formidable gate. 'What's going on?'

'Ah, well, see,' said the red squirrel, 'the nuns have taken vows of silence. They're not allowed to speak to anyone, not even to each other. And the others, well I suppose they're quiet because they're sick.'

Mawk said suspiciously, 'What others?'

'The animals who've got the mange.'

Mawk recoiled at these words. 'I knew it, I knew it,' he said. 'This is a mange colony. There's squirrels and other creatures rotting to bits in there, aren't there? That's why they've got the high fence and the gate, to keep 'em from getting out and infecting normal animals.' He shuddered. 'I'm not going in there. I don't want my fur to fall out in clumps. I don't want my eyes to go all gooey and my ears to bung up.'

'Be quiet Mawk,' said Sylver, severely. 'Those poor animals are just as "normal" as you are and the fence is probably to keep other animals from wandering in. The creatures inside just happen to have caught a rather unfortunate disease, that's all. So long as we take the proper precautions we won't be in any danger. Try not to touch those who are infected and make sure we scrub down properly when we get back.'

Miniver added, 'And you should be ashamed of yourself, Mawk. Those nuns in there have to live with the possibility of catching the mange every day, yet they tend to their patients without a thought for themselves. You would do well to try to copy their selfless attitude.'

'Would I?' grumbled Mawk. 'Well, just because they're daft enough to risk their lives, doesn't mean I have to be silly too, does it? I'm not going in and that's that. Some weasels are scared of snakes and spiders, I'm scared of the mange. Simple as that.'

Sylver said, 'You're the only weasel I know who's scared of snakes and spiders, Mawk – and you're coming in, and that is *definitely* that.'

'Oh,' whined Mawk. 'Don't make me, Sylver. I admit it, I'm scared. Why do you always make me do things I don't like?'

'Because you're a member of the outlaws and if you want to stay one of us you must do your part.'

Link stared at Mawk and rolled her eyes. The red squirrel then turned to the huge gates, within which as usual there was a smaller gate, cut to size for the creatures who now used it. On this small gate was a doorknocker made of iron in the shape of a black sun. Link used this knocker to call attention from within. The sound of the knocking seemed to echo throughout the courtyard behind the doors. Eventually a figure in a habit came and opened the gates. Her eyes enquired though her lips remained tightly sealed.

'Could we come through?' asked Link. 'Some weasels want to see the secret passage. I have something here.'

Link held up the brown parcel she had obtained at the inn.

The nun shrugged and opened the gate wider.

Link led the way across the courtyard into the main building on the far side. This was a long narrow structure with a door at either end. Once the four had entered they found themselves in a room dimly lit by cheap tallow candles. Down each side of the room were rows of mammals – not just squirrels but other animals too – and it was obvious they were sick with the mange. Nuns in dark habits hovered about them, giving them water when they asked for it, attending to their various needs.

Link the poacher passed between these rows and the weasels followed her. Mawk's complexion was waxen. He looked even sicker than the nuns' patients. He smooled between creatures in various stages of the dread disease, shrinking into himself as he passed by them.

Link stopped to talk to one or two of them in her chatty style, while Mawk hopped anxiously from one foot to the other. Eventually they all reached the end of the ward. There stood a pot-bellied stove. It was unlit. Link pulled the damper knob with a clunking sound. After a few moments there was the sound of machinery within the stove. Wheels turned, pulleys pulled, winches winched and springs wound and unwound themselves.

There was a faint grating sound from beneath the stove.

'What's happening?' asked Mawk, his voice booming through the stillness in the ward. 'What's going on?'

No-one answered him.

The nuns glared at him severely, as if he had been responsible for them breaking their vows of silence. The mangers on their biscuit-thin mattresses of straw regarded him with solemn faces. The other two outlaws frowned and shook their heads as if to say, There's always one, and it's usually Mawk. Link sighed and said, 'Tsk, tsk.'

'I only asked,' whispered Mawk.

Suddenly the pot-bellied stove swung sideways to reveal a hole in the floor. The outlaws could just see steps descending down that hole. Link went down first, followed closely by Miniver, then Mawk and finally Sylver. At the bottom of the steps Link pulled a lever and the stove swung back into its original place, leaving them in utter darkness.

Link seemed to know what she was doing. She used a tinderbox in the dark. Sparks flew up each time the flint struck the steel. Soon she had lit three normal-sized candles and gave one to each of the outlaws. A fourth, much larger candle, she took for herself.

In the passage the walls ran damp with water. Moss grew in the cracks between the bricks. Beetles scuttled over these padded stones.

One particular stone looked a little bit looser than the others. Link pulled it out and reached inside where the others could see a wire. She tugged on the wire once. A tinkling bell sounded faintly further down the tunnel. She replaced the brick, carefully, in its own particular slot.

'To warn them we're coming,' she murmured.

Who it was she was 'warning' she did not say.

They began walking. Eventually at the end of the first section of the passage, during which time Sylver studied the walls for any clues, they came to a small cell filled with light. Inside the cell sat three squirrels around a barrel-shaped table. They were playing some sort of memory game, whispering quotations to one another from books.

When they saw they were not alone they looked up. Link silently handed the brown package to them. They muttered their thanks, then turned away, intent on getting back to their task.

'Who are they?' asked Sylver, once they had gone further down the secret passage. 'What are they doing?'

'They're priests, memorizing passages from the Good Book,' said Link. 'They went underground when the New Religion became law. They're rather fond of the old one, but it's illegal. So we have these priest-holes in various places, where they hide. I bring food and drink to these three from time to time.'

'But who would stop them practising their old religion – not Clive of Coldkettle, surely?'

'No, not him. The stoat Torca Marda.'

'But isn't Torca Marda inside the castle?'

Link nodded. 'The Grand Inquisitor's got these long forelegs. He can reach out into the town and slay anyone he pleases. His spies are everywhere. Rosencrass and Guildenswine, to name but two. Those three priests would not survive the assassin's blade for long if they preached openly. There's a hefty price on their heads as it is.'

'How much?' asked Mawk, a little too quickly.

Link stopped and stared at him in the light from the candles. 'Why?' she asked. 'You thinkin' of collecting?'

'No, not me,' replied Mawk, swallowing hard. 'I – well – just curious, that's all.'

'I suggest you make yourself uncurious, friend,' said Link in a voice she had not used before. 'Otherwise you might find yourself in serious trouble.'

Mawk nodded swiftly.

At that moment Sylver made a little sound. He had been inspecting the walls in the light of his candle. The four were now in a large round chamber the walls of which hurtled up into the darkness

151

above. It was a rather frightening chamber simply because of the feeling of infinity all around them. Sylver could see something etched into the stone-work high above his head, at about the height a tall human might stand.

'There are words written up there,' he said to Link. 'I can't quite see them from here. Do you know what they say?'

'No, I've never been this far down the tunnel before. No-one has to my knowledge. Not for decades.'

'Mawk, get Miniver on your shoulders, then climb up my back while I brace myself against the wall.'

'What for?' asked Mawk.

'So I can see the words, ninny,' replied Miniver, who was one of the few weasels who could read.

Mawk did as he was asked though not without a murmured protest or two.

Eventually Miniver was high enough to hold a candle out and read what was written.

'Is it the clue?' asked Sylver, straining against the wall as he bore the weight of the other two. 'What does it say?'

'It says: THERE IS NOTHING TO FEAR IN THE DARKNESS OF THIS VAST CHAMBER — EXCEPT THE DARKNESS ITSELF.'

Sylver let the other two climb down his back. He was disappointed. It did not sound like the clue they were seeking.

'I suppose it would have been too simple for us to get it straight away.'

'Are you *sure* that's not what you want?' asked Link.

'Pretty sure. Unless it's cryptic. We'll ask Wodehed to have a think about it, once we get out of here.'

152

Mawk was still staring at the words, his paw with the candle in it outstretched. He shuddered as if someone had stepped on his grave. 'What's it mean do you think?'

Link shone her candle on the stone flags of the floor. 'I guess there might be some traps around, some pits of darkness to fall into. It's a bit like that other saying, isn't it? You know, *there is nothing to fear but fear itself.* Someone's sort of copied it.'

'Or,' Mawk said in a quietly hysterical tone, 'there's some sort of supernatural meaning.'

Sylver was about to tell his cowardly outlaw to pull himself together when he saw a strange thing happening. Mawk was vanishing, very gradually, bit by bit. His hind legs and hips had disappeared already. An inky substance, unaffected by the light, was creeping up his body, even as he stared at the words on the wall. It flowed up the weasel like a thick fluid, a black oily matter. As it crept over his bodily parts it took on their shape, took on *his* shape, becoming as it were, another Mawk-the-doubter of a different hue.

Mawk was being engulfed by darkness!

Before Sylver could shout a warning, the stuff had shot up Mawk's outstretched arm, and doused his candle with a *phut!*

Chapter Sixteen

'It's a swamper!' Link cried.

Sylver looked to the squirrel for guidance in dealing with this strange being, since she seemed to know what it was called. But for the moment Link appeared to be paralysed.

Mawk felt as if his body were being swallowed by tar: if it covered his head he was sure he would be suffocated. He was sensible enough to know that if Link were frightened of this creature, then he should be too. After all, Link was a local.

'Help me!' he cried. 'Get it off!'

Mawk was like a weasel drowning in a barrel of malt, attempting to keep his head clear of the surface. He tried to lift his forelegs but the swamper was as sticky and binding as treacle, gluing his limbs to his sides. He was being eaten by darkness and he knew that he only had a few seconds to live.

'It won't let me move,' he said in panic. 'Do something, Sylver!'

But it was Link who was jolted out of her frozen state by Mawk's plea. She leaped forward, with the large candle in her claws. She applied the flame to the bottom of the creeping darkness. Sylver and Miniver, seeing this, did the same with their candles. Immediately the swamper began to flow downwards, rushing to its hem to extinguish the candle.

At first the supernatural creature seemed to be winning against the flames, gathering in a mass at the point where the flames touched. It wriggled and squirmed, still managing to retain the shape of Mawk, but using some of itself to form puddles of darkness to douse the candles.

'Is it in pain?' asked Miniver, wonderingly.

Link said, 'No, it's not the heat, it's the *light*. This thing is made of darkness. Darkness hates light. It's as simple as that. In a battle between the two, light will always defeat darkness.' She paused before adding, 'Though swamper darkness is much thicker than ordinary darkness.'

'You mean, you can't tell who's going to win here?' cried Mawk, his eyes starting from his head. 'This sludgy darkness might defeat your little lights!'

Link was very clever for though the creature managed to douse Sylver's small candle, Link kept drawing the flame of her candle back every time the swamper surged forwards. She applied the flame, then withdrew it quickly. By this method, she gradually compelled the swamper to leave Mawk's body.

Link drove the swamper towards the side of the chamber with the candle flame. When she got it to the edge, she picked up a loose brick and plonked it on top of the creature. It wriggled, struggled for a while, then was still. It lay flat as an abandoned shade on the floor of the chamber, still half of it in the shape of Mawk. It was as if Mawk had cut his own shadow loose and left it behind him like a piece of litter.

Link came back, shuddered, then relit the candles of the other two.

Mawk was still in a state of shock.

'What *was* that thing?' asked Sylver. 'I know you called it a *swamper*, but what does that mean?'

'It's a phantom, the ghost of one of them animals who treated mangers badly when they was alive,' answered Link. 'Their cruelty on earth has been rewarded by eternal sufferin', by having to wander the underworld, never knowing peace, because of the nasty things they did during their lives.'

Miniver stated, 'You said something about "light will always defeat darkness" – what did you mean exactly?'

'Well, we animals don't look at stars much, because they're so far away, they don't mean much to us. But stars are actually little points of light in a huge darkness – a darkness so big it doesn't have a beginning or an end – yet one of those little stars sends its light to us through that darkness from a distance which would make your head spin if you thought about it.'

'So one tiny bit of light can cut through billions of miles of darkness?'

'That's right.'

Sylver asked, 'How did these swampers come about?'

'It was in the time when we hadn't got a hostel for mangers, like we've got now with the nuns. They had to walk about with a sign round their necks saying UNCLEAN and ring this bell to warn people they had the mange. Some animals used to drive mangers off, throwin' rocks and things at them, instead of leaving food on their doorsteps. Those are the ones what became swampers after they died.'

'Plagues are frightening things,' agreed Sylver, 'though that doesn't excuse their tormentors.'

'That's right. Those animals who had been cruel began gathering darkness and depression into their

156

spirits 'til it was a thing you could feel and touch, a substance of sorts. When their bodies was put down into the grave, they still kept soaking up the darkness of the earth, 'til one day they was swampers and rose up out of their tombs.'

'How do you know about the swampers?' asked Sylver. 'You said you've never been this far down the passage before.'

'I once met a dormouse who came down here. She told me what had happened to her. That was before she went mad of course.'

'My sanity is in danger,' wailed Mawk. 'I'm going to spend my twilight days walking around burbling nonsense.'

'So what's the difference?' said Miniver.

'Thank you very much,' replied Mawk, testily. 'No sympathy around here, is there?'

'There'll be more swampers about,' said Link. 'We should've brought brands wiv us. We'll just have to be careful. If you see a spot in the passage a bit darker than the rest of it, then don't go near it. And keep weaving your candles around you, to fight off any dark shapes movin' in on you.'

'Oh Gawd!' moaned Mawk. 'I never should have come.'

The four continued down the passage until finally they came to a fork.

'Which way, left or right?' asked Sylver.

'Search me,' said Link. 'Let's go right.'

So they went right and finally came into another great chamber, a place of horror, filled with bones. They did not bother to go in. They simply stared at the corpses, some still with decaying rags clinging to them, which lay about the chamber floor in disarray. Bits of rotten coffin wood lay here and there, as if there had been a shipwreck of sorts. This last chamber was directly under the mangers' cemetery itself.

It was as if a great wave had washed through the graveyard above and carried dead bodies with it like so much flotsam and jetsam. Which was in a way what had happened, though not quite so dramatically. Rain had filled the coffins and graves, making them heavy, so that their weight caused them to crash through a metre or so of earth, through the ceiling of the chamber from the graveyard above. The coffins had smashed on the chamber floor, scattering their grisly contents over the great room.

'Ghastly place,' said Miniver, clutching her candle tightly. 'Are we going in?'

'Not on your life,' murmured Mawk. 'Look at all those swampers!'

It was true; the whole chamber was crawling with the supernatural creatures, like cockroaches in swill. One paw inside that chamber would be enough to have them swarming over the owner of that paw.

Link motioned for the group to draw back. 'Let's get out of here,' she said. 'Let's take the other fork and see where that leads.'

They went back to the fork and turned right, penetrating deep under the houses of the town. At one point they came to a massive chamber, a room off the main passageway. It *looked* innocent enough, but there was a drone, a kind of murmuring, coming from within the room. Miniver stuck her head in, to look for any clues written on the walls, but immediately withdrew it again. She was bemused.

'What's the matter?' asked Mawk, nervously. 'Why did you pull out like that?'

'I – I saw figures, animals and birds, swirling about inside the room. It was strange. They seemed to be enticing me to enter. If I hadn't just stuck my head around the doorway, I might have gone in. It was hard to resist.'

Miniver stared through the open doorway, the light from her candle playing on the opposite wall. 'It looks empty enough, though,' she said.

Sylver said, 'Maybe you were seeing things that aren't there?'

'Well that's obvious enough, since there *isn't* anybody there,' Mawk retorted.

Link said, 'Best not to go in.'

'But we have to check to see the clue isn't there,' replied Miniver. 'I couldn't see the wall behind the doorway. I shall have to go in.'

'Why you?' asked Link. 'Why not Sylver – or Mawk?'

'No – no, not me,' cried Mawk, backing off. 'I've done enough. I've fought with a swamper. It's somebody else's turn. In fact, I don't think you should let *anybody* go in, Sylver. Just for once, listen to me. Let's move on.'

Sylver said, 'I should be the one.'

'No,' said Miniver, thoughtfully, 'this time it really should be me. I'm the smallest and lightest. What we have to do is form a chain, by linking forepaws. Somebody, perhaps the two on the end of the chain, must stay *outside* the room, while allowing me inside, so that I can look around. If there's any threat, you can yank me out quickly.'

Sylver thought this over and though he did not like the idea of risking Miniver's life, it seemed the most sensible and sound solution. Miniver was a finger-weasel, light of frame, and it would be quite easy to pull her from the room. Sylver himself was muscled and Mawk was plump. They could not ask Link to do it, for she was simply a guide, not a searcher.

'Right,' he said, eventually, 'everybody grab the

paw of the one next to them. Let's get this over with.'

So, they formed a mammal chain, with Mawk on one end, holding the left paw of Link. Link's right paw gripped Sylver's left paw, while Sylver's right paw held little Miniver's belt. In this way they gradually allowed Miniver to enter the chamber, ready at a moment's notice to yank her out.

Slowly Miniver entered the chamber on the end of Sylver's outstretched forelimb. Once inside she dripped some molten wax on the floor and used it as a stand for her candle. Then she straightened again and stared around her.

'What can you see?' asked Link, from behind Sylver. 'Describe it.'

Miniver's voice was full of wonder. She sounded completely spellbound. 'It's – it's like the whole room is a huge lake, with a whirlpool in the centre of it, only it's not made of water – it's made of these shapes of creatures, animals and birds of all kinds. They must be wraiths, they're so flimsy, like mist. The whole room is full of them. They're all around the walls, on the ceiling, washing around the floor, all of them moving in a swirling motion, those on the outside are going slower than those in the middle of the room – just like a whirlpool . . .'

'Get her out of there!' cried Link, sharply, pulling on Sylver's paw. 'Quickly, make her come out!'

'They're calling to me,' Miniver said in a strange tone, 'asking me to join them.'

'I see them too,' said Sylver, in a faraway voice. 'I hear them as well.' He was now halfway through the entrance to the chamber and seemingly as entranced as Miniver. 'It's enchanting. I can hear their voices murmuring in my ears. "Come to us, come to us . . ." I think I have to go in there with them. It looks so lovely, all those colours whirling, all those little

160

paws outstretched for me. You should see it, Mawk. It's all so very *beautiful*. There are blossoms and mossy banks, streams flowing silver and bright in the sun, snow on the mountains, leafy glades, woods and meadows full of wild flowers, mushrooms a deep velvety brown – oh, you should see it, Link. And the animals, they're having such a time, dancing, running across the leas, burrowing in rich brown bottom land. Let me go, Link, I have to go in, I have to go in.'

Sylver began to sound annoyed at being held back. He struggled to free his paw from that of Link's. Link held on grimly, pulling him back gradually, Sylver's claws scratching on the floor, grooving the dust as she tugged at his forelimb.

'Glistening blackberries,' Miniver was saying, 'plump blackberries dangling from the brambles . . .'

Mawk began pulling with Link now, the pair of them trying to wrench Sylver and Miniver from the chamber.

'You don't understand,' yelled Sylver. 'We have to go in – you don't understand. There are bright white castles, sparkling in the moonlight. Horses thundering over the drawbridges – palominos, piebalds, greys, bays, chestnuts – dancing to music that lives in their heads. Fabulous creatures. Griffons, gargoyles, dragons, unicorns. Lumbering monsters with a multitude of legs and a host of wings. And wide blue lakes. A tall black ship with a hundred sails. There are fairies on the deck, bearing the body of a pale dead knight. A one-eyed giant is striding over the mountain-tops. They're calling for us, asking us to join them. Let me go, Link, will you?'

Sylver bent his head down, trying to bite Link's forelimb, but stretched between two animals he could not reach. Miniver was quiet now, simply pulling to get away from Sylver. Link thought it a miracle that Sylver had not leg go of the finger-weasel's belt, but some small part of his brain must have told the outlaw leader that there was danger here, which he must keep Miniver from entering, even as he himself struggled to go in.

'Yes!' cried Miniver, in tones of ecstasy. 'Yes, yes.'

Suddenly Mawk and Link shot backwards, pulling Sylver with them. The three creatures ended piled up against the far wall of the passage in a tangle of limbs and bodies. When they sorted them-selves out, Sylver looked down despairingly to find he had Miniver's belt in his claws. It had been undone at the buckle. She had finally reached down and released herself.

Sylver rushed to chamber doorway again, staring inside, but without entering.

Miniver was nowhere to be seen.

To Sylver the room looked dull and empty once more. There were no bright scenes whirling around the walls, no pool of wraiths in the middle of the floor, no paws beckoning, enticing him to join them. Only that faint unintelligible murmuring which was the only indication that the chamber was magical.

'We've lost her,' said Link, coming up beside him. 'She's been swept away to the Land of Lost Dreams.'

'Gone where?' asked Sylver. 'Can we get her back? What is this place? Why didn't you warn us?'

'Didn't know it was here. I've heard about it, in stories and such, but it's one of them things you think's just another myth, another tall tale.'

'The Land of Lost Dreams,' repeated Mawk. 'Is that where she's gone?'

Link nodded, sadly. 'I'm almost positive that this here, what you described, Sylver, was the Pool of

162

Lost Dreams. If you fall in, you get sucked down in the vortex, the whirlpool, and then taken off, swept away on the currents of night to the Land of Lost Dreams.'

'Can we get her back?' asked Sylver, frantically. 'If only I hadn't let her go.'

'You didn't let her go. She let herself go,' replied Link. 'She undid her belt. You couldn't stop her. It's lucky we was able to save *you*, or you'd have gone with her. There's nothing we can do. She's gone now. I've never heard of any way of getting animals back, once they've been swept off. We'd best be gettin' on. We can't do any more now.'

Sylver stared into the room, feeling wretched. He had allowed Miniver to go into the chamber and all for nothing. There was no clue written on the walls. He knew that from time to time his outlaws would be killed or hurt, or captured and imprisoned, and that was all part of the life they led. They were aware of the risks and accepted them, or they would not be members of his band. Yet still he felt responsible each time one was lost. Now Miniver had disappeared in this whirlpool, this maelstrom which had pulled her down and carried her off into oblivion.

A paw touched his shoulder. He turned to see it was Mawk, tears running down his whiskers. Mawk too was in the throes of grief.

'We have to be getting on,' said Mawk, in a broken voice. 'Link's right, there's nothing more to do here. If we could do something, I'd do it, even though I'm a coward.'

'You were right to be scared,' said Sylver. 'I should have listened to you this time. But I didn't, more's the pity. We'll move on then, before any more of us are drawn into that chamber. We don't need any more casualties.'

163

Three candle flames moved solemnly along the passageway.

The fourth was left burning in the middle of the chamber, fighting away the darkness, like a tiny star keeping back the forces of infinite night.

Chapter Seventeen

Dispirited as they were, the trio were on the alert when they came to a bend in the passage and saw lights ahead. Then yet another set of lights appeared to the left. The three groups seemed to be converging at a central point.

'What's this?' asked Sylver. 'More trickery?'

'Ho!' came a voice which echoed hollowly throughout the passage. 'Who's there?'

Sylver cried, 'Identify yourself first, stranger.'

'No,' cried someone in the third group, 'you give us your names and then we'll reveal ourselves.'

All three groups had stopped now, at a far enough distance away from each other to allow retreat if necessary. They seemed to be at a stalemate. Sylver realized that if someone did not break the ice they would be there for ever.

'Sylver the weasel here, with Link the squirrel and Mawk.'

The voices that came back were joyous with relief.

'Luke, Wodehed and Alysoun here!'

'And Bryony, Icham and Scirf over here!'

The three sets of weasels ran towards each other and everyone began talking at once. It seemed that the other two groups had travelled through their passages with various minor adventures, but nothing on the scale of those experienced by Sylver's group. Unfortunately no-one had found the clue they were all seeking.

When things had calmed down a little Sylver told the others what had happened to Miniver. Naturally there was an expression of grief from the weasels. Questions were asked about whether the accident could have been avoided or not. It was not that they were looking for someone to blame, but so they had all the information necessary to avoid it happening again.

The atmosphere became very subdued. Weasels were always upset when they lost one of their number, but Miniver had been liked by everyone, being such a bright and enthusiastic creature.

'Wodehed,' asked Alysoun, 'can you do anything to get Miniver back from the Land of Dreams?'

The wizard of the outlaw band looked doubtful. 'You know what my magic is like,' he said, admitting its flaws for once in his life. 'It's – it's not that reliable. What if something were to go wrong and I condemn her to oblivion for ever? You would never forgive me. I would never forgive *myself*. What about the soothsayers in Stormtown?'

'I wouldn't like to trust those moles,' said Link. 'They're not the sort of creatures who help animals. They're more inclined to create mischief.'

'Well then, there's nothing we can do about it for the moment, I suppose,' Bryony said. 'When we get back to Thistle Hall maybe Lord Haukin will be able to give us some hope. With all his book learning he may have an answer. Perhaps there's something we can do to get her back from this place, the Land of Dreams. Providing – providing she's still alive, that is.'

Clive of Coldkettle was equally sympathetic when he heard of the incident, but again stressed that the coven of moles was not the place to go for assistance in the matter.

'You might as well go to Torca Marda himself,' said Clive. 'Speaking of which, we must ready ourselves for the tourney tomorrow. Tonight I must keep vigil in the town chapel. I would be honoured, Sylver, if you would join me.'

As a weasel, Sylver was indeed pleased to receive this invitation. He understood that the tourney would be between grey and red squirrels. There would be a few other animals there – the weasels themselves, perhaps Torca Marda and his two stoats, and the ferret spies, Rosencrass and Guildenswine – but any competition between these creatures would be merely sideshows to the main events. It was essentially a squirrel tournament.

Sylver said it was he who should be honoured and agreed to accompany the knight on his vigil.

The tournament would be a dangerous set of games. Those taking part were often injured, though it was rare someone was killed. Amongst the events would be archery, dart-throwing, slingshot, stave-fighting and most important of all, singlestick. It would be peasants' and merchants' sons and daughters taking part in the first four events, while the knights saved their strength and skill for singlestick.

Singlestick is the art of swordfighting, but using wooden swords with leather pommels. One could be bruised and beaten at the end of singlestick, but since the swords were short poles without a point, at least one could not be stabbed to death. A broken head, or bones, but not a pierced heart. In this way knights could prove themselves without forfeiting their lives for the opportunity of testing their mettle.

A good knight undergoes many rituals, but the main one is the vigil, in which he tries to cleanse his spirit ready for contest or battle. Many knights make vows to remain poor and chaste, in order to keep themselves pure. Clive of Coldkettle was such a knight. He had no personal wealth and he was a jack without a jill. When he went to kneel in the chapel that evening, to offer his sword to his god, he was as pure as a knight could be when on his vigil.

Sylver sat by his side, enjoying the peace of the squirrel chapel, which was formed from the bole of a giant hollow oak. There were oak leaves carved into the round walls. In the centre of the chapel stood an old drey used as an altar, a point of focus for the praying knight. It was said to be the den of the first squirrel ever to be born. Her name was Mohic and she had been a dappled squirrel, both red and grey.

Mohic had given birth to six young, three of which were grey and three of which were red. These young squirrels quarrelled with each other over who wore the most natural and proper coat. Eventually their arguments reached such a fever pitch they separated into two tribes, the reds and the greys. All of this gave their mother much sorrow, but since she had brought them into the world in order for them to make their own way, she could not interfere and things went from bad to worse.

Finally, no red would have anything to do with a grey, and vice versa. The two sets of rodents – for squirrels are related to those rats who besieged Castle Rayn – went their different ways. As the tribes grew in size, so did the need to extend territory, and it was inevitable that some day the reds and the greys would clash again. Thus, having been driven south by their ratty cousins, the reds and the greys found their frontiers meeting each other in the grounds of Castle Storm.

Mohic's drey now just looked like a ball of sticks and straw, but to knights like Clive and Pommf it was a holy relic and a nut of contention between them. The chapel was in the town, which meant it could be used by Clive and his fellow red knights, but Pommf de Fritte, Foppington, Derrière and the other greys felt they had an equal right to worship at the shrine of the First Mother of all squirrels. One of the reasons for the tournament was to decide whether the altar would remain in the chapel, or spend some time in the castle proper.

Clive and Sylver finished their vigil early in the morning and then went off to sleep. Clive went to his cold kettle and Sylver to the corner of the house they had been given.

Sylver woke to the sound of trumpets. Clear high notes cut through the air two hours before noon. The heralds were at work making sure everyone was aware that it was a tourney day. The reds stood in the market square of the town blasting away and the greys on the battlements of Castle Storm, blaring with equal vigour. Valorous knights and their squires rose from their beds and began to don their armour. Those who would be heroes were taking up their weapons before going down to breakfast.

In the market square the pastry-makers, bakers and grocers were preparing light midday snacks for those who became peckish: nut cutlets, nut kebabs, nut sweetmeats. Since there was a feast in the evening no-one would want a full lunch, except possibly Scirf and Link. The needs of these two gannets was considered relatively unimportant on such a day.

'I hope we'll be given the opportunity to fight in the tournament,' said Icham. 'Although I would have preferred to do it on some good red meat –

169

some volison or mouse stew – but beggars can't be choosers.'

Mawk was buckling his belt but his head came up quickly. 'What? Take part in the fighting? Not me.'

'Well, we didn't expect *you* to want to,' sneered Icham, 'but the rest of us do.'

'That's not quite true,' replied Alysoun. 'I don't mind taking part if it'll get us into the castle – but not just for the sake of breaking someone's head with a staff.'

A debate followed with everyone giving their own opinion on the matter. Sylver did not join in but equally he did not try to stop the argument. He felt it was good for his outlaws to get rid of some of their pent-up frustration. One needed a cool head for a tourney.

They went out when they heard the drums and fifes playing the two leaders of the squirrel clans to their boxes. The reds had some kind of martial dirge and the greys a kind of piping jig or sea shanty. Of the two Sylver actually preferred the music of the greys, but there was no judging character from an animal's musical preference.

The tournament was in a field outside the town walls. It was therefore neutral to both sets of participants, the reds and the greys. There were some gay looking grey and cream bell-tents with stripes and some scarlet ones with gold or silver trim. Banners were flying from centre poles and from the grandstand where the spectators were gathering: the greys on the left and the reds on the right.

Pie-sellers, pickpockets and knick-knack vendors moved through the crowds, plying their wares or their trade. It was a very festive occasion and though mammals minded losing a few groats to cheats and cutpurses, they knew there was a price to pay for a day of jollity and fun.

Round the back of the tents, wrestlers and jugglers were limbering up on the grass. One grey squirrel had a savage shrew on a lead. The creature looked bad-tempered and appeared to want to bite off the head of any animal who looked at it.

Sylver did not approve of keeping creatures on leads or in cages, no matter what their status in the animal kingdom. It seemed to demean the owners as well as the creature itself.

The first contestant the outlaws saw was Clive of Coldkettle himself. In his right hand he carried a knobbed and gnarled blackthorn knobkerrie. In his belt was stuck a willow-wand swordstick. He still had his brush-topped tin cup on his head, but now he also wore a splendid breastplate made from what appeared to be a cheese grater . . .

'My Sunday suit,' he said, bashfully. Then he squinted at the outlaws as if noticing for the first time that they were armed. 'Are you taking part in the contests?'

'One or two of us might,' replied Mawk, quickly. 'Depends what it is.'

'We'll definitely try the dart-throwing and sling-shot,' Sylver said.

'Definitely those,' said Mawk.

'But as to the rest,' continued the outlaw leader, glaring at Mawk, 'we'll see what happens.'

At that moment the trumpets sounded in the castle. Looking up through the open town gates, Sylver saw the portcullis rattling upwards and the drawbridge lowering, both at the same time. Then over the drawbridge marched a regiment of grey squirrels with a sergeant-at-arms leading them.

171

Following these disciplined troops came a figure resplendent in chain-mail armour made of walnut shell halves, painted black and hooked together. The hollows of the walnut shells were on the inside, so the effect was of a grey squirrel covered in cockroaches. On his head was a black-painted horse chestnut casing complete with spikes. Like Clive the figure was armed with a knobkerrie and swordstick.

This character appeared very sinister to the onlooking outlaws, green figures from the forest. The black knight was of course Pommf de Fritte himself. He was followed by his fellow knights. Clive informed the outlaws who was whom amongst de Fritte's retinue.

'That's Derrière, the thick-set one in the boxy armour. Foppington's the stylish grey sauntering along in floppy leather boots, loose white shirt and a wide-brimmed hat topped with a robin's feather. Don't be fooled by his casual appearance, he's a very dangerous fighter. Poisson d'Avril's the character with the stern look and the helmet that sort of wraps itself around her face. Ah, there's La Belle Savage, the female in the armour that looks as if it's made of fish hooks. It is, so don't let her embrace you in a clinch, if you fight her . . .'

The grey knights passed through an avenue of onlookers, both grey and red, as well as a few stoats and ferrets. Some cheered, some jeered, but only one squirrel got upset – Derrière tried to fight his way into the crowd when he heard someone call out 'Bum-features' which he knew was intended for him. He was dragged back by his fellow knights who kept patting him on the shoulders and saying it was not worth it.

'You great bottom!' yelled the same member of the crowd, when Derrière had been persuaded to carry on. 'You squirrel's rear end!'

The enraged knight, whose sense of humour should have been larger than it was considering his name, once again hurled himself into the crowd, who proceeded to pelt him with the rotten pies they had been sold by hawkers.

'You shouldn't bait people,' whispered Bryony to Scirf, the weasel responsible for shouting the insults from the back of the mob. 'Now you've started a riot.'

'Well, the pompous idiot deserved it,' replied the unrepentant weasel. 'Look how he struts around in that silly square-plated armour. He looks a right ass.'

Mawk giggled at this but was silenced by a glare from Bryony.

'Don't encourage him, Mawk,' she said. 'He doesn't need it.'

The grey knights, on reaching the tournament green, were greeted politely and ceremoniously by the red knights. Besides Clive there was Blodwin, Imogen, Wivenhoe, Eric Rood, Will Splayfoot and Goodsquirrel. Cold but courteous remarks were exchanged about the good fortune they had with the weather and how they hoped the other side would do well in the contests. It was all a lot of hot air, because the outlaws could see the greys disliked the reds intensely and the reds loathed the greys with venom.

So grand had been the parade of knights that the outlaws had not been watching the figures who followed them. Now they heard a cold imperious retort from one of these creatures, a stoat dressed in a scarlet robe. The tone was shrill and menacing, though was never raised above that of normal level of conversation. It was a voice which would have started a stunned hare from its trance and made a rabbit's blood run as cold as a rill from an ice-capped mountain.

'Why, look who we have here! Some rebels from the north. Perhaps we ought to have raised a gallows on the green, along with our magnificent tents? Certainly a gibbet or two would not be out of place considering the low nature of our visitors.'

Two creatures, stoats in holy robes, stood by the speaker and sniggered at his words.

A chill went through the outlaws as they recognized the stoat who had spoken the words.

'Torca Marda,' murmured Luke. 'The Grand Inquisitor – and his henchmen, Orgoglio and Furioso.'

'And one other,' added Sylver as a figure crept from behind the billowing red robes of the inquisitor. 'It is the Mad March Stoat, our old friend Sheriff Falshed!'

Chapter Eighteen

Pommf de Fritte had heard the stoat inquisitor's remarks. He called Orgoglio to his side.

'Tell your master,' said the black knight, 'that today is not the day for such language. There is a truce on and we must treat the reds and their guests with civility. There must be no talk of gallows and gibbets until after the tournament is over and we return to normal hostilities. Is that understood?'

'Perfectly,' called Torca Marda. 'My priest understood your royal command.'

Although Torca Marda had spoken in a low pleasant tone, all who knew him realized he was absolutely livid with anger at being told off by Pommf de Fritte. He was being sarcastic when he called it a royal command and everyone knew he had gone too far. Pommf de Fritte gave him an equally cordial reply.

'I am not royal, as well you know, Grand Inquisitor; I am merely a noble. You would do well to remember it, or find yourself without a roof over your head. Do not forget you have been exiled, banished by your own kind, and are living under my protection. Try not to sting the paw which assists you.'

'Yeth,' called Foppington, as he casually beheaded an innocent dandelion with a swish of his wooden sword, 'be very careful thtoat, or you may be thorry for your thtinging wordth.'

'Lisping fool,' muttered Torca Marda, but under his breath, for there wasn't an animal alive who wasn't afraid of Foppington's deadly swordplay. 'Born with his head in a bucket of syrup.'

The knights and the priests passed on, leaving Falshed to face the outlaws.

He flinched as they crowded round him.

'Hey nonny-nonny no?' he tried, weakly.

'Less of that,' said Sylver. 'We know you're not mad.'

Furioso, standing nearby, cried, 'Do you need some assistance with those weasels, Sheriff?'

'You keep your whiskers out,' said Scirf, 'or you might find yourself in trouble.'

'Ho?' cried Furioso, coming nose to nose with Scirf. 'And what would you do about it, smelly?'

'Right,' said Scirf, darkly. 'You an' me at single-stick, today.'

Furioso sneered. 'I'm not fighting a rhubarb dung-watcher. Who do you think I am? I'll fight Sylver – at wrestling.'

Since stoats are a great deal larger than weasels, he stood a good chance of winning, but Sylver shrugged.

'I'd rather fight with staves, but if you want to wrestle, then we'll do it.'

'I'll fight you with staves after we've wrestled,' replied Furioso, without thinking. 'Best of three. Let's do knotted clouts as well.'

'You're on,' Sylver cried.

The day began with the castle gongs – mostly empty suits of armour battling it out with maces and swords. The noise made by these hollow beings beating each other was appalling. Dents appeared all over their bodies. They knocked off each other's heads, bashed off legs and arms, and generally reduced each other to heaps of scrap iron. Soon the better fighters amongst them were wading knee-deep in loose bucklers, visors and cuirasses, their straps hanging limp and their fasteners broken.

This initial battle between metal people served to whet the appetite of the flesh-and-blood creatures who were to copy the performance of the gongs soon afterwards. Once there was not a suit of armour standing, sweepers came on to the field, swept and gathered the bits of metal into carts, and trundled them away somewhere for squirrels expert at jigsaws to put them back together again, ready for next year's competition.

Then began the individual contests between the squirrel knights. Pommf de Fritte won his singlestick competition against Clive of Coldkettle, as did Foppington against Wivenhoe, but the rest of the greys lost their battles with the remainder of the reds. In the grand finale, where the red and grey knights charged at each other en masse, as in a mock battle, Clive managed to best Pommf and so even up the score between the two of them. At the end of the overall contest between the knights, wherein much cheering and jeering took place, and Derrière had to suffer further the slings and arrows of outrageous insults, the reds managed to retain the Holy Drey for yet another year.

Then came the open competition, when everyone and anyone could take part. The knights retired to nurse their wounds and the peasants and serfs had their go. Sylver was matched against the false priest in wrestling, but after a goodly struggle had to succumb to the stoat's superior strength. Three falls and no submissions saw the end of that leg of their contest.

'Now, staves,' cried Bryony. 'Choose your staff.'

Sylver chose a slim staff, almost a wand, while Furioso inevitably went for a stout oaken staff. They had a good rattling time, with blow and parry, until finally Sylver's skill with the lighter staff allowed him to slip over Furioso's guard and land the stoat a telling strike to the head. The stoat dropped his staff with a yell and staggered away, his head cut above the brow.

He was soon back again, however, to battle the third time with knotted clouts of rope soaked in water. These flexible 'maces' could deliver a stinging blow when wielded by an expert. Bruises were the main outcome of such a fight, and both participants were soon sporting a number of plum-coloured welts on their pelts. Eventually, they became exhausted and had to call it a draw, and both retired with honour.

'To the slingshot and dart-throwing,' cried Bryony, and the outlaws thronged towards their favourite weaponry competitions.

For the slingshot a thrower had to hit a rotten apple balanced on a bottle-top, without breaking the bottle.

Alysoun won this competition outright, much to the chagrin of the red and grey squirrels, who all thought they were pretty good at slingshot. The dart-throwing was won by a grey squirrel with one foreleg – the other having been lost when a block fell from a castle tower and crushed it – and she was absolutely brilliant at her sport, knocking the outlaws out of the competition one by one, until she stood alone.

The outlaws did not go in for the archery, which

was not a favourite of theirs. Since they were small willowy creatures with rather short forelimbs their bows had to be small too and could not be drawn very far. Consequently their arrows did not go as far as those shot by squirrels or even stoats. They watched and applauded when targets were hit, but showed little interest other than that in what was a rather glorious and interesting sport to other creatures.

Finally, just as the sun was going down, and the day was coming to an end, the stoat Orgoglio came to the outlaws and challenged any one of them to a battle of singlestick.

'I'll take 'im on,' said the eager Scirf. 'Let me have a go at him.'

'Have you ever used a singlestick?' asked Sylver of Scirf.

'Hundreds of times,' replied that dauntless weasel.

'Honestly?'

'Well – once or twice.'

'When?'

Scirf shifted his paws petulantly. 'Awright, never – but I learn quick!'

'No,' said Sylver, who could not fight himself because of the cuts and bruises he had been given by Furioso, 'it shall be one of the others.'

'Me,' Wodehed said. 'I'll fight the false priest.'

'So be it,' replied Orgoglio, letting the insult pass for the time being. 'I'll make you swallow your own tail in fright.'

The two contestants were padded up with shoulder protectors made of leather and voleswool and given wicker facemasks. They were then taken to a wide circle drawn on the grass. There they faced each other with their stick swords.

The competition aroused a lot of interest. A stoat

and a weasel battling at singlestick. It added to that interest that one of them was a priest and the other an outlaw. Even the red and grey knights came to watch. A referee was chosen: Will Splayfoot of the red squirrels, whose unimpeachable honour and integrity was well known throughout town and castle. This squirrel would ensure fair play.

'No opponent may strike below the waist,' droned Will Splayfoot, 'nor punch, kick or gouge with the free claws. Three successful thrusts to the heart, head or stomach ensures victory to the thruster. A blow with the cutting edge of the weapon counts as one-third of a thrust. Thus nine slashes to vital areas of the body, including the kidneys, counts as three successful thrusts.

'On your guard, gentlemammals . . .'

The combatants crossed their blunt wooden swords.

Will Splayfoot, who carried the traditional truncheon in case there was *not* fair play, swept it upwards between the sticks and the battle began.

'. . . and so to it.'

Wodehed and Orgoglio got stuck in. There was much cheering and yelling from the spectators. Some even threw applecores and nutshells, which was allowed so long as nothing struck the referee.

Wodehed was not an especially good swordsmammal, but he had a certain number of tricks which he used to good effect. He would at some point in the fencing, look sharply to the left as if he had seen something untoward and drop his guard a little. His opponent instinctively glanced in the same direction. Then Wodehed would suddenly bring his sword up from under, striking his adversary with a short thrust under the ribs.

He did this now, gaining the first successful thrust.

'Not fair, not fair,' yelled Furioso from the sidelines. 'Come on, ref! Are you blind?'

'There's nothing in the rules that says he can't do a dummy,' Scirf yelled back. 'You can fake it if you want to – more fool the stoat for falling for it!'

The referee remained impassive during this hot exchange of opinions. He took no notice of the calls of spectators. He knew his job, which was to watch the contestants. The rules were planted in his head like potatoes and when he saw an infraction he acted immediately. So far as could be told from his expression, no infringement of the rules had yet taken place, or Will Splayfoot would have cried 'Foul' and deducted thrusts or strokes from the offending swordsmammal.

Orgoglio, who had been known as quite a blade at one time, now began to come into his own. With a cool head and a skilful forelimb, he managed to gain the next two thrusts. Wodehed was clearly being outmatched here and the outlaws groaned inwardly. They still kept yelling for their side, but inside there was the sinking feeling that Wodehed was going down.

Then Orgoglio trod on Wodehed's paw. It did not look like an accident. It looked deliberate.

'Hold!' cried Will Splayfoot in an official voice, bringing his truncheon down between the stick swords. When they had stopped fencing, he pointed his truncheon at Orgoglio.

''Ponent to my left, below the waist foul, deducted one slash!'

'Oh, surely *two* slashes,' cried Icham. 'At least two for a foul like that!'

'An accident,' cried a grey squirrel. 'Couldn't help it anyway. The weasel stuck his foot out. He was *arskin'* to be trod on . . .'

Will Splayfoot again took no notice of these interruptions. He motioned that his judgement had been made and was irreversible. Down came the truncheon. Swordplay was to continue. Orgoglio leaped forward, trying to score while Wodehed was distracted. Indeed, he managed to get back the slash he had lost only a few moments ago. The outlaws audibly groaned now, seeing their champion was going to lose.

Then those who knew him best saw Wodehed muttering to himself and they knew something was going to happen. Wodehed was, after all, a wizard. He was not very good at it, his spells often went wrong, but he had received training in the art of magic. Fencing away with his opponent, parrying and thrusting, and yelling 'Have at ye' and '*Touché*' when he felt it were necessary, to the astonishment of the onlookers he suddenly let go of his stick sword and walked away.

Orgoglio hardly noticed the difference, for Wodehed's stick sword still fenced with him, and rather cleverly at that. The false priest had to parry like mad in order to prevent himself from being stuck or slashed, while he actually had no combatant to hit back at. Wodehed strolled around the circle, smiling at the spectators, and holding up the palms of his paws as if to say, What can I do? My stick wants to fight on its own.

The outlaws began clicking their teeth in amusement. So did the red squirrels. The greys began booing and yelling at the referee to stop the fight. Furloso shrieked for justice and fair play. Torca

Marda watched with cold eyes, saying nothing, his lips in a thin line.

And all the time, Orgoglio was battling away at an invisible enemy, gradually tiring.

'Help!' he cried. 'Witchcraft! Ho!'

Will Splayfoot was turning over all the potatoes in his mind, trying to find whether there was an infringement of the rules or not. This sort of thing was outside his experience and his status as a referee would be in question if he made a hasty decision. So far as he could recall there was nothing in the rules which said a combatant could not walk away from his sword and leave it to do the fighting for him.

Suddenly, Wodehed's stick sword jumped out of the ring and began beating a grey squirrel about the shoulders and bottom. When the squirrel had been soundly thrashed, it went on to the next animal, who happened to be Scirf.

'Hey! Ow! Stop that! What's going on, Wodehed?'

The wizard weasel stared in horror as another of his spells went haywire. He was helpless to intervene. He could do nothing but goggle at his wayward stick.

The stick began to flay the whole crowd, who were now dispersing, running away from the spot on all fours. Squirrels, ferrets, stoats and weasels were being walloped on their backsides as they fled from the renegade stick sword.

'FOUL!' shouted Will Splayfoot at last. 'Dirty rotten foul! Rogue stick on the loose!'

With that the stick came weaving over to the referee and started to lay into him with great vigour, while Wodehed watched in dismay as his magic once again went awry. The furious Will Splayfoot fought back with bravery and vigour, whacking the stick sword with his truncheon, trying to break it. For a while it seemed like the referee might win, then the stick started to use all Wodehed's sneaky tricks and got under his guard.

It was Torca Marda who put an end to it.

He spoke some words with a dark and cryptic mouth. His throat became the dry pit of a cuckoo pint, his tongue the ditchweed leaf of a ragwort. Had he not been an archbishop, a holy stoat of the highest order, some might have said it was the language of evil magic, of devils and demons and things that made devious sounds in the night. He was however a stoat opposed to such heinous practices, and therefore was above suspicion.

Whatever the harsh guttural words meant, they were effective. The stick sword suddenly shattered into a thousand splinters, which fell like gentle rain upon the earth beneath. Those running away stopped to witness the act. All were mightily impressed. Sylver was especially fascinated and a chill of fear went through the leader of the outlaws.

Chapter Nineteen

'It seems,' said Torca Marda, 'that our rebel friends cannot be trusted to behave themselves.'

'It was a joke, Grand Inquisitor,' replied Sylver. 'Don't try to make it any more than that.'

'Animals may have been hurt,' said Torca Marda smoothly. 'I think some sort of punishment is called for. What do you say, Lord of the Castle? Does this act call for some sort of retribution?'

Pommf de Fritte had been as badly beaten by the stick as anyone else amongst the spectators. Inside he was boiling with rage. It had been an undignified exhibition. He felt humiliated.

'I think something has to be done,' he agreed.

Torca Marda nodded, then to everyone's astonishment the stoat inquisitor began to remove his scarlet robe.

'The weasel will have to fight *me*,' he murmured, flexing his forelimbs. 'Let us see if his puny magic can outwit a formidable opponent – someone other than a fool.'

Orgoglio, having been called a fool, opened his mouth to protest but Furioso stepped on his paw to shut him up. Nothing could be gained by arguing with the likes of Torca Marda. If the Grand Inquisitor called you a fool, that is what you were, and no amount of protestations would change the fact.

Torca Marda stepped forward to select a stick

sword from amongst those lying on the grass.

He said, 'I have no objection to the former referee, if my opponent has not.'

Wodehed looked absolutely terrified. He had no idea whether or not the inquisitor could use his sword with skill, but he knew the creature's reputation. Torca Marda would not challenge him unless he knew he could thrash the life out of him. Wodehed felt dizzy and faint. He clutched at Bryony's shoulder for support. She patted his paw.

'I shall fight the inquisitor,' she said. 'Wodehed has battled enough for today.'

'No you won't,' cried Icham, leaping forwards. 'I shall be the one to fight him. I'm second-in-command, behind Sylver. Since our leader is in no condition to fight, it should be me.'

'Come, come,' interrupted de Fritte, 'one of you, one of you.'

But by this time Icham had got his hand on a stick sword and was standing before Torca Marda. The stoat had a sneer on his face, as he whipped the air with his wooden blade.

'So, Icham, you fancy yourself at singlestick?'

'As much as you do, Grand Inquisitor. You'll find this is a bit more energetic than strolling around in a red gown.'

'I have dug graves in my time as a lowly sextant,' murmured the inquisitor, dangerously. 'My muscles were built in those years and I keep them exercised. You think torturing is light work? Lifting stones to press an animal to death, or turning the wheel on the stretching rack? Even wielding a branding iron keeps one fit and flexible. You forget my profession.'

'Yes, I suppose I did overlook the fact that you deal in pain and death.'

'Best not to forget those, especially the second one.'

The sun was casting long purple lanes across the green now, as it dipped down below the lake beyond the castle. Tall lean shadows mingled as the crowd moved in for a closer look. A cool wind had sprung up from behind a distant rise and was whiffling through the high grasses of the hinterland.

'*En garde!*' cried Will Splayfoot. 'Take your positions, gentlemammals!'

The two combatants made ready and were soon fencing furiously. As Sylver and perhaps some of the other outlaws had guessed, the inquisitor was no slouch when it came to singlestick. He had obviously practised fencing in his time. However, it seemed that the two were fairly evenly matched, for Icham was actually the best of the outlaws at this sport. He was nimble and agile. He also had some good strokes. Lord Haukin, when younger of course, had been an expert at singlestick and Icham had taken lessons from the old noble.

'Very good, very good,' murmured Torca Marda, holding up his paw. 'You fight well – for a ditch weasel.'

A red silk handkerchief was tossed from the crowd into the raised paw and the inquisitor wiped his brow with it, even as he fenced with his opponent. It was a bit of showmammalship. The greys clicked their teeth and clapped. The reds screwed their faces contemptuously. They wanted to see a strike of some kind, not this fancy paw-work and neat fencing. At the end of the day it was hits that counted, rather than style or flair.

Suddenly, the inquisitor scored two hits in a row. His sword paw moved swifter than lightning. The blunt end of the sword striking Icham on the chest robbed the weasel of wind. Two small bruised bumps appeared under his white bib. Icham blinked, water came to his eyes, but he said nothing. He fought on valiantly without a murmur escaping his throat, though the hits must have been extremely painful.

'Had enough, weasel?' asked the inquisitor softly. 'Or do you want the final thrust?'

'Just stop talking and fight,' muttered Icham, shivering and hunching a little against the cool evening wind. 'I shall battle until one of us wins.'

The inquisitor raised his brow and eyed the crowd, getting the response he wanted. The greys yelled and shouted for him to finish it. The reds remained defiantly silent.

Then something happened which everyone saw but no-one quite believed for a moment. Torca Marda's eyes narrowed to slits. He seemed – though no-one afterwards could swear to it – to utter a strange dark sound. Icham was moving in, looking like getting his first hit on the inquisitor's wicker mask and thus scoring a head thrust. The weasel stepped forward, crying, 'Touché!'

The word was hardly out of his mouth when he staggered backwards, an expression of agony and horror on his face.

Somehow, in the whirlwind of strokes, Torca Marda's stick had snapped a quarter of the way from the end. It was an oblique split, running a good two inches down the stick, leaving a sharp point where there should have been a blunt end. This point had penetrated Icham's chest and gone into his heart.

The weasel dropped his own stick and fell to his knees, clutching a wound which pumped blood on to the brown earth. He looked at the horrified outlaws with a pleading expression, as if asking them silently to staunch the flow. Bryony rushed forward, but the others were too stunned to move for the moment. They hardly believed what they had witnessed.

'I am most dreadfully upset,' murmured the Grand Inquisitor, staring at the bloodied end of his stick sword. 'I cannot apologize enough for this terrible accident. How on earth did that happen?' He held up the broken stick sword for all to see. 'Faulty workmammalship, I'm certain.'

Sympathy and remorse dripped from his very whiskers.

The outlaws took no notice of Torca Marda. They were too concerned with the plight of Icham.

'A physician?' cried Sylver at the silent crowd of greys and reds. 'Where will we find one?'

Clive of Coldkettle came forward. 'Follow me,' he said. 'There's the house of a stoat physician just inside the walls.'

'Not a stoat,' yelled Mawk. 'It was a stoat who did for him.'

But Sylver, Bryony, Luke and Scirf had already hoisted the bleeding Icham onto their shoulders. They ran with him, following Clive at a trot across the green and through the town gates. The other outlaws came up behind.

Darkness fell rather more sharply than usual, as the sun dipped suddenly below the horizon. Inside the gates Clive turned left. The weasels went with him. Lamps began to be lit in houses as the weasels passed with their precious load. Those who had not gone to the tourney were making ready for the return of those who had attended.

Finally they came to a large wattle-and-daub

house tucked in amongst some smaller ones. A lamp was burning yellowly in the glassless window, lighting a sign which read: TOMUS CULPIN, PHYSICIAN. Beyond was a room cluttered with bottles, sinister-looking copper instruments, drying herbs, charts and books. A sort of soapy, acidy smell was wafting through the gap.

Clive hammered on the door.

A few moments later the door opened abruptly and a peevish-looking stoat stood there. 'What is it? What is it? I'm busy.' Then the physician noticed the weasel with the mortal wound and motioned for him to be carried inside. 'Quickly now,' he said. 'Lay him on the table. What was it? The tournament?'

'A stick sword broke and penetrated his chest,' replied Bryony efficiently. 'We can't staunch the blood.'

The stoat nodded, going immediately to a cupboard and taking out some green stuff. 'Dried moss,' he murmured.

After washing round the wound he padded it quickly with the moss, then wrapped it around with a bandage. All the while Icham's breathing was becoming shallower and shallower. The wounded outlaw's eyes had taken on a funny look.

'We must try to get him to chew some of this,' said the stoat physician, taking some leaves from a jar. 'It will help stimulate his heart – make it beat a little faster for the moment. That particular organ has gone into a state of shock and needs to be properly restarted.'

'It wasn't an accident,' blazed Mawk, 'it was done deliberately – by a stoat.'

The physician looked mildly over the prone form

of Icham at the heated face of Mawk. 'Then you must bring the individual stoat responsible to account, for his or her actions, weasel, but your tone has no place in here – this is a sickroom. It will do your friend no good to rant and rave at every stoat in sight.'

Sylver said sharply, 'Mawk – get out.'

'But . . .'

'Get out.' Then to the physician, 'I'm sorry.'

'Please,' replied the physician, raising a paw. 'Your friend is obviously overwrought, but he should indeed go outside to cool his emotions a little.'

Mawk left the room in the firm grip of Scirf.

Unfortunately, they could not get Icham to chew the stimulant. He gradually slipped away from life. He felt no more pain. A faraway look came on his face, the heart movement in his chest became slower and slower, fluttered softly once, and finally he was gone. The physician tried to wet the stimulant and squeeze some drops between his half-open lips, but there was no help for it. Icham had lost too much blood. It was unlikely that an animal could survive with a punctured heart, but the physician took it personally, and was ashamed of his failure.

'I'm sorry,' he said, drawing a sheet over the body. 'I did try.'

'There was not much you could do,' acknowledged Bryony. 'There wasn't anything anyone could do.'

'Do you wish me to do anything with the corpse?' asked the physician. 'I can at least lay it out. Would you like me to embalm him? No charge of course.'

'No,' replied Sylver. 'We don't do that. Perhaps you'll keep the body of our friend Icham here, until we come for it? We need to give him a kalkie.'

'Ah yes, the weasel wake,' murmured the stoat. 'I know.'

'There's no time at present, but later, when the body has dried, we'll burn it on a bonfire.'

'Certainly. He'll be here when you come for him.'

The weasels trooped out through the front door, to where Clive of Coldkettle was waiting with Scirf and Mawk. Mawk took one look at the faces and then burst into tears. Scirf put his foreleg around that weasel's shoulders. Clive hung his head for a moment, then nodded thoughtfully.

'My condolences,' he said. 'An unfortunate accident.'

'You think it was an accident?' asked Bryony.

Clive of Coldkettle looked taken aback. 'It was – wasn't it? We were all there. I have no love for the Grand Inquisitor, but I fail to see how it could have been anything else. The stick broke just as he was making his thrust. There was no opportunity to make it deliberate.'

Sylver said, 'I don't think we're ever going to know, are we? It all happened so quickly. But a stoat who can make a wayward stick shatter to a thousand splinters with just a word, can surely split a cane when he wishes.'

'But where's your proof?' asked Clive, with a helpless gesture.

'We have none,' replied Sylver, despairingly. 'And if we did, I'm not sure we would be taken seriously. I know one thing. That stoat will be watched very closely from now on. If I ever get the opportunity . . . but never mind that now. Icham has gone. Miniver has gone. We must do what we can to make their sacrifices worthwhile. There is a

192

banquet at the castle tonight, isn't there? Will we be invited?'

'You'll come as my guests,' said Clive. 'I'll make sure you get in.'

'Thank you.'

The weasels parted from the squirrel and trudged back to their living quarters, each lost in their own sadness.

Chapter Twenty

Later that evening, almost midnight, the weasels accompanied Clive of Coldkettle over the draw-bridge and into the castle. They passed through the gatehouse and barbican to the outer ward. Thence they went past the two great towers and into the inner ward, to the South Hall behind the round church. At each stage they were watched over by surly-looking guardsquirrels. One of them gazed too long at Clive's extraordinary tail.

'See something?' asked the red squirrel gruffly. 'Want to say anything – anything at all?'

'No,' growled the guard, catching the look in Clive of Coldkettle's eyes.

'Just as well.'

The party had by now reached the doorway to the great hall, which was lit by flaming torches.

The feasting had already begun amongst the greys. Though they had lost the competition overall, there were always a few individual victories to savour. One of the important achievements so far as they were concerned, was that Pommf de Fritte had beaten Clive of Coldkettle in single combat. So if there was nothing else to toast, that one would do.

Sylver and the outlaws had to swallow hard and bite their tongues when they went in, for there was Torca Murda at the head table, quaffing honey dew and clicking his teeth. He looked up as they entered,

194

but Sylver could read nothing from his eyes. Had the inquisitor looked smug, or something like that, Sylver might well have forgotten himself. As it was he was a whisker's breadth from leaping over the tables and sinking his teeth into the throat of the red-robed stoat.

Sitting with Torca Marda and his henchstoats was Falshed. To give him his due the sheriff was looking a little shamefaced. Despite his long-running feud with the outlaws Falshed was not a cruel stoat. He was weak and nasty by turns, but could sympathize with Sylver over the death of his best friend. The death of Icham did not have him grieving but he could understand why others were doing so.

Pommf de Fritte had risen from his seat on seeing Clive and the weasels enter the hall. He was a big muscled grey squirrel, with a heavy jaw and strong forelimbs. Had he been born a serf instead of a knight, he might have been a roadworker or a tree-feller. Pommf was not very bright when it came to poetry or mathematics, but put a sword or a mace in his paw and he would fight with intelligence. In short his brain power was used to assist his physical deeds, but for nothing else.

'Ah, the red champion and his visitors,' cried Pommf. 'I bid you welcome, gentlemammals. Clive of Coldkettle, worthy opponent, come you up here by me. There's no reason two foes can't drink together on one evening of the year without insults or claws flying. You weasels, find yourselves a space somewhere and enjoy the wassail.'

Clive accepted the invitation to the top table graciously and said he would meet up with the weasels later. A moment later he was sitting with reds and greys ripping apart nut cutlets with his claws and swilling down honey dew. Scraps of food were thrown under the table for the savage guard-shrews to eat. Sometimes a small chunk of food fell down a gridded pit called an 'oubliette'. Piteous sounds of joyous moans came from the bottom of the pit on such occasions. Down there were kept forgotten prisoners, who licked drops of moisture from the mossy stone walls and ate only what fell through the grill above.

The squirrel knights fought hard and played hard. There were no niceties on the top table, no fine etiquette. You grabbed, you stuffed food into your mouth, you swigged it down with a goblet of raw honey dew. If some came out of the sides of your mouth so be it. No-one on the top table was concerned about pleases and thank-yous or even pass-the-pepper.

If you wanted to find good table manners you went to the far end of the room where the leather-tanner apprentices and candlemaker journeysquirrels sat and gossiped. Coming from humble homes they had been taught not to lick their knives or dribble their soup. Their poor misguided mothers were under the impression that gentle-mammals of high birth were born knowing how to use their cutlery and not to put their elbows on the table.

These mums had drummed such knowledge into their unwilling offspring so their sons and daughters would not make their dutiful parents ashamed of them should they ever have the good fortune to eat at the castle.

It was here, on these lower tables that you heard, 'I say, would you mind awfully passing the cumin-shaker?' and 'Is that the last sprig of rosemary? Can I offer it to anyone else first?' and similar phrases. The tables here were clear of elbows and no-one ate with their claws. All the unseemly grabbing and snatching and gobbling went on amongst the aristocrats and gentry.

Since they were in mourning, and grieving for absent friends, the weasels did not throw themselves into the feasting. Instead they looked around for creatures of their kind amongst all the squirrels. They saw two ferrets, distant cousin to the weasel, sitting at the end of one long bench. A clutch of candles stuck in a pot of sand lit their features. Although the weasels would not usually consort with such low-life as ferrets Sylver felt they might learn something from them.

'A brace of rabbiteers,' Scirf said, sitting next to one. 'Steal the scut off a bunny every time, eh?'

'I beg your pardon,' replied one of the ferrets, putting down his cup with a haughty expression. 'I'll have you know we're warreners, me and my jill, Guildenswine, here. That's a respectable profession that is.'

'Warreners? Amongst a load of nut-cutlet squirrels?'

'We look after the rabbits owned by the meat-eating section of the community,' said the other ferret, just as snootily. 'We serve the stoats and ferrets of town and castle, and the occasional gypsy fox, don't we, Rosencrass?'

'Ah,' said Sylver, 'Rosencrass and Guildenswine. I heard you two were dead.'

'Well we're not,' said Rosencrass hotly. 'We just went away for a while, that's all.'

'Things got too sticky for you in the north of Welkin?'

The two ferrets did not answer this question. They simply looked away. A few moments later they were in low conversation with one another. Each picked

197

at a plate of vegetable sweetmeats in front of them, and sipped their honey dew. The outlaws were served with some of the same, but few of them felt like drinking at all. They simply sat there and gazed around the room. Sylver was making a mental list of the entrances and exits. The positions of the windows were also noted.

Finally, Guildenswine leaned over and spoke to Scirf. The ferret had a sly expression on her face. 'So, I hear you are looking for a secret passage? We could be of use to you, my jack and I.'

Scirf was shocked by the news that these two spies knew why the outlaws were in the castle. 'I don't know what you're talking about, friend,' he replied. 'We're simply running away from the oppression of the tyrant Prince Poynt.'

'Yes, that too. And from the rat hordes. But you're also looking for a passage, the one with the Alice clue in it.'

'How do you know all this?' gasped Scirf, giving the game away.

Guildenswine touched her nose with a claw. 'It's our business to know things, isn't it, Rosencrass?'

'Absolutely,' replied the other ferret. 'Starve without it.'

'Sellers of information, that's what we are.'

'Quite. Anything you want to know? Shipping forecast? We've got it at our clawtips. Tomorrow's weather? Just ask. Secret passages? Memorized every one between here and Timbukthree.'

The two ferrets nudged each other and clicked their teeth in amusement. Then Rosencrass caught Torca Marda's eyes resting on them. He gave a quick swallow and his face assumed an expression of fear. Another nudge, this one not in merriment, and he and his partner tended to their own business. Scirf was left wondering whether they were indeed serious. Did they know all the secret passages in the castle? As they had said, it was their profession to know things.

Sylver spoke to Bryony in a low voice. 'When the time comes for everyone to go home, Scirf, Mawk and I will hide ourselves in the castle. You take the others and go back to the town. Make as much noise as you can and sort of move around a bit so the guards don't see that the group leaving is much smaller than the one which came in. Contact these two ferrets when you get out. You don't have to trust them but they probably know even more than Link about any passages that run under the town.'

'Will you be all right?' asked Bryony anxiously. 'I mean, Luke, Alysoun, Wodehed and I can handle things outside, but you'll be in terrible danger in here. Pommf de Fritte is bad enough, but Torca Marda . . .'

'We'll be fine,' replied Sylver, with more conviction than he felt. 'You just make sure you explore all you can in and around the town. Mawk, Scirf and I will do the same here inside the castle.'

'Why Scirf and Mawk?'

Sylver shrugged. 'I don't know, really. The three of us made a good team when we went to find Thunder Oak. Mawk has got a lot of cunning, even though he's often scared . . .'

'Probably he's cunning *because* he's frightened.'

'Right. Anyway it comes in useful sometimes, to have a devious mind working on your side.'

'And Scirf?' asked Bryony. 'I thought you didn't like him much.'

'Hmmm. He sort of grows on you, doesn't he? Like rhubarb on dung. Anyway, he's got sagacity. You know what I mean? He's shrewd and clever. It's a pity his personal habits are not what we'd like them to be, but you can't deny he has courage and resourcefulness.'

'Right,' said Bryony, clicking her teeth. 'That's all settled then. Let's hope we get away with it.'

''Ello, 'ello,' said Rosencrass, his eyes narrowing, 'what's afoot down that end of the table then? Plotting against Pommf de Fritte, is it?'

'No,' replied Bryony, sweetly. 'We're just discussing the best way to dispose of a ferret's body after a foul murder. My friend Sylver here thinks a lime pit is probably the easiest. I'm more inclined towards chopping the corpse up into little pieces and throwing them to river pike.'

'That's not very nice,' said Guildenswine, scowling. But then her natural curiosity, of which she had huge gobbets, forced out the obvious question. 'So which one would you recommend?'

'Well, since there are two of you,' Bryony replied, coldly now, 'we could test out both.'

The two ferrets glowered.

There was a great noise from the top table now, as two grey knights, Derrière and Foppington, were having an argument as to whether a third grey knight, namely the female Poisson d'Avril, could cross the ceiling of the great South Hall without touching the floor. The subject in question was quietly watching the two champions yell and bawl at each other, while she quaffed honey dew and waited to be asked to do the deed.

'Tho, thall you do it, Poithon?' lisped Foppington. 'I think you could do it thimply by thwinging from the thandelierth.'

Poisson d'Avril, female of weighty but muscled proportions like most of the knights, rose to her hind paws. 'Piece of cake,' she said. 'Stand back.'

200

So, while the leather-tanner apprentices and candlemaker journeysquirrels were quietly talking about the finer points of cricket and whether or not poetry that didn't rhyme was really poetry, Poisson d'Avril leaped up on to the table and launched herself at the nearest chandelier. She reached it and clung on, while it listed and swayed, dropping lighted candles down onto the middle tables of the burghers and merchants. Animals screamed and jumped about as hot candle wax splattered on their fur.

'Oh thweetly done,' cried Foppington, unconcerned by the hysteria from merchants and their kind. 'Thwing it now – thwing to the nektht one.'

Poisson swayed her large-bellied form and got the chandelier swinging back and forth. When she had it going like a trapeze, she threw herself through the air and caught the second chandelier, causing another rain of lighted candles to fall upon the tables beneath. Roars of disapproval came from the animals below, including the outlaws and the two spy ferrets. Small fires were starting and being stamped out by civic minded mammals.

On the top table the knights, including Clive of Coldkettle, were on their feet and stamping their approval of Poisson's efforts. She was a *squirrel*, one was saying, and had not forgotten her squirrelly skills. Once upon a time they had all had the dexterity to run amok through the trees, leaping from branch to branch, balancing on the end of a twig. That was before they became hefty knights. Now Poisson was showing them that the talent was still there, deep in her bones.

'How's this, you ground-lubbers?' she cried, as she swung back and forth, ready to leap for the third and last chandelier.

'Oh, thuper, my brave little thauthage!' cried

Foppington. 'None tho agile ath you!'

Alas, the iron staples holding the chains of the last chandelier were the weakest in the hall, owing to damp, crumbling brickwork in the ceiling at that point. Some spilt cauldron of oil in a siege now long forgotten was responsible, its contents seeping down from the floor above and wreaking havoc on the mortar. When Poisson landed heavily on this chandelier, the staples ripped out. She fell, along with a lot of ironmongery, slap in the middle of the apprentices and journeysquirrels, splashing garlic soup everywhere.

Well brought-up as they had been, this intrusion on their genteel manners was too much to bear. The youthful squirrels went in with flying paws, pummelling the female knight responsible. Down from the top table came the other knights, yelling for fair play, and throwing chunks of turnip and parsnip. Up rose the burghers and merchants between, happy at last to show they were not pansies when it came to a fight, even if they did sew a good seam. They waded into the knights. Seeing this, the guardshrews scampered from beneath the tables, squealing like mad and sinking their teeth into any available leg.

There ensued a delightful brawl, while the squirrel sentries looked on, cheering their favourites and booing those they disliked. It happened almost every year and was therefore a sort of standard end to the feasting. Everyone sort of looked forward to the brawl and would have been disappointed had the day ended on any other note.

While all this was going on Sylver had motioned to Scirf and Mawk and the three weasels had crept away.

Chapter Twenty-One

While the guards were safely occupied watching the brawl in the South Hall, Sylver, Mawk and Scirf slipped away to the end of the hall. There they found a small animal door within the larger human-sized door. Sylver tried the handle, but could not turn it. Then Scirf nudged him and pointed out a large rusty key hanging on a hook. Sylver took it down and tried it in the lock. Eventually, after much grating and grinding, the lock turned and the door opened. The weasels slipped through and locked the small door behind them.

They found themselves in the South-east Hall, attached to the South-west Hall. This was a square room with a half-wall in the middle, forming a partition. It was gloomy in there at first, the only light coming in through loop windows from a pale, fairly uninterested moon. Whether its light was good enough for the outlaws was not its concern. It had a duty to remain in the sky all night, but not to any purpose.

When his eyes became used to the dimness, Sylver perceived a number of statues of humans and mythological creatures clustered in the room. They were all sitting or standing around looking down in the mouth.

There were several busts there – those statues the weasels called 'chunkies' – as well as gongs (hollow metal statues), blocks (solid stone statues), puddings (plaster statues) and stumpers (wooden statues). They were the normal sort of collection of statues you might find in any castle and grounds, except they should be scattered over the whole area.

'Why are you all lumped together in this room?' asked Scirf, never short of a question. 'What's goin' on?'

The statues – of human knights, of kings and queens, of conquerors and their horses – looked away miserably.

'Come on,' ordered Scirf, 'answer the question!'

Scirf, in his long association with statues, had found that they could be bullied. They were on the whole a shy slow-thinking lot, who were only interested in one thing: their First and Last Resting Places, the spots from which they had been mined, quarried, cut down or gathered as wet clay. They wanted to go back there and lay down to sleep for ever.

A pudding, nearest to Mawk, was the first to break the silence. 'One for sorrow,' he moaned. 'Two for joy. Three for . . .'

'Stop that,' said Mawk, 'we're weasels, not magpies.'

Then a statue of a king with a chipped and cracked crown, a block, spoke with a grave and cheerless voice. 'They locked us up, you know. The squirrels. Said they couldn't stand the moaning and groaning.'

'And was you moanin' and groanin'?' asked Scirf.

'All the time,' admitted the king, receiving a few murmured encouragements from his fellows. 'It's our duty to moan and groan, until we get what we want. That is . . .'

'We know what you want,' replied Scirf, quickly throttling what would have been a long boring speech. 'You want to find your First and Last whatsit.'

'We want to be *free* first,' said the king, indignantly. 'We were better off as statues standing in the gardens and hallways. At least then we had no expectations. Oh, yes, we had the pigeons to worry about. They never leave us alone. But apart from that we were not too badly off.'

The rest of the statues now began to put their case forward for freedom. These statues were much better at speech than other statues the weasels had known, no doubt because they had had a lot of time to practise, being locked in a room together for so long. In the normal way they would not gather together, but strike out across the countryside alone, speaking only when they wanted the answer to their eternal question.

A gargoyle with a hollow lead throat now suddenly rushed at the weasels, to emphasize a point. At the same time all the statues in the room wanted to speak. They came forward to cluster around Scirf, moaning and groaning. Scirf shushed them and told them to back off. They did as he asked, timidly backing away, making the same awful noise.

A griffon cried, 'We want to be free, like the birds.'

'Free,' repeated a stone lion, 'like the deer.'

'Listen,' said Scirf. 'You lot were never meant to be free in the first place. You were built to stand and gawp at the world, and to let the world gawp at you if it wanted to. But you was never meant to flit around like birds, or dash here and there like live deer. You're *statues.*'

'Even statues are entitled to a bit of fresh air,' muttered a unicorn with a broken horn. 'We were never meant to be stuck in a place like this. I'll stand still for a bit, if they let me out.'

Sylver, having let Scirf handle the situation until now, finally said a word. 'We'll find a way to come back and open the big door to let you free before we leave the castle.'

Scirf was fond of his leader, but he had been leading up to something, and felt Sylver had interrupted a little too early. '. . . but you got to help us in the meantime,' Scirf said. 'We're looking for a particular secret passage. What we want to know is whether there's any actually in the castle.'

'Bad news and good news,' replied the king. 'Bad news first. There are lots. The place is riddled with them. Like a wormery it is.'

'I was afraid of that,' sighed Sylver. 'And the good news?'

'They nearly all join up somewhere. You get into one, you get into them all.'

'That sounds more like it,' said the relieved Sylver. 'Which is the nearest entrance?'

'Under one of the great bread ovens,' said the unicorn with the broken horn. 'You have to push it out of the way. It's on a swivel. Underneath there's a hole which leads to the network of secret passages.'

'How do you know all this?' asked Mawk, suspiciously. 'You're a garden statue.'

'I told him,' said a pudding in the shape of a princess. 'I used to be standing not far from the ovens, when I was just fired clay. We tell each other everything in here. It's the only thing we've got to do.'

'You saw this passage being used?' asked Sylver. 'Did you ever see any children go down there?'

'All the time. The children of the castle would play in all the secret passages. They knew where such tunnels went better than the adults did.'

'How do we get to these ovens?' asked Sylver.

'Go through that door there on the north side of this hall and you'll find yourself in front of the ovens,' said the princess. 'But, look here, you won't forget us will you? You promised to do something for us you know.'

'A promise is a promise,' Scirf said. 'I'll be back.'

'Thank you,' murmured the princess.

The unicorn, lion, king and the rest of the statues also murmured their thanks.

The three weasels then passed down through the avenue of stone, metal and wooden statues, to a small door on the side of the South-east Hall. There were torches in iron rings on the walls of the inner ward, which flickered and blew in the night breezes. On the walls of the battlements and towers above there were one or two sleepy sentries. The noise of the brawl in the South Hall confirmed that the fight was still in progress. The weasels drifted across the ward and found the ovens by the West Hall, in a nicely shadowed corner.

There were two great ovens which towered over the three slim weasels.

'Let's try this one first,' whispered Sylver, pointing to the left oven. 'Here, give me a paw.'

The three outlaws put their backs against the huge oven, but it was a hopeless task. It would not move an inch. It was a huge solid affair of stone and iron. It would take more than three weasels to shift it. They tried the second oven, just in case they had been attempting to move the wrong one, but encountered the same strong resistance.

''S'no good,' puffed Scirf. 'Won't budge.'

Mawk said, nervously, 'Let's give it up. If we're caught out here we'll end up in a dungeon. I've had enough of dungeons – and torture.'

'Torture?' said Scirf. 'You 'aven't been in the

clutches of Torca Marda yet. Now *there's* an animal what knows his torture.'

These words did nothing to cheer up the frightened Mawk.

Sylver said, 'We need that unicorn.'

'An' some rope,' Scirf agreed, nodding. 'I know where to get that.'

'Where?' asked his leader.

'The round church over there,' replied the ex-dung watcher, pointing with a claw. 'It'll have a bell rope inside.'

'Right. Mawk, you go and get the bell rope. Scirf and I have got to get the big side door open so that we can let the unicorn out into the ward.'

'Me?' squeaked Mawk. 'On my own?'

'It's going to take two of us to get that door moved,' Scirf confirmed. 'An' we'll make a bit of noise doing it. You've got the easy bit. All you've got to do is sneak into that church and pinch a bit of old bell rope.'

'I remember the last church we went into,' muttered Mawk. 'It was full of flying stone angels. I nearly got killed, several times.'

The sound of a crash came from the South Hall and voices rose to an uproar.

'Sounds like they're having a grand time in there,' said Sylver. 'I hope our weasels are giving as good as they get. Come on, Scirf, let's have a go at this door while they're still making a racket.'

Mawk went off now, slipping through the shadows, keeping close to the walls. Sylver and Scirf went back through the door to the South-east Hall. Once inside the statues clustered around them again.

'What's this, come to set us free already?' asked the king, in a delighted voice.

'We hope so,' said Sylver, 'but we want a favour from the unicorn once you're outside in the ward.'

'What can I do?' asked the unicorn.

Scirf said, 'We need to harness you to the oven. We can't shift it on our own.'

'Oh!' exclaimed the princess, sarcastically. 'Us statues are good for something after all.'

'Course you are,' replied Scirf. 'Never said you wasn't.'

'Where's the key to the *big* side door,' asked Sylver. 'The one the humans would have used? When we get the great door open you can all make a dash for it. All except the unicorn, of course. Once he's helped us, he can go too.'

'I think it's in the South Hall, hanging on the wall,' replied the king. 'I used to stand in there, at the end, and that's where it was always kept in those days.'

'Heck, we've got to go back in there again,' said Scirf. 'I'll do it. In the meantime you lot spit into the keyhole of that lock up there.' He pointed to the rusty lock on the big door, high above his head. 'It's prob'ly not been opened for a century. It'll have rusted solid. We need to oil it with somethin' and spit's as good as anythin' else.'

'Yuk!' the princess replied, wrinkling her plaster nose. 'Anyway, we can't do things like that. We're statues, remember? We don't have spit in our mouths.'

'Forgot that,' muttered Scirf. 'What do you suggest, Sylver?'

'Vegetable oil, from one of the tables.'

'Good thinking, leader.'

Scirf then went to the small door to the South Hall, unlocked it with the little key, and then opened it quickly and ducked through. A nut cutlet hit him full in the face the second he was inside the hall.

'Hey!' he yelled, wiping the sauce from his fur. 'Watch it!'

There was pandemonium in the hall. A serious food fight was in progress. Knights, merchants, burghers and serfs had taken sides and were lobbing anything to paw. Clive of Coldkettle was covered from head to foot in butter. Pommf de Fritte had cream dripping from his whiskers. Foppington was giggling like mad as he launched a custard pie at a peasant.

The only animals who were not taking part in this delightful orgy were Torca Marda and his two priests. They sat aloof from the whole thing, the missiles magically missing them by fractions, never once striking any of them.

The rest of the outlaws were engaged on the side of the serf weasels, those energetic field workers. Guardshrews harried their efforts to pelt the knights with plums and pears, snapping at their ankles. Scirf tried to signal the weasels but they were too engrossed in the battle to notice him. He had to weave through the throng, run the gauntlet as it were, which ensured he was hit with everything from apricots to zucchinis.

'Quickly,' he murmured in Bryony's ear. 'I need your help to get that key.'

At that moment the Grand Inquisitor looked directly at Scirf, who then proceeded to scratch his ear instead of pointing at the wall by the door.

'What key?' asked Bryony, a little impatiently. 'You haven't got a key in your lughole have you? Aren't you supposed to be helping Sylver?'

'I am helping Sylver,' said Scirf through gritted teeth, as a lettuce struck him full in the chest. 'We need the big key over there by the door. I can't reach on my own. Come and help me prop a bench up against the wall.'

'Oh, sorry. Let's go then.'

Fortunately for the two weasels, at that moment Torca Marda and his henchstoats rose from their seats and made for the entrance at the far end of the hall. Again, they seemed to bear charmed lives, as they walked resolutely through the hail of cabbages and carrots, to reach their destination. It was as if they had an invisible barrier around them. Scirf watched them with some suspicion.

'Dark magic,' he muttered.

But then his attention was taken by Bryony, who was tugging at his bib. He went with her through the mass of battling animals, back to the end of the hall. There the pair of them found a bench and propped it up against the wall like a slide. A young squirrel nearby asked them in an excited voice what they were doing.

'Just getting a bit of height,' said Bryony. 'So we can lob stuff over the heads in front.'

'Good idea,' squeaked the squirrel. 'Can I use it too?'

'In a minute,' Scirf said in a peeved tone. 'Let's have a go first.'

The squirrel nodded, just as he got a stick of rhubarb in the neck. He turned to seek out his adversary, on the far side of the hall. In that moment Scirf ran up the bench, snatched the big key. Then he shot down again and was about to return to Sylver when he remembered the vegetable oil.

'Oil,' he said to Bryony. 'Quickly.'

She ran forward and grabbed a jug of sunflower oil from the paw of a serf-squirrel who was just about to pour it over the head of one of the town burghers.

'Hey!' cried the serf. 'That was mine!'

'Find another,' snarled Bryony, 'unless you want it over *your* head.'

The serf stared at her nervously for a moment, then moved off into the thick of the mob, glad to get away from this savage jill weasel.

Giving the jug to Scirf, she asked, 'Will that do?'

'Good as any,' said Scirf. 'See you later.'

He slipped back through the door to the South-east Hall, where Sylver was waiting on the other side.

'Did you get it?' was the weasel leader's first question.

Scirf held up both paws, one with the key in it, the other bearing a jug of sunflower oil.

'Well done,' cried Sylver. 'You are an ingenious weasel.'

'Ain't I just,' said Scirf, pleased at the compliment. 'Now for that lock. We can't pour it from the jug, the spout's too thick, so here goes . . .'

He took a big mouthful of oil from the jug and with bulging cheeks leaped onto a chair and thence onto the unicorn's back. The unicorn carried him over to the big door which led to the inner ward and the ovens. Scirf put his mouth to the large lock and spat the mouthful of oil into the works.

'Yuk!' exclaimed the princess.

'Give it a few minutes to work its way in,' said Sylver, 'and then try the key. By the way, what's happening in the South Hall?'

'Food fight,' said Scirf. 'Everyone's in on it. Makes a good diversion for us. Wouldn't be surprised if our lot started it during the brawl. A food fight lasts longer than a straight battle with pawsicuffs.'

'You said everyone's in on it? Even the Grand Inquisitor and his two minions? I can't imagine that.'

'No,' replied Scirf. 'Those three left.'

'To go where?'

Scirf shrugged. 'They went out of the end door – the one we came in by. The one that leads to the castle gate.'

'The one that opens out onto the round church?'

'Yep,' replied Scirf. 'That's the . . .'

He stopped and stared at Sylver. They had both come to the same realization. A ghastly hue had come into Scirf's eyes.

'Mawk,' said Scirf. 'He's probably tryin' to break into the church just at this minute . . .'

Chapter Twenty-Two

Mawk found the small door to the round church unlocked. He entered warily. There were lighted candles on the altar on the far side of the aisle, so he was able to see his way fairly well. But Mawk did not like empty churches. He always associated them with dead humans, because of the graveyards, and found them spooky and creepy places. Even now he half expected a rotting corpse to leap out from behind the pulpit and shout 'Gotcha' while clamping a bony hand on his shoulder.

'Hum-hum-hum-hum,' he murmured tunelessly to himself. 'Tum-tum-tum-tum.'

The bell in this particular church, because the building was such an unusual shape, was behind the altar and to the left. A silken bell rope hung down between two windows. Mawk made straight for this stop, almost tripping over a lectern in the process. When he reached the rope he looked up to see how it could be removed without actually ringing the bell.

'I could climb up the rope,' he told himself, 'but that delicate little clanger, looking like an iron tongue, would strike the side of the bell as soon as I touched it.'

He thought some more.

'I could climb up on the altar, then onto the windowsill, and cut it in half – but then it would probably be too short. What to do, what to do?' he mused.

At that moment he was electrified into movement. The door to the church had swung open again. Mawk leaped for the altar and just managed to get under the cloth when someone entered and began walking up the aisle. There was more than one animal. They were talking together. Mawk recognized who the voices belonged to as they got closer to where he was hiding. He almost choked on his fear when he realized that the creatures were Furioso, Orgoglio and Torca Marda himself.

'Such childish horseplay,' Torca Marda was saying. 'And a waste of good food. Every year it's the same. Yet they think because someone different starts it each year that it's an original game. How very stupid of them.'

Suddenly the pawsteps stopped, close to the altar. Mawk heard a heavy-sounding sniff. Someone was smelling the air.

'Garlic,' said Torca Marda. 'There's an odour of garlic in here.'

Then Orgoglio's voice came drifting down to Mawk, who was cowering under the altar cloth. 'All I can smell is incense.'

'That's because you have no sense of smell,' retorted Torca Marda. 'Now why would there be garlic in here?'

'Holy stoats use garlic,' offered Furioso, 'to keep away the vampire bats.'

Again, the voice of the Grand Inquisitor, patient-sounding on the surface, but with a veiled anger beneath.

'We're the only holy stoats in this castle and I don't remember hanging strings of garlic anywhere, do you?'

'No,' replied Furioso in a timid voice. Then, 'I've got it – you remember Poisson d'Avril fell in the garlic soup. She splashed those apprentices. Some of them must have been in here for some reason. Shall I have a look round? You never know, Your Grace, those apprentices might have planted a booby trap, to get back at you for asking Pommf de Fritte to confiscate the nuts they cached away last season.'

Mawk curled up into a little ball and pretended he was somewhere else.

'They wouldn't dare,' replied the Grand Inquisitor. 'Booby trap *me*?'

There was silence for a few moments, then the same voice came back with, 'Perhaps you'd better just check in the corners and behind the curtains . . .'

It was a miracle that Mawk did not cry out, or leap up and run for the door, but that was probably because he was not there; he was in Halfmoon Wood, dancing around a bonfire, being happy and carefree, out of harm's way.

There were some sounds around the altar, as Orgoglio and Furioso made a search of the church. He could hear them clumping around, lifting things. Mawk was brought back suddenly to his present position when a high wailing note suddenly pierced the interior of the room. It was like the cry of a beast in mortal pain. His eyes bulged out of his head and he whimpered, his own sounds luckily being drowned by the wail.

'Do you have to, Furioso?' said Torca Marda. 'Leave the organ alone.'

'Sorry. Accident,' said the false priest. 'Didn't mean to touch it.'

'Liar,' murmured Orgoglio. 'You always touch it when you pass it – you can't help it, can you? Playing

216

with the stops, pumping the bellows, messing around with the keys.'

'You shut your trap,' replied Furioso. 'What about you and the bishop's mitre. You always put it on when you think no-one's looking. I've seen you, parading up and down in front of the mirror . . .'

'Please,' murmured Torca Marda, 'you'll give me a headache.'

Finally, Orgoglio came to the altar. Mawk could see his hindpaws in the gap below the altar cloth and the floor. The weasel held his breath.

'Pooh-ahhh, the garlic smell's really strong over here.'

'Is there anything missing from the altar? Chalice? Plate? Whatever?'

'No – all here, 's far as I can see.'

'Come,' said Torca Marda, 'we're wasting time here – let us get on . . .'

There was a grating noise, the sound of padding paws, followed by silence. When Mawk finally poked his head out and looked around, the stoats were gone. Where they had disappeared to he had no idea. At that moment the door to the church opened again and Sylver and Scirf came in.

'Mawk?' said Sylver as he crawled from beneath the altar. 'Did the Grand Inquisitor come in here?'

'Yes, but he's gone now. I don't know where he went.'

'You had a lucky escape,' said Scirf, drawing his finger across his throat. 'We came to warn you.'

'You came too late, they've been and gone.'

'Well, let's get this rope,' said Sylver. 'Scirf, can you climb up there?'

Scirf looked at the sheer walls of the church interior. 'Piece of cake,' he said.

He started up, clinging to bits of projecting

masonry and decorative knobbles on the bricks. Mawk admitted to himself that he could never have done that. Scirf was a superb climber, sure-pawed and nimble. He found small cracks in the stonework and little ledges around the edges of windows. Finally he was at the bell. He unhooked the clapper and dropped it, with the words, 'Catch, Mawk!'

Mawk just managed to catch the clapper before it hit the stone flags.

With the clapper out of the way it did not matter what Scirf did to the bell. He actually hung on to it, swaying back and forth, while he untied the rope. The rope was dropped. Sylver gathered it up and immediately left the church. Mawk waited for Scirf, then the two joined their leader, creeping around the walls to the ovens on the far side of the ward. Here they were joined by the stone unicorn who allowed himself to be harnessed to one of the ovens.

Fortunately it was the right oven and when he strained against the harness it slid over the flags on a swivel, revealing a hole beneath.

'Once we're down there, I want you to drag the oven back to its original position,' said Sylver to the unicorn. 'Then get one of your own kind to untie the rope. After that, you're on your own. Good luck.'

'And to you, weasel,' murmured the unicorn. 'If you hear a mighty thundering, it will be us, making a mighty charge at the gate. Heaven help anyone who gets between me and my freedom. If they close the gates we'll smash through them. We have the weight and the force to do so. We couldn't get a good run at the door to the hall, but we have a good two hundred metres over the inner ward. We'll trample down any creature who gets in our path . . .'

218

The unicorn was still talking when the three weasels dropped down into the passage beneath the ovens. Shortly afterwards there was a rumbling overhead as the oven was replaced. Then they were in pitch black.

'We should have brought a light,' said Mawk. 'I hate darkness.'

A spark suddenly lit up the tunnel. Then a small flame flared. Sylver had used his tinder-box. Scirf had produced a candle stub from his belt pouch. Soon they had light enough to see their way. Mawk was saying, 'I could have brought those, if I'd thought of it,' while the other two went on ahead, moving northwards along a passage which must have taken them under the West Hall towards the North-West Tower.

Sylver found some arrows chalked on the floor of the passageway. It was a low and twisting tunnel, certainly not big enough for a human to enter, so Sylver knew there would be no clue in this particular section. It must have been built by some creature other than humans, but then many animals were good at burrowing. Eventually they came to a crossroads, a sort of wheel, off which were many passageways.

Sylver decided to continue to follow the line of arrows, which seemed to be leading them directly under the tower.

'They may have been put here for us – that is, searchers of the clues – to follow.'

After squirming and crawling along a very narrow section, Sylver could suddenly smell fresh air. Some sort of exit lay ahead of them. Since it was night he had no idea how far this exit lay along the passage. He simply had to keep going, feeling in front of him every two or three paces.

'What's happening?' asked Scirf from behind him. 'Can you see anythin' yet?'

'I'm not sure,' began Sylver. 'I thought I could . . .'

The sentence was cut off in the middle as Sylver suddenly found himself dangling in mid-air. He had gone down a steepish slope, then slipped over a ledge. It was to the edge of this ledge that he clung by the tips of his claws. The candle had gone spinning downwards into blackness, snuffed by the night winds, for below them were the rocky shores of the lake.

'Help!' he cried to Scirf. 'Give me a paw.'

Scirf had managed to jam himself against the walls of the tunnel and so prevent himself from sliding down the same slippery slope which had fooled Sylver. Mawk, dragging his paws as usual, was some way behind and perfectly safe.

Scirf clung to the walls with three good paws and reached out to grab Sylver's outstretched right paw.

'Got you,' he said. 'What's below?'

'About one hundred metres of nothing,' gasped Sylver, 'so don't let go.'

Mawk was crying, 'I've gone blind. Oh my Gawd, I've gone blind.'

'Be quiet, you silly dolt, we've dropped the candle,' said Scirf. 'Quick, come up here by me, my forelimb's being wrenched from its socket.'

'Where are you?' cried Mawk, miserably.

'Just ahead of you. Don't come too fast. Creep along and grip the sides of the tunnel. When you feel my fur in your face, get hold of my rump and start pulling.'

Mawk did as he was asked and eventually Scirf's unwholesome fur tickled his chin. He gripped Scirf around the thighs and began to back up slowly, digging his claws into the edges of the tunnel, where the walls met the floor. Gradually, centimetre by centimetre, the pair of them managed to pull Sylver to safety. Sylver's last view of the outside world was when a light from above, possibly torches on the battlements, lit up the drop down to the rocky fangs in the foaming waters below.

'Who's down there?' came the voice of a sentry from above. 'What's going on?'

Sylver refrained from replying to this question, having little breath with which to do so anyway. Once he was back inside the tunnel and in no danger of falling, he leaned back and rested.

'Thanks, Scirf, thanks, Mawk, that was a close call,' he gasped. 'I could see myself dashed on those sharp rocks down below. Thane of County Elleswhere? I was nearly seagull tidbits and pike meat.'

The other two were too relieved to speak for the moment.

Chapter Twenty-Three

Up in the north-west of Welkin the prince of stoats was still surrounded by a sea of rats. It was now over a week since the weasels and the deserters had brought food. Stores were beginning to get low again. The prince himself would be the last to starve of course, but his soldiers were becoming embittered creatures, complaining night and day.

There was more to contend with than just lack of food.

Flaggatis had been at work with his magic again. This time the Lord of the Rats had conjured up a horrible smell. It came from the ooze at the bottom of the moat and broke in gaseous bubbles on its surface. Several million years of organic sludge lay under the moat: rotting cockles, mussels and whelks, left there by an earlier sea. This foul decaying slime was now releasing its odours to envelop the castle.

The stench wafted over the castle battlements, through windows and under doors, making everyone feel quite sick. If one might imagine a thousand rotten eggs mixed with pig's manure on a hot day, then that would probably be halfway to the strength and rottenness of the stink which found its way into every crevice of the castle.

Stoats had taken the pawkerchiefs off their faces and put clothes-pegs on their noses. Noblestoats all went about speaking as if they had severe colds or bad adenoids, saying, 'Gudd borning, wad a terrible spmell!'

The soldiers and lower ranks hung over the battlements, careless of the missiles aimed at them by the rats below, gagging and trying to suck some clean air from any passing breeze.

Sibiline was contemptuous of those who swooned and vomited all over the place. She had fashioned a long tube from a hollow washing pole, which she stuck out of an arrowloop. With this device she could breathe clean air from outside the stink zone whenever she felt the need.

The lower orders of life, the garderobe and sewer weasels, were the only ones who did not bother with wearing pegs, since they carried bucketfuls of smells about every day and this new stench was just a wee bit more on the bracing side.

Prince Poynt wore a scented veil over his nose, which he refreshed every so often from a small blue vial.

His Royal Highness wandered the battlements of his castle in his white coat, shivering in the heat of the summer, staring gloomily out over the multitude of rat encampments. The rats had built high watchtowers now, of sticks covered in vole hides, far enough away from the castle to be out of range of rock catapults, but near enough to be able to peer in the window loops and over the battlements.

The prince was locked in a windowless library in the inner ward of the castle. Stuffy though it was it was the only place where he was not overlooked by watchtowers. He hated the smell of musty old books, ink and damp paper. If he had any time when all this was over he promised himself he would make a bonfire of the lot and have done with it. What good were books anyway? They just cluttered the place up and made it look untidy.

'I feel like I'm being stared at night and day,' groaned the poor prince. 'I can't even go for a breath of stinky-fresh air without some rat looking in and shouting a remark. I can't sleep in my bed without their eyes boring into me. I can't eat breakfast without them looking down my throat. It's awful.'

'It's bad, my prince,' agreed Pompom. 'The night has a thousand eyes.'

'And the day ten thousand. But what are we to do? Their beady little red eyes follow us everywhere. I see the horrible smirks on their ratty faces, their whiskers quivering in malice. There's nothing we can do to get back at them. Nothing at all.'

'We could get all the weasel slaves and servants to stand on the battlements and stare back at them,' suggested Pompom. 'That might rattle them a little.'

'No, no. That won't do. Oh, I wish I hadn't sent Falshed away. He always has good ideas.'

To the east things were somewhat different.

Lord Ragnar, Thane of Fearsomeshire, was managing to contain things, but he was as yet unable to send relief to the prince. Halfmoon Wood and Thistle Hall had been overrun by a rat advance which had swept round in a claw-shaped movement from the north-east. Fortunately Lord Haukin, Culver and the rest of his household had managed to escape and join up with Lord Ragnar.

The two lords did not, under normal circumstances, get on well together. Lord Ragnar was a big bluff fellow, absolutely fearless in battle, but bone-headed and stubborn. He had few refinements, though he called himself a gentlestoat, and his conversation tended towards hunting and fishing, rather than books and music. Lord Haukin found him a bit of a boor. Lord Ragnar thought Lord Haukin was a ninny.

A meeting between the weasel servants, Culver on the one paw, and Gritnal, Lord Ragnar's servant, on the other may serve to illustrate the differences in their masters.

'My master,' said Gritnal, 'has killed a hundred rats, cut them up with his own bloody paws, and thrown the bits to starving voles.'

Culver was not impressed by this piece of intelligence. 'If he had eaten them himself, then I should be fascinated,' he remarked, 'but voles will eat dead horses if they're hungry enough. On the other paw, *my* master has won the admiration of many for his skill at chess. He is the chess champion of all Welkin. Now that takes true nerve.'

Gritnal sniffed contemptuously. 'I expect he's good at flower arranging too.'

Culver surprised Gritnal by answering, 'Yes he is. At the last county show his "Poppies with tortured willow" won first prize. The theme was the bloody massacre of the weasels at the Battle of Koptin Ridge, you see. The red poppies represented the blood of the fallen on the battlefield, and the twisted willow twigs their pain, both physical and spiritual.'

'Huh!' exclaimed Gritnal. 'Who cares about a load of old weasels that died *that* long ago.'

'It is our history. It was the last of the battles between the stoats and weasels, when the flower of weasel nobility was broken. You as a weasel yourself should appreciate that. If that battle had gone differently, we weasels might have been free and perhaps even ruling Welkin ourselves this day.'

'If I remember rightly,' said Gritnal, 'some of the fieldland weasels fought on the side of the stoats. I'm descended from fieldland weasels myself. You, on the other paw, are probably a woodland weasel. We've never seen eye to eye, nor bitten tooth to tooth, on these matters. I suggest we leave them well alone before we come to blows.'

'Fair enough,' Culver said, through gritted teeth, 'but let me tell you something . . .'

And so it went on, the two weasels each entrenched in their own view on these matters of state.

Their masters, being stoats and the ruling class at that, were less directly hostile with one another. Lord Haukin was of course clever enough to realize that it took boneheads like Ragnar, with their glorious if foolhardy charges at the enemy, to win wars. Lord Ragnar on the other paw, was secretly pleased to have a brain like Haukin about the place, to assist him with confusing things like maps and strategy.

Ragnar was all right with tactics. That was on-the-spot, seeing-how-things-lay, making-an-instant-decision. Strategy however was deeper stuff. It was before-the-battle-planning and involved looking at charts, remembering similar battles fought in the past, and reading biographies on great generals. All that sort of thing made his head spin a little. Such stuff was right up Lord Haukin's alley and that good thane was not too proud to spill everything he knew about strategy when asked.

So things in the middle east of Welkin were, if not progressing at a healthy pace, at least stemming a further advance of the stinking hordes from the unnamed marshes. There was word too that Jessex was moving up from the south-west with an army of ferret mercenaries. Once Jessex's mercenaries joined with Ragnar's army of stoats Lord Haukin felt that substantial progress could be made in the war against the rats.

Even after a wind came and chased away the smell, however, things were not good in Castle Rayn. Food was in even shorter supply, though the stoats had not eaten very much when the stench had been present. On top of that Prince Poynt was finding himself strangely missing Sheriff Falshed. When Falshed was around the prince tended to become irritated with him a great deal, but now he was not there seemed to be a hole in the prince's life. To cheer himself up Prince Poynt had arranged a game of tennis with some of the noblestoats.

Lord Elphet was Prince Poynt's opponent, with Lord Wilisen as the umpire. A net formed of kitchen weasels stretched across the battlements. For rackets the two royal and noble stoats were using frying pans from the kitchen. Their balls were inflated water vole's bladders, which had a bounce of sorts, though were not ideal for the game. Hit too hard they tended to burst on contact with the bronze frying pans.

'My service,' said Prince Poynt. 'We start the game at fifteen–love.'

'I thought we were supposed to start love–love,' grumbled Elphet, 'but you're the prince, so you know the rules better than me.'

'I know *everything* better than you, Elphet, so don't forget it.'

The prince served the ball which appeared to be whizzing straight for the net, but somehow cleared it when two kitchen weasels ducked. Elphet was so surprised it came over, he failed to hit it back.

'*Rrrroottteeen shhhhirttt!*' shrieked the rats, watching from the watchtowers.

Prince Poynt glowered at the rats, who had now

built effigies on the top of their watchtowers.

These figures were of their horrible god, Herman, who appeared to be a fearsome white rat character who demanded blood sacrifices quite often.

Like other savage hordes the rats were not above executing their own kind in midnight ritual killings. The rat shamans put on grass masks with hollow eyes and sniffed out victims who carried bad demons in their heads. They dragged screaming rat soldiers from their reed mattresses during the dawn hours. They held mock trials over which Herman watched with lustful eyes. The shamans spoke with Herman, nearly always agreeing with the god that the victims should be slaughtered. Hoods were put over the victims' heads and they were led to a place where they were garrotted with a piece of greasy knotted string.

News of these horrible rat rituals, supposedly encouraged by Herman, had reached the ears of those in the castle. This made the stoats and weasels wonder what would happen to *them* once they fell into rat claws. If the rats were prepared to treat their own kind with such barbarity, then what price stoats?

'What on earth are those rats talking about?' snarled Prince Poynt. 'Root and shirt?'

'I think, my prince,' said Pompom, coughing politely, 'they mean rotten *shot*.'

'Oh. Well, that's their opinion, which is worth absolutely nothing so far as I'm concerned.'

Down the other end of the court, Lord Elphet was not happy. 'Hey!' he cried. 'That's not fair. The net ducked. Did you see that, umpire?'

Wilisen said, 'See what?'

'Oh, it's going to be like that is it?' Elphet grumbled. 'Well I hope they duck for me too.'

However, having won the first game, the prince was ready to receive the serve from Elphet. Suddenly all the weasels went up on tiptoe and the net was much higher than before. They knew on which side their bread was buttered. Elphet was no fool however. He began lobbing the ball at every opportunity and began winning points that way.

Once more Prince Poynt grieved for the missing Falshed. The sheriff would have immediately taken over from Wilisen as the umpire and ensured that Prince Poynt won every game. As it was, who knew where the sheriff was now?

What would the sheriff recommend in this case, thought Prince Poynt, if he *were* here?

He tried to imagine Falshed standing by him, advising him, and heard a little silent voice in his head.

'Of course,' muttered Prince Poynt. 'That's what Falshed would tell me to do.'

Next time, when Prince Poynt did a little chip over the net and Elphet went rushing in to chop it back over again, the prince swung hard at the ball and 'accidentally' let go of his racket.

The frying pan went whizzing at the net who scattered and parted in the middle.

Lord Elphet was not so quick. The frying pan caught him a donging blow on the forehead. He staggered back and fell to his knees. Suddenly the game was over. Since they had not finished the set the umpire proclaimed it 'Even Stevens' and the prince gave his apologies.

'Sorry, Elphet. Sweaty paw. Handle slipped in my claws.'

'Of course, my lord,' muttered the wounded lord. 'I *fully* understand.'

Elphet went off to bathe his bleeding head.

The rats seemed delighted at Elphet's defeat and shouted, '*Chhhheeeet. Heeee eeeess chhhheeeet!*' at Prince Poynt in a reverent tone, seemingly as a compliment. Cheating, to the rats, was obviously very character building. They looked on it as something to which every animal should aspire.

'I am not a cheat,' replied Prince Poynt, huffily, who did not like being accused of deceit. 'It was an accident.'

But this served only to raise the voices of the rats in the watchtowers, who seemed to be pouring praise on the prince for his underhand tricks. Incensed, Prince Poynt went back to the stuffy library. Once there he sent for Falshed's stoat-servant, Spinfer, who wisely answered the call immediately.

'In the absence of your master,' said Prince Poynt, 'I want you to think of a way of getting back at the rats, for peeping at us all the time.'

'I shall give it my best attention, my prince,' murmured Spinfer, silkily. 'Leave it in my claws.'

Chapter Twenty-Four

Sylver, Scirf and Mawk retreated back along the tunnel with the arrows on the floor. It was obvious to Sylver that the arrows had been placed there to lure unfortunate animals to a horrible death on the rocks below the castle. Some devious mind was at work in these underground passages.

'We must be more careful,' he said, as they came to the multiple crossroads again. 'We were being led by the nose there – let's try another passage, but be more careful this time.'

This time they chose a passage which looked as if it might collapse at any time. Some of the support beams were cracked or bent and some earth had already dropped from the ceiling to form mounds on the floor. The three outlaws followed this passage along until they came to a curve. Sylver saw something flicker on the walls as he approached and he immediately doused his own candle.

'What is it?' whispered Scirf. 'Seen somefink?'

However, it was quite obvious now what had made Sylver wary. A light was coming from round the bend and further down the tunnel. A flame was flickering on the walls. The outlaws crept forward until they could hear voices coming from a cavern ahead. Flattening themselves on the floor they snaked along until they were behind a mound of earth, then peeked over.

At first all they could see was something which looked like a shrine. Several candles burned in niches cut into the rock face. Then Sylver made out the shapes of three stoats, crouched below these candles. One was wearing a scarlet robe and was armed with a sword. Even in the poor light he was recognizable as Torca Marda. This made Sylver suspect that the other two figures, in the flickering shadows, were Orgoglio and Furioso.

Then one of the figures spoke and Sylver knew it was not either of those two false priests, but indeed the old enemy of the outlaws, the High Sheriff of Welkin.

'Your Grace,' Falshed was saying in a thick, frightened voice, 'you can't let this creature loose. He – he might do something awful to an innocent stoat. Of course,' a tinny sound of clicking teeth came out of Falshed's mouth, 'I have no love for weasels, nor squirrels for that matter. But to let this monster roam free, why, anything could happen.'

'Falshed,' murmured the soft warm tones of the Grand Inquisitor's voice, 'you are far too finicky. Your ambitions have always outweighed your scruples. You worry about other animals, about whether innocent creatures might be hurt. I, on the other paw, have no such principles, which is why I shall one day rule Welkin, while you remain a minion.'

The three outlaws, hidden behind the pile of soil, watched this scene with narrowed eyes. Still the third stoat had said nothing, but simply lay stretched out on all fours, seemingly waiting to be addressed. Sylver was intrigued by this figure, which had a mottled and what appeared to be rather flea-bitten appearance. A strange smell wafted down to the outlaws now, of putrid flesh and some other unpleasant odour.

'Grave earth,' whispered Scirf, the weasel who recognized such odours. 'Rotting flesh and grave earth.'

Mawk shuddered and would have whimpered if he had not been so scared. His eyes were bulging out of his head. He shivered from the tip of his nose to the end of his tail. This was a nightmare as far as he was concerned. He did not like sinister shrines with horrid black candles – for that was their colour – and stoats like Torca Marda swishing about in robes.

Then two more mammals came out of the darkness, having been waiting silently in the wings. Once in the light they were recognizable as Rosencrass and Guildenswine, the two ferrets who would spy on their own mothers if it brought any reward. They looked almost as distressed as Falshed. One of them stretched forth his paw.

'Payment,' said Guildenswine, 'for the corpse.'

'Yes,' Rosencrass said, 'we've got to pay the moles. They went and dug it up and now they want their groats.'

'Was the exhumation done according to my instructions?'

Guildenswine nodded. 'The moles waited until midnight. Then they burned four black candles, one on each corner of the grave, before chanting the words you gave them.' Here Guildenswine shuddered a little. 'Once they'd carried out the rituals they dug down and found the body. It was as you said it would be, almost like new . . .'

The candleflame in Torca Marda's paw was now shone on the mysterious creature stretched on the floor of the cavern. Sylver was startled to see it was the corpse of a big black-and-white badger. True, the badger's fur was patchy and moth-eaten, with small holes everywhere, but essentially the carcass was whole, including two glassy eyes which stared dead ahead. The corpse's mouth was open, revealing white fangs. A small red tongue poked between the front two teeth.

'A badger's cadaver,' whispered Scirf. 'Oh my Gawd – what's that fiendish inquisitor going to do with that?'

Mawk indeed gave a little whimper now, which caused those in the cavern to turn their heads.

'What was that?' asked Torca Marda, crisply. 'Did any of you hear something?'

'One of the support beams creaking, I think,' said Rosencrass. 'Are you sure this is safe?'

'Of course it's not safe,' replied Torca Marda, still staring down the tunnel. 'This passage could collapse at any time. But do you want me to revive a corpse up in the castle where everyone can see and hear what we're doing? Do you think that oaf Pommf de Fritte would allow me to work my magic and bring a corpse back to life?'

Apparently satisfied that what had been heard was indeed the shoring timbers of the tunnel, the Grand Inquisitor again turned his attention to the matter in paw. He paid off the two shaken ferrets and they scuttled away down another passageway. Falshed, looking miserable and frightened, stayed with the evil and ambitious stoat in the scarlet robes.

'I will need some assistance,' he told the quaking sheriff, 'which you will provide. Bringing a dead animal back to life again after it has been long in its grave is not an easy thing to do. I want you to remain here with me during the ceremony. You will help with the rituals. Understand?'

'Yes,' replied Falshed hoarsely.

'Once we have our ghoul, we can send it in search of Sylver. He's in this maze of passages somewhere – I can feel it in my bones – and the ghoul is the only creature who can sniff him out. This dead badger will be my Minotaur. He will work to my command, to bring me the body, dead or alive, of that outlaw Sylver.'

Torca Marda sighed. 'I wish the outlaw leader had stepped forward instead of his minion, Icham, when I challenged them at single combat. I expected him to. None of this would have been necessary then. However, since that did not happen we have our work to do. Are you ready, Sheriff?'

'As much as I'm ever going to be,' answered that unhappy stoat, staring at the decomposing corpse on the floor. 'But if I run screaming from this place, you won't blame me, will you?'

'I'll do more than blame you – I'll quarter you myself with a blunt knife – now pull yourself together.'

The Grand Inquisitor began chanting and sprinkling some kind of grey dust on the prone form of the corpse. Sylver thought he heard a low moan coming from the ghoul's throat a moment later, but it was in fact Falshed making the noise. The sheriff was shaking so badly, holding a salver of magic dust in his paws, that he was liable to scatter the precious stuff all over the floor of the cavern. Sylver felt he had to talk to the two weasels with him and motioned for them to follow him.

When the three of them were some way back and in pitch darkness again, Sylver gave voice to his thoughts.

'We have two choices. We either leave the Grand Inquisitor and his "helper" to do their magic, then deal with the ghoul of that badger later. Or we interrupt them now.'

Mawk said, 'Later, much later – let's get out of here. Let's go back to the castle.'

Scirf spoke too, after this. 'Much as I don't usually agree with Mawk, I do this time. If we go bargin' in there, Torca Marda will skewer all three of us on that deadly blade of his. We've got a few darts between us, but there's not much room to throw them, is there? And he's an expert swordstoat – we wouldn't stand a chance.

'Better to wait and get that thing he's sending after you – trap it somehow, or keep out of its way.'

Sylver sighed. 'I suppose you're right. Let's go back and see what's happening. If I give the signal to attack, move in quickly to support me. Otherwise, run away when I do.'

'Can't we run away now?' suggested Mawk.

'No, I want to see how Torca Marda works. Don't worry, Mawk, the ghoul's after me, not you.'

'Yes, but it might have to get past me to get to you.'

Nevertheless, the three weasels flowed and rippled over the floor, back to the pile of fallen earth behind which they had been hiding. When they peered over the top they saw that Torca Marda's chanting had ceased. He was bending down and, with his mouth to that of the ghoul's, was breathing air into its lungs, much as one might do to revive a drowned mammal. The creature stirred, coughed harshly, something oozing out of the corners of its mouth looking suspiciously like the slimy green juice from the regurgitated cud of a ruminant beast.

Torca Marda stood up and wiped his mouth on the corner of his red robe. Falshed stepped away, his eyes white and rolling with fear. The three weasels could hear the sheriff's teeth chattering and none of

236

them thought any the worse of him for being so scared. They themselves had never seen anything like this. Mawk only stood his ground because Scirf was deliberately standing on his tail.

Soon the ghoul was up on its hind legs, standing there, swaying before its master, Torca Marda. Falshed now moved to one side, into the shadows, and gawped at the monster.

The ghoul took a few tentative steps, staggering forward, its forelimbs hanging loosely like lead-weighted plumlines. Its lower jaw hung down and its eyes stared vacantly. A thin green slip of drool fell from the corner of its mouth. Only its forepaw claws were working at all, opening and closing slowly, as if trying to grip the throat of some poor hapless creature. The ghoul's nostrils flared as it spoke its first few words.

'Master,' it grated, much in the vein of a stone statue, 'give-me-my-orders.'

Torca Marda seemed for the moment to be wallowing in the pleasure of having a large ferocious beast like a badger addressing him as "Master". He tapped his own chin with a foreclaw, as if musing on the beauty of his labours. Having created life out of death, he was at that moment feeling rather godlike and invincible. Clearly he had not enjoyed giving mouth-to-mouth resuscitation to the creature, but it seemed to have been worth what amounted to kissing the dead.

Now that the dead badger was on his feet, he looked even more ravaged and mouldy than before. He seemed to have shrunk from the large figure he had been in real life, as if all the moisture had dried up in his body. He was like a mangy lump of weather-beaten pelt, which has been hung from a gibbet for an age in the sun and rain. His fur hung

237

like knotty bits of string. His ears looked chewed and twisted. There were still bits of peat stuck to him here and there, like crusty scabs on his pelt. There were gaping holes in places where something had bored its way through his body and out the other side.

In a word, he appeared quite ghastly to mammal eyes.

'Lovely,' said Torca Marda, murmuring softly. 'Beautiful creature.'

'Thank-you-master.'

'You are my creation,' murmured the Grand Inquisitor, 'my wonderful monster.'

Suddenly the ghoul's mouth twisted and its lip curled back. 'Do-not-call-me-that-word. Do-not-speak-that-word.'

Interesting, thought Sylver, as he saw the shocked expression on Torca Marda's face, and the enraged look on that of the ghoul, this creature who had been revived from the world of darkness, from the world of the dead, did not like to be considered a monstrosity. Its face had been all light and pleasure when the Grand Inquisitor called it 'lovely' and 'beautiful' but the word 'monster' angered it.

'You – you don't like to be known as a monster?' asked the Grand Inquisitor, risking the word again.

The ghoul howled in rage and swiped the air. 'Not-monster,' it cried. 'Not-monster.'

'No, no, of course not,' soothed Torca Marda. 'Falshed was only joking, weren't you, Sheriff.' He turned to look at Falshed as if it had been he who had used the word and not Torca Marda.

Falshed finally dropped the salver of dust, let out a terrible cry of terror, and fled along the passage in the wake of the two ferrets who had gone before.

The Grand Inquisitor let his assistant go with a

mild look of amusement on his face, then he turned back to the ghoul and gave it its instructions.

'Find the outlaw Sylver,' he ordered. 'Sniff him out, my fine – creature. Bring him to me, alive or dead. I have given you life – now you must give *me* life, that of the weasel whose body will be my gift to Prince Poynt. I shall soon be back in the good graces of the prince – then who knows, perhaps greater things even than that lie in store for Torca Marda?'

Amongst the three weasels, down the passage-way, there was silence, save for the one sound of Mawk trying not to swallow his own tongue in fright.

The ghoul turned its glassy eyes and its pitted nose in the direction of the tunnel. It sniffed, long and slowly, like an animal drawing in the aroma of a good meal. Its eyes rested on the mound of earth behind which the outlaws were crouched.

'Meat,' said the ghoul, in a satisfied voice, and began to amble forwards.

'Run,' cried Sylver.

And the three weasels ran like a draught of air escaping from a punctured balloon.

Chapter Twenty-Five

Somehow, in the darkness, the three fleeing weasels managed to stick together. Down narrow passage-ways, squeezing through holes, round bends, and into straights they flew. Finally, Sylver saw a glimmer of light ahead of them. He headed towards this with the other two in tow. The light came from a chink, which appeared to be the edge of a slab of stone, where it did not quite meet the hole over which it had been placed.

'Help me with this,' said Sylver, reaching up.

The other two did as they were bid. Between them the three weasels managed to move the slab aside. Scirf bunked the other two up through the hole, then they in turn reached down and pulled him up to safety. The slab was quickly pushed back into place, this time properly, so that no light would get by it.

Scirf let out a gasp of relieved joy. 'Did you *see* that thing? I never saw nothing so horrible in all my life. Plug-ugly, wasn't he? Wouldn't win no queen of the tourney competition.'

'How can you be so – so amused,' cried Mawk, in a distressed state. 'I was terrified. I think I ran so fast I left my tail behind somewhere in that tunnel.'

'Never mind,' Sylver said, breathing more easily, 'we got away from it. But we mustn't forget it's roaming around down there somewhere, when we have to go back.'

'Go back?' cried Mawk. 'I'm never going down there again in my life. You can threaten me with red-hot pokers, I'm staying up here, in the fresh air . . .'

As he spoke he looked around him, realizing he was not above ground yet. They were in some kind of crypt, a room below ground without windows, though not the kind you might find in a church. In those sorts of places you find dead bodies walled up, with stone figures of knights and ladies. Here, probably in the heart of the castle, they could see a group of old polecats in leather caps and woollen gowns, sitting at high desks, all scribbling away in massive books and on huge parchments.

Now that they were safe, temporarily, from the monster, the three weasels relaxed a little. They needed to knit their unravelled thoughts into a recognizable shape and gather together their shredded spirits. A few minutes for reflection would not be out of the way, and who knew, perhaps one of the venerable old scribes might know the where-abouts of the clue they were seeking. Sylver decided to cast around, once they had introduced them-selves, for any information on the matter.

Polecats normally have a dark overcoat which hides a thick cream undercoat. When the polecat moves, its soft fur parts like corn in a breeze to reveal the lighter colour beneath. They have this kind of bandit mask edged with white patches on their faces, which makes them look quite sinister some-times. These polecats, however, tended towards grey, being ancient in years and with the person-alities of sages.

The polecats seemed to have taken little notice of their visitors, so intent were they on their task. However, when Scirf wandered over to a grey-whiskered old fellow, whose claw held a quill as neatly as if it had been a hand, the creature glanced up with an irritated expression.

'What is it you want?' it asked, in imperious tones. 'Can't you see I'm busy?'

Scirf looked at the parchment on the desk. The polecat was drawing a beautiful illuminated letter. When Scirf looked at it more closely he could see it was made up of different sorts of insects. There were dragonflies, damselflies, bees, wasps, mayflies and crane-flies, all going to make the letter E. It was a work of art and the ex-dung-watcher appreciated such skill. Scirf had wanted to draw since the age of dot.

'That's not bad that,' he said, looking over the elderly polecat's shoulder. 'But – well, what about a flea or two in there somewhere. I'm rather partial to fleas as companions. They always seem to get missed out.'

'Please,' murmured the polecat, wiping a paw over his eyes. 'Do you *mind*?'

Sylver wandered over too, to see what the polecat was drawing, but like most of the outlaw band he could not read or write. Only Scirf, who had spent time studying during the boring hours of his dung-watching period – and Miniver – had any idea of what to do with the letters of the alphabet. The rest of the weasel band had been raised in a wood, with no opportunities to learn how to read and write.

Sylver regretted this and was always impressed when he saw someone using either of those skills.

'What's he writing?' he asked Scirf, as the polecat scratched away in the candlelight, like the rest of his kind, as busy as a hare scraping out its form. 'Is it interesting?'

The polecat slammed his pen down on top of his desk. 'What *does* one have to do to get some peace and quiet around here?' he demanded.

'Answer a few questions,' replied Scirf.

The polecat raised his eyes to the ceiling and folded his forepaws in resignation. 'Continue, weasel.'

'Well, for starters,' Scirf replied, 'where are we?'

'You are in the South Undercroft, which the squirrel lord Pommf de Fritte has kindly allocated to us scribes in order that we may do our work – uninterrupted. We chose a crypt because, even though it lacks air and light, it is out of the way of normal animal activity. We need complete silence to concentrate on our letters. We cannot afford to make a mistake. Our task is too important. Here, we were told, we would not ever be disturbed. Am I getting through to you?'

Scirf however was one of the most thick-skinned creatures on the great island of Welkin – or pretended to be. 'So what's your name then?'

'My name, if it is of any consequence whatsoever, is Wwwillliammms.'

'Williams?'

'No, Wwwillliammms.'

The polecat wrote it down for him on a spare scrap of parchment.

'That's an unusual name for a polecat,' interrupted Sylver, when Scirf spelled it out loud.

'That's because we're not polecats – at least, the polecat sighed, 'we *are*, but they don't call us that where we come from. We are from a far western peninsula, an area known Wwwalllesss. There we are called *ffwlbart*.'

'Cor, can't get me tongue round that one,' said Scirf, impressed. 'How does it go?'

'Ffwlbart. It is derived from the word "foumart", which has its origins in the phrase "foul smell".'

'You stink, is that it?' said Scirf, more interested than insulting. 'I mean, I stink too – though it's not sort of natural with me – it's more a chosen thing, if you know what I mean. I like it this way. Keeps the flies off. Well, I s'pose it doesn't – those are interestin' flies you've got in your picture. Are you sure you don't want to put a couple of fleas in, considerin' you're, you know, sort of stinky like me. I adore *my* fleas. They're my constant companions. They don't sweat and whine about their condition. They don't lie awake in the dark and whine about their sins. Not one of them kneels to another . . .'

The polecat put his paws over his ears. 'Who *is* this creature? Where is he from? The Otherworld?'

'No, from a little village to the north-west of here, but you might call it an Otherworld,' replied Scirf, 'if you had to sit and watch rhubarb dung all day long.'

The scribe looked as if he was about to scream, so Sylver stepped forward.

'Might I ask,' he said, 'what you polecats – you ffwlbart – are doing with these manuscripts?'

These words of enquiry seemed to put the polecat in a calmer and more rational mood. He stared at the parchment before him with a kind of reverence in his eye. His claw touched the edge of the reed document, ran along it, possessively, as a mother might run her paw through her kitten's fur.

He was obviously proud of his work and quite rightly so, for Sylver saw that it was of the highest quality. No crossings-out or blots, no accidental scribbles, nor forgotten t's uncrossed nor i's undotted. It was as perfect as one might wish it.

'We are writing the history of the world,' said the scribe Wwwillliammms. 'Every detail of animal history is in these manuscripts. Once we have finished the world will end, history will cease at that point.'

Scirf knew his opinions were not wanted, that his views on things were considered with contempt by the polecat, but there seemed to be some sort of funny logic here.

'Wait a minute,' he said. 'How do you know when you've got to the end of history? I mean, it's not as if the world will burst into fragments like a pancake hittin' a rock, is it? How do you know when it's all over?'

'When we reach the end of it,' replied the exasperated polecat. 'That's when history ceases. Our work will be finished. We can go to our Maker in the knowledge that we have written a full and complete account of animal history.'

Scirf gave a little apologetic cough and then spoke again to the venerable polecat. 'Wouldn't it sort of be better if you let the world end first, *then* finish the history?'

The polecat looked at him as if he were stupid. 'How will we finish it, if we're all dead?'

'I see what you mean,' replied Scirf, 'but it won't necessarily go off bang. It might sort of die slowly and give a little whimper before it flops over and lies still. You could sort of write history up to the whimper. Anythin' that happens after that ain't really worth recording, is it?'

Some of the other scribes had left their benches and desks now and were gathering around, listening to this idiot weasel trying to change the great plan of the universe. They folded their forelimbs and shook their heads as if in disbelief. One of them, even more elderly than the rest, spoke in a voice like cracked leather being shaken out by apprentice tanners.

'My dear weasel, it is we in this little room who

control the destiny of the world. We receive news from the outside from our agents and we record it. We never leave this undercroft, even for a few breaths of fresh air. We eat, sleep and work down here, our food brought to us, our water transported from the castle well. We record the information our agents bring us, but when the time comes I shall put the last full stop.

'This flat world of ours will then fold itself up like a piece of paper, starting at the corners, until it's a small thick wad. The wad will then cast itself into oblivion – that's a place from which nothing returns.'

'And your name is?' enquired Scirf, politely.

'I am the head clerk, Bead.'

'Well, listen, venerable Bead – it behooves me to tell you that you're spoutin' rubbish, me old poltroon. You might put your last little dot on the parchment, but animals outside won't just roll over and die. They'll just carry on doin' what they've always done, an' you won't even know about it. If you've been down here for years, beg yer pardon, but you'll know less about the world than a bunch of toads stuck down a well.'

Before the aggrieved looking Bead could respond to this tirade from Scirf, Mawk came over.

'So,' said Mawk, 'who're these agents of yours that bring you the history of the world as it is taking place?'

Bead said, haughtily, 'Not that it's any business of yours, but their names are Rosencrass and Guildenswine.'

Sylver clicked his incisors. Mawk clacked his molars.

Scirf began to read the parchment over the shoulder of Wwwillliammms.

'So,' said the ex-dung-watcher, 'what's happening up there in the big wide Welkin at the moment, eh?'

Bead raised his brow. 'Animals are all at peace with one another. The rat lies down to sleep alongside the dove, the mink helps the rabbit build her burrow, the wildcat collects wool for the birds to build their nests. Everyone is using this time of peace to build cities. All the woodland has gone and with it the fields and lakes. Only stone remains, building stone, cut into blocks. Those blocks have been put together to make long straight roads, build palaces, turn wilderness into thriving townships.

'A horseless carriage has been invented and will soon be transporting goods and animals all over Welkin. Kites are being built which are big enough to fly without their strings. They too will soon be carrying animals and cargo, just as such things were once transported by mouse-cart. However, there is a mad hare somewhere, inventing a world-folding machine. Once this device has been built the earth is doomed, for an invention cannot be uninvented, even if one wishes it.'

'How much time have we got left?' asked Scirf. 'Give or take a couple of days?'

'Many decades. According to our agents the hare has only just begun on the blueprints. We have oodles of time left.'

'Good. Well, these two agents of yours . . .'

'Rosencrass and Guildenswine.'

'. . . that's the pair. A brace of truth-gatherers, whose hard work and dedication has let you put all this down on parchment, all this history happenin' to the world right now – well they ought to be proud of themselves.'

'So we frequently tell them,' said the venerable Bead. 'They are our eyes and ears. Without their true and accurate accounts we should have no work. They travel the land, they toil, they labour for the good of our cause. In the normal scale of things those two self-sacrificing ferrets are head and shoulders above the rest of animalkind.'

'And you pay them well?' asked Mawk.

'A modest sum, considering the amount of work they have to do to provide us with our information. Travel expenses only. The mere amount of a thousand groats a month.'

'Well,' Sylver said, 'cheap at the price. But that's Rosencrass and Guildenswine for you. They would give their own lives if they thought it necessary.'

'Quite,' said Bead, 'now if you'll excuse us, we have our work to do as well, so that theirs is not wasted.'

The polecats returned to their desks and were soon sharpening their goose-feather quills in order to scrive away again, writing down pure fiction which came from the vivid imaginations owned by two ferrets, who probably never had to even get out of bed to collect their thousand groats a month.

'Some animals,' said Scirf, looking round him, 'were born daft.'

'And others born to take advantage of them,' added Sylver. 'Those two ferrets are into everything, aren't they? One of these days they're going to get their comeuppance. Anyway, for the moment we need to walk amongst these scriveners and ask them if they've heard of or seen our clue. Come on, you two, work to be done, or the world will end before we manage to save it.'

Chapter Twenty-Six

The three weasels strolled around the South Undercroft, having a word here and there with the scriveners, asking them if they had heard of any passage containing a clue as to the whereabouts of the humans. Each time the question was answered with a shake of the head or a definite 'No'. Gradually the scribes were allowed to get on with their work of writing what was a false history of the world, supplied to them by two unscrupulous ferrets with vivid imaginations. The outlaws did not have the heart to inform the polecats that they were writing a fictional story and not a true history.

'Well,' said Sylver, once the three had gathered again in the corner of the room, 'we have to go back down.'

'Back down?' cried Mawk, his voice vibrant enough to start bells ringing in belfries all over Welkin. 'Who's going back down?'

'We are, chum,' said Scirf, placing a forelimb around the doubter's shoulders which was both brotherly and restraining. 'Me and you, an' Sylver here.'

Mawk struggled to get free of the forelimb.

'I can't,' he whispered hoarsely. 'There's – there's that *thing* down there.'

'The ghoul? You saw how slowly he moved. We could outrun him every time. He's sort of jerky and stumbly. You an' me, Mawky, we can run like the wind.'

'Not when I'm scared.'

' 'Specially when you're scared.'

Sylver had slid aside the flagstone with which they had blocked the hole leading to the underground network of passageways. He took some lighted candles from one of the holders on the wall and gave one each to Mawk and Scirf, keeping one for himself. He then stuck his head and shoulders down the hole. Waving the candle around he searched for signs of the ghoul below. A few moments later he told the other two it was all clear.

'Here we go,' said Scirf, 'under the top.'

He pushed Mawk towards the hole first and then lowered the unfortunate, trembling doubter down into the darkness below. Then before Sylver could follow, Scirf pushed the grating flagstone over the hole, saying, 'Bye, Mawk. Have a good time.' He then winked at the puzzled Sylver before removing the stone again and yelling down, 'April Fool – just kidding, Mawk,' to the weasel below who had been reduced to a blubbing ball of fur.

Once all three weasels were down they peered about them, their flickering candles making the shadows dance on the rough tunnel walls.

'Let's try this way,' whispered Sylver, pointing in the direction they had been running when they found the South Undercroft. 'Let's see where it loads.'

They kept Mawk in the middle. He was likely to run at the least jump of a shadow. This was a wise thing to do, because they had only travelled a few hundred metres before they heard a worrying sniffing sound.

'What was that?' cried Mawk.

'Ssshhhhh!' ordered Sylver. 'I think the monster's up ahead of us.'

'Oh Gawd,' muttered the unhappy Mawk.

The three began to retrace their footsteps quickly. It was obvious before too long that the ghoul was on their trail. They could hear its shambling gait coming up behind them. They could hear its horrible snorting, smell its rotting flesh. Sylver was in despair. How could they search the secret passages of the castle if it was full of supernatural beasts like this? They would have to surface again, quickly, and make some sort of plan to get rid of the creature.

A while later, with the ghoul gaining on them every second, they came upon some roughly-hewn stone steps at the side of the tunnel. These led to a wooden door above the weasels' heads. Sylver flowed up the steps, stood on his hind legs, and tried the iron ring handle. For a moment it did not seem as if it would budge, but then it suddenly gave with a loud 'clack'. Scirf and Mawk came up behind him then and all three pushed the door hard. Just as the monster came round the corner and its eyes settled on them, the door swung outwards. They scrambled through and slammed it shut behind them.

Scirf found a bolt and quickly shot it into its bed. 'There,' he said, 'that ought to hold him.'

They found themselves in another, narrower passageway, leading to some more steps and a second door. Sylver lost no time in showing the others the way. This door would not open no matter how hard they twisted the handle. It was obviously locked on the inside. 'Well, we can't stay here,' he said. 'We'll die of thirst or starve.' He picked up a loose brick from the floor and used it to hammer on the door.

After several knocks the door flew open and an

incredulous chamber-jill stood there, peering down at them. 'What are you lot doing behind the book-shelves?' she said. 'Good job I found the lever or you'd still be here.'

She had apparently found a switch which made a bookshelf swing open in the room behind her.

'We – we got lost after the feast,' explained Sylver. 'Took a wrong turning on our way back to town and found ourselves in some sort of maze. Can we, er, come in?'

The ghoul was now hammering on the door further down the passage and making loud moaning noises.

'What's that?' asked the servant, peering over their shoulders.

'It's the plumbing,' replied Scirf, waving his paw in the general direction of the sound. 'Makes that noise all the time.'

'Doesn't sound like the plumbing to me,' she argued. 'Sounds more like something's trapped in there.'

'Oh, right,' Scirf said, looking over his shoulder, 'maybe it's somethin' which crawled out of the depths of the earth, or from the bottom of the lake. When we came over another lake we saw a dragon-fly nymph suck the innards out of several rats and leave 'em looking like soggy bits of cardboard floatin' on the water. Maybe it's the dragonfly nymph.'

The chamber-jill stared for a few more moments down the dark passageway, then motioned for the group to enter. 'Come on in, but go right through,' she said. 'This is Pommf de Fritte's bedroom. If he catches you in here you'll end up as streamers flying from the flagpole on the North Great Tower. His bedroom's private quarters.'

'So they should be,' said Sylver, hurrying past a great four-poster bed with posts the size of tree trunks. He paused and stared at the bed for a moment. 'Clive sleeps in a cold kettle,' he said, 'and Pommf de Fritte sleeps in this great bed. How different are the reds and greys.'

'Each to his own,' shrugged Scirf. 'Personally, I don't think you can beat a nice warm mound of horse dung . . .'

They hurried on through the room, which was decorated throughout with weapons both for hunting and fighting. Once outside they found themselves on the battlements. One or two of the sentries walking up and down raised a brow at their presence, but Sylver tried to look as if he was entitled to be there, and strode purposefully towards the South Great Tower.

He intended to find his way down to the inner ward again and thence to the ovens where they had first entered the underworld of the castle.

Scirf and Mawk scurried after him, wondering when someone would twig that they were not supposed to be there and call them to halt. They reached the tower however and found a door by which to enter. Inside there was a spiral staircase. They followed this down, quickly, flowing over steps and rises made for human legs, until they reached another door. Opening it, they entered, and found themselves in a room only halfway to ground level.

'What have we here?' asked Sylver, peering round at a fantastic sight of bottles, glass phials and tubes. Round bobbles of glass full of strange liquids were bubbling and hissing over candle flames.

There was an oven, or more likely a furnace, roaring somewhere at the other end of the room, which was making the place unbearably hot. Sure enough when Sylver looked around some bottles he could see a kiln. The iron door was open below it and flames licked out into the room.

Around several benches and on racks on the walls were hundreds of tools. These ranged from small callipers to large hammers. There were balls of wire and spools of thread scattered around the bench tops.

Leather-bound books, as thick as castle bricks, lined another wall. The covers of these volumes were decorated with strange markings – moons and suns, stars and planets – some in silver, some in gold, some in red velvet.

This was clearly a craftmammal's workshop of some special kind, for what candlemaker or wood-carver would need books like these? Not for the first time Sylver felt they were entering territory into which they had never before ventured. He was a weasel who liked adventure, but the pace at which new discoveries were taking place was leaving even him breathless. However, he prided himself on being able to absorb new findings without losing his sense of mental balance.

They were about to leave when an elderly squirrel in a leather cap and apron stepped from behind a frozen fountain of glass and copper. He stared at them from beneath grey brows. Since his face was completely clear of malice – quite a nice face really and similar to that of Lord Haukin's – Sylver decided to risk remaining in the room a little longer.

'Good morrow, sire,' said Sylver to the elderly squirrel, 'are you the proprietor of this fine establishment?'

The old squirrel nodded. 'I am Kloog, the

alchemist,' he replied, 'and who might you weasels be?'

'What's an alchemist?' whispered Mawk.

'Some sort of goldsmith,' explained Scirf.

'More than a goldsmith,' said Sylver, staring at the glass and copper contraption behind which the squirrel stood. 'An alchemist searches for the secret of turning base metals like lead into gold.'

'More even than that, my fine weasel friend,' said Kloog. 'We alchemists are also searching for the elixir of life and the universal solvent.'

'What's them?' asked Mawk, still mystified.

'Why,' continued the squirrel, 'two of the three great secrets! The universal solvent will be able to dissolve any other substance, thus rendering all wars impossible. We would spray it on weapons and castles and these machineries of war would melt before our very eyes. Of course,' he added reflectively, 'so would the creatures in them and holding them, but perhaps just having the solvent would make it all unnecessary, if you see what I mean.'

'But,' pointed out Scirf, who was quick to pounce on to theories like this with huge flaws in them, 'once this stuff had melted a castle it would go right through the world and out the other side, wouldn't it? You'd have animals fallin' through holes and never seen again!'

'We'd just have to be extra careful.'

'And what would you keep it in? Eh?' argued the ex-dung-watcher. 'It'd melt anythin' you put it in – glass bottles, wooden casks, metal drums . . .'

The sound of grinding teeth came to the weasels.

'We'd freeze it solid until we needed it.'

'You have to invent somethin' to freeze it with first.'

'We're working on it,' replied the elderly Kloog, grinding his teeth even more. 'We're working on it very hard.'

'The elixir of life,' murmured Mawk, catching on to the other work of the alchemists. 'You mean, something to make us live for ever?'

'Eternal youth,' replied the squirrel. 'To be young and lusty for ever.'

'Going to get a bit crowded, ain't it?' argued Scirf. 'New animals comin' along all the time and no-one dying.'

The alchemist stared very hard at the three weasels. 'Just exactly what is it you want?' he asked. 'Why do you interrupt my important work with your silly objections? This is my room. I was given it by Pommf de Fritte. Does anyone know you're here? What are weasels doing in the castle in the first place? I could call the guard.'

Scirf growled, 'You do that and I'll . . .'

But Sylver stepped in front of him and addressed the old squirrel himself. 'Look, sir, we mean no harm. My young companion here just loves to argue a point with friend and stranger alike. We are looking for a message, supposedly written on the wall of a secret passage which runs under the castle. Now we know there are many of these passageways, having been down there, but wondered if you knew of any writings to do with where the humans have gone?'

The alchemist appeared to calm down a little. 'Human writings? I know of none such. I spend most of my time here in this little room, delving for the secrets about which we just spoke. I seek those hidden paths which we oftimes lose, only to turn and find again. You would do well to go down and look for yourselves.'

'We would do,' explained Sylver, 'except there's a monster on the loose down there.'

Kloog's brow was suddenly a map with thousands of wrinkles. 'Monster? What kind of a monster?'

'A ghoul. It's the revived corpse of a badger.'

Kloog stroked his chin with his paw. 'A ghoul you say? Sounds like the work of that charlatan Torca Marda. If I had my way we would have thrown the Grand Inquisitor into a pit of leeches many summers ago . . .'

'That sounds good,' remarked Scirf. 'I like that idea.'

'Don't interrupt, scruffy one,' warned Kloog, 'or I might not put my alchemist's brain to your problem. A ghoul, you say?' He stroked his chin again. 'There is, if my memory serves me well, a way of getting rid of ghouls. Now which book did I see that in?' He turned away to look along a shelf of parchments and books. 'One of these, I'm sure – ah-ha! Here we are: FABULOUS BEASTS.'

He opened the volume and began to pore over the pages, while the three weasels waited patiently for him to find the right place and give them the information they wanted.

'Hmmm, ah, yes – here,' the alchemist's paw traced a line of words on the page. *'To rid oneself of a persistent ghoul, use an arrow, the point of which has been tipped with a talon drawn from the left claw set of a dead murderer, preferably a bird of prey, known as the claw-of-glory. The arrow must strike the ghoul in the heart. If these instructions are carried out to the letter, the ghoul will fall dead, destroyed once-and-for-all, never to be revived again.'*

He paused and looked up with a tight click of his teeth.

'There you are – nothing to it – all you have to do is find a murdering hawk or falcon, kill it, and remove a claw.'

'Simple,' said Scirf, hollowly. 'Why didn't we think of that?'

Chapter Twenty-Seven

Scirf's snorted reply seemed to wound Kloog the squirrel alchemist quite deeply.

'You asked me a question,' he said, huffily, 'and I answered it for you. Is it my fault that the object you require might be difficult to obtain?'

Sylver said, 'Take no notice of Scirf here – we appreciate your assistance.'

Scirf twitched his nose at this mild reprimand, but said nothing further. Sylver considered the problem. As leader of the outlaw band he often felt a little inadequate when it came to brain power. He was fine on points of action, making quick decisions, leading his friends out of difficult places and into new territories. But sometimes, when the problem required deep thought, he had to rely on one of the others.

Bryony was probably the brightest of the band, with – he hated to admit it – Scirf coming a very close second. Bryony was not here, so it would have to be Scirf whom he consulted. The trouble was, if you asked Bryony something she told you, and that was that. There was no feeling that she was judging you and thinking you were a little wanting in grey matter. With Scirf it was different. He seemed to swell. There was something of the sin of pride in his bearing.

'I know what you're thinkin',' said Scirf,

suddenly. 'You want to ask me where we get a murderer's claw, but you think I'm going to crow over you when I give you the answer. Well, I'm not, see . . .'

'I'm glad about that, Scirf,' said Sylver, startled to know his thoughts could be read so easily, yet relieved that it was all out in the open. 'So – what shall we do?'

'I don't know,' replied Scirf, humbly and simply. 'I haven't the foggiest.'

'Wha – what, you mean you haven't thought it out yet?' asked Mawk, anxious to get the monster out of the way and done with. 'You mean you need a bit more time?'

'Don't need no more time,' replied Scirf sniffily. 'I've been thinkin' about it for the last ten minutes. Got no idea where to get one of these murderer's claws. I know who might have an idea, but you won't like it.'

'Who?' asked Sylver. 'Come on, out with it, weasel.'

'Rosencrass and Guildenswine. Those two know everythin' about everythin' it seems to me. If anyone knows where to get a rotten claw, it's them.'

'I fear your friend is right,' interrupted Kloog. 'I too have no love for those two ferrets, but they are twin founts of undesirable knowledge.'

Sylver considered his position. They could not search the passages under the castle thoroughly unless they got rid of the ghoul. The monster's powers of 'sniffing' out the weasels were quite considerable it seemed. So there did not appear to be a great deal of choice in the matter. They had to seek out the two ferrets and see if they could help in obtaining a claw-of-glory. Sylver could see no other path to follow.

In the meantime, he felt weary. They had been up all night, running around underground passageways. It was time for some rest. He could see Mawk swaying on his feet, the way that doubting weasel did when he was very tired. Scirf looked bleary-eyed too. Sylver decided to take a chance on the alchemist, who stood watching them.

'Kloog,' he said, 'from what you said earlier I understand that there is no love lost between you and Torca Marda?'

'None whatsoever,' said the grey squirrel, firmly. 'He called me a fake and a fraud in front of my lord and master, Pommf de Fritte. He said the art and science of alchemy – changing base metals into gold – was fantasy. I can never forgive him for that. It is my life's work. The other day I almost got a piece of lead to glint a bit yellowish when it was held up to the light . . .'

'Yes, I understand,' Sylver said, feeling that although Torca Marda was a villain, the inquisitor was not stupid. Alchemists had been searching for the secret of changing lead and other metals into gold for decades, and Sylver too believed they were chasing rainbows. 'I understand you are aggrieved at being insulted. The Grand Inquisitor does not favour us very much either, hence the fact that he has raised a creature from the dead to hunt us down. Would you help us in thwarting him of this goal?'

Kloog's brow wrinkled like a grey sea in a light breeze. Finally he said, 'Yes – why not. Just so long as it isn't too dangerous – and I don't want to do anything which might anger Pommf de Fritte or Foppington! Those two would have my ears scorched if I annoyed them.'

'All I want you to do is get hold of Rosencrass and Guildenswine and bring them here. We have to

261

sleep for a while, since we've been awake all night. Would you do that for us?'

'Curl up under one of my tables,' said Kloog. 'I shall hie me hence and find those two agents of darkness.'

With that the squirrel left the room in the tower and they could hear him going down the spiral staircase.

'Can we trust him?' asked Mawk, anxiously, fighting to keep his eyelids from closing. 'What if he brings back the Grand Inquisitor?'

Scirf shook his head and yawned. 'No, don't worry, me old Mawky. Sylver made the right decision there. Kloog won't bring back the demon priest. Alchemists and inquisitors don't make good companions. They're deadly rivals in the art and science of *mystery*. Now let's get some sleep.'

So saying the ex-dung-watcher lay down on the sawdust below one of the benches, above which bubbled and hissed a strange concoction in a green glass bubble, and fell instantly and deeply asleep. The other two followed his example. Soon nothing could be heard above the sound of their whistling snores, which weasels always seem to make due to their tiny nostrils.

Sylver was deep in a dream about rushy glens, mossy banks and ruined priories with lots of hidey-holes. He gambolled over lichen-covered blocks of stone, fallen from high arches and tall windows. He bathed in a brook where aspens trembled and elders dripped their berries. Suddenly, there in his dream, he thought he saw another weasel, a small shape, just emerging from an arbour. The figure slipped in and out of shadows, seemingly desperate to reach him, to be recognized by him.

But before the dream could proceed any further he

felt himself being roughly shaken out of it. He opened his eyes to focus on the ferrety face of an amused Guildenswine.

'He's awake,' she said.

'Yes, I'm awake,' replied Sylver, scrambling to his feet.

Scirf too had stirred and was staring with distaste into the eyes of Rosencrass, who had awakened him.

Mawk continued dozing, his mouth open and his tongue vibrating noisily between his little white fangs.

'So,' said Sylver, 'did Kloog explain what we want?'

Guildenswine folded her forelimbs. 'Seems a bit strange to me. I mean, we helped Torca Marda to revive the dead body of a badger in order to kill you – now you want us to help you put it back in its grave again in order to thwart his plans. Do you think we have loyalty to no-one?'

Sylver nodded, his mouth grim. 'Yes – that's exactly what I believe. I think loyalty and honour are plucked very quickly from your minds, like unwanted weeds from a garden, whenever they grow there. I think you would sell your own mothers on the open market for a few groats.'

Guildenswine clicked her teeth in amusement. 'How well you know us – and in such a short time.'

'Well?' asked Sylver. 'I assume Kloog explained to you what we wanted? Do you have it?'

'No,' replied Rosencrass, tickling the sleeping Mawk's nose with a piece of paper. 'But we know someone who does.'

Kloog, standing by the doorway, seemed a little anxious. 'I would rather you were all out of my room very soon,' he said. 'So please conduct your business and go your separate ways. I certainly don't want to

263

be caught by my lord and master entertaining such a gathering of reprobates and rebels. It smacks of conspiracy. De Fritte would have my tail for a feather duster.'

'A *fur* duster, I think,' murmured Rosencrass. 'Let's not mix our fur and feathers.'

Sylver was weary of the games the ferrets were playing with his precious time. He said to Rosencrass and Guildenswine, 'Have you got what we want, or not? If you don't settle with me in the next three seconds, you'll find yourselves tossed out of the nearest window.'

'Steady on, steady on,' muttered Rosencrass, backing away a little. 'We haven't talked about payment yet.'

'You'll have to trust me for that,' replied Sylver. 'I don't carry money on me, not the amount you'll want. When we get back to Halfmoon Wood I'll make sure you are paid. You have my word of honour on that. A hundred groats. How does that sound? Just as soon as all this is over.'

Guildenswine frowned. 'I dunno about that. You can't spend someone's honour. Cash in paw. That's how we always work – don't we, Rosencrass?'

'Always,' said her mate.

'Well, this time you'll have to make an exception,' replied Sylver. 'Lord Haukin will stand the amount. You can apply to him any time you're in the district of County Ellesswhere. He'll settle the debt with no questions asked.'

Guildenswine brightened. 'Ah, Lord Haukin? That's a bit different from a few scruffy weasels. Lord Haukin is highly respected and a great gentlemammal. All right, wheel in the witch, Rosencrass.'

The jack ferret went to the door and opened it to

reveal one of the velvet soothsayers from the town.

'Hail, Sylver,' the crone screeched, 'Thane of County Elleswhere!'

'Not this again,' groaned Sylver.

'Hail, Lord of Thistle Hall!' shrieked the hag, coming into the room. 'May you live as long as you can!'

The two ferrets were looking at Sylver with a new light in their eyes now.

'You didn't tell us you were destined for greatness,' said Guildenswine, silkily. 'This changes everything. You can have the claw thingy for free.'

'You place a lot of trust in the prophecy of some old subterranean hag,' said Sylver.

Rosencrass nodded. 'They've never been known to be wrong before. If she says you're going to be an aristocrat, then polish up your accent, weasel. We'll settle for half the silverware in Thistle Hall, when you're the lord and master of the manor.'

'Never mind all that now,' said Sylver, irritated by all these omens, 'where's the goods?'

'Tarrraaarraa,' cried the crone, whipping something from beneath her rags. 'Behold! The claw-of-glory.'

She held forth an object more gory than glorious. It was the foot of a sparrowhawk. Some of the skin was peeling away where it was rotting. However, the talons were intact. Sylver reached out and gingerly took the claw from the paw of the soothsayer. He held it out at forelimb's length, studying it in the dim light of the alchemist's chamber.

'Don't worry about the hag,' said Guildenswine, 'we'll settle with her later.'

'I wasn't worrying about her,' replied Sylver. 'I was wondering – how do we know this is the real thing? I mean, we apparently need the foot of a murderer. This is a bird of prey – it kills other creatures all the time.'

Rosencrass shook his head. 'No, you have to kill your *own* kind to be a murderer. This hawk was a bandit and a rogue. A slashthroat and skywaybird. It used to wait and attack other sparrowhawks on their way to feeding their young, robbing them of their prey. Once, it went too far . . .'

That was enough for Sylver. He motioned to Scirf to wake the sleeping Mawk. Scirf shook the slumbering form. Mawk snorted and sat up, staring about him indignantly. When he saw the room was crowded with crones and spies he blinked. Scirf hauled him to his paws and they joined Sylver, standing by the door.

'Let's go,' said Sylver.

Before they left the alchemist slipped a phial of fluid into Sylver's paw. 'You will need this,' murmured the squirrel, 'to complete the deed.'

Sylver put the phial in his belt pouch. The three weasels then slipped out quickly, leaving the alchemist, the crone and the riff-raff ferrets behind. They hurried down the spiral staircase, anxious to get to the entrance to the underground maze. On the way down, Scirf threw a sidelong glance at Sylver, who said, 'What?'

'So you're going to be Thane of Elleswhere?'

Sylver clicked his teeth, though he was feeling far from amused. 'You don't believe that rubbish, do you? It's just a lot of old soothsayers dreaming up shocking prophecies. Lord Haukin's the thane. He's not going anywhere. Why would I ever get to be Lord of Thistle Hall?'

'I dunno,' said Scirf, 'ambition's a funny thing.'

'It's claptrap,' replied Sylver, as he now caught Mawk staring at him in a peculiar way. 'I have no desire whatsoever to step into Lord Haukin's sandals. Those crones – they'll say anything to get attention. You know.'

'If you say so,' said Scirf, in a voice which revealed he was not entirely convinced. 'You got to live with your own conscience, squire.'

Sylver was upset by this remark but he did not feel it was the time or the place to hold a discussion on the subject. He decided to let it drop for the moment. In his paw was the claw-of-glory. This grisly object still had to be turned into usable weapons. Then the three outlaws had to reach the ovens and get below without being noticed.

There were three darts in the pouch on his belt. He would replace the points of these with a talon from the claw and arm himself, Scirf and Mawk with a single dart each.

Thus equipped they could go hunting for ghouls.

Chapter Twenty-Eight

Once the trio were down in the maze of tunnels again, Sylver paused to fit the strange hooked points to his darts. After which he threw the disgusting claw away, not having any further use for it. He then handed out a dart each to Mawk and Scirf. Scirf looked at his claw-tipped dart and shook his head.

'I hope this works,' said the ex-dung-watcher. ' 'Cause if it doesn't, we're all ghoul meat.'

'Don't *say* that,' said Mawk. 'Why do you always say things like that?'

Sylver's mind was on the immediate future too. Ever practical he was wondering what was the best plan for attacking the ghoul. Down in the world of darkness and shadows once again, where beetles scuttled away and cockroaches hid in cracks, schemes came and went in his head, some leaving traces behind them, others vanishing like mist into heather.

It made sense for the group to split up and search as individuals. In this way they would probably find the monster much more quickly than if they remained as a bunch. However, he knew Mawk would never agree to that and when he was honest, he himself did not relish the thought of tackling the ghoul alone. So he suggested they stay and tackle the beast together.

'Wouldn't have it any other way,' said Mawk,

shivering. 'Otherwise I'd definitely go home.'

'I shall lead,' said Sylver. 'Scirf, you back me up –
and Mawk, take up the rear.'

Thus, they began their search of the system of
passages under the castle. It did not take long to
locate the monster, who was after all searching for
them too. They heard it sniffing down the corridors
ahead of them, coming towards them. Mawk gave a
little whimper but stood his ground. Sylver braced
himself, being the first in line. It was up to him to
throw the first dart. He placed his candle on a con-
venient ledge, then backed away a few paces, so that
the monster would walk into its light while the
weasels would be in half-darkness.

'Get ready,' he said, as the snorting and sniffing
became louder. 'Here we go.'

Around the corner came the corpse of the badger,
standing tall on its hind legs, its blackened, yellow
fangs bared. The shadow it cast on the tunnel walls
was bad enough, but when the black-and white fur
came under the candlelight, they saw how formidable
was the fiend. The badger had frightened enough
weasels when he had been alive, by his size alone.

When the creature's glassy eyes caught the
candlelight, it shambled forward letting out a
tremendous scream of triumph.

At last Mawk turned and ran back about twenty
metres, his heart pounding in his ears. He wanted to
be a million miles away. Some basic instinct stopped
him from running further however. It seemed
sensible to wait and see what happened to the
monster before trying to outrun it.

Sylver waited patiently in the shadows. He knew
the monster was aware of him. It did not go by
sight but by smell. The weasels had been smelled
out by the dead badger. It ambled towards the

weasel-scent, its forelimbs swinging. Sylver drew back his forelimb with the dart in its paw.

The ghoul was fully illuminated now by the candlelight.

'Have at ye!' cried Sylver, in the manner of a tourney knight.

He launched the dart at the monster's heart. The monster moved surprisingly quickly for once, jumping to one side. The dart caught it in the shoulder. A cry of pain went hurling down the passageway, rolling like thunder before a storm, hurting the ears of the weasels. Scirf stepped forward then and threw his dart. This would indeed have struck the monster in the heart, had not the lumbering beast stumbled right at that moment. Instead the missile caught it in the throat, bringing forth this time a strangled cry of agony.

The ghoul blundered on, sweeping Sylver aside with one blow of a forelimb. The supernatural beast actually trampled over Scirf, who was trodden down into the dust. This left Mawk who was frozen to the spot with fear. Running now, the monster went straight at the third weasel and took him in a bear hug, perhaps intending to squeeze the life from the smallest of the three weasels, before going back to deal with the other two. It bent its foul head to get a grip on Mawk's neck with its fangs. Poor Mawk could smell the stench of its disgusting breath.

'Help me!' cried Mawk 'It's – uh – it's crushing me to death!'

The fur of the ghoul was coarse and stiff, like an old doormat left too long in the wind and rain. Mawk could feel holes in the creature's body, which seemed to be alive with something. Mawk knew what that would be. There were pockets of maggots still working on the corpse. Other parasites were running through its coat, too numerous and perhaps too ugly to mention their names.

Had Mawk not been in fear of his life, he might have found time to be revolted by it all, but as it was the forelimbs were squeezing the breath out of his body and his head was giddy and swimming.

'Please, stop,' gasped Mawk. 'Don't . . .'

The monster gripped him even harder and crushed him to its bony chest.

Amazingly there was a loosening of the creature's limbs.

Suddenly the monster had begun to stiffen. It let out a terrible moan of despair. The sound went moaning down the tunnel, echoing like the note of a horn in a hollow morning. Such a cry might have come from the mouth of a dying god. In a winter world it would have awakened every dormouse, every hibernating hedgehog, every cold snake asleep in its hole. Such a cry would have touched the heart of the cruellest wolf.

Had it been any other creature, the weasels might have felt pity for it, so full of sorrow was its call.

A wave of odious breath was expelled into Mawk's face and the weasel gagged. The ghoul's tight grip on him slackened and fell away altogether. The creature let go, staggering back a few paces. It looked down at its chest. There was Mawk's dart, protruding from its breast, the hawk's-talon point in its flesh. The doubting weasel realized he had stabbed the creature through its ribcage and punctured its rotten heart.

'I – I did it,' whispered Mawk, amazed.

How he had done it he hardly knew, until he was given space to think about it. The dart had been in his paw when the monster took hold of him. In trying to crush him, the ghoul had pressed its own

271

breast on Mawk's dart hand. The hooked point had gone in like a dagger, piercing the creature's heart. Thus the beast of the underground night had destroyed itself, rather than Mawk having any real paw in the act.

In a few moments the monster lay still and lifeless. The dark magic of the claw-of-glory had worked. Sylver got to his feet. So did Scirf. These two weasels came to Mawk and patted him on the back with their paws.

'Well done,' said Sylver.

Scirf added, 'Good for you, Mawk.'

For once Mawk did not feel he could claim credit. He was so relieved to be still alive. 'I – I didn't do it on purpose,' he admitted. 'The beastie fell on my dart.'

'Still, you held on to it,' Scirf said. 'You didn't chuck it away and run.'

'That's the important thing,' agreed Sylver. 'You didn't run.'

'I was scared . . .'

'We all were. But you stood your ground and you got the job done. That's what it's all about. Never mind dashing courage. That sort of bravery is just spur of the moment stuff – but you – you stayed calm and reasoning. That takes *real* courage . . .'

Mawk did not feel he could argue against Sylver's logic any longer and took on the burden of praise. 'Well, if you say so,' he replied, modestly. 'But what are we going to do now – with the corpse I mean?'

Sylver realized that if they just left it as it was Torca Marda would only revive it again with dark magic. Remembering the phial of viscous liquid given him by the alchemist, he now took the little bottle out of his pouch. He uncorked it and smelled the fluid. It was lamp oil. Now he knew what the alchemist had meant about completing the task.

'Stand back,' he said to the other two.

He sprinkled the lamp oil over the fur of the life-less ghoul and then put a candle flame to it. Soon the dead pelt was burning as furiously as any pyre. They left it, hurrying along the passage ahead of the smoke, not wishing to be choked by the fumes which came from the fire. Sylver felt quite triumphant at having bested Torca Marda, though he knew there would have to be a meeting of the two of them before long. Sylver could not leave his best friend unavenged.

The three friends now continued to search the passages under the castle, but without success. They found no messages, no icons, no symbols which would lead them to the discovery of the where-abouts of the humans. Sylver might have despaired had he been a weasel who was easily depressed. As it was this initial failure only made him more deter-mined to find what they had come looking for. The outlaw band had been through a number of adven-tures to get to and inside the castle. No doubt there would be more before they returned to Halfmoon Wood. They simply had to keep looking.

He said as much to his two companions, but Mawk sowed a seed of doubt.

'Of course,' said Mawk, 'we could have got the wrong castle – perhaps there's another castle in the region with a sort of stormy weather name?'

Sylver had not thought of this possibility before now and it worried him a little. 'Is it possible? I suppose it is. Perhaps we should try to look at a few maps of the area – if there are any.'

Scirf said, 'I'm sure that alchemist squirrel has got a few of them around. Shall we go back to him? It's a bit dangerous, keeping on going up top and wanderin' around the battlements, but I can't see us getting anywhere down here. What d'you think, Sylver?'

'I think you're right, Scirf. Now that Mawk has raised the question, I think it has to be answered. We'll go up top and see our friend the alchemist just once more. If he hasn't got a map he'll know where we can find one.'

Sylver led the way once again along passages which were becoming more familiar with every hour.

Chapter Twenty-Nine

Back in Castle Rayn, things were faring a little better for Prince Poynt and his besieged stoats. The lower orders of the castle were now down to eating their voleskin sandals, but Flaggatis had gone back to his home in the marshes. The Lord of the Rats had decided that the siege was going to be protracted and had left orders with the rat warchiefs to send for him when those inside the castle surrendered.

The last act of magic by the rat lord had been to conjure up a hurricane-rainstorm which had showered the castle with small snails and slugs, torn from trees and plants in that damp and dreary western region.

The noblestoats, elegant and finicky as they were, disliked the idea of snails and slugs everywhere, crunching and squirting under their feet. It was distasteful to the gentlestoats to find slick creatures making their homes in their water jugs, hand basins and chamber-pots.

Those who were not so fussy went around gathering the lower orders of life who left slimy trails on their walls and floors. These were cooked and eaten. In the cruder and more vulgar quarters of the castle, snail soup was a delicacy and slug pie was a welcome addition to the menu. Encouraged by this new diet, others began prodding around in the garden for worms, centipedes, maggots and earwigs and other tasty delights.

Prince Poynt was a little happier too.

The admirable Spinfer had come up with the idea of raising a screen of hessian sacking all round the battlements, so the rats could not see over the top. Thus Prince Poynt and his noblestoats could walk around without being stared or jeered at by the rodents. Occasionally Prince Poynt would raise the edge of the sacking and blow a raspberry at those who were making his life a misery. It was a little thing but it made him feel more in control.

And at least the prince did not have to look at the horrible effigies of the rat god Herman all day long.

'Ugly, ugly creature,' he told himself, shuddering. 'Choosing that wan, pasty rodent for a god is beyond the pale.'

He clicked his teeth in amusement when he realized he had made a pun.

The hunger thing was getting the better of everyone though, so most stoats remained testy and irritable.

'We need a distraction,' said Prince Poynt. 'Come on, Pompom, think of something.'

Now the court jester was good for a clack or a click, most of the time, but his jokes were never very original. Besides, he was not an ideas-weasel. His comedy was more of the slapstick kind. Give him a banana skin and he would keep his audience in fits of clickter for hours. He was cruelly good at picking on unfortunates and making fun of them too. Show him someone with a limp or a speech impediment and he would mimic them until the tears ran from noblestoats' eyes.

However, he was no great thinker, and rack his

weasel brains as he might, he could only come up with old games.

'Blind Stoat's Buff?' he suggested weakly. 'Postweasel's Knock?'

'For goodness sakes,' muttered Prince Poynt, 'can't you come up with anything better than that? I think I'd rather watch a weasel deep fry in vole fat. Now *that* at least has not been done before . . .'

Pompom swallowed hard. 'That – that doesn't sound very entertaining to me, my liege. I mean,' he gave a little false chuckle, 'you might get fat splashed on your nice bib.'

'It might be worth it, weasel,' muttered the prince, darkly. 'Now come up with something *good*.'

Spinfer who had been witnessing this exchange with some hauteur (Spinfer was never less than haughty when he was dealing with his intellectual inferiors, which on the whole tended to include most mammals), now decided to intervene and rescue Pompom. Not that he liked the weasel, but more that he enjoyed displaying his own talents.

'My liege,' he murmured, 'perhaps I could be of some assistance.'

'Yes,' snapped the prince, irritably, 'speak up.'

'What about a game of cards?'

Prince Poynt looked at Spinfer with narrowed eyes. You could see by his expression that he was disappointed in his sheriff's valet. There was a time, quite recently, when he thought Spinfer was the brightest star in the firmament, but it seemed that the stoatservant had burned himself out. 'And you think – you think that a game of *cards* is an original idea, do you?'

Pompom watched this exchange with a vicious smirk. However, Spinfer spoke again. 'Not as such, my liege, but I was thinking of a variation in theme. What if your nobles, and yourself of course, were to dress up in costumes which represented playing cards. You yourself could be the king of hearts, for instance . . .'

'Jack of spades. I hate kings.'

'A one-eyed jack, then. Yes, I think the role might suit you. Not that you are any sort of a *knave*, my liege, but you have a certain flair for dark characters. One can never quite penetrate the enigma of the knave of spades, can one?'

'Penetrate the enigma?'

'Pierce the mystery, the complex nature of that particular individual card. A dashing knave, but what is his other eye looking at? There's the rub.'

'I don't know what you're babbling about now, Spinfer, but the basic idea is brilliant. A dressing-up game. I *love* dressing up. My sister Sibiline and I used to do it all the time when we were kittens . . .' He became a little misty-eyed and his voice was wistful as he spoke of his kittenhood. 'Anyway,' the prince continued, brightening, 'well done, Spinfer. I'll·get the royal seamstresses – is that a word? – I'll get them on to it right away. In fact, you can do that, Pompom.'

Pompom, jealous of Spinfer's success, was foolish enough to forget himself. 'Why me? I'm not a messenger-weasel, am I?'

Prince Poynt stared at his jester. 'You'll be a fried and battered messenger-weasel in about two seconds.'

Pompom waited around no longer. He was off, down to the rooms which housed the females of the castle. They were having a coffee morning – or rather nutmeg morning – when he burst in on them with

278

the news. They grumbled a little, saying it was about time jack stoats learned to do their own needlework (useless lumps) but were soon hard at work, sewing and stitching.

At the end of one morning there were fifty-two fine outfits of black and red cloth. Prince Poynt himself was full of excitement as he donned his satin knave's suit with a black spade on the pocket over his heart.

'Whist. We'll play whist. I'm going to be the trump card,' he announced. 'Whenever I meet anyone in a passageway or room I'm going to trump them and take the trick.'

Thus when he came across Lord Wilisen and his jill, one the king of hearts, the other the queen of the same suit, he cried, 'You're trumped, Wilisen. Get to the bottom of the pack,' and clacked his teeth in amusement.

When all the cards had been allocated the king of clubs had been left over. There was no noblestoat for it. Thus Pompom had become a face card, the king of clubs. The heights of power went immediately to the jester's head. By the time he had stalked the castle corridors and disposed of a number of lower cards, he was feeling like a *real* king.

'Off with his head,' he shouted at those cards of his suit which he took prisoner. 'And off with hers, too! Into the dungeons with them. Let them rot in the oubliettes. Death to all other common cards. I am king, I am king, I am king.'

Noblestoats rolled their eyes and gritted their teeth as they too began to fall prey to the king of clubs.

Finally, the overexcited Pompom saw a figure in the bailey and ran up to clutch its shoulder with his claw.

'Ho, got you, you sneaking cur – get thee to a bakery and bake thy fat head!'

When the victim turned, Pompom suddenly found himself under the glare of Prince Poynt.

'Ho yourself, King of Clubs. Sneaking cur?' murmured the prince, silkily. 'Fat head?'

An electric feeling of fear rippled through Pompom's body making even the tip of his tail quiver.

'My liege – I – I – I thought you were someone else.'

'Obviously. Now I think *you're* someone else, King of Clubs. I think you're one of Flaggatis's rats in disguise. I think you're a spy. Do you know what we do with spies? We bake *all* of them in the oven. Not just their heads, but the whole spy, until it's cooked right the way through.'

'Ahhhh,' sighed the jester in despair. 'My liege, I – I'm not a spy. I'm your funny little Pompom, whose jokes keep you sane in this time of terror.' Pompom whipped off his king of clubs costume. 'Look, see, it's me underneath. Please, sire, may I be excused the rest of the game? I'm not feeling too well. I think I've had a touch of the sun.'

'I think so too, Pompom. Why don't you go and lie in a bath of icewater to cool yourself down. Don't get out until I've got time to come and see you and make sure this fever has departed your poor body.'

Pompom's lip curled up in distaste. 'Icewater, my liege?'

'Icewater, from the deepest well in the castle. I shall come and test the temperature at any time, so don't try to fool me, will you, Pompom. Off you go now.'

The jester left the game and went to take his punishment with a banging and a whimpering.

Others were playing the game according to its

merits. Little twos, threes and fours of any suit, mostly kitchen paws and milkmaids, were trying to hide in nooks and crannies, to avoid being leaped on by picture cards – nearly all noblestoats and their wives – or perhaps a sergeant-at-arms who was a nine or ten of clubs, hearts, diamonds or spades. It was indeed fun and Spinfer was praised for his originality.

Fun for everyone, except the prince's sister, Sibiline.

'Why can't I play?' she demanded of her brother. 'How comes it's just you jacks and the married jills?'

Now Sibiline, who was not a raving beauty but was quite attractive in a sharp sort of way, was not the sort of stoat who was left out of games without protest. Sibiline had a strong personality. She was the sort of jill who could wear a silly hat with such aplomb that when she walked into a room full of nobles she made them feel as if they should be wearing exactly the same style of headwear. She was a presence.

Her brother was eternally exasperated with her.

'You can't because you're a princess. There are no princesses in a pack of cards. Only kings, queens and jacks.'

'Well, there are no princes either.'

'The *jack* represents the prince,' replied her brother, repeating what Spinfer had told him. 'The knave is the son of the king and queen. They have no daughters. I'm an only child.'

'You're nothing of the sort,' snapped his sister, 'you're not a human so you can't be a child and if I'm your sister how can you be an only?' She stamped her four feet, one at a time. 'I *want* to play. You must make a princess card, just for me.'

'I can't do that, it wouldn't be right,' he argued,

wilting under this barrage of words. 'Please, Sib, don't cause such a fuss. We were enjoying ourselves till you came along.'

'I know,' she said, brightly, 'let's play Happy Families instead!'

The prince was genuinely shocked, given the way he felt about his relatives. 'You must be joking,' he winced.

'I want to enjoy myself too,' snapped Sibiline, her face changing again as she screwed up her pretty features into a hideous expression of fury. 'You invent a princess in the pack or I'll make your life unbearable.'

Sibiline was not the sort to mince words.

Spinfer was consulted for a solution.

'It's true there are no princesses in a deck of cards,' replied that able valet, 'but I'm sure we can accommodate Her Royal Highness. What about the ace of hearts? There's no reason why aces should not be female. I think it an entirely suitable card. A single blood-red heart! The symbol of faithfulness and constancy. It is purity and worth combined. One heart, standing alone, strong yet with a sense of vulnerability, our princess, Sibiline . . .'

'You talk a lot of tosh, Spinfer,' replied Sibiline, 'but I get the drift. All right, I'll be an ace – the ace of hearts – but bear in mind that in this game aces are high and hearts are trumps.'

'I'm a trump,' whined her brother, 'and I'm spades.'

'Spades have been trumps long enough,' replied Sibiline. 'Hearts are trumps now. That makes me the strongest card in the pack. Any king or queen, of any suit, who gets in my way will be taken without mercy. Lesser cards will be swept aside. And puny jacks of spades? Why, I eat *them* for breakfast.'

'It's not fair,' howled her brother. 'You always spoil my fun!'

But he had to put up with it. Sibiline was the only stoat in the princedom who could bully Prince Poynt. She now sailed around the castle, digging out all sorts of hidden cards – from under beds, behind toilet doors, amongst the boxes in the attic – and subjected them to merciless takings. Soon she had piled tricks up in the throne room, where Poynt sat and sulked, and they milled around listlessly wondering when the slaughter would be finished and they could start a new game, perhaps canasta or bridge – something really complicated which would put Sibiline off from playing any more.

In the middle of all this misery, a guard came bursting into the throne room.

'My prince,' he cried, falling on his belly, 'the rats!'

Prince Poynt shot up in his throne. 'What about them?'

'Look!' cried the guard, pointing to a window loop.

All eyes in the room stared at the spot.

Outside the rats had built a tall spindly tower which swayed like a pine above the battlements. From the top of this tower half a dozen rats were leering at those in the castle.

With a cry of anguish Prince Poynt rushed outside onto the battlements. It was true. The rats could now see over the hessian screens from the top of their new tower. They jeered and sneered at the prince, calling him foul names, accusing him in their own tongue, saying that he had betrayed his own brother, King Redfur, for the crown of Welkin.

'I did not,' cried Poynt, desperately. 'Don't you say such untruths.'

'*Asssssassssseeeen!*' they jeered.

283

'Am not, am not, am not.'

But they clacked at his protests. More and more rats climbed the tower, to shower him with insults and provoke his anger. They wound him up and watched him skittering about the battlements, trying to defend himself. In his acute distress the prince sent for Spinfer, feeling the stoatservant had failed him now in both the cards and the rat problem.

'Look what's happening,' moaned the prince, 'I won't even be able to go to sleep without their watching my every move.'

Spinfer surveyed the situation as more rats climbed the tower and added their tongues to the growing tumult. 'Not so, my liege – this will be very short-lived.'

'What do you mean?' asked Poynt, with hope in his voice.

Spinfer replied, 'I mean that the physics of the situation will soon return things to our favour.'

'Are you talking drivel again?'

'No, my liege, good common sense. Watch the tower.'

Prince Poynt stared hard at the hated rats as they swayed on top of their tall structure. They were a massed ball of writhing bodies now, the inmost rats gripping the top of the tower and those on the outside gripping their comrades. Prince Poynt shuddered. To him they were like a ghastly ball of maggots or something. It made him sick to look at them.

They screamed abuse. They called him names. They attacked his character.

Then, suddenly, as he continued to stare, there was a terrible cracking sound. The rats began screaming in a different tone now. Some fell to the ground immediately, dropping from the ball at the top of the tower like maggots falling from a piece of suspended meat. They plunged to their deaths, hitting the hard earth below with horrible thumps. Then the whole tower began to keel over.

With cries of terror the ball of rats went crashing to the earth, some of the rodents escaping with their lives when they fell into the moat. Soon Prince Poynt was left standing on the battlements, once again hidden by his hessian screens.

'Spinfer, remind me to promote you one of these days,' he murmured. 'I'd like to do that.'

'Yes, my liege, and might I suggest you change the game now? What about "Snap"? Aces have no power in snap. No single card does. You just wander around looking for jacks or whatever you might be yourself and shouting "Snap!" whenever one comes into view. I should think you would be good at that.'

Prince Poynt rather thought he would be good at it too. After all he created such fear in everyone except Sibiline they would be scared to open their mouths when they saw him coming. And Sibiline was an ace, so he would not have to snap her.

'What brilliance, Spinfer. I used to think your master the tops, but now . . .'

'Now you know where he gets it from,' muttered Spinfer, out of the prince's hearing, 'but let's not crow too much, for the sheriff has his uses too.'

The prince did not hear of course. He was not meant to. He was on his way to see how Pompom was soaking in the bath of icewater he had prescribed earlier. By the time the prince got to him the jester had a good fierce cold flowing, which might have turned to something nastier if he had not been released.

Chapter Thirty

In the town below Castle Storm the rest of the band of outlaws were beginning to get worried about Sylver, Mawk and Scirf. They themselves – Luke, Alysoun, Wodehed and Bryony – had with the help of Link investigated every underground nook and cranny below the town streets. They had found nothing. Now they were concerned that Sylver's presence in the castle had been discovered and that he and the others had been imprisoned.

'Perhaps they've been captured by Pommf de Fritte, or even Torca Marda,' said Luke. 'We ought to be doing something.'

'We were told to wait here,' Bryony said, biting her bottom lip. 'I think that's what we ought to do, though I agree it's horrible to sit here doing nothing while they may be in great danger, but there's no other choice.'

Finally, Bryony went to ask the advice of that fine sturdy knight, Clive of Coldkettle, as he left his copper kettle nest one morning. The red squirrel with the eye-patch and inward-curling tail was concerned. His reaction to the news, as with most things, was to Bryony a little alarming. She wished she had kept her fears to herself.

'So the greys may have my friend Sylver in their dungeons, eh?' He struck the air with a balled claw. 'This calls for all-out war. We shall storm the battlements and settle our differences once and for all.'

'Er, isn't that a bit extreme?' queried Bryony. 'I mean, a lot of grey – and red – squirrels might die. After all, we haven't any proof of anything. Perhaps we just ought to wait a while?'

'Nonsense,' bellowed the sturdy pear-shaped squirrel, his red eyebrows and white whiskers quivering, 'we'll overrun and sack the castle. My knights will engage with the greys and eliminate them once and for all. We'll see who are the best out of the reds and greys. Who likes grey dawns? No-one. Who likes red sunsets? Everyone. Those greys are a blot on the colour of the landscape. They have to go.'

Bryony tried to plead with the swashbuckling red knight, but he would not listen. He roused everyone in the town and made them strap on such armour as they had. Some merely had breastplates and shields of wicker, being too poor to own metal trappings, but there was great excitement in the air. There was to be a full parade in the town square followed by an attack on the castle. Castle Storm was about to be stormed.

Even the coven of moles was roused from its musty hideout. Griselda, Mathop, Osmand, Gowk, Spavin and the rest of the flea-bitten, moth-holed witches were told to report to the parade. They turned out reluctantly. War was not their thing. They were better at turning creatures into puddles of candle wax from the comfort of their lair. They offered to do this very thing to Pommf de Fritte, rather than take up the sword, but Clive of Coldkettle would not hear of it.

'Dishonourable,' he said. 'Anyway, you've tried it before and it never worked. De Fritte has Torca Marda's magic to protect him. No, you get out here with the rest of the sprogs and if you can't march in time then shuffle your feet to a tune in your heads.'

The parade was a magnificent affair. Clive of Coldkettle loved military parades. He would have one every day if he could have roused the same enthusiasm from his fellow knights. He liked to see gleaming spears all in neat rows. He liked to see his officers in polished armour that flashed in the sun, standing quietly at the heads of their squadrons, their colourful jay-feather helmet plumes waving in the wind. There was enjoyment for him, walking around the ranks inspecting his troops, commenting on a polished button or a leather harness.

'This is the stuff,' he told Bryony. 'This is what animals were made for. Pomp and circumstance. Showing off. Jolly good. Excellent. Lots of brisk orders flying around. Lots of clashing of weapons. Buckles glinting. Silent ranks of determined mammals. Fear and expectancy in the air. The bagpipes stirring, slowly rising to a wail, until suddenly you can recognize a martial air. The kettledrums rat-tatting. The trumpets and sackbuts blaring.'

His eyes were shining as he wiped away a tear from his good eye with a quick paw. Brimful with emotion, but holding himself tightly in check, Clive continued.

'Then the parade itself begins. Ranks of animals moving as one, like a single great menacing beast on the march. Crunch, crunch, crunch, crunch, crunch – paws and claws on gravel, marching in time. The tunes of glory on every animal's lips as they strut with puffed chests and proud faces. Plenty of "left wheels" and "by the rights" and "eyes fronts" Banners flowing, flags fluttering. Love it. Love it.'

'Well,' she replied, cautiously, 'I don't mind

the *parading* part so much as what follows.'

'Blood and gore?' he queried, raising his famous red eyebrows. 'Guts and stringy bits? Heads bursting like rotten fruit, leaving pips and juice all over the ground? Stuff of life, young weasel. Not squeamish, are we?'

'Well, just a bit,' she confessed. 'I mean, I know we have to fight for our rights sometimes, but I must admit I don't altogether look forward to all-out war.'

'Nonsense. Make a weasel of you.'

'I'm already a weasel,' muttered Bryony, but she did not want to provoke the red knight, so she said it under her breath.

Those on the castle walls saw the preparations for war being made down in the town and there was a call to arms there too. Grey squirrels began appearing on the battlements in businesslike attire. Pots of hot dishwater were lined up, ready to throw down on the invaders. Turnips were piled up as ammunition beside the siege catapults. Flags went up on flagstaffs and window shutters were closed.

By the time the troops in the town were moving towards the castle walls, the battlements were bristling with armoured squirrels bearing pointed and blunt weapons.

Before the order to attack could be given, something quite nasty happened to spoil Clive's fun. A huge cold shadow appeared over the town. There was a whirring sound in the air, like a thousand hornets on the wing. The shadow was shaped like a cross with a long tapering stem.

Looking up, with everyone else, Bryony was horrified to see a giant blue emperor dragonfly hovering above the town. Its vicious-looking jaws were masticating in anticipation, gooey stuff dripping from them to splatter on the cobbled square.

Normally a dragonfly eats insects, but this one was capable of taking a squirrel in one quick chew and gulp. Its face was hideous and its eyes were everywhere.

'It's the nymph from the lake,' cried Wodehed. 'It's hatched.'

The silence that immediately followed this remark was broken by a shout of despair from the battlements.

'Oh Gawd!'

Which told Bryony that at least Mawk was alive, if not Sylver and Scirf.

Hawker dragonflies are extremely efficient hunters who can fly at speeds up to sixty miles per hour. This one was no exception. One moment it was there above the town, hovering on its four massive wings, the next it had darted away somewhere out of sight. Then it was back again, its feet resting lightly on the roof of the guildhall, one of the tallest buildings in town. Its huge eyes, covering most of both sides of its head, were black and glittering, seeing everything.

'Run!' cried Clive, waving his sword. 'Get under cover!'

Already many red squirrels and other creatures were scuttling away to the safety of the houses. The dragonfly swooped and snatched up a squirrel in its mouth. There was no time to see who it was. The poor creature was gone in a single swallow and the dragonfly on to another red victim in the streets, then streaking upwards, snatching a grey from the battlements. It seemed the monster's appetite could not be satisfied.

'Do something!' cried Pommf de Fritte, hurrying to the safety of a tower. 'Somebody kill it.'

But no creature living had had experience of

dragonflies before this attack. The skies above the town had never darkened before. The beat of translucent filigree wings had not been heard prior to this terrible happening. What was more, when animals rushed into houses they blundered into stoves and knocked them over. Soon fires were raging throughout the town. No-one could get to the wells or pumps because the dragonfly snatched up anyone who went outside in the open.

Finally the creature had eaten enough and went away, leaving the town free to draw breath. Gradually they emerged from their houses and soon bucket lines were formed to help put out the fires. Even the greys from the castle walls came down to help, since the flames threatened to engulf the castle too. Choking black smoke was everywhere. Under this pall which screened their movements, Sylver, Mawk and Scirf joined their friends.

'What did you find?' asked Bryony in a lull. 'Did you get the clue?'

'No,' replied Sylver, sadly. 'Not a sight of it.'

'Oh well, we'll have to keep looking I suppose, once these fires are under control.'

The outlaws of course pitched in with the squirrels and other animals in order to quench the flames. There was not a creature in the town or castle, apart from Torca Marda and his two false priests, who were not there. Even Falshed was in the bucket line from the well, doing his best to help. The smell of singed fur was in the air and cries of 'More water here' were heard until deep into the night hours.

The next day, when the exhausted townsquirrels and others were clearing away the mess, the dragonfly returned to take yet more victims. It came without warning this time, not bothering to hover above the town to select the fattest prey. It simply flashed in from nowhere, out of the glare of the sun, and took one, two, three creatures, just like that. Then it was gone again, into the blinding east of the morning.

Griselda, the leader of the mole witches, then came to Clive of Coldkettle. 'We have to give it sacrifices,' she said. 'There's an old whipping-post, outside the town gates. I suggest we tie the victims to this post, then the dragonfly will not need to enter the air above the town.'

'Who do we give it?'

'Why, the old and sick of course,' said Griselda. 'Survival of the fittest. The halt and lame should be the first to go. They're a drain on the economy. Then those who can't see or hear, or are too old and senile to be able to look after themselves. When we run out of those, we'll look around for strangers – animals not from around here – creatures no-one from the town or castle will miss at all.'

Bryony was suitably appalled and not because she was one of the 'strangers' who might be sacrificed. 'You can't do that. Just because someone is sick or elderly.'

'Why not?' cackled Griselda. 'They're no use to anyone. Better off without them. Chuck 'em to the monster. We'll make a ritual of it. Turn it into a kind of festival, once a month. When we've run out of unwanted creatures and strangers, we'll ask for volunteers amongst the young.'

Torca Marda, now that the monster had recently eaten and was gone, had appeared on the scene. 'I agree with Griselda,' he said. 'We could make a festival of it.'

'What's that, *stranger*?' asked Sylver. 'You approve of this revolting plan do you?'

'I'm not the sort of stranger Griselda means. I have

my uses. We're quite close, the members of the coven and I. While you – you weasels have nothing. You're a burden on the town. You simply eat our supplies but do no work. You brought nothing with you and you have nothing to offer. I think you should be the first on the post myself.'

'I'll decide that,' said Clive of Coldkettle. 'You keep your nose out of our affairs, stoat.'

Torca Marda glared at Clive but wisely kept his peace.

'Wait a minute,' Wodehed said, breaking the silence. 'There are other things we can do. All right, it seems too big, too fast and too much in the air to be attacked with swords and clubs, but what about getting it on the ground? We could use magic, or hypnotise it, or something. Once we've got it on the ground we can swarm all over it and destroy it.'

'You think it would work, Wodehed?'

The wizard shrugged his shoulders. 'We could give it a try.'

Chapter Thirty-One

To Torca Marda's disgust the arrival of the dragon-fly had the effect of uniting the reds and greys against a common enemy. It was to his advantage that they remained hostile to one another, so that he could ensure support in capturing Sylver and his band. However, Pommf de Fritte would not hear of imprisoning the outlaw weasels because it would seem like an act of bad faith to Clive of Coldkettle. The weasels were Clive's guests, not his, and were therefore untouchable.

The Grand Inquisitor had even tried getting into de Fritte's good books by offering his usual services with a click.

'Is there anyone you wish tortured at the moment, sire?' he murmured to the grey knight while they were at dinner. 'Anyone you would like to hear screaming for mercy? My assistant priests and myself are free at this point in time. Anyone you would like put in the Iron Maiden, or burned with red-hot pokers, or put under a dripping tap until they go mad?'

'No-one I can think of,' replied de Fritte, looking at the inquisitor as if he were a garden slug. 'But if I ever think of someone, I'll let you know.'

Foppington, who had overheard the conversation, had a look of disgust on his face. 'I thwear you are a nathty little thtoat, Grand Inquithitor. One of theath dayth you'll end up under one of your own torture machineth.'

'Merely doing my duty,' murmured Torca Marda, silkily. 'Merely offering my services to my lord, Pommf de Fritte. My loyalty to him is unquestioned.'

'Are you thuggethting my loyalty ith not?' said Foppington with narrowed eyes.

Torca Marda was aware that Foppington's paw, as ever, was on the handle of his deadly sword.

'No, no, of course not,' he replied hastily. 'We are all, I am sure, dedicated to the lord of the castle.'

That had been a nasty moment for the Grand Inquisitor and he finished his meal quickly then excused himself.

Later, Torca Marda paced the chapel floor, with Orgoglio and Furioso trotting along behind him.

'Maybe we should make sure the weasel Wodehed's magic doesn't work,' suggested Orgoglio. 'Then Clive of Coldkettle will be upset with them.'

Torca Marda thought about this for a moment, then decided it was not good enough.

'The menace of the dragonfly will still be here and the squirrels united in their cause. What we have to do, somehow, is ensure that the weasels *worsen* the situation.'

'How do we do that?' asked Furioso.

Torca Marda glared at his priest. 'That's what I'm trying to work out, you idiot. I don't have instant answers for everything. Put your own brain to work on it, such as it is.'

Furioso gulped and stared at the floor. 'Yes, Your Grace.'

Falshed was also there, sitting in the corner, looking as gloomy as he felt.

'And you too, Sheriff – you can think, can't you?'

'That's what I'm doing,' replied Falshed, but he was not thinking about how to discredit the weasels. That would only make the inquisitor's position stronger. He was trying to work out how to capture Sylver himself, so that he could steal a march on Torca Marda.

'Your Grace,' said Orgoglio, 'please consider – we don't have to do anything – nothing at all – that is, we can assist matters to continue as they are.'

'How do you work that out?' asked Torca Marda.

'It's well known,' replied Orgoglio, 'that Wodehed is a poor magician. His spells almost invariably go wrong. Left to Wodehed's devices the outlaws are courting disaster, by giving that creature Wodehed licence to use his magic.'

Torca Marda ceased his pacing to think about this.

'Do you know,' he said, 'I do believe you're right. Just to make sure, we'll interfere a little in the process, but secretly. I don't want to be accused of warping Wodehed's efforts at destroying the dragonfly. Good, good. Let's get our heads together and think about this.'

The impatient Furioso asked, 'What can we do then?'

'I was thinking,' said Torca Marda, idly crushing an innocent little beetle which had been quietly travelling along one of the chapel's windowsills, 'that we might double, triple or even increase Wodehed's efforts ten-fold.'

'You mean,' sniggered Orgoglio, 'that whatever he does wrong will be made ten times worse by us. But secretly, so no-one knows about it.'

'Exactly,' murmured the Grand Inquisitor, popping the shattered shell of the beetle into his own mouth. 'That's precisely what I mean.'

*　　*　　*

Wodehed, however, had no intention of relying on his own magic alone. He knew he could not stop the dragonfly with his unreliable magic. But being a magician he knew where he might be able to obtain the right help. Torca Marda was to be disappointed if he thought he could interfere.

While Torca Marda's evil conference had been in progress, the outlaws had been reunited. Bryony and her crew met Sylver, Mawk and Scirf just outside the castle walls. There was no great demonstration of affection – weasels are a bit reserved that way – but their eyes showed they were pleased to see one another again.

'No luck then?' asked Luke.

Scirf shook his head. 'We searched the whole maze and got nowhere, chum. We was even attacked by a ghoul, but we soon dealt with *him*. He's not even maggot meat now.'

Alysoun then explained to the three from the castle that Wodehed had put the band on the line.

'He's promised we'll deal with the dragonfly, using his magic, so now we have to support him.'

Scirf looked at Wodehed. 'You sure you can do this, mate?'

'He's got to now, hasn't he,' said Sylver, 'whether he's sure or not. What's the idea, Wodehed? How do we go about this?'

'Special plants,' said Wodehed. 'Herbs known only to wizards and witches. There's one called *shrinkage*, which we might use to make the dragonfly smaller. And another called *shatter*, which would dash it to a thousand pieces. Yet another named *stretch* would turn it into something long and thin. Many, many more . . .'

'Have you got any of these special herbs?' asked Sylver, fairly sure of the reply even before it came.

'No,' said Wodehed predictably. 'We'll have to find some.'

Scirf said, 'The first place to try is those moles – if anyone's got anyfink like what we want, they have.'

There was a general murmuring of agreement. The whole band trooped off to find the coven of moles. They were heartened to see when they entered the gloomy place where the moles resided that there were dried herbs and plants hanging from the rafters. Wodehed spoke to Griselda, telling her what the outlaws wanted. The soothsayer shook her head.

'Don't keep any of those. Most of our herbs are for curing illnesses and such. We're *good* witches, we are. We just tell sooths. They only place you'll find a herb of the kind you want is in the secret garden.'

'What secret garden?' asked Wodehed, hopefully. 'Where?'

'Sessile's garden. All plants ever known to the world grow there. But nobody is aware of where it is except Sessile.'

'Sessile? Where does this Sessile live?' asked Sylver, taking over the questioning. 'We have to find him quickly.'

'*Her* – she lives in the Forest of Lost Birds. There is a forest, east of here, where those migrating birds who fall behind their leaders, or get lost in mists and fogs, finally find a resting place from their wanderings . . .'

'I often wondered what happened to them,' said Scirf. 'After all it stands to reason some of 'em are goin' to lose their way when they're flying halfway across the world.'

'Well,' Griselda replied in that grating voice of hers, 'now you know. Sessile's forest is like a tall landmark, you see. She herself stands forty-five metres high in her stockinged feet. The exhausted birds – geese, starlings, whatever – can see her from a long way off in the air, and know they can find refuge and food in her forest, no matter what the time of year. But you'll never find her from the ground.'

'Why?' asked Scirf. 'What's she look like?'

Griselda cackled. 'Sessile is an oak tree. She's hidden in a forest of oak trees. How are you going to find a tree hidden in a wood?' The soothsayer cackled again. The other witches in the coven cackled with her. They seemed to enjoy a good cackle.

'Never mind that,' said Sylver, a little irritated by their attitude to a serious request, 'how do we get to the Forest of Lost Birds?'

'Just follow a lost bunting, or wayward petrel, and you'll be on the right flight path.'

Mathop, Osmand, Gowk and Spavin fell about, rolling on the floor, cackling like demented hens.

Once outside the coven's den the outlaws took stock.

Sylver said, 'The soothsayer told us the forest lay in the east – we'll set out in that direction and hope for the best – Bryony, Scirf, Wodehed and myself. The rest of you stay here. Keep out of the way of the Grand Inquisitor, but keep a weather eye on him and on Sheriff Falshed. Keep asking about secret passages too. We'll be back as soon as we can with the herbs Wodehed needs to destroy the dragonfly – speaking of which . . .'

They could see the terrible creature now, darting swiftly through the air above the town. The outlaws ducked into doorways as the dragonfly shot down for a victim. It found a grey squirrel attempting a short dash between towers on the battlements of the castle. In an instant all they could see of the poor grey was his or her tail, sticking out like a bottle brush from the corner of the dragonfly's mouth. Then that too disappeared down the maw of the monster.

Bryony shuddered. 'We have to deal with that fiend soon, or there'll be no-one left in the town or the castle.'

The following night, while it was still dark and they had the shield of the night to protect them from the dragonfly, Sylver and the three outlaws he had chosen to accompany him set out eastwards of the castle. This was across a lonely moor with very little to offer in the way of food. There were forests of oak there, but these were stunted little groves hidden amongst the clusters of rocks. They were dwarf oaks, covered in lichen and moss, hunched down in clefts in the landscape where they were out of the way of the vicious freezing winter winds.

The weasels followed narrow paths across the moor, travelling past ancient tors with strange shapes that made their fur stand on end. Becks running through craggy gullies hindered their passage, as did boggy areas around which they had to travel. In the night they slept in such hollows on the bleak landscape as they could find. One morning Sylver woke with the dew on his pelt to discover they were not alone.

They were surrounded by at least a thousand ptarmigan.

'Egg-stealers,' said a huge cock bird, kicking Scirf awake with his sharp claws. 'Nasty little egg-stealers.'

' 'Ere, watch it,' said Scirf, rolling away from the ptarmigan's talons. 'Don't be so free with your feet.'

Now normally a weasel would not be afraid of a ptarmigan, but the outlaws were surrounded by the birds. Not only that, many of the ptarmigan were indeed cock birds – big yellow fellows with shiny white wings and black stripes through their eyes – who looked very formidable. There were sharp beaks a-plenty amongst these barrel-chested yard birds and their glittering eyes were not the friendliest the outlaws had ever encountered.

'Hold on a bit,' said Scirf, 'I've never pinched an egg in me life.'

'So *you* say,' grated another large male. 'But can you vouch for your mother?'

There seemed to be nothing the outlaws could reply to this and they slowly got to their feet wondering if they could make a run for it. The big cock bird who had first spoken read their body language and shook his head.

'Don't even think about it,' he said. 'Don't move a scratchy inch. We've been waiting a long time to get our claws on one of you fellows. Now we've got four of you – all together – and you're not going to get away lightly.'

Chapter Thirty-Two

The leader of the ptarmigan clan was called Colin and he was a big mean fellow with heavy-lidded eyes. Colin and his clan of ground birds came from the mountainous isle of Rood, far out in the North Ocean where the animals spoke an older language, had a culture quite different from that of Welkin. There were older mountains there, like worn teeth, covered in purple and white heather. There were good tall pines and forests of bracken. Deer shared the same land, eagles the same sky.

The islanders considered themselves fairly superior creatures. Rood Island poetry had a lot of words like 'saywhut' and 'wisna' and 'pattle' which meant nothing to weasels from the mainland. They were known to have a good oral tradition: stories of myths and legends passed down from father to daughter, mother to son, by word of beak. They were usually sad tales of love in the snowy mountains, or fierce tales of clan wars.

The clan had been shipped to Welkin by the humans, when they ruled the land, but were at last planning to return to the home of their ancestors. Rood was in their blood. Welkin was rich in many things – corn for instance, which was precious fare – but they would rather starve out on the isle than live a wealthy life in a land they did not know or love. The breezes smelled sweeter there; the skies were a paler blue; the winters were crisp and cold and clean on the feathers.

Sylver and the other outlaws were told to lie down in a peat hollow while their future – if any – was discussed by the clan council. They could hear Colin ranting and raving, arguing with some of the female members of the council. Though his accent was such they could not understand the words at a distance, they had no doubt he was calling for the death sentence.

Finally there was silence as the ptarmigan sat around a camp fire and stared into the flames. The light gleamed on their brown feathers, making them look as if they were formed from burnished bronze. All around were hundreds of ptarmigan, all patiently waiting for the judgement of the council. Finally, Colin stood up, stretched his wings, and then walked over to where the outlaws were resting their heads.

'Well,' he said, 'first the good news: you're not going to be pecked to death – in fact, you're to be allowed to live. It's against my better judgement, mind, but I've been overruled by the council. If it were on our own isle you'd certainly be scratched off the face of the earth. But I suppose I have to agree that this is your country and we're the visitors here, so the bad news – from your point of view – is it's been decided you should be enslaved instead.'

'Slaves?' cried Scirf. 'I'm not goin' to be no slave to a ptarmigan, and that's that.'

'Who will you be a slave to?' asked Colin.

'No-one. I'm not going to be a slave to anyone.'

Colin clucked and shook his head, pecking something invisible from the dust at his feet. 'That's where you're wrong. You're to run the gauntlet and then to become slaves. When – or rather if – we ever get back to our homeland, you're to come with us. Egg-stealers like you are getting off lightly with a bit of a pecking and a slave collar, that's for sure. Of course . . .'

Here Sylver leaned forward to listen, for he knew there would be a loophole somewhere. If the ptarmigan had decided not to kill the weasels – and it must be remembered that in general weasels had stolen the eggs of ptarmigans since time began – then there must be a reason for it. Now he was going to learn from Colin what the council had said.

'Some of us are not of the clan, so to speak,' said Colin. 'Some of us, you may have noticed, are not even ptarmigan as such, but capercaillies and red grouse. That huge rufous fellow over there is a capercaillie. He spoke up for you, said our first priority was to get back to Rood. Well, here's your chance to help us. If you can find us enough apples to make a skin for our boat, then you'll get off with just running the gauntlet.'

'Skin for your boat?' repeated Bryony. 'What are you talking about?'

The ptarmigan cock bird took on an air of superiority. 'Even ignorant Welkiners like you must surely have noticed how waterproof the skin of an apple is?'

Bryony shrugged and looked at the other weasels, who all raised their eyebrows. 'Haven't even thought about it,' she said. 'I suppose it is – but what of it.'

'Not *suppose* it is – it's jolly well certain sure it is,' snapped the ptarmigan. 'An apple hangs out there on a branch in the pouring rain, day after day, but it doesn't fill up and get all spongy and soggy inside, does it? So the skin of an apple *has* to be waterproof. Stands to reason. We plan to cover our boat with apple peel before setting sail for Rood.'

'What boat?' asked Scirf.

Colin looked at him with narrowed eyes. 'Oh, yes, you'd like to know that, wouldn't you, eh? What, so's you can ambush us at the launch? Or maybe send out a pirate ship to board us on the high seas? I've got your number, weasel, don't you worry about that.'

'How will you get the apple peel to stay on the shell of the craft?' asked Sylver.

'Overlap it. Stick it on with tree sap,' said the ptarmigan, nodding as if he were the greatest genius of all time. 'Tree sap, you may have noticed, has certain waterproof properties in itself and is certainly very adhesive. Try to get it off your claws after you've been scratching a tree trunk! No problem. We'll get back to our native isle, that's for sure, weasels. The thing is, can you save your own lives by helping us to make it?'

'Why don't you fly back to Rood?' asked Bryony. 'You've got wings.'

'Too far,' replied Colin. 'Some of us might make it, others definitely wouldn't. We're not distance fliers, us mountain birds. Better to go by boat than risk losing some of the clan to the cruel sea.'

The rest of the council had begun to crowd round the four weasels now, including the big capercaillie and one or two rather tough-looking red grouse wearing false wattles on their heads.

'Up yours,' snorted Scirf, before Sylver could stop him. 'Go fly into a mountain.'

One of the red grouse rushed at Scirf and stood menacingly before him, staring him in the eye.

There were cries from amongst the ptarmigan.

'Go on, put the head across him, Robbie.'

'Let him have it a-tween the eyes.'

'Give him the Rood Island nut.'

But the capercaillie stepped forward, strutting out determinedly, putting one claw in the front of the other until he was alongside the red grouse.

'There's to be none o' that here, Robbie,' said the capercaillie, quietly. 'No unnecessary violence. The weasel will be running the gauntlet. You'll get your chance.'

Still the red grouse did not move, as if he were making up his mind whether or not to make a swift lunge at Scirf with his head. Scirf was certainly in danger of losing an eye. His mouth, ever hasty, had got him into trouble before.

Sylver stepped swiftly forward. 'What my friend meant to say, in his awkward way, was "Up your apple tree" or rather, up *our* apple tree. Then you can fly into your mountains with – with the help of our apples. We have many, you see. Or at least our patron does, Lord Haukin. His vast orchards are a sight to behold.'

'Granny Smith's?' queried Colin the ptarmigan, with an excited note in his voice. 'Cox's Pippin? Golden Delicious?'

'Braeburns,' interrupted Bryony, who knew of apple matters. 'Braeburns with good tight thick skins.'

'Braeburns,' repeated the ptarmigan, as if intoning a prayer to the god of morning. 'Why, they've got the best skins of any apple out there.'

'Is that so?' said Bryony. 'I hadn't realized. Well, they're Braeburns all right. Not your russets with nasty browny crinkly skin, nor your softy costards.' The knowledgeable Bryony, who knew more about cultivated and wild fruit than a respectable meat-eating weasel should, was just getting into her stride. 'Of course, you could say the slack-ma-girdle apple has a good skin, or even cap-of-liberty. John-apples aren't too bad in that area either, nor Laxton's epicure, but I suppose I have to agree that there's really nothing to beat an unblemished Braeburn . . .'

'Braeburns.' The word went out softly amongst the ptarmigan like a leaf on the wind. 'They have Braeburns.'

It was a sacred word, worthy of a priest's mouth.

The capercaillie came forward now and the red grouse went back to his place in the council. 'How do we get these Braeburns?' he asked. 'Do you have some with you?'

Sylver shook his head. 'None with us – but we'll bring you seven barrelfuls in the autumn.'

Colin cried out, 'That's very likely. Let them go and we'll never see them again.'

'You have my word as an honourable weasel,' stated Sylver. 'I will return.'

He kept the words simple, but spoke them with conviction, and the capercaillie believed him.

'The weasels must be set free,' said that particular councillor. 'We have to let them go on the promise of seven barrels of Braeburns.'

One of the red grouse rushed forward. 'No – no – you know what happened when we let that stoat loose last year. *He* promised to come back again, with some Rosamunds. We never saw him again.'

'We never *expected* to,' snorted the capercaillie, 'you know that. A *stoat's* word?' If a capercaillie could have spat on the ground in contempt, this one certainly would have done. 'In any case

307

Rosamunds can't even compare with Braeburns – they're not in the same league. A Rosamund is a throwaway apple, while a Braeburn is worth its weight in corn. I say we let them run the gauntlet and then release them.'

'Can't you just sort of release us?' asked the venerable Wodehed. 'I've got a soft skull. I'm not sure it'll stand up to a lot of pecking.'

'No, I'm afraid that part is unchangeable,' said Colin the ptarmigan. 'You have to run the gauntlet. The stoat had to do that. Every carnivore we get our claws on has to do it. You have stolen our eggs for centuries, taken our young, destroyed our families, interfered with generations of ground birds.' He turned to look sympathetically at the elderly wizard. 'How old are you? You might get off on age.'

Wodehed told them his years at his last birthday.

'Hmmm, in that case perhaps you should stand aside, old weasel – but the rest of you – prepare for the run.'

The ptarmigan, red grouse and capercaillies now formed two lines with an avenue between them. They were very excited, pecking the ground to sharpen their beaks, scratching away at the dirt to hone their claws. This was the famous gauntlet run and they were going to get their corn's worth.

'Ready, steady, GO!' cried Colin, who was first in line.

The three weasels dashed down through the two lines of birds, who pecked at their heads, slashed with their claws at shoulders and bodies as they ran past. The weasels were fast and snaky, managing to avoid many of the vicious beaks and claws, but they could not dodge them all. When they finished the run they were covered in marks, their pelts missing chunks of fur where the hairs had been plucked out.

'That hurt,' said Scirf, rolling down on his stomach, exhausted. 'That flippin' well hurt.'

'Not as much as losing a chick,' remarked a hen bird, passing them by. 'Believe me.'

The weasels set off once more, but someone came running after them. When the bird got closer they saw it was Robbie, the red grouse. The grouse cleared his throat and then spoke to Sylver.

'Look, see, I was wondering . . .'

'Yes?'

'Well, could you get me a couple o' dozen of them apples for me, myself. See, I thought I'd make a swimsuit out of the skins – you know, cover my whole body with apple-skin – so's I'd be waterproof like one of they penguin birds. I could swim to Rood ahead of the boat, so as to get things ready for them when they arrived back at home. Arrange a welcome party, like.'

The grouse looked intently at Sylver, as if trying to gauge how his wonderful idea had gone down with the weasel.

Sylver sighed, stood high on his hind legs, and put a paw on the bird's shoulder. 'Take my advice,' he said, sympathetically. 'Go on the boat with the others.'

Robbie the grouse tried to look a little disappointed, but in truth was somewhat relieved. Having thought of this wonderful idea he had felt obliged to go through with it. But in truth the idea of swimming a hundred miles or so in cold water scared the living daylights out of him. 'You really think so?'

'I'm sure of it. Give the islanders a surprise.

Getting home will be enough for the rest of them, without the party, believe me.'

Robbie nodded his thanks, bid the weasels goodbye, and walked thoughtfully back to the ptarmigan feeding grounds.

Chapter Thirty-Three

Before they left the ptarmigan camp the outlaws obtained directions to the Forest of Lost Birds. Sylver asked Robbie how they would find Sessile and her secret garden once they got there. The red grouse said the soothsayers had been wrong about Sessile being lost and hidden amongst the other trees.

'You can't miss her,' he told them. 'She stands head and branches above the rest.'

The four weasels crossed the moor without further incident, finally sighting the tall oaks in the far distance around dusk. They decided to camp the night outside the forest and enter it in the morning when there was light. Soon they had a blazing camp fire, which kept the darkness at bay. Shadows danced with the flames. Each of them had some white crumbly vole cheese in their belt pouches which they ate, wistfully dreaming of better fare. They washed it down with stream water.

'I'd give my right forepaw to be in an inn right now,' sighed Scirf. 'A bed wiv clean sheets, a roast haunch of mouse and a foaming tankard of honey dew at me elbow.'

Bryony said, 'I'd settle for warm hay and hot apple juice.'

'My needs is simple,' replied Scirf, 'but yours is simpler.'

'Hang on,' Wodehed interrupted, 'let's see if we

can do anything about this. I'm supposed to be a wizard after all. Apple juice, eh, Bryony? I'm sure I should be able to conjure up something as simple as that. It doesn't need to be a barrelful after all – a bottle or jug would be enough.'

'Go on then,' said Bryony, looking interested. 'See if you can magic us some juice.'

Wodehed stood up. He took some powder from his belt pouch and threw it in the flames of the fire. There was a flaring of blue and green. He performed certain gestures with his paws and forelimbs, magic symbols which he traced in the air. The moon slid behind a cloud and the breeze grew in force. Taking these as good signs, Wodehed then spoke the words of the spell.

He intoned: *'Lord of Darkness and of Light, give us some apple juice tonight!'* He made several more gestures in the air with his paws, spat into the fire ('Is that absolutely necessary?' asked Bryony) and shuffled his feet.

A whistling noise was heard out on the moor, which swiftly became louder. A serious wind struck up, swirling old leaves into a pillar, then dispersing them again. A wolf howled in the distant hills, calling for the moon to return.

Finally, something came whirling out of the darkness of the forest trees and struck Scirf on the back of the neck.

'Oi!' yelled the ex-dung-watcher.

He picked it up. It was a gnarled old crab-apple with a withered skin.

'There's your apple juice, wizard,' clicked Bryony in merriment. 'Still inside the apple.'

Wodehed grumbled, 'Why can't I ever do things properly?'

At that moment the sky rained shrivelled

crab-apples by the thousand, thundering down on the weasels and the earth around them like hailstones. The apples only stopped falling when the weasels were up to their necks in them. The group emerged, bruised and shaken, and stared at the mountain of wizened-skinned crab-apples that had fallen from heaven.

'Well I knew I was bad,' said Wodehed, 'but not *that* bad.'

'You don't know your own magical strength, you don't,' complained Bryony.

Sylver said, 'I suggest we all try to get a little sleep. We have a long day ahead of us tomorrow.'

They got their heads down, but sleeping did not come easy. The wind was beginning to gust. Clouds scudded across the face of the moon. The trees tossed their heads this way and that, thrashing each other. Perhaps it was this violence among the branches which had flung the crab-apple at Scirf. In any case it was impossible to sleep deeply. The outlaws tossed and turned by the flaring embers of their fire, dozing fitfully the whole night long, until dawn crept from behind the forest.

It was then they slept more soundly, for the wind died with the coming of the light. Consequently the sun was quite high above the horizon when Sylver actually woke. He was alarmed by the lateness of the morning and tried to get up. Something held him tightly down however.

He felt as if he had been bound paw and claw.

'Help me, someone. I can't move.'

There were the sounds of struggling around him as others woke and attempted to get to their feet.

'Neither can I.'

'Nor me.'

'Me neither.'

313

All four outlaws had been trussed in the early hours and were now at the mercy of any hostile traveller. Who had done this thing, and why, was unknown to them. They were so well bound they could not even raise their heads to look at the ropes, where the type of knot used might have told them something of their captor or captors. They were securely pinned to the earth. Sylver could not see any wooden or metal stakes, but he supposed they must be there somewhere.

They lay there helpless for what seemed a century, then voices were heard. Sylver saw no point in keeping quiet. Even if the voices belonged to enemies they could be no worse off than they were now.

'Help us!' he called. 'Over here!'

The chatter stopped and footsteps were heard scampering over the dead leaves on the edge of the forest.

'Well, well, look at this!'

Sylver, who had been straining with his bonds and had his eyes closed, opened the lids to see a mammal towering above him. It was a furry creature, a ferret to be precise. One of two ferrets he knew well. The other came into view now, staring down at him with an amused expression.

'Who is it?' called Bryony. 'I can't see.'

'Rosencrass and Guildenswine,' Sylver said, 'two dubious ferrets from Castle Storm.'

'Now, now,' said Rosencrass, 'there's no need to be insulting. You're in no position to insult anyone, are they, Guildenswine?'

'Not at all,' replied the other, clicking her teeth.

'What are you two doin' here?' asked Scirf. 'Aren't you supposed to be up to mischief?'

'We are,' said Guildenswine, 'and you're the

314

object of the mischief. We've been paid handsomely to despatch you. You've made it very easy for us. We hoped to catch you asleep last night but we had some trouble with a troop of ptarmigan. All we were doing was taking a few eggs for a feast and they chased us to kingdom come.'

'We got away though,' sniggered Rosencrass. 'And we sent one of them to his maker.'

'You killed a ptarmigan?' gasped Bryony. 'You could have talked yourselves out of it with little more than a few pecks after running the gauntlet.'

'He got in my way,' snarled Guildenswine. 'Anyway, he wasn't a ptarmigan. He was some sort of grouse. A red one with a wig which fell off.' The ferret held up a false wattle and flapped it back and forth in amusement. 'One of those who came up after called him Robbie, or something. He died like a good 'un. They seemed pretty concerned about him. Gave us time to get away.'

Sylver groaned. 'You killed Robbie? There wasn't much harm in him.'

'So *you* say, squire. He wouldn't let us alone.'

'No,' said Rosencrass. 'The other birds seemed willing enough to let us go, when they couldn't catch up, including a big capercaillie, but this Robbie character wouldn't stop the chase. Oh no, not him. When he *did* catch up to us, he kept burbling something about apple-skins, pleading with us for an opinion on some idea he had about swimming to Lord knows where. Got on our nerves. So we did away with him. How about *them* apples, I told him, as he breathed his last. He didn't seem to see the funny side of it.'

'You murdered him – for *annoying* you?' gasped Bryony.

'Just as we're going to do away with you four,'

315

admitted Rosencrass. 'You lot cause too much trouble. Plenty of animals want you out of the way for good.'

'Plenty of animals?' Sylver muttered. 'You mean Torca Marda and his priests.'

Rosencrass gave a click of his teeth. 'Well, at one time Torca Marda thought he might take you alive and present you to Prince Poynt. It seems the Grand Inquisitor has now given up on that idea. Instead he's paid us to do away with you. He can still claim the credit for your disappearance. He's hoping Prince Poynt will let him go back to Castle Rayn. Then who knows? When you have Grubelgut's address, anything can happen, can't it?'

Bryony gasped. 'I get it. Torca Marda is going to have Prince Poynt poisoned. That's all that apothecary Grubelgut is good for – manufacturing poisons in those chambers of his.'

'Grubelgut is brilliant,' agreed Rosencrass. 'He can make a deadly poison you can't see or taste, or even detect in the food after it's been eaten. You simply drop dead from it several days after you've swallowed it. Some foam at the mouth first, or clutch their chest and cry out in pain, but most just go glassy-eyed and drop stone dead where they stand.'

Guildenswine said, 'A bit of destroying angel toadstool here, a smidgen of death-cap mushroom there. A touch of deadly nightshade. A soupçon of adder's venom. A pinch of peppered laburnum seeds. The whole dish garnished perhaps with some very unsavoury rhubarb leaves. Makes a nice going-away meal.'

'I hadn't realized what dangerous creatures you two were,' growled Sylver, 'or I would have taken you more seriously.'

'I should have thought,' sniggered Rosencrass,

316

'that you would have been glad to get rid of Prince Poynt.'

'Not that way,' Luke said. 'Not by poisoning his food.'

Guildenswine became impatient now, to get the dirty business done and out of the way. 'Have you got your dagger out, Rosencrass?'

'I have, Guildenswine.'

'Then let's chop them about a bit, cut their throats, and then go back to Torca Marda to collect our reward.'

'Suits me, Guildenswine.'

A knife flashed in the sun above Sylver. He waited for it to descend, to be plunged in his breast. The blade never came down. Instead there was a swishing noise followed by the sound of someone choking. He turned his head slightly to see something wrapped around Rosencrass's throat. It looked like a hairy rope with a tapering end. Rosencrass was trying to peel it away, without success. It was a few moments before Sylver realized that the rope was in fact a tree root.

The dagger had fallen to the ground beside Sylver. Rosencrass disappeared from sight, still gagging and coughing, probably trying to speak. There was a dragging sound as if the ferret were being pulled away somewhere. Sylver guessed it would be into the forest. There were no tree roots other than came from the woodland behind him.

'Are you three all right?' called Sylver, after a while. 'Still there?'

Each of the other outlaws confirmed they were still alive.

Scirf added, 'Guildenswine was near me. She got whipped away by somefink. Some sort of rope.'

'Tree root, I think,' replied Sylver, trying to get

317

hold of the dropped knife with his fingers, but finding it was just out of reach. 'Did she leave anything behind?'

'Her dagger,' replied Scirf. 'It dropped onto me chest. 'I'm just trying – to – jiggle – it – down – near – my – ah . . .'

'What?' asked Sylver.

'Got it! Got it in me paw.'

Scirf was silent for a few minutes, obviously trying to get his breath back. Finally he spoke again. 'Look, I've been thinkin', Sylver. If them two scruffs was whipped off by tree roots, then that's what's probably got us tied up, ain't it? No point in trying to *cut* through a tree root, especially when I'm all trussed up like this. Tree roots is as tough as the tails on grandfather pigs. I'm going to try to get the blade of this dagger into the embers of the fire. I'm lying right by it and I think I can reach . . .'

'Good thinking,' replied Sylver.

There was another period when no-one was speaking but everyone was hoping.

Scirf finally spoke again. 'Right. The blade's red-hot. I've still got it by the handle. If I squirm – a – bit – I can press the blade against the root around me wrist – there – ha, it don't like it. It's peelin' off. Now another one – yes – here we go. Soon be out of this lot. And another.'

Within a few minutes Scirf was free. He reheated the knife blade then dashed around getting the others loose. The tree roots which had bound them were curling away as if in pain, like long tentacles of grey-white hairy flesh. These octopus-like arms disappeared into the forest, to be dragged down holes and beneath the soil, from whence they had come. The outlaws moved away and were soon out of range of the forest.

318

'Look, this is no good,' said Sylver. 'How are we going to find Sessile if we can't enter the Forest of Lost Birds. She and the other trees are obviously protecting the birds. They won't let us near the place. I'm at a loss as to know what to do.'

'We could go back to the ptarmigan camp,' said Bryony, 'and ask whether one of them will act as our messenger. After all, if the forest is protecting birds, then a ptarmigan should be able to get through all right.'

'After those two ferrets have killed a red grouse?' Sylver said, shaking his head. 'We won't even be asked if we have an excuse. I'll bet the whole ptarmigan camp is just waiting for the next unfortunate weasel, ferret or stoat to wander into the region so they can fall on it and peck it to bits.'

'Sylver's right,' said Scirf, shivering. 'Colin is going to be as mad as a snake with backache. He's not going to ask whether we had anyfink to do with them two ferrets. He's just going to give out a blood-curdling war cry and urge his horde of mountain birds to trample over us and stamp us into the ground. To him we're weasels, cousins of them murderin' ferrets, and he'll want revenge for the death of Robbie the red grouse.'

'So?' asked Sylver. 'Any more ideas? Anyone?'

Chapter Thirty-Four

The weasels decided they had no choice but to attempt to enter the Forest of Lost Birds. If they were forced out, then they would have to think again, but they had to try at least. Sylver led the way, followed by the other three.

As they slipped under the first row of trees and entered the half-light of the forest, those roots of trees which were showing above the surface soil quivered. Deeply bedded clay shuddered beneath their feet. Fungi, ferns and wild flowers trembled. The whole woodland was alive, truly alive, and it stirred like a huge prehistoric beast disturbed at its supper. The weasels felt as if there were a thousand eyes on them. Scirf uttered what sounded suspiciously like pagan curses. Sylver remained silent and watching.

When nothing untoward happened the forest settled back down. The weasels could sense that it was still a prickly beast, its pine needles standing on end, spiky and spiny. But for some reason it had decided to let the outlaws proceed.

'I think it threw out its roots to hold us hostage when the ferrets killed the red grouse, maybe thinking we were also to blame. But now it has the true culprits,' said Sylver, 'it's prepared to be less hostile towards us.'

That might have been so, but still, four weasels in

a wood filled with birds would not leave everyone at ease, and they knew they were being watched closely.

Deeper into the green world they went. Here there were shafts of sunlight like golden pillars thrust through the leafy ceiling of leaves. The undergrowth was mostly browning bracken and briar, but not a hindrance to weasels who could slip through the densest patch of brambles without being scratched.

Soon the weasels were aware of many birds around them.

There were arctic terns, cuckoos, sand martins, fieldfares, swallows, barnacle geese and redwings: many different kinds of birds that migrate for summer and winter. These were those who had fallen behind, become confused, had lost themselves. They had been guided by some unknown star or carried by a friendly wind, into this magical wood to rest their weary bones.

These lost souls chattered to each other from branch to branch, bough to bough, each trying to tell the story of how they got lost. Others shouted their more exciting tales back. No-one was really listening. When you have been through a terrible experience you expect others to listen to you. You do not have much time for their personal yarns.

'Anyway,' a cuckoo with a strident voice was yelling, 'I suddenly found myself in this thick cloud. I tried to listen to my body compass – which way shall I go? Which path shall I take? – but I couldn't find the direction . . .'

'What happened was,' screeched a redwing, 'the sun was slanting off the sea, blinding me you know, and before I knew it the others had wheeled away out of sight . . .'

A barnacle goose bellowed from a pond in a glade,

'I was supposed to be the leader, but someone said, "You fall back for a minute, get your breath, I'll take over." The next thing I knew I'd fallen asleep and dropped into the ocean. Narrowly missed being eaten by a great white shark, but I managed to peck it on the nose and drive it off . . .'

Suddenly there was utter silence as this remark found a home in every other bird's ear.

A swallow said slowly and carefully, '*You* drove away a *great white*?'

The goose shuffled and riffled its feathers in embarrassment. 'Well, I suppose that's a *bit* of an exaggeration, but I did see a shark – at least I think it was a shark – it was a sort of pointy thing in a lump of foam . . .'

The noise started up again, now this liar had been exposed for who she was. One was allowed to embellish the truth a little, but it had to be within reason. An outright lie was not considered good form amongst the lost birds. The goose was hunched and silent for a while, but soon found her voice again, and before long was battling again to get her story heard.

The weasels made their way underneath the trees full of noisy feathered creatures. They knew they had to reach the centre of the wood, where the oak Sessile had her glade. They passed many other oaks, and large hornbeams, elms, twisted elders and alders, horse chestnuts and feathery ash trees. At one point they followed a stream into a clearing where a mossy bank invited them to lay their heads for a while.

Sylver was resting, lying on his stomach and staring at a pair of twin hornbeams ahead. Gradually he saw some something in their trunks. Clouds scudded over the sky ahead, like boats over a blue pond. The light kept changing, creating different moods with its shadows.

Suddenly the leader of the weasel band knew what he was looking at and he gasped, 'Do you see those faces – in the trunks?'

The others stared. Scirf got up and wandered over to the two gnarled tree trunks. Sure enough, now that he was close, he could see the shapes of two faces like wooden masks moulded in the bark. And there were the faint outlines of their bodies, below the masks. The mouths of these masks were slightly open, as if they were calling, crying for help. The eyes were wide with fear, the nostrils flaring in terror.

'It's Rosencrass and Guildenswine,' Scirf said, amazed. 'They're inside the tree. They're under the bark. You can see where they've had a bit of struggle, where the two trunks are knotty and twisted. Good grief, they're trapped inside – they can't get out. They're part of the trees now.'

The others crowded round, horrified. Sure enough they could see what might be a gall forming on the bark, but was really Guildenswine's nose. And a twiggy growth on the other tree was actually Rosencrass's ear. The trees had formed hollows in their trunks, sucked the two murderers into their boles and had closed their bark around them.

'What a prison!' whispered Bryony. 'I wonder if they'll ever get out? It would be no good trying to cut them out with an axe. You couldn't be sure of not hurting them. They'll have to live as trees now . . .'

The two terrified masks, one of Rosencrass, the other of Guildenswine, stared out at her mutely. Scirf, Wodehed and Sylver could see they wanted to scream, but they had no mouths with which to do it. Their efforts towards freedom were frozen in wood.

They might as well have been carved from real timber. Someday perhaps some human would come along and chop down the trees, cut these interesting faces from the bark, and use them as garden ornaments to decorate a lawn or flower-bed.

The weasels moved on, now knowing what their fate would be if they upset the Forest of Lost Birds.

Finally, after fighting their way through bramble and thicket, brake and briar, they reached a glade in the middle of the forest. There stood Sessile, mighty and majestic, overshadowing all else. There were no nests in her branches. She was far too stately to allow mere birds to decorate her limbs. Even the wind was respectful as it blew through her green locks, gently lifting the hem of her green regal gown. You would need to go a long way before you found another tree as august and splendid in age as Sessile. She was almost as old as her hidden roots, and they went back many decades.

Sylver stood before her, not at all embarrassed by talking to a tree, though he had guessed he would be.

'Sessile,' he said, 'Grand Lady of the forest. We come here to seek your advice . . .'

While the other outlaws stood a respectful distance, Sylver went on to explain to the elderly oak the reason for their visit to her forest. He told her about the dragonfly and its destructive attacks. He said he had no wish to kill such a creature, even though it was daily taking lives, but wished to put it out of action somehow.

After Sylver's speech the wind picked up speed and soon the weasels could hear a voice whispering from the foliage of the oak. Sessile was talking to them with her leaves.

'Weasels,' she said, '*you must take the herb called*

shatter *from my secret garden and burn it on a bonfire.
When the dragonfly passes through the smoke it will
splinter into a thousand fragments. I shall open my trunk.
You will enter to seek the secret garden of Sessile.'*

Soon the bark on Sessile's trunk opened and a
cave-like opening appeared. Clearly Sylver was
being invited inside. Bryony told him not to go in, to
remember what he had seen only a few minutes
before. She was of course referring to the prisons of
Rosencrass and Guildenswine.

'I must trust this ancient oak,' said Sylver. 'If I do
not return . . .'

'Then we'll chop it down,' Scirf said. 'Leave just a
rotten old stump.'

The oak tree shivered in disapproval at these
words and Sylver made Scirf promise this threat
would never be carried out, even if Sylver disappeared for ever.

Scirf agreed, sulkily, that he would not take an axe
to the trunk of the tree, even if she deserved it. The
trouble with Scirf was that he had no respect for
authority. He recognized no-one as being superior to
himself. In Scirf's eyes all creatures were of equal
status. Anyone who thought they were better than
the ex-dung-watcher got short shrift.

Sylver now stepped inside the maw of the oak and
soon vanished from view. To Bryony's relief the
trunk did not close around the departed Sylver. Scirf
remained suspicious and kept a weather eye on the
oak, but the other two were convinced of the tree's
willingness to help them. They lay down on the
grass and waited for the return of their leader.

And return he did, within quite a short time. With
him was a strange creature the like of which the
outlaws had met once before. This one had his arms
full of some kind of plant.

'This is a Green Man,' said Sylver, introducing the earthy, woody being. 'He normally lives in Sessile's secret garden, but he kindly offered to help carry some bundles of the herb for me, since my forelimbs are so small.'

The Green Man, a figure whose face was covered in warty projections that on closer inspection looked like twigs, fruits and fungi all tangled together to form his features, muttered some earthy words, which might have been, 'You're welcome,' or 'Least I could do'. Some effigies had never mastered the art of speech, not to any degree of usefulness. This Green Man, this mythical folklore hero of the forest, was one of those. In his world there was no need for words.

A Green Man was part of the forest itself. One never knew where the undergrowth ended and the Green Man began. He was a twiggy, leafy, fruit-mouldering figure formed from an oak's mat and mask. No flesh and blood covered his bones, but mud, peat and humus stuck to them. And the bones themselves were of stick and stone, not living matter.

His hair was a coot's nest and his eyes chanterelle mushrooms. His mouth was an overripe plum, split along the seam. In place of nostrils were two empty acorn cups, side by side. Hands, feet, legs and arms were clay that creased with every movement. Body was of mashed nuts and fruit, plastered together with green leaves. Painted over various parts of his figure was a natural blue dye called woad.

Sorrowful were his eyes and sorrowful his mouth, for the Green Man is not an outwardly happy creature, though some weasels say contentment lies at his core.

Once the Green Man had passed his share of the herb over to Wodehed and Scirf, he quickly re-entered the oak. Sessile closed around the creature, lovingly. Sylver had tried to thank the Green Man, but the figure was gone before the words left the outlaw leader's mouth.

'What was the secret garden like?' asked Wodehed, a little envious of not having seen it. 'Was it beautiful?'

'Like no garden you've ever seen before,' said Sylver, nodding. 'It was autumn, summer and spring all rolled into one. There were ripe apples and pears, dripping from the trees. There were daisies springing from the green turf. There were blue cornflowers blowing in the breeze.

'I followed a golden path through a wood, across a silver stream, down into a lovely vale. Every kind of plant known to mammal was there, cared for and tended by the Green Man and other mythical creatures of the garden.' Sylver sighed. 'It's the sort of place you hope you're going to, when you die . . .'

Now the outlaws set out again for Castle Storm, passing without incident through the region of the ptarmigan clan, for the birds had moved to a new grazing ground further north. The band noticed one small mount with a feather like a banner stuck on top of it. This was no doubt the grave of Robbie the red grouse and they went by it with the prayer for a dead stranger rolling between tongue and fang.

When they reached the town below the castle they found the dragonfly still wreaking havoc amongst the population of squirrels. The rest of the outlaws welcomed them back and there was a joyous reunion. Then they set about forming a plan to rid the skies of this menace.

Clive of Coldkettle told them, 'We will help you

all we can – just say the word. Pommf de Fritte has suspended hostilities until this fiend has been destroyed, so I'm sure if you needed anything from him you would not go away empty-pawed. Torca Marda has been promising every day to rid us of the dragonfly, but so far his efforts have come to nothing.'

'I would think it in the Grand Inquisitor's interest to keep the dragonfly on the wing,' Sylver responded. 'He thrives on chaos. Torca Marda likes nothing better than living in a place which is ruled by terror.'

'You might be right, Sylver,' Clive replied, 'for I've seen nothing positive come from his actions.'

'What about the coven of moles? Have they got anywhere?'

'They seem to be waiting for your return. Griselda has locked up the barn where the soothsayers live and has not poked her nose outside. In fact she maintains that since she and her kind are creatures of the underground, this villain of the skies is not her concern at all.'

'So, it's as we thought,' said Sylver to his outlaws. 'It's up to us to clear the air of this monster.'

Chapter Thirty-Five

Sylver decided the decoy would have to be him.

Scirf protested saying that *he* wanted to do it. He stated that he had actually wanted to be a decoy all his life; that he had been *trained* for such work; that he was being prevented from doing the very thing he was good at. In fact he offered every argument in favour of himself being the decoy you would have thought that Sylver was denying the ex-dung-watcher his birthright.

'I used to practise at bein' a decoy by laying on the ground lookin' dead,' Scirf told his leader, 'when I was not much more than a kitten, tempting eagles and hawks, so to speak. I was really good at it. Much better than what you'll probably be, you not having any training as such. Some raptor – that's what birds of prey is called – some raptor would come along and when they swooped on me I'd jump up and run like a devil . . .'

Sylver took no notice of the protests from the ex-dung-watcher. He knew that Scirf was being noble and that the other weasel considered himself the most expendable of the band of outlaws. Scirf thought they could do without him if the need arose, but Sylver had decided a long time ago that the courageous Scirf was one of the most valuable of creatures.

They asked Pommf de Fritte's permission to use

one of the towers on the battlements. On such a high place Sylver could attract the dragonfly's attention easily. Also it was important that the smoke from the magic herb did not touch anyone else, otherwise they would get the same treatment as they hoped to inflict on the dragonfly.

The leader of the grey squirrels gave his consent immediately.

'Anything to get rid of that monster,' said de Fritte. 'We're losing squirrels at the rate of one a day. I had thought that Torca Marda's magic would have destroyed the dragonfly by now, egad, but the Grand Inquisitor has proved worse than useless in this matter.'

'Speaking of the Grand Inquisitor,' said Sylver, 'where is that eminent gentlestoat?'

'Oh, somewhere in those tunnels he likes to frequent,' replied de Fritte, airily. 'Let us not worry about the inquisitor – let us concentrate on the monster.'

Sylver found it difficult not to worry about Torca Marda when the outlaw knew that the stoat was planning some way of killing him.

The outlaws built a huge bonfire on the top of the North-west Tower. The wind was blowing offshore over the lake and would take the smoke away from the castle and town. Sylver intended to climb the flagpole in the centre of the tower to attract the dragonfly when that creature was coming in over the lake.

Bryony was positioned near the bonfire with a tinder-box, so that she could light the fire when the time came.

The dragonfly was fond of coming at dusk and dawn, when the light was poor and he could be on the town before they knew it. Of course he did not fly in every evening, or they would all have remained indoors. Instead he came at irregular intervals, so that some of them decided to chance it. They ran through streets or across the market-place to attend an important appointment, only to be snatched by the jaws of death leaving unfinished business behind them.

Sometimes the dragonfly would leave it a week before he came again. But just when you did not expect him to, he came the following morning. He was a most unpredictable creature. And there is always one mammal who decides the run is worth the risk – that they lead a charmed life. Being chewed and eaten by a dragonfly is not a pleasant experience. Bits of you stick out of the sides of his mouth as he flies away with your body: an arm wriggling here, a leg waggling there. Other half-eaten bits, perhaps like fingers and toes too small to get a firm grip on with large chomping jaws, fall off and drop to the ground.

So Sylver spent three evenings up the flagpole on the North-west Tower, waiting for something to swoop out of the scarlet sunset and attempt to snatch him from his perch.

On the fourth evening Sylver had managed to find a perch on that knobbly bit on the top of the pole, when something indeed swooped from the sky like a giant hawk. The dragonfly had come without warning. Bryony, on seeing the creature dive from the heavens, shouted a warning to her leader. Then she used the tinder-box, striking a spark which lit the lint. At last she made the flame with which she started the fire of faggots.

On top of the faggots was the magic weed.

Too late, for Sylver was yelling, trying to beat off the dragonfly with his paws.

The smoke from the fire was taken by the natural evening offshore breezes out over the lake. The dragonfly, its transparent wings whirring wildly above, fanned the flames. It hovered there as Sylver hung on the other side of the pole, using it as a barrier against the flying monster. Eventually the dragonfly whipped around the post too fast for Sylver to swing away and grabbed the weasel by the belt. It backed away ripping Sylver from the post. Then the creature headed out over the water with Sylver dangling from its mouth.

'Watch out, Sylver,' shrieked Bryony, beside herself with anxiety. 'The smoke!'

Sylver realized the dragonfly was flying right into the pall of smoke, just as they had wanted him to. However, the weasel outlaw leader had not intended to be with the creature when it did so. He reached up with his paws and desperately tried to cover the creature's repulsive eyes with his paws.

At the same time the other weasels had come out from hiding and under Alysoun's guidance were pelting the monster with slingshot stones. Still it flew on, blinded and troubled by flying rocks, towards the building column of smoke. Nearer and nearer it came to that area, while Sylver kicked out with his hind legs, trying to unsettle the creature further.

Finally, just before it entered the smoke it decided that enough was enough. This creature it had in its mouth was not worth the effort. The dragonfly opened its jaws and let the weasel fall down into the water. Sylver struck the surface of the lake with a splash and immediately started swimming, his nose above the surface like a water rat, towards the bank. Weasels are not that fond of water.

The dragonfly disappeared into the smoke.

Moments later there was a shattering sound, a sort of explosion of glass, then ten thousand normal-sized azure dragonflies came zipping from the cloud. They were like splinters of lapis lazuli with wings. They clustered like bees at first, soaring down on to the town that they had – as a single dragonfly – terrorized. Now they were harmless creatures, only able to eat tiny insects from the air. Within seconds they had cleansed the air above the town of midges, flies and mosquitoes.

Bryony was concerned about Sylver, who was swimming towards the harbour gate.

'Are you all right?' she called. 'Are you hurt?'

Sylver pulled himself out of the water and shook his fur free of water droplets. 'I'm fine,' he called back. 'Did we get it?'

'Yes,' she replied joyously. 'It shattered into thousands of bits.'

Above the outlaw leader the wind was beginning to disperse the smoke. It blew it out over the lake, scattered it, sent it skywards until it trailed into the darkening evening sky. Scirf had already doused the faggots. The fire was harmless. All in all the operation had been wholly successful.

The news quickly spread around the town and castle. Squirrels came out of their houses, their hearts light. They ran through the streets, calling to each other. Red squirrels danced across the drawbridge to embrace grey squirrels. Grey squirrels skipped through the alleyways of the town. Enemy hugged enemy, friend greeted friend. Flags were raised on poles, banners fluttered in celebration. Tables were soon dragged out into the streets, to be filled with nuts and raisins and other kinds of fare. Great barrels of honey dew were rolled down from the castle cellars. There was feasting.

'Hurrah for Sylver!' cried the populace. 'Hurrah for the weasel band!'

Clive of Coldkettle and Pommf de Fritte both came to see Sylver at the same time. The red and the grey knights stood either side of him. Almost as one they said to the weasel leader, 'Anything you ask shall be granted. You have saved town and castle from a terrible fiend. Tell us what you want and we shall endeavour to give it to you.'

Sylver took a red paw with his own right paw and a grey paw with his left. He joined the red and the grey together, so that the two knights were left shaking paws. They looked embarrassed by this demonstration which had been forced upon them by the weasel, but they nodded to one another.

'Now you are friends,' said Sylver. 'My wish is you should stay so and all the squirrels under your separate commands. There should be no more fighting amongst neighbours. What does it matter that one has a red coat and the other a grey? If you can't live amongst each other you should at least live peacefully side by side, trade honestly, do not cheat each other, and treat each other with the respect and dignity all animals deserve.'

A mighty cheer went up from both reds and greys on all sides.

Pommf de Fritte looked very grave. 'This is all very well,' he said, 'but what happens when there is a dispute? We shall fall to warring again.'

'I don't expect there to be agreement between you for all time – it can't be all sweetness and honey. What I suggest is that you set up some kind of mixed squirrel council, to discuss such disputes before they get out of paw. It's important to diffuse such situations. They must not be allowed to develop into feuds which involve the whole population on both sides.'

'You mean we should talk first,' Clive of Coldkettle said, 'and only take action at the last resort.'

'I would like you to consider settling your differences by discussing them,' agreed Sylver.

Once again the two knights shook paws and nodded to one another.

'If this is the weasel's wish, then we must obey,' said de Fritte.

'Agreed,' replied Clive.

The celebrations in town and castle were renewed with great vigour. Most squirrels were pleased with the outcome. There were some, of course, who were not. You cannot please everyone, no matter how hard you try. There will be those who will always have a dislike of others who are different from themselves.

But these are small mean creatures who do not matter in the general scheme of things – so long as they are not given the time of day when they speak of such things, so long as they are ignored when they talk of their hatred for those in red, or for those in grey, or when they harp on about silly differences in taste or culture. These shallow animals are frightened and insecure, worried that their way of life will be changed by the nearness of others who do things a little differently. They are not to be heeded, not to be given any importance.

'Personally,' said Scirf, 'I like different cultures. You get to taste all sort of new foods, listen to new kinds of music, hear unusual stories. You get to learn stuff you don't know about. Sometimes some animals do things a better way and sometimes not.

You get to swop ideas, see which is quicker or easier. That's my opinion, for what it's worth.'

Someone who had come down from the castle while all the celebrations were in progress, stood over Scirf and made a rude noise accompanied by a sneer.

'What silly drivel you talk, weasel,' said the newcomer. 'How uneducated is your reasoning. Creatures were born for strife. It is how they learn to defend themselves. Survival of the fittest. How does an animal become the fittest? By defeating all those around him, so his strength is the greater, so none dare attack him, so that any who oppose him are crushed and beaten down, afraid to rise again.'

The other outlaws and Scirf turned to see Torca Marda and his two false priests standing behind them.

'So you believe in brotherly love?' sneered Orgoglio.

'And sisterly affection?' jeered Furioso.

Scirf shrugged. 'You don't need to *love* your neighbour, not in that way. I believe you should tolerate those who are different from you. Live and let live. Nothin' wrong in that, is there? Better than bashing their heads in.'

Clive of Coldkettle and Pommf de Fritte had come to listen to the debate now.

'You mean,' said the Grand Inquisitor in a sinister voice, 'the way you broke the skulls of Rosencrass and Guildenswine? Those two innocent victims of your foul prejudices against stoats? Did you murder them out on the trail because of your vindictiveness towards Prince Poynt? Speak up now? Why have you killed two fellow travellers out on the road?'

Sylver spoke up now. 'We killed no-one. Those two agents of yours attempted to kill the four of *us*.'

'So *you* say,' snarled Orgoglio, 'but our reports are different. We heard you fell on them while they slept and clubbed the poor creatures to death. Our sources say you showed them no mercy, gave them no chance. You murdered them most foully, without giving them a chance to defend themselves.'

'That's a lie,' cried Wodehed, hotly. 'We never did any such thing.'

'So *you* say,' cried Furioso, 'but we hear differently.'

'Our witnesses,' smirked Torca Marda, 'tell us that it was a cowardly deed of vengeance towards creatures a little different from themselves, simply because they themselves had suffered under stoat rule. I say we hang these weasels from the gibbet now, before any more innocent creatures are murdered in their beds. I say we show them we are not prepared to tolerate blackguards and cutthroats in our midst. I say we hang them for a month, then burn their dried and crusted pelts, to warn other *strangers* not to enter the walls of Castle Storm, unless at their peril.'

Chapter Thirty-Six

'Just a minute,' said Clive of Coldkettle. 'This smacks a little of sour grapes to me. The inquisitor could not rid the castle and town of the dragonfly. Now that Sylver has done so, Torca Marda accuses the weasel of murder.'

'Yet,' Pommf de Fritte said, 'the two ferrets *are* missing – and have been so since the weasels left for the forest.'

'They're alwayth mithing,' interrupted Foppington, scornfully. 'They're alwayth up to thomething deviouth, thomewhere. I thuthpect they're thtuck thomewhere in the thecret pathageth under the carthel.'

Other squirrels both red and grey began to offer their opinions on the missing spies. Blodwin, Imogen and Eric Rood were inclined to think that they had gone north to Castle Rayn. Wivenhoe, Will Splayfoot and Goodsquirrel said they were almost certainly heading south. Derrière and Poisson d'Avril were sure that the two had gone east. La Belle Savage was inclined to agree with Foppington (whom she was secretly and desperately fond of) and supported his theory that the two ferrets were somewhere right under the feet of the crowd.

'They are dead, I tell you,' insisted Torca Marda. 'Let the weasel deny it if he dare.'

Sylver nodded. 'I think they are dead . . .'

338

'There you are!' cried Orgoglio. 'Condemned out of his own mouth – I say we hang them . . .'

'Let him finish,' growled Clive of Coldkettle.

Sylver nodded at Clive. 'Thank you. I was about to say the two ferrets followed us to the Forest of Lost Birds. On the way they ran into some ptarmigan, who had with them a red grouse. When the red grouse challenged Rosencrass and Guildenswine, they killed him and ran off.'

'How do you know all this?' sneered Furioso.

'The two ferrets told us so themselves. They never expected us to get back here alive. We were trapped by the roots of trees at the time and only managed to free ourselves by good fortune. When we later went into the forest we saw the faces of the two ferrets. They were trapped under the bark of trees. If they were not dead they were certainly imprisoned where no-one could reach them.'

'This fantastic story must be checked,' said Torca Marda. 'I shall send someone to examine these trees. If the evidence bears out what the weasel says, then he and his band shall go free. Otherwise they stand trial for murder. Rosencrass and Guildenswine were my guests at the castle. I shall defer to the judgement of the lord of the castle, Pommf de Fritte.'

Pommf de Fritte looked undecided. On the one paw he had clearly seen the weasels save the town from the scourge of the dragonfly. On the other paw he had to ensure justice was done, or there would be nothing but anarchy in the land. The weasels were the guests of his newly-acquired ally and friend, the red squirrel, Clive of Coldkettle. This knight had to be consulted when making the final decision.

'I think it would be best,' said Pommf de Fritte, finally, 'if the weasels are held under lock and key temporarily at the castle. They shall be confined to a room in one of the towers until we get proof of their story. If the tale they have told proves to be untrue, then they shall hang on the gibbet.'

Torca Marda looked smug and beamed at his two false priests, now sure of a victory.

'Yet,' said de Fritte, a hard note to his voice, 'if their story proves true, the Grand Inquisitor, Orgoglio and Furioso shall take their place on the gibbet, for bringing false witness against them.'

Now Torca Marda's expression changed to one of fury. 'You dare to question my authority?' he snarled at Pommf de Fritte. 'I am the Grand Inquisitor.'

'You are in the castle and town of the squirrels,' said Pommf de Fritte, coldly. 'You will abide by our rules and regulations while you are here. I have given my judgement. Clive of Coldkettle, you have some part in this decision, how say you? Shall this judgement stand, or not?'

Clive of Coldkettle was sure that his guests, the weasels, were speaking the truth. He decided there could be no harm in their being confined in the castle for a day or two. He nodded, staring hard at Torca Marda. 'I think it a very wise judgement. Who shall we send to the Forest of Lost Birds?'

'I know exactly who to send,' said Torca Marda, triumphantly. 'The Sheriff of Welkin will go.'

'Falshed?' cried Scirf. 'He hates us!'

'The sheriff is Prince Poynt's law-keeper,' replied the Grand Inquisitor. 'He is the Thief-taker General and is above suspicion, being the highest authority in the land when it comes to the law. The prince makes the laws of Welkin and the sheriff sees they are carried out to the letter. There could be no-one better suited for the task of discovering the truth.'

'I'm afraid the inquisitor is right,' said Pommf de Fritte. 'Sheriff Falshed is the law so far as stoats and weasels are concerned.'

Despite some reassurances from Clive of Coldkettle, the weasels were then taken to the castle and locked in a room in the North-west Tower. There they were left to languish, though Pommf de Fritte saw they did not go short of food. There was straw on the floor on which to sleep and a garderobe, or toilet, on one side of the room. Their spirits would certainly perish if they were left there for a long, long time, but anyway Sylver hoped Falshed would meet with an accident on his travels. It would be nice to think of the sheriff ending up locked inside a tree trunk, like Rosencrass and Guildenswine.

Three of the red squirrels – Wivenhoe, Imogen and Blodwin – promised the outlaws that if the sheriff came back with the story that the two stoats had been murdered by the weasels, then they themselves would set out and discover whether the report was accurate or not. This was heartening news to the outlaws, who could do nothing but sit around and stare out of arrowloop windows at the lake.

Wodehed of course tried to use his magic to free himself and his companions. He attempted to change Mawk into a bird, so they could let it fly through the arrowloop, promising Mawk he would change back into a weasel within twenty-four hours. But all that happened was that Mawk remained in weasel shape but was covered in feathers for a whole day. The plumes tickled his nose and armpits, but he was in no mood to laugh. After one or two more experiments with his magic, Wodehed was forced to give up, the others being concerned that he would do some real damage to one of them before he found any answer to their problem.

Two days later the weasels were surprised when the door to their prison was opened and someone thrust inside. The door was then locked again. They were astonished to see that the creature now imprisoned with them was none other than Sheriff Falshed himself. The stoat looked at them, appearing somewhat abashed. The weasels stared at the stoat. Finally, Sylver asked the sheriff what was happening.

Falshed got to his feet and dusted down his pelt with his paws. 'I'm a prisoner like you,' he said, disgustedly. 'And all because I've turned honourable.'

'You – turned honourable?' cried Bryony. 'That'll be the day.'

'It *is* the day, the hour, the minute,' said Falshed, dramatically. 'I am made honest.'

'How did that happen?' asked Luke, thinking there had been holy intervention. 'I mean, it's a miracle.'

Falshed looked awkward. 'Well, I went to the forest, as Torca Marda asked me to. It was a very dangerous journey, but I made it, though I was chased by ptarmigan and whipped about by tree roots. I saw the two ferrets, trapped in their tree trunks. Then I came back to report to the Grand Inquisitor.'

He paused and cleared his throat.

'It was my intention,' said the sheriff, shamefaced, 'to lie to the squirrels and say that I found the bodies of the two stoats with weasel-darts in them.'

'That sounds more like you,' said Alysoun. 'So what happened to change your mind?'

'The Grand Inquisitor repeated to me what he had said to Clive of Coldkettle and Pommf de Fritte –

how the Sheriff of Welkin was above suspicion and the highest authority in the land on the law.' Falshed's eyes suddenly had a light of defiance in them as he continued with his story. 'Torca Marda clicked his teeth in amusement as he told me that my office bore a sacred duty – the duty to uphold the truth – and therefore my word would not be questioned. If I said you were guilty, you would be hung from the gibbet, without fail.'

'So,' interrupted Wodehed, 'why didn't you pronounce us guilty then?'

Falshed looked proud. 'Because you were not. As Torca Marda was jabbering on about his great conquest over the truth, I began to see what a noble position I had and how I *did* have a sacred duty to uphold the law. If the prince had appointed me to do this work because he saw in me a scrupulously honest stoat, then I would be demeaning myself. I would be lowering myself to the level of the basest slug in the land, if I denounced you falsely.'

Scirf thumped the sheriff on the shoulder. 'Well done, Fally, well done. You've come good at last.'

'I wouldn't go so far as to say that,' answered Falshed, coldly. 'If I can capture you all and drag you before Prince Poynt, then I will do so. But I will not allow the inquisitor to bring me down to his level. You know he intends taking your head and presenting it to Prince Poynt, Sylver? And a number of other heads too, I've no doubt. In this way he hopes to wheedle himself into the prince's good graces. Once there he plans to employ the poisoner, Grubelgut, to dispose of my beloved master . . .'

Once Falshed was on a roll, there was nothing to do but interrupt him, or he would go on all night.

'Yes, quite,' said Sylver, 'but is de Fritte now with

Torca Marda? Why does the inquisitor have a key to this room?'

'De Fritte does not know I'm back,' replied Falshed. 'I suspect Torca Marda means to do something with us all before the grey knight discovers and questions me.'

'We've got to get out of here,' said Scirf, pacing up and down, 'before that fiend burns down the tower or somefink.'

He looked around him in frustration. Scirf felt responsible for getting them out of the room. He was the weasel with the quirky mind. It was up to him to think around corners and find a way to escape. He started by studying the drop from the arrowloop window. It was a massive distance to the ground and even if one of them was lean enough to squeeze through the thin arrowloop, they would be killed by the fall.

Next he looked around the room.

'The door to the stairs is too thick,' he muttered, as the others watched his brain at work, 'but what's behind this other door? The garderobe thing. Yeeessss. Now where does that go, I wonder?'

'Straight down about twenty metres,' answered Falshed contemptuously. 'Where do you expect it to go?'

Scirf did not answer the stoat. Instead he opened the door to the garderobe and inspected it. There was a stone seat, with a hole in the top. Scirf ignored the pong and stared down this hole into the depths below.

'I wonder,' he said. 'It's got to come out somewhere. Prob'ly into the lake. Anyone got a tinder-box?'

Bryony fiddled with the pouches on her belt and came up with the required fire-lighting equipment.

With Falshed's scorn still ringing in the room, Scirf lit a piece of rag and then dropped it down the garderobe hole. It fell, fluttering, down into the blackness. When it reached the bottom it burned very briefly then went out. Scirf nodded and put the tinder-box in his own pouch.

'Not twenty metres – about ten – then it slides off somewhere west – into the lake – must be.'

'What are you planning to do?' asked Sylver.

'Well,' said Scirf, 'I might hurt meself if I drop all that way down, even if it's soft and squidgy at the bottom . . .' Bryony and Alysoun winced and looked at each other. '. . . but if we form a weasel rope, so to speak, each weasel holdin' on to the tail of the one above, then we could get rid of about four metres.'

'I'm not forming part of any rope,' cried Falshed, backing away. 'You won't get me hanging down there.'

'You'll do as you're told, fellah-me-lad,' said Wodehed, the frail old magician. 'I've thrown bigger striplings like you down holes in the ground before – and you won't get the benefit of an animal rope if we have to lob you down, that's for sure.'

'Are you positive about this?' asked Sylver of Scirf. 'You don't have to do it, you know.'

'Can you think of any other way of gettin' out?' queried the ex-dung-watcher.

'No,' admitted the outlaw leader.

'Right then. Don't worry about me, I've fallen in the stuff before and it's as soft as rice pudding. I was on the barn roof once and fell down into the rhubarb dung. It didn't hurt a bit.'

Again, Alysoun and Bryony winced, and wrinkled their weaselly noses.

Mawk stared down the black hole in terror. 'I'm not doing it,' he said, flatly.

'Right,' said Scirf, completely ignoring Mawk. 'Me first. Falshed – you sit on the edge of the garderobe and let me hang down from your tail. Then you grab Mawk's tail . . .'

'I can't do it, I can't do it, I can't do it,' cried Mawk, hysterically, letting the words all come out with a whoosh of air which he had been holding in his lungs.

Scirf rapped him on the head with his paw to silence him. Scirf rarely took Mawk's fear seriously. He felt there was a courageous weasel somewhere deep inside Mawk, struggling to get out, and all you had to do was tell him so.

'. . . then Mawk, you grab Wodehed's tail, and so on, until we're all dangling down, with Sylver last, holding on to the edge of the seat . . .'

Falshed found himself forced forward into position. Soon Scirf was hanging from his tail. He then grabbed Wodehed's tail, who took hold of Alysoun's tail, who clutched Bryony's tail, until the animal rope was as long as they could get it. Sylver could hear Falshed's muffled groans of terror, somewhere down in the darkness of the deep hole. Then the rope got lighter.

Scirf had let go.

There was a kind of muted *splodge* sound, followed by silence.

'Get me out of here,' cried Falshed from the bottom of the living rope, 'I can't hold on much longer.'

Mawk, who was the next one up from him, gave out a stifled whimper.

'How do you think *I* feel,' said Sylver, straining, pulling himself and several others out of the hole. 'My tail is about to become dislocated!'

Finally, the rope was up and they were all out – all

except Scirf of course – and their heads ringed the smelly hole of the garderobe, staring down into the blackness.

'You all right?' called Sylver, his heart in his mouth. 'You there, Scirf?'

While this drama was unfolding in the south, in the north another dramatic event was taking place. Lord Ragnar and Lord Haukin had taken the field against a massive rat onslaught. The rats had been met with fierce resistance from the armies of the two stoat lords. Eventually, the stoats began to gain the upper paw, and soon afterwards the rat warchieftains turned and were on the run. Their warriors followed them, screaming at the tops of their voices, scrambling over each other's backs to get out of the way of the charging victorious stoats.

Unfortunately Lord Ragnar, being a big strong stoat, was quite an athlete. Consequently this lord found himself way out in front of his own troops. He was, as always, over-eager to get at the retreating rats. It was his intention to personally 'bag' as many rats as he could before his troops and the rest of the generals caught up with him – especially that 'namby-pamby Lord Haukin'.

' 'Ware the rat rearguard!' cried Lord Haukin to Lord Ragnar. 'You have no protection!'

Lord Ragnar took no notice of this warning, being the thick-skulled but courageous idiot he was.

At last the thing that Lord Haukin had feared might happen did so. On seeing one stoat way out in front of the others, some fifty retreating rats turned on Lord Ragnar. In their fury they overwhelmed the general, biting him in a thousand places. He struggled valiantly, roaring out his anger at their insolence. There were too many of them though.

They swamped him with their disgusting bodies. They tore at him with claws, struck him with blades and beat him with blunt weapons. He went down under a welter of blows from which no stoat could recover.

By the time Lord Haukin and the rest of the troops reached his corpse, Lord Ragnar was not even fit to be a doormat. He was holed in a hundred places. There was barely a patch of fur left on his body. The rats had taken out their spite for being bested in battle on the one they hated the most. They had literally cut, beaten and torn his pelt to pieces. Lord Ragnar was now only crow meat.

'You stupid bone-headed noblestoat,' growled Lord Haukin to the ragged, tatty bit of stoat hide lying on the ground, 'all you had to do was wait a bit . . .'

The fleeing rats flung back insults, crowing and boasting over the killing of Lord Ragnar. They had lost the day on the field, but they had taken Ragnar with them. Even as more of them were caught and captured, they chortled their glee.

Chapter Thirty-Seven

Prince Poynt was covered in beautiful white fur, except for the end of his tail, which was tipped with black. He liked this small difference in his coat – which was no different from that of the meanest serf, since all stoats keep a tar tip to their tail after changing to ermine – because it reminded him he was mortal. Princes get so puffed up with their own importance they often come to believe they are so special they will live for ever. They get to thinking they are gods. Prince Poynt knew that was a dangerous way to think. Such thoughts had been partly responsible for the death of his elder (by a few minutes) brother, King Redfur.

He was having his tail combed, and then trimmed with nail-scissors by Pompom, when a messenger burst into the hall.

'My liege!' cried the messenger, falling on his face and burying it in a volehair rug.

Prince Poynt was alarmed. He did not like messengers falling on their faces. It usually meant bad news was on the way.

'What is it? Speak up, stoat. You won't be harmed.'

'My liege,' said the messenger into the rug, 'Lord Ragnar is dead.'

Prince Poynt jerked upright so quickly that Pompom accidentally snipped off the tip of his tail.

There was no wound to the flesh but half the precious tar tip had gone. Pompom gave a strangled cry and stuffed his paw into his mouth. The jester was certain he was going on the gibbet. But the prince had not even noticed, so distraught was he by the news.

'Lord Ragnar? Dead?'

'Killed in battle by the rats, my liege,' mumbled the messenger deep into the thick pile hair. He had once been kicked up the bottom by Lord Ragnar for being slow with pouring the honey dew. 'They are dancing on his grave.'

'Aaagghhh!' cried the prince, jumping up, his head in his paws. He paced the floor biting his claws, absolutely stunned by the news. He had been sure that Lord Ragnar of Fearsomeshire would triumph. At school Raggy had been a big bully. He was brilliant at making animals confess to things they had not done, then punishing them for their confessed crimes. Raggy was a great friend, but a terrible enemy. Those who had snitched on Raggy were already neighbours with worms. Raggy had been the cause of half the suffering in the kingdom. He was so good at being nasty. Everyone was afraid of him and with good reason. If you upset him he would get you even if he had to sacrifice his mother to do it.

'Raggy dead? I can't believe it.'

'They have his head on a pole,' said the messenger, unable to keep a touch of glee out of his tone.

Raggy had been such a wonderful braggart, so terrifically uncouth. He could spit vole bones the length of the great hall. He could drink honey dew until he was violently sick, then start again on a new barrel. When Raggy blew his nose into his paw (then

350

wiped his paw on his companion's shoulder) you could hear it in the next county. Raggy could hunt, shoot and fish after being up half the night drinking, and make all the other nobles do the same, though they felt like death.

'My best friend, gone?' wailed the prince.

'They tossed his legs to the four winds,' sniggered the messenger.

Prince Poynt rounded on the fellow, glad to have a target to distract him. 'You're enjoying this, aren't you?'

'No, my liege,' moaned the messenger, realizing he had gone too far. By now he was so deeply buried in the volehair rug he was in danger of disappearing. 'But there is worse news.'

'What? What could be worse than the news that Lord Ragnar is dead? Now the rats from the east will join this lot outside my walls and before you know it we'll be overrun.'

'Precisely, my liege.'

Pompom shrieked, 'Oh, my prince, we'll be overrun. The rats will eat me. They're cannibals. They eat anything on four legs. They'll roast me and eat me. Save me, my prince.'

'Shut up, Pompom. Messenger, how do you know all this?'

'Lord Ragnar's stoats sent a message with his hunting-robin – it arrived just minutes ago.'

'The news could be false.'

'There are celebrations going on outside the walls. Flaggatis and his rats are joyously parading through their camps. They carry the wicker god they call Herman – they are shouting that they are going to burn him soon. Oh, and by the way, my liege – that's the rest of the bad news.'

Prince Poynt was becoming very irritated with

351

this messenger, but now the hall was beginning to fill with noblestoats, jacks and jills, who had got wind of the news. His sister Sibiline had also come into the hall. Everyone seemed to be there, from the scullery weasel up to the Lord Chancellor. They were staring at Prince Poynt, expectantly, waiting for him to give them some idea of what to do next.

'What is? What?'

'The note from Lord Ragnar's stoats. It said Lord Ragnar had found out that Herman wasn't really *Herman*, as such.'

'I don't care what the creature's name is. Who is he then? What difference does it matter?'

The messenger buried himself deeper into the rug. 'His real name is "Ermine". It's just that the rats can't pronounce it properly. You know what they're like, my liege, "Ermine" comes out sounding like "Herman".'

A chill went through Prince Poynt. Feebly, he said, 'I don't understand. What are you trying to say?'

The messenger lifted his head. 'It's *you*, my liege. You're the God of the Rats. You're their Great War God. Once the battle is over they will take you north and burn you on a huge fire. But they think you won't feel anything, because you're a god, see? You're immortal to them. They think we've been keeping you prisoner here, that you belong to them, and they want to turn you into smoke and send you back up to the heavens where you belong.'

Under his fur Prince Poynt went dreadfully pale. 'That disgusting wicker effigy covered in birdlime is supposed to be *me*?'

'The rats think it a good likeness,' murmured the messenger's voice, from the depths of the volehair rug.

'Flaggatis! He did this,' cried the prince. 'I thought it was a white rat. It looks like a revolting white rat. But it's actually – me.'

'It seems so, my liege. He told them we had captured you long ago. They want you back. It's really what this war is all about, what they're fighting for. They want to retrieve their god and send him back as smoke, up to his rightful place up on high. It's the hot seat for you, my liege, and the gibbet for us.'

Pompom let out a strangled cry. 'I say we let them have what they want,' he cried, wildly. 'Give them their god back – then they'll go home.'

Earl Takely gave Pompom a clip around the ear. 'Be quiet, weasel, this is no time for jokes.'

Pompom had not been joking, but he wisely fell silent.

'Is there any hope?' moaned Prince Poynt, collapsing onto his throne and draping himself majestically over the arm. 'Who will save us now?'

Sibiline stepped forward, calm and serene. She had her hunting-robin on her arm, with its head covered by its hood and the jesses hanging from its legs. Sibiline was fond of robinry, for it got her out into the countryside, when the rats were not there of course. Her robin brought her juicy worms to eat, which she cooked on an open fire with the Jill Guides group of which she was the leader. 'Twist' she called the meat.

'I have been in communication with Lord Haukin,' she said. 'Ragnar is not the only one bright enough to use hunting-robins as message-carriers. All may not be lost. We have a few days yet, before the rat army which destroyed that blustering fool Ragnar arrives outside our walls. Lord Haukin is on his way south to make contact with Sylver and his band of outlaws. They will then move north-westwards, to the sea . . .'

'What good will that do?' cried Prince Poynt, testily. 'All is lost. The rats are chattering about royal kebabs. I'm about to be barbecued.'

Sibiline shook her head impatiently. 'Listen, brother, stop feeling sorry for yourself and think just a minute. Lord Haukin and the weasels are aware that the dykes around the island are crumbling, which is why they want to bring the humans back, so the sea walls can be repaired. It's Lord Haukin's intention to break down the dykes even further, in selected spots, to flood the land. Hopefully the rats will be caught in the flood and swept away.'

Prince Poynt sat up quickly, as a murmuring went through the hall amongst his noblestoats. 'Will it work?' he cried. 'What about us? Won't we be drowned too?'

'Castle Rayn is on a mound. We'll be surrounded by water, but we should be high enough to be safe. Lord Haukin and the weasels will be the only ones at risk and they'll take great care . . .'

'I'm not worried about *them*,' snapped the prince, 'so long as we don't drown.'

The messenger who had first brought the bad news felt it prudent to stand up now. He sneaked through the noblestoats and was out the door in a twinkling. Later, if it all went wrong, he would not be punished. Prince Poynt could not tell one common soldier from another. Now that he was out of the prince's sight, he was away and clear.

Sibiline had not finished with the prince yet. 'There's just one stipulation,' she said. 'Lord Haukin wants some assurances from you first. Then I send this robin with the message that you agree.'

'Agree?' said the prince. 'Agree to what?'

'A pardon for the weasels. A *real* one. None of this going back on your word later. All your noblestoats are here, remember, to witness your word.'

Prince Poynt made a face and then nodded. 'All right, the weasels will be pardoned – if I live. If I die they are to be hung, drawn and quartered – and,' he remembered something the messenger had said about Ragnar, 'their graves danced upon.'

'And Lord Haukin had some addenda to that.'

The prince drew himself up to his full height of ten centimetres. 'Sib, you're my *sister*. Don't use big words like addenda. You know I'm not very bright.'

'And you'd do well to remember it. A postscript, some additions. Now, Lord Ragnar is dead. His county is the richest and most fertile in all Welkin. Lord Haukin wants it to be given to him. Lord Haukin is to be the Thane of Fearsomeshire.'

'And what happens to Elleswhere?' asked the prince, his nose twitching with irritation. 'Not that it's much good to anyone. All it comprises is a few woods, streams and fields, with Thistle Hall in the middle.'

'It should be given to Sylver the weasel. Sylver should be made Thane of Elleswhere.'

The prince sprang from his throne. 'Are you mad? Give a weasel a whole county? Why, they'll be thinking they're as good as stoats next.'

The hall started buzzing with the protestations of the noblestoats and the gleeful chatter of kitchen weasels.

'I'm merely passing on the message,' said Sibiline. 'I've no love for weasels as you know, brother, but this seems to be our only hope. If we want to live – if you don't want to be skewered like a shish – then

355

we have to agree to Lord Haukin's terms. He wants you to make the announcements of the promotions now, before I send off this robin.'

'Well I won't, so there,' said the prince, petulantly. 'I'd rather be roasted.'

Pompom howled. Noblestoats and their jills pleaded with the prince. Kitchen weasels set up such a wailing that the prince could not hear himself think. He knew he was going to have to knuckle under, but it hurt his pride deeply. He tried one more ploy with his sister.

'Couldn't we lie, Sib? Couldn't we just *say* we've made the proclamation and not do it?'

Sibiline now drew herself up to her full height on her hind legs. '*You* may have lost all honour, brother, but the integrity of the family is still strong in *me*. All that is noble has rested in the female bloodline of the royal family. If we are going to do this thing we are going to have to swallow our pride for once. So a weasel becomes a thane? So what? I hear this weasel intends seeking out the humans. That means Sylver will soon be sailing from Welkin. We shall probably never see him again. There are tempests out there – storms and squalls which take the most expert of sailors – and weasels are not sailors.

'Brother, you will make him a lord, he will build his boat, and set sail, and that will be the end of it.'

'By heaven, Sib, you always were the brains in the family.'

'Of course,' she said, simply.

'So be it,' cried Prince Poynt in his Town Crier's voice. 'Oyez, oyez, oyez. Hear it now and mark it well. Should Lord Haukin vanquish the rats, he is to be made Thane of Fearsomeshire. Should he be assisted in this endeavour by the – the – the . . .'

'The *weasel*,' prompted Sibiline, before her brother could choke on the word.

'. . . the *weasel* Sylver, of Halfmoon Wood, that said weasel – may his soul rot in the other place – shall be made Thane of Elleswhere. So let it be said, so let it be done. Right, that's all settled. Tea and biccys anyone?'

'There are no biscuits left,' said a weasel cook with her forelimbs folded over her breast. 'You ate the last one yesterday – my *liege*.'

Prince Poynt's face twisted. Already the weasel servants were becoming uppity. Next they would be sleeping in beds and asking to use the proper toilets. Give a weasel a stone, he thought, and they'll take a castle. Well, he would soon sort some of them out. 'If I don't get my elevenses,' he growled, rounding on the crowd of kitchen weasels cluttering up his nice hall, 'certain weasels will be baking biscuits in the torturer's furnace, down in the dungeons.'

There was a scuffling and scuttling as the hall suddenly emptied of weasels, leaving only noblestoats, guards and the prince and his sister.

'Now where was I?' said the prince, looking over his shoulder at his tail. 'Pompom was trimming . . .' The prince let out a wail of anger as he noticed that his precious tar tip had been severed in two. 'POMPOM!'

But the jester was nowhere to be seen.

Chapter Thirty-Eight

When the outlaws and Sheriff Falshed got no reply from Scirf they assumed he was dead. Mawk began to whimper something about drowning in muck, but the others quickly shut him up. Everyone was depressed enough as it was, without Mawk making things worse with his vivid imagination. Sylver stood by the arrowloop window, staring out at the sky, until the evening came. Then he gently suggested that everyone should get some sleep, to keep up their strength.

'What for?' moaned Falshed. 'We're going to rot here for evermore.'

Sylver was too depressed even to answer him. He had lost three of his band now, on this expedition, and still had nothing to show for it. They had not discovered the whereabouts of the humans and the whole thing had been a failure. It was not one of the outlaw band's best ventures. He fell asleep on the straw, his head tumbling with thoughts.

He woke when he felt paws on him, dragging him across the floor. 'Wha . . . what's going on?' he cried.

But before he knew it he had been bundled outside the door to the room in the tower and the lock turned behind him. He was being firmly held by two stoats, now recognizable as Orgoglio and Furioso in the light of the burning torches which stood in iron cages along the passageway. In the room behind him there was a commotion going on as the weasel band and Falshed woke to find him gone.

Furioso, who was carrying an inflated goose bladder attached to his belt like a balloon, clicked his teeth as they marched Sylver along the passageway to a door leading to the battlements.

'It's the high jump for you, my friend,' said that false priest. 'You're lucky. The Grand Inquisitor tossed a coin between torturing you to death or simply throwing you over the battlements down on to the rocks of the lake shore. The coin came down heads. You get a quick end.'

Soon Sylver was forced out into the night air, where he found Torca Marda waiting for him. Orgoglio had a sword out now, pointing at Sylver's chest. Torca Marda was also armed with a similar weapon. Sylver was forced to stand on the crenellations, in the gap between two stone teeth. Three swords were now at his throat. He looked back and down from the dizzying heights of the battlements to see the lake foaming around the rocks below in the near darkness.

'So, it's come to this,' said Sylver. 'I'm supposed to jump to my death.'

'How quick you are,' said Torca Marda, softly. 'Such a lively brain.'

'Bit of a waste, wouldn't you say?' said Sylver, an attempt at humour. 'Better to save it for a rainy day.'

'I'm so glad you can make light of your own death,' replied the Grand Inquisitor. 'Unfortunately you stand in the way of all my plans. In case you're wondering where the guards of the tower are, we have left them getting roaring drunk in a room down below. All it needed was a barrel of honey dew. If any of them come up within the next few minutes, it's been decided that you fell while trying to escape.

There's a rope hanging from the battlements. Clever, eh?'

Sylver glanced down. There was indeed a rope attached to the crenellations. He thought about trying to grab it when he was forced to jump, but it looked too close to the wall. Still, it raised his spirits a little, to think there was some slim chance of outwitting the Grand Inquisitor. 'And then?'

'Then the three of us will go down and collect your remains by means of a boat. But we will not return to the castle with them. Instead we'll make our way to Castle Rayn where I will present your head to Prince Poynt on a trencher. He will forgive me all my past transgressions of course and I will once more be a member of his court.'

Sylver said nothing. There seemed to be nothing left to say. Torca Marda pressed the sword to his throat.

'Jump, weasel, or be run through!'

Sylver was about to let go of the battlements and try for what would have been a hopeless and desperate lunge at the rope below, when a door creaked open somewhere and an apparition appeared on the battlements. Torca Marda and his two minions turned to look, expecting to see one of the drunk guards. What they saw instead was a hooded shape, a figure in a monk's habit about three sizes too large for it. Folds of cloth hung down, trailed after the creature, giving it an even ghastlier appearance than had the robe fitted.

There was an offensive odour in the air now, which clearly signalled that something was rotten about the creature. When the animal shuffled closer they could see a sign around its neck which was just readable in the moonlight. The word sent a chill of panic through the three assassins.

It read: MANGER – UNCLEAN.

The figure, whose face was completely hidden inside the hood, then rang a small copper bell.

'Unclean!' moaned the poor animal, which to the Grand Inquisitor stank of rotting flesh. ' 'Ware of the mange. Unclean. Unclean.'

Torca Marda stepped away from the figure as it approached him, a strange sound welling in his throat. When it seemed that the manger was heading towards the Grand Inquisitor, Orgoglio and Furioso jumped aside. They then scuttled away towards the other side of the tower, well away from the diseased creature who had interrupted their plans for murder.

Torca Marda was stumbling backwards, jabbing the air in front of him with his sword. His eyes were starting from his head and there was a look of sheer and utter horror on his stoatly features.

'Keep away from me!' screamed the inquisitor. 'By heaven I'll run you through . . .'

But the figure appeared to be blind, simply staggering forward on some inner impulse, perhaps half out of its mind, its brain eaten away by the dread disease. Torca Marda's blade went out, but he was shaking so much with fear it simply pierced through the monk's habit under the manger's armpit. It caught there as the poor sick animal continued to lurch forwards, its forelimbs outstretched, reaching for the Grand Inquisitor.

'Help me!' it croaked. 'Help me, Master of the Church of King Redfur, save me from my suffering. Give me your blessing! Let me kiss the ring on your paw . . .'

The hood went down towards the paw which held the sword and the Grand Inquisitor let go of his sword. He gave out a cry of terror, staggering backwards. His hind legs caught the edge of the battlements, his forelimbs windmilled as he fought to keep his balance, then with a last long terrified wail he was gone over the edge, his expression a rigid mask of fear.

Sylver watched his body fall down through the night air to crumple on the rocks below. The weasel could do nothing to save the inquisitor. Waves from the lake, whipped white and frothy by the wind, washed at Torca Marda's remains as his body lay there wedged between two jagged stones. The Grand Inquisitor was grand no more, but simply a pathetic rag-like figure with his soul now on its way to a place of harsh judgement.

Orgoglio let out a thin cry. 'Master!'

But at that moment the door to the tower opened and Pommf de Fritte, Clive of Coldkettle, and other knights of castle and town came pouring out.

'We heard someone yelling,' said de Fritte, 'while we were in the North-west Hall discussing the terms of our peace . . .'

Sylver turned to the two false priests, who without their master were nothing. They cowered against the side of the tower, their faces sullen. 'You two had better explain to the knights what happened here this evening,' he said. 'And make it the truth, or it'll be worse for you both in the long run.'

'It wasn't my fault,' cried Furioso, stepping forwards. 'I was just obeying orders . . .'

The two stoats gave a garbled account of what they had been 'forced' to do by the Grand Inquisitor. They ended with the statement that they were glad he was dead because they had lived in fear of him all their lives. They said they wished they had left his service, but were frightened he would track them down and murder them. Torca Marda was responsible for everything, they told the squirrels.

Pommf de Fritte ordered that the two stoats should be taken away, to await further interrogation and possibly punishment.

Sylver said, 'I would simply send them away. They are what they say they are, just stupid creatures who followed the wrong master. Without him they're harmless.'

'Possibly,' Pommf de Fritte replied. 'I'll bear what you say in mind when we come to sentencing them, but my inclination is to throw them in the oubliette and forget them . . .'

Furioso looked horrified. He stepped forward, undoing the string to the goose bladder attached to his belt. He held the goose bladder in front of him, his claws on the seal to the opening.

'In here,' he cried, wildly, 'is smoke from the herb *shatter*. I took some from amongst the ashes of the fire Sylver built on the battlements, when he destroyed the dragonfly. You saw what happened to the dragonfly. If I break this seal, the bladder will spurt the smoke in your direction.'

'You'll all burst into splinters,' Orgoglio cried triumphantly, stepping up beside his compatriot. 'You'll shatter to bits!'

It seemed like a stand-off, with the weasels and squirrels on one side of the tower and the two stoats on the other side.

Orgoglio and Furioso began to edge towards the door to the spiral staircase.

'Stay back!' warned Furioso. 'I'll open the neck to the balloon and pump some at you if you move.'

There was silence. Nobody stirred. Weasels and squirrels alike were afraid and unsure. Then after a long moment one of their number stepped forward with an elegant leg. It was Foppington. This gaily-dressed knight now wet a foreclaw with his lips and then held it up with a flourish in the air, as if testing something. He nodded, thoughtfully. 'The wind,' he said to the stoats in a sad voice, 'ith blowing in your direction.'

Furioso and Orgoglio, the stupidity showing in their expression, exchanged slack-mouthed looks. Then Foppington's paw went like lightning towards his weapon. In an instant his sword was out. He made a quick lunge – actually *lunge* is a sort of awkward word for such a swift and graceful flash of the blade – and the bladder had been pierced by swordpoint.

'La!' said the suave squirrel.

The blade was back in its scabbard before the amazed weasels and squirrels heard the 'pop' of the bladder.

Their balloon having been burst, the smoke which had been trapped within billowed over the two stoats, who stood there helplessly coughing and spluttering.

In the next moment there were dozens and dozens of tiny Orgoglios and Furiosos, minuscule stoats the size of pine needles, running around the floor of the tower. They made tiny squeaks as they ran. They found cracks and holes in the stonework and disappeared from view. Soon, it was as if the two – sorry, the very many – false priests had never existed. There was no trace of any of them. The smoke itself drifted over their side of the wall and harmlessly out into the night.

'So much for them,' snarled Pommf de Fritte. 'Well done, Foppington. Blade as deadly as ever.'

'My pleathure,' murmured that debonair sword-squirrel with an exquisite bow to his admirers.

Then Pommf de Fritte turned as if he had

forgotten something. 'But what's this fellow doing here? Hie there, you! Who are you?'

This remark was addressed to the offensive-smelling manger, who now stepped forward, his stink coming with him in waves, the flies gathering about his person, buzzing like mad. Everyone else backed away a pace and held their noses. The figure then threw back its hood to reveal none other than Scirf.

'Fooled that ole inquisitor, eh?' he said, clicking his teeth. 'Phew, what a pong! But it just goes to show that nuffink but good can come from fallin' into a nice bit of dung, don't it?'

Sylver gave out a yell of delight. 'Scirf, you old rogue. But why didn't you answer us when we called down to you?'

'Couldn't. Had me mouth full.'

Sylver did not care to delve any further into this line of enquiry. 'But later?'

'By that time I'd slid down the chute and into a bog at the bottom. Then I found me way into the town, then into the castle again. Got these togs from Griselda and the witches on the way, thinkin' no-one would stop a manger. On me way up the tower I saw you bein' hustled out on to the battlements by them stoats – and the rest you know.'

'What a brilliant weasel you are. I'd give you a hug, you know, but . . .'

Scirf looked down at himself and clicked his teeth again. 'Know what you mean, squire. Don't worry about it.'

The rest of the weasels and Sheriff Falshed were then freed from their prison room and the weasels went with Scirf down to the lake to make sure he was thoroughly scrubbed. He did not like it, saying the smell was not as bad as they thought it was and it reminded him of his old job, but they insisted.

There was feasting then, throughout the night. The weasels were given the thanks they should have received earlier, for vanquishing the dragonfly. When the first rays of the morning sun struck the castle walls they were on their way to real beds, down in the town, happy in the thought that they were free again.

At noon, they were woken by an excited Clive of Coldkettle, to learn that Lord Haukin was in the town. 'He says he wants to talk to you right away,' said Clive. 'He's got some of his servants with him. And there are quite a few stoats and weasels from County Elleswhere camped outside the walls of the town. I think Lord Haukin has got a job for you.'

Chapter Thirty-Nine

Lord Haukin stated his business briefly and with the preciseness Sylver had come to expect of him.

'Ah, what's-his-name, there you are. Things are grave, young jack, very grave. The rats have destroyed Lord Whatsit's army and are now threatening to overwhelm Castle Thingummy. We must set to, lad, and save the day. We need to break through the sea walls in one or two places – let the flood cascade over the land – and wash these rats back to where they came from.'

Sylver said he and his weasels were ready to do whatever was required of them.

'Good, good,' replied Lord Haukin, briskly. 'Well, let's be off then – westward ho!'

'What about County Elleswhere, though,' asked Bryony. 'Will that be flooded too?'

'Oh, shouldn't think so, young jill. Flood waters from the western region won't reach that far inland. There's a wide shallow basin around the river Bronn, which will be under a metre or so of water. The castle will stand proud, but all around it will be sea, and only Prince Poynt will be isolated. No big loss. The rats are concentrated in and around that basin now. Most other places will be fine, so long as we don't encourage the crumbling dykes along the inland rivers or the sea walls to the east and south to break open and flood the rest of Welkin.'

The outlaws were actually quite ready to leave Castle Storm. They were missing their Halfmoon Wood.

They went first to the house of Tomus Culpin and collected Icham's body. This had been dried by the good doctor and was light enough to be easily carried by two weasels. Scirf and Mawk took it between them on a makeshift litter.

The outlaws had to say their goodbyes too and went first to the castle greys, then through the town bidding farewell to the reds.

Even the coven came to see them off. Griselda, Mathop, Osmand, Gowk and Spavin muttered their mole farewells, ending with the chant, 'Hail Sylver, Thane of County Elleswhere! Hail Sylver, Lord of Thistle Hall!'

Sylver was embarrassed by this, especially since Lord Haukin was standing near enough to hear them.

'I'm sorry about that, Lord Haukin,' said Sylver, going over to the venerable stoat. 'They've been chanting that nonsense ever since I arrived.'

To the astonishment of the band of outlaws Lord Haukin clicked his teeth and told them it was not nonsense. 'You're the new Thane of County Elleswhere,' he said. 'Or will be, once we get rid of the rats.'

'But – but – what about *you*?' asked Bryony of the lord.

'Me? I'm the new Thane of Whatsit, Whojamaflip – you know, Thingummybob.'

Culver, standing near his master, raised his eyes to heaven. 'He means Fearsomeshire,' said that faithful weasel servant. 'He'll be the new Thane of Fearsomeshire. Big county. Very rich in land. Excellent library at the Great House. Lots of bottle dumps close at paw. Lord Ragnar is dead, killed by the rats. Fearsomeshire was up for grabs.'

Sylver tried to let all this sink in. He was at an absolute loss for words. His weasel band crowded round him, bursting with excitement.

A little way off, Sheriff Falshed stood blinking away his tears. He had heard it all. It had been his cunning intention to capture the weasels single-pawed once the flooding had been accomplished. But it seemed his plans had once more been dashed. Lord Sylver of Halfmoon Wood? It made Falshed wince.

The sheriff wanted to crawl away somewhere and cry – or bite someone very hard in a tender place. Preferably the prince. He wanted to bite the prince, for promoting this outlaw weasel above his loved and trusted sheriff, who had no lands, estate nor even a proper title. All he had was a rank: High Sheriff of All Welkin. It simply was not fair. It made one choke on one's own spittle.

Luke said to Culver, 'The prince must be dead, surely, for this to happen?'

'No – a little mad perhaps – but it was forced on him by his sister. Lord Haukin put the proposal to the prince; he tried to find a way round it, but Princess Sibiline eventually told him he had to agree to Lord Haukin's demands. It's true enough, but don't forget we have the work to do first.'

'I don't want to be lord of anything,' said Sylver. 'I'm happy as I am.'

Lord Haukin disapproved of this attitude. 'You don't like the system, do you – stoats always at the top, weasels at the bottom?'

'No.'

'Then you have to change it from within. You have to accept the position and use the power it gives you

369

wisely. It's time we had a meritocracy in this land of Welkin . . .'

'What's that?' asked Mawk. 'The merit thing.'

'It means,' explained Lord Haukin, 'that those who deserve to achieve a high position actually get it. At the moment high positions are pawed out to sycophants – flatterers of Prince Poynt – and stoats of little worth, so long as they are stoats. Under a meritocracy you would all get your chance. But it's not here yet, don'cha know. We have to work for it.'

Sylver decided to let come what may and put his efforts into the task in paw for the moment.

Finally, at the town gates, the outlaws said their farewells to Clive of Coldkettle, that able red knight. He and Pommf de Fritte were preparing to march north with their knights. They were at last going to do battle with the rats. It was their intention to strike at those rats who had overrun County Elleswhere and drive them north.

'Good luck to us all,' said Clive, adjusting his eye-patch and fluffing his famous reversed tail in order to keep from appearing too emotional. 'May you fare well in your new venture and may we vanquish the foe from the doorstep on your new home, Lord Sylver.'

'Thank you, Clive,' replied Sylver, feeling rather peculiar at being addressed in such a fashion, 'and thank you indeed for all your help while we were your guests.'

'Think nothing of it, young jack. Just sorry you didn't find this clue thing you were looking for.'

Sylver's heart sank as he remembered his failure, but Scirf pushed forward now, full of self-importance. 'Ah, that's where you're wrong, squire. We did find it. At least, I did. Bin savin' it for such an occasion as this.'

Sylver gasped and stepped back. It was not like Scirf to lie about something so important. 'Where was it?' he asked the ex-dung-watcher. 'Where did you see it?'

'Down at the bottom of the North-west Tower's garderobe,' Scirf said, clicking his teeth. 'You remember I said I found a tunnel to the lake. Well, there was another tunnel which branched off that one. I took that route, rather than the stinky one. At the end of this second tunnel was a ledge which was just above the water . . .'

'Get to the point, Scirf,' said Mawk.

'I'm comin' to it. Be patient. This is important. Now, that ledge must have been used for swimmin' from by children at some time, 'cause there was all sorts of things scrawled on the walls of the cave inside. Things like "Billy Wittle can't dive for toffee," stuff like that. One of these writings was a rhyme.'

Scirf paused for effect, obviously loving the idea that many eyes were upon him, and that weasels were hanging on to his every word.

Scirf cleared his throat and continued. 'The rhyme went somethin' like this:

"Goodbye, goodbye, we're off to sea,
Leaving Welkin, you and me –
We're going to cross the stormy foam
To Dorma Island, our new home."

'It was written in big scrawly letters and signed – listen to this – signed TOM.'

'Tom!' cried Bryony. 'That was the name of the child Alice's cousin. You found the clue, Scirf. You're wonderful!'

Scirf drew a circle in the dust with his claw, saying bashfully, 'Oh, I don't know.'

Lord Haukin shook his head sadly. 'I never understood how this fellow learned to read. His grammar is appalling, his sentence construction quite extraordinary and his slang offensive to the ear.'

But Sylver was not concerned by the way Scirf spoke. He was only delighted that the ex-dungwatcher had discovered the clue for which they had all been searching for so long. It made everything worth it. Almost everything. They had lost Miniver, gone to the Land of Lost Dreams, and Icham, killed by the sword of a villain. Sylver wished these tragedies had not occurred, but he could not change history and he knew that both Miniver and Icham had been prepared to accept the risks. He promised them a great kalkie when things were back to normal.

The other outlaws had begun nipping Scirf on the back – the equivalent of a human slap – for having helped them achieve what they had set out to do.

There was one last farewell to make. Link the poacher appeared from somewhere and voiced her goodbyes to the outlaws. She gave Mawk a squeeze and then much to his consternation said she had just been to visit the nuns at the mangery. She'd hugged Mawk on purpose of course, to watch him squirm.

'Oh, and by the way, Sylver,' she told the outlaw leader, 'the priests of the old religion – they're now able to leave their priest-holes and come out in the fresh air. They send their thanks to Scirf for killing Torca Marda.'

'Didn't actually kill the Grand Inquisitor on purpose,' said Scirf, uncomfortable with these words. 'Was a bit of an accident.'

'Well, they've been locked up for so long and they appreciate being allowed out again.'

Then it was time to go. The little workforce of weasels and stoats set forth north-westwards. It was a longish forced march, moving during the night as well as day to save time, and they reached their destination in good time.

They chose a place where the river Bronn came close to the sea walls. Here they employed their claws to dig away at a weak part of the dyke. The spot they chose was between two sturdy hawthorn trees, which straddled the top of the dyke. The position of these two trees would prevent the gap they were going to make from eating away at the dyke on either side and growing too wide. To make doubly sure they transported rocks and placed them around the roots of the hawthorns to strengthen them.

Once this had been done they set to clawing away the clay in the small space between. Soon they had breached the dyke. Water started pouring through the narrow channel in a silver stream and filling the river Bronn.

'Look at that water go!' cried Mawk.

The water in the river rose and a tidal wave which Lord Haukin called a 'bore' swept both ways, up and down the river.

'When that upward bore reaches Castle Rayn it will cause the river to overflow its banks and flood the countryside around – the rat encampments will be swept away,' said Lord Haukin.

'I didn't know you were good at engineering, squire,' said Scirf, impressed. 'And you helped Lord Ragnar too, at strategy and what-not. You're not just a forgetful old codger, are you?'

'When you read as many books as I do, young whatsit,' said Lord Haukin, deciding to overlook Scirf's lack of respect for his title and person, 'you get to be good at most things. There's not many tasks that can't be solved by reading books.'

The water poured forth in a steady stream, funnelled now by two large boulders which had been under the clay. The operation had been successful. Sylver stared with satisfaction at a job well done and thanked his luck for having a friend like Lord Haukin, whose brains were invaluable.

Upstream the river burst its banks and swept across the land. In the early hours of the morning the sentries on the battlements of Castle Rayn suddenly let out shouts of alarm. They pointed. A big shining wave was coming from the direction of the river, foaming at its crest. It rolled over the land, gathering loose debris as it came: dead wood, tree trunks, even large stones. By the time it reached the rat camp outside the castle they could hear its roar. Prince Poynt and most of the inhabitants of Rayn were up in the towers, watching it come.

'It'll go right over us!' shouted Pompom. 'We'll all drown. We're doomed. We're doomed.'

'Be quiet, you stupid jester,' snarled Prince Poynt, 'or I'll have you flung into the maw of that thing. You realize what that wave represents? It represents the loss of stoat sovereignty over the weasels. One of them has been made a thane. Our supremacy will be whittled away, bit by bit, until we're no better than the serfs out in the fields.'

'I'm a weasel,' murmured Pompom, calmer now. 'I could be a thane one day.'

'You?' growled the prince. 'Over my dead body.'

Pompom said nothing on hearing these words. But a bright light came into his eyes as he stared at his lord and master. And then he began humming a little tune.

Down below the castle walls, the rats were frantic. They had seen the wave now. They could smell the briny. They realized they were about to be engulfed. Many of them were grabbing siege platforms to use as rafts. Others were running, futilely, eastwards. Flaggatis, that mad stoat whose plans had now been smashed on the eve of success, was in the back of a cart drawn by thirty hysterical mice. Unfortunately for future generations of stoats, weasels, and it has to be said, rats, it looked like he had a good start and would reach high ground before the wave struck.

When the foaming wave washed up against the castle walls, it climbed high to soak those on the battlements, then swirled around the corners of the towers and out into the fields behind the castle and the rats went with it. Many of them were swimming vigorously, allowing the current to take them inland. Others had clutched spars and other floating objects, hanging on for grim life. The valley of the Bronn was a natural funnel for the water and the rat hordes were carried, struggling and thrashing, along this channel and away.

'Good riddance,' muttered Prince Poynt.

The water still washed around the castle walls, flowing in from the sea. Prince Poynt watched as a wickerwork god named Herman – or as he now knew, *Ermine* – was picked from its perch and smashed against the stonework of the castle. The blow merely distorted the shape of the creature and it went bobbing away in the direction of its worshippers, looking like a twisted basket with eyes and ears. Its tail stuck up out of the water like a mast, a rag end waving like a flag from its tip.

'And good riddance to you too,' added the prince, glad that his so-called likeness was beyond recognition, even to those who hated him and pointed out to each other the similarities between the wicker god and Prince Poynt. It had been a caricature, now it was just a ball of twigs, a squirrel's drey.

There was a whinny from beside the prince and he turned to see that the bronze horse was there.

'Now-Wodehed-come,' she said, 'tell-me-First-and-Last-Resting-Place. Soon-we-say-goodbye-prince.'

'I'm devastated,' snarled the prince, sarcastically. 'Absolutely tragic. Won't know what to do with myself. Goodbye.'

At that moment Sibiline came up to the top of the tower from below. She was dressed in an orange-coloured costume. Prince Poynt raised his brow in a query.

'Miss Clapirons, the Dungeon-master's Daughter,' she said in answer to his silent question. 'We're going to play Happy Families, brother. Do go and choose a costume. It's such fun.'

'Urrggghhh,' replied her brother. 'Whose idea was this? Spinfer's? Pompom's?'

'No, there's a new fellow arrived, just swam into the outer bailey below.'

'Swam?'

'He's an otter. *Nice* young jack. He's called Sleek.'

Prince Poynt was piqued. 'What's he doing here?'

'Says he makes clothes. Wants to make your court the envy of the fashion world.'

'Does he now? *How* exciting.'

Once again the prince's voice was thick with sarcasm, but his listener did not care. Sibiline was happy. She wanted everyone else to be happy. If her brother wanted to go into one of his silly moods, that was up to him. So far as Princess Sibiline was concerned, this young otter Sleek was going to transform life in the castle. He was so enthusiastic, so passionate about fabrics and colours. They were going to drape everyone in beautiful gowns, fabulous cloaks, pretty lace and nice gingham. It was lovely. It was wonderful. It was everything she wanted out of life.

She left the prince looking moodily out over the great sea in the middle of which stood the castle.

'So I'm stuck here now with a stickleback-eater who flirts with my sister and waves silk pawker-chiefs under our noses, am I? Oh my brother, Redfur, why did I ever let you give me the princedom. You should be here, king of it all, and I off somewhere hunting rabbits in the tangled blue forests, by rushy brooks, under the bright moon . . .'

The prince's voice trailed off and he sank to the floor, his chin resting in the gap between two stone teeth, as he stared out over the waterland which was now his garden.

Chapter Forty

The first thing Sylver did when he became Thane of County Elleswhere and Lord of Thistle Hall was to send thanks to Clive and Pommf. Those good knights, with their small but able army of squirrels, had charged the rats with pike and halberd and had driven them out of County Elleswhere before the rodents had done too much damage to the estates. On the borders of the county those same rats had then been caught up in the general retreat of their kind, sweeping them all back to the unnamed marshes.

To the chagrin of all creatures other than the rats, Flaggatis had escaped being caught in the flood. His mouse-cart had outrun the wave. The Lord of the Rats had survived to gather the remnants of his evil hordes around him. Since rats increase their numbers rapidly, it was his intention to strike once more, as soon as the rat population reached the proportions of an army again.

At Thistle Hall they were not yet concerned by the possibility of another invasion. They were too busy celebrating their victory of the last one. Seven barrels of Braeburn apples were sent to the ptarmigans. Sylver also sent words of condolence on the untimely death of Robbie the red grouse. A message was received back that both were much appreciated.

Thus the outlaws' commitments to the clans out near the Forest of Lost Birds were carried out.

It took him quite a while to get accustomed to living in a house again. In fact he never quite got used to it. He would sneak out some nights when the servants had gone to bed and spend his sleeping hours in the hollow of a live oak, listening to the sounds of the woodland around him. The other outlaws too, began by sleeping in the great hall, but before long they had drifted back out into Halfmoon Wood. Only Bryony remained, to keep him company, faithful despite her own yearnings for the greenwood.

Sylver thought it ironic that Prince Poynt believed he had given the weasel outlaw leader a great gift, while Sylver actually could have very well done without it.

In fact it was just one more reason for getting the humans back. He and the outlaws were planning on becoming mariners. Already Lord Haukin was studying various diagrams in books for the building of a great windjammer, a ship which would take the weasels to Dorma Island. The outlaws were practising their knots and how to reef sails and splice ropes.

Scirf was practising his sea-dog oaths. 'May ye rot like wormy timbers washed ashore on the Skeleton Coast, ye unsalty landlubbers, ye!' rang out through the greenwood trees.

In November, when the first frosts were on the ground, they had a kalkie for Icham. There was a great roaring bonfire on top of which sat the dried body of their former friend. Sparks flew from the logs and twigs up in the dark night. The scent of woodsmoke was breathed with great satisfaction.

Other animals came from miles around to watch the activity.

The weasels threw stones at Icham and chanted and yelled good-humoured insults, though as ever Lord Haukin – who of course attended – could not bring himself to carry out this ritual. He never did understand that a kalkie was not a solemn funeral for the dead, but a celebration of the weasel's life.

After it was all over, Sylver went back to the hall, to a bed. His fur smelled of woodsmoke. He was pleased at having given his best friend Icham a good send off. Next they would have to do one for little Miniver. It was with the finger-weasel in mind that he drifted off to sleep. It was the first time he had allowed himself to dwell on her image.

Once asleep he found himself wandering into dreamland, where Miniver stood waiting impatiently for him.

'Where have you been?' she demanded. 'I've been waiting for one of you to come for me!'

'I – we didn't know we were supposed to,' said Sylver.

'All you had to do was dream about me, to get to the Land of Lost Dreams and find me again.'

'We didn't realize. Everyone's deliberately not been thinking of you. We were sad.'

'Well, now you're here at last you can lead me out again. I don't care if you haven't had a lot of sleep after Icham's kalkie, I'm dying to see Halfmoon Wood again. I want to smell the wild flowers and the mushrooms. I'm missing all my friends.'

Sylver marvelled at the fact that they were going to see Miniver the finger-weasel again, have her back amongst them, but he felt he ought to warn her of the changes which had occurred, before he now took her with him to the land of living.

'I'm actually asleep in Thistle Hall,' he said, beginning to wake up. 'You see I've been made Thane of Elleswhere . . .'

THE END

ABOUT THE AUTHOR

Garry Kilworth was born in York but, as the son of an Air Force family, was educated at more than twenty schools. He himself joined the RAF at the age of fifteen and was stationed all over the world, from Singapore to Cyprus, before leaving to continue his education and begin a career in business, which also enabled him to travel widely.

He became a full-time writer when his two young children left home and has written many novels for both adults and younger readers – mostly on science fiction, fantasy and historical themes. He has won several awards for his work, including the World Fantasy Award in 1992, and the Lancashire Book Award in 1995 for *The Electric Kid*.

His previous titles for Transworld Publishers include *Thunder Oak*, the first title in the Welkin Weasels trilogy, *The Electric Kid* and *Cybercats*; and *House of Tribes* and *A Midsummer's Nightmare* for Bantam Press/Corgi Books. The third title in the Welkin Weasels trilogy, *Windjammer Run* will be published in 1999.

Garry Kilworth lives in a country cottage in Essex which has a large woodland garden teeming with wildlife, including foxes, doves, squirrels and grass snakes.

THE WELKIN WEASELS
Book 1: Thunder Oak

by Garry Kilworth

Long ago, before Sylver the weasel was born, the humans all left Welkin. Now life for a weasel – under the heavy paw of the vicious stoat rulers – is pretty miserable (unless you happen to be a weasel who *likes* living in a hovel and toiling all hours for the benefit of the stoats).

It's certainly not enough for Sylver. Or for his small band of outlaws, both jacks and jills. But slingshots and darts can only do so much against heavily-armed stoats and life as an outlaw has a fairly limited future (probably a painful one, too). That's when Sylver comes up with his plan – a heroic plan that could destroy the stoats' reign of power for ever. He will find humans and bring them back to Welkin! And the first step is to follow up a clue from the past – a clue that lies in a place known as *Thunder Oak* . . .

The first title in an inventive, highly imaginative and often very funny trilogy, *The Welkin Weasels*.

ISBN 0 552 54546 5